A Red Hot New Year

A Red Hot New Year

Cynthia Eden, Diana Mercury,
Virginia Reede, Denise Rossetti

AVON

An Imprint of HarperCollins Publishers

This is a work of fiction. Names, characters, places, and incidents are products of the author's imagination or are used fictitiously and are not to be construed as real. Any resemblance to actual events, locales, organizations, or persons, living or dead, is entirely coincidental.

FIRST EDITION

Designed by Elizabeth Glover

Library of Congress Cataloging-in-Publication Data
A red hot new year / Cynthia Eden . . . [et al.]. — 1st ed.
    p. cm.
  ISBN-13: 978-0-06-145147-8
  ISBN-10: 0-06-145147-9
1. Erotic stories, American. 2. American fiction—Women authors. 3. American fiction—21st century. 4. Erotic stories, Australian. I. Eden, Cynthia
  PS648.E7R437 2007
  813'.6083538—dc22   2007037430

07 08 09 10 11   OV/RRD   10 9 8 7 6 5 4 3 2 1

Contents

Part 1

New Year's Bites

CYNTHIA EDEN

If Anna Summers hadn't been busy fantasizing about wild New Year's Eve sex with the man of her dreams, she might have been able to sense the danger that waited for her.

But when Anna stepped out of the elevator onto the ground floor of the parking garage, her mind was completely on Jon York.

Tall, strong, sexy-as-hell Jon York. The man with the midnight black hair and the bright blue eyes. The man that made her mouth dry up and her sex cream.

The man who was way, way out of her league.

Anna sighed as she walked, her keys clutched lightly in her right hand. She'd known Jon for two months now. Her boss, the curator at the Richmond Natural History Museum, had contracted with Jon to spruce up the museum's security. So she'd been sitting in countless meetings with him since then, drinking up his scent, searching for a flash of his dimples.

And wishing that she had the guts to ask him for a night of wild sex.

Her cell phone vibrated with a peal of sound. Anna dug it out of her purse, wincing when she saw the name on her caller

ID. Veronica. *Ronnie*. Hell. Guilt gnawed at her. Why had she stayed in the museum so long? She'd promised her best friend that she'd be at her New Year's Eve party just after nine—arriving in plenty of time to help with setup.

But, oh, no, she just had to stop by and log in a few more items for work.

Idiot.

Taking a quick breath, she answered the phone. "Ronnie, I'm so sorry! I'm on my way, I—"

A low growl sounded from the shadows.

The rumble froze Anna in her tracks.

Then the growl came again. Louder. Closer.

A shiver traced down her spine and fear rose, bitter and hard, on her tongue. She could vaguely hear her friend's voice, rambling softly, but all of her attention was on that menacing sound.

A growl. What the hell? Was there some kind of animal in the garage with her?

"Anna? Anna, are you listening to me?"

No, she was focused on the growl. "I-I've got to call you back, Ronnie." She ended the call, shoved the phone into her purse, and began to move faster. Much faster. Her Jeep was waiting. Maybe twenty feet away. Parked under that nice, bright, slightly flickering fluorescent light and—

Glowing silver eyes stared at her from the darkness.

Anna skidded to a stop.

A howl echoed through the garage and the beast stepped forward. Huge, covered with thick, matted black fur. A dog of some kind—one of the ugliest beasts she'd ever seen. Its mouth was open, filled with teeth that dripped with saliva and were far, far too sharp for her peace of mind.

Oh, no. "Uh . . . n-nice, d-dog." He was stalking forward, getting between her and her Jeep. Not a good sign.

She saw his nostrils flare, his muscles tense.

Anna took a quick step back.

The beast's head lowered toward the ground.

Could she run around him? Jump in her Jeep and—

The creature sprang forward, mouth open, teeth glinting.

She screamed, turned to run, and felt the razor-sharp lash of his teeth sink into her right calf.

Then he was jerking her down, and Anna slammed into the concrete, the impact stealing the breath she'd drawn for a second scream.

This isn't happening. Can't be. It's a dream, a nightmare. There's no dog attacking me—

His teeth sank deeper.

Anna swiped out with her keys, managing to twist and aim for his eyes.

The beast jumped back. She scrambled to her feet, all too aware of the wet warmth trickling down her leg.

Anna started running. Not toward the Jeep; the ugly dog was still blocking her. No, she went for the elevator. She could hear the animal thundering after her, feel his hot breath on her back—

With a soft chime, the elevator's doors slid open. Anna caught a glimpse of a man—tall, muscled, dark-haired, *familiar*—

"Help me!" She screamed.

The beast took her down again.

Sonofabitch.

Jon York stared down at Anna's face. Her eyes were closed, her face pale.

She'd been bitten.

Dammit.

He pulled in a slow breath, catching her scent, the lush smell of roses and woman. His hand brushed aside a curling lock of her red hair.

Her hair had been the first thing he'd noticed about her. Shining like fire, the strands had been trapped in a knot at the nape of her neck.

Anna. Anna of the big, dreamy green eyes, the soft mouth, and the sweet face.

He'd noticed her the first day he walked into the museum and found her bent over a box of dusty artifacts. He'd touched her shoulder and she'd spun around, her lips parted in surprise.

Jon had wanted to kiss her then. To taste those red lips and see if they were really as soft as they looked.

But Anna had been all business. Assistant curator at the museum, she'd obviously taken her job seriously, and she'd ignored the sexual overtures that he'd witnessed a few other guys make to her.

The lady was smart, dedicated to her job, and sexy. Damn, but he'd always had a thing for smart women.

He'd run a background check on her, as he always did when he had to work closely with someone he didn't know. For him, it was just too dangerous to take chances. So he'd gotten one of his men to check her out.

Anna Summers. Age thirty-one. No criminal record. Single. Her parents had been killed when she was just a child, barely seven years old. After that, she'd bounced around a series of foster homes until she was legal. Then she put herself through college and grad school with student loans and scholarships. She'd eventually taken a job at the museum, following somewhat in her paleontologist father's footsteps.

Jon admired Anna. She'd turned her life around, gotten herself a nice home, a good job.

Yeah, he admired her. Respected her.

And wanted her like crazy.

It was a pity, really. If he'd arrived in that garage five minutes sooner, he might have been able to save her. Now, well, now. . .

Her life was about to become hell and she didn't even know it.

Anna's lashes began to flutter. He tensed. "Anna? Anna, are you all right?"

Her eyelids lifted slowly. She blinked, and her gaze focused on him. "Jon?" She sat up, pushing against the leather couch cushions.

He'd taken her back into the museum, back to her office. Good thing he knew just how to get inside the place. "Easy." His fingers wrapped around her upper arms. "You've been out for the last ten minutes."

She frowned at that, a line appearing on her forehead. "What did I . . . God, that dog!"

Not a dog, not really. "Do you remember what happened?" He asked carefully.

"Uh . . . I heard something growling. I looked up and saw that—that thing. It lunged at me." Her hand dropped to her calf. He'd taken the first-aid kit from the security desk and bandaged the wound. "He bit me."

Yeah, unfortunately, he had, and because of that bite, things were about to get really scary for her. Jon's nostrils flared as he inhaled her scent. It was already becoming stronger, her pheromones becoming more powerful.

His cock began to swell.

He realized that his fingers were caressing her arms with long, slow strokes. With an effort, he managed to release her. Jon stood and paced a few steps away from the couch, *away from her*.

Anna looked up at him. She was wearing a black dress with a scooped neckline that showed a hint of her cleavage—and the woman had damn good cleavage. Firm, round breasts that he bet would fit perfectly in his hands and taste like heaven on his tongue. The dress stopped at her knees, but it had bunched up, and he could see a nice, tempting expanse of pale leg.

He'd always been a leg man.

And Jon could all too easily imagine Anna's legs wrapped around him as he pushed her into the cushions of that couch and took her, long and hard.

Not the time. The lady had just been attacked—she didn't need him pouncing on her, too. "Anna, how do you feel?"

She blinked. "Uh, my leg hurts a bit, but other than that," she gave a little shrug. "I actually feel pretty good. Weird, huh?"

Not particularly.

"Do you know where my glasses are? I was wearing them when that *thing* jumped me."

He pointed to the nearby table.

She scooped them up and perched the glasses on her nose, looking so cute she made him ache. "Uh, Jon, did you carry me up here?"

Jon gave a slow nod. The woman had felt damn good in his arms. He'd been doing his best to play the gentleman with her, but it looked like the rules of the game had just taken a serious turn.

He'd have to stay with Anna now, at least for the next twenty-four hours. It was important to make certain she didn't turn feral.

Anna rose slowly to her feet. At six foot three, he was much taller than her own five-foot-five frame, so she had to tilt her head back to look into his eyes. "Bringing me up here, carrying me—that was very kind of you." Her voice was breathless and stroked right over his skin like satin.

He swallowed, hoping that she wouldn't glance down and notice the growing bulge in his trousers. "No problem."

Her lips lifted into a faint smile.

Jon had to fight the urge to kiss her.

But he knew that later he'd be doing a hell of a lot more than just touching those lips.

Yet now wasn't the time.

"Anna, that dog . . . can you tell me what he looked like?" Important, very, very important. Because the beast had gotten away, and all Jon had been left with was the creature's rank stench, filling his nostrils and turning his stomach.

"Big. Black. Really ugly." Her nose wrinkled. "Its eyes were so weird—silver, but almost—" She broke off, laughing. "You'll think I'm crazy."

"No, I won't."

Her smile faded. "It was almost like—like his eyes were glowing." She shook her head. "I know it was probably just a trick of the light. I mean, the thing's eyes weren't glowing, right? This isn't some kind of horror movie, and it *was* just a dog."

He didn't speak. Sometimes, it was just easier not to lie.

"We need to call someone," she murmured, "animal control or something. We can't just let that thing stay loose in the parking garage."

"I sent two security officers down there—they'll make sure

the area's safe." As for the beast, well, he was long gone—for now.

Anna exhaled heavily. "That's good to know. I've got to go back down there and the thought of running into that thing again . . ." She shuddered. "Not exactly how I plan to spend my New Year's Eve."

"And how do you plan to spend the night?" The words came out sounding suggestive, and he hadn't meant them to, not really.

She blinked, her eyes widening behind the glasses. "Uh . . ."

He almost smiled. Almost. Instead, he reached for her hand, running his fingertips over the slight rise of her knuckles, then over the smooth skin below them.

He was close enough to see the slight flaring of her pupils and his enhanced senses let him hear the sudden racing of her heart.

Good. She felt the same lust he did. It would make things easier.

"How are you spending your night, Anna? And are you planning to spend it with someone in particular?" Not another man. He couldn't allow that. It would be too dangerous for anyone else.

"I-I'm going to my friend Ronnie's. She's having a New Year's party. I promised I'd stop by." Her eyes narrowed. "Why? Are you—are you asking me out?"

He should have asked her out weeks ago. When he'd first wondered how she tasted and what she looked like without those thin, wire-framed glasses. Or even what she looked like with them on, in bed. "Maybe I am," he told her, twining his fingers with hers. Damn but her skin was soft, and that seductive scent of hers was just growing stronger.

Soon, the other changes would begin. They'd come—faster and faster as the night progressed.

A slight flush stained her cheeks. "You could come with me. If you wanted, that is." Her gaze dropped to the floor, then lifted quickly to meet his. "You did save me from a dangerous beast, after all."

She had no idea.

Her hand felt good against his. Delicate, but strong. He'd like to feel that hand on other parts of his body, stroking him.

Soon.

For now, he had to make certain she was safe.

Anna had been targeted. Why, he didn't know, but attacks like the one she'd had weren't random. No, they were *never* random.

"Jon?" There was a flicker of worry in her eyes and the red in her cheeks deepened. "Do you want to come to the party?"

He brought her hand to his lips and pressed a kiss just above her knuckles. "I'd like that." All the better to protect her, and those who crossed her path.

She smiled at him again, and the sight was like a punch in his gut.

Damn, why did it have to be her?

He felt something for Anna Summers, a stirring, a need.

If only he'd arrived in that parking garage five minutes earlier.

Then Anna wouldn't have been attacked.

He could have just been a man who wanted a desirable woman. Things could have been so simple, so easy.

But that game was screwed to hell and back.

Because Anna hadn't been bitten by just a wild dog.

The beast that attacked her had been a werewolf.

Once bitten, humans changed—and soon Anna would feel

the full power of the bite.

Some couldn't handle that power. Some went mad, driven beyond sanity by the bloodlust. Those people—well, they had to be stopped.

That was Jon's real job. He was a hunter, of sorts.

He'd just never thought that sweet Ms. Summers would become his prey.

Jon's scent surrounded her. Warm. Rich. Masculine. It made her think of dark nights and warm sheets. Naked flesh and moans.

Anna pulled in a deep breath as she walked beside Jon. She still couldn't believe she was with him. Her heart was racing like crazy and her skin seemed to literally burn with excitement.

So it had taken a dog attack to get the man's attention. She would have preferred something a lot less painful, but well, she hadn't exactly been given a choice in the situation.

Music spilled into the night. Laughter. Voices. The empty lot next to Ronnie's two-story brick colonial house was filled with cars, and it was barely ten o'clock.

Ronnie had always loved a good party.

Anna had always loved a good book.

If they hadn't both wound up in the same foster home at sixteen, they probably never would have been friends.

But they'd been confidants for years now, and they were closer than sisters.

Anna stopped at the front entrance and Jon rang the bell. Ronnie opened the door, her heart-shaped face bright, and her long black hair pulled high into a twist. "Anna! About time!" Then she was hugging her and trying to pull her inside.

"Uh, Ronnie, wait—this is my date." God, that sounded good. "Jon York."

Ronnie tensed. Her eyes narrowed as she eyed Jon. "You brought a date?" Her voice was a scandalized whisper.

Anna frowned at her. Well, she did date occasionally. She wasn't an old maid—she was only thirty-one!

"But I invited Steven . . ."

Ronnie's guilty words made Anna flinch. Steven Phillips. Steven of the two-minute, boring-as-hell sex. The guy she'd had the misfortune to date for an entire six months of her life. "You didn't."

A quick nod.

Thank God the dog had bitten her. Otherwise, she'd have been there alone. But with Jon by her side . . . She glanced at him, shoulders straightening. Well, Steven wouldn't be dumb enough to come near her.

She hoped.

Anna turned back to Ronnie and realized that she couldn't see her friend anymore. Not really. Just a vague, blurry outline. She blinked. Once, twice.

Fear whipped through her blood.

She reached for her glasses. Maybe something was wrong with the lenses, maybe—

The instant she lifted the glasses away, her vision was perfect. Far more perfect than it had ever been in her life.

What the hell?

"I'll take those," Jon murmured, his breath blowing lightly against her ear and sending a shiver down her spine.

"But I—" *need them.*

Yet she could see perfectly. What was going on? How could—

Ronnie tugged on Anna's hand. She told Jon it was great to meet him, and then dragged them into the mix of laughter and music inside the house.

It was starting, Jon realized. The changes were rippling through her body.

Enhanced vision always came first.

Anna wouldn't need her glasses, not anymore. She was confused by her suddenly stronger vision. A small line dotted her brow, and she kept rubbing her eyes.

The other changes would come, soon.

She'd begin to feel the heat. The steady buildup of desire.

The need would rise to an almost uncontrollable level—he'd have to make certain he stayed close by her side.

Her other senses would sharpen. Her sense of smell. Taste. Touch. Then, finally, hearing.

She'd also have other modifications.

He wondered how she'd respond to her new self.

Wondered how he'd respond.

Jon reached for a glass of champagne, and knew it wouldn't be long before they both found out.

She was too hot. Anna rubbed her hand over the back of her neck and felt the slick touch of sweat against her palm. Her heart was racing, much too fast, and the music seemed loud—so loud her temples were pounding in a matching beat.

Jon was beside her, standing so close that his arm brushed against hers. Even that small touch rippled through her sensitive body. A hard yearning filled her.

God, she wanted his hands on her.

Her head tilted back. Her breath expelled in a hard rush. Voices drifted over her, around her, and—

"I want you to kiss me." There. She'd said it. Bald. Desperate. She didn't care. She wanted him, no, *needed* him to kiss her then. So badly she was aching.

Jon's brows rose at her words, and he set down his drink. His fingers wrapped around her wrist and he started to pull her toward the balcony doors.

She didn't move. "No, here." She wanted his mouth on hers, wanted those lips pressing against her and his tongue driving deep.

What was happening to her?

His blue eyes met hers. His head lowered and his mouth covered hers.

Yes. Her fingers clenched around his shoulders and she rose onto her toes. Her lips parted, and his tongue swept inside.

A growl rumbled in her throat.

More. Her tongue met his, rubbing, teasing, tasting. And he tasted so good. Rich, but sweet, like the champagne he'd just put into his mouth.

God, she wanted more. Her nails dug into his flesh and heat pooled low in her belly.

She wanted to rip his clothes away. To feel his hard flesh against her, to feel the strong length of his cock nudging against her opening—

The sound of ripping fabric reached her ears.

Anna jerked away, gasping. What was happening? She stared at Jon, horrified. Her nails had torn the sleeves of his shirt. "I- I'm sorry, this isn't—" *me.* She swiped a hand across her forehead. It was so hot.

Her gaze darted to the balcony. Outside. Yes, yes, she needed to get outside. She pushed past Jon, humiliated. She'd ripped his shirt like some kind of sex-crazy nympho—in the middle of a crowded room of people.

She grabbed a champagne flute, drained the sweet drink in one gulp, and shoved the glass back on the tray. Then she was pushing open the glass doors of the balcony and stepping outside. No one else was out there, and the slightly cool night air feathered over her skin. It should have calmed her, taken away some of the desperate heat, but it didn't.

Seconds later, Jon stepped behind her. She knew it was him without even turning around. She could smell him. His cologne, the darker scent of man.

She could see perfectly without her glasses.

She could catch a man's scent and know instantly who he was.

And she was so damn hot. Burning, from the inside.

Jon touched her shoulder and she had to bite back the moan that rose to her lips.

She wanted him so much. Her panties were wet, soaked with cream, and her breasts pushed hard and tight against her bra.

"It's all right." He turned her toward him.

"No, it isn't." Anna didn't want to look into his eyes. Her gaze stayed on his throat, on the powerful pulse that she could see, pounding. *Pounding.*

She could almost hear that strong beat.

He caught her chin between his thumb and forefinger, forcing her head to lift. When she finally met his stare, her breath expelled in a hard rush.

Lust. Hunger. The same desire raging through her blood— she could see it in his eyes. She licked her lips, tasted him.

"S-something is happening to me." Making her desperate, al- most wild for the feel of him against her.

He lowered his head, brushing his lips over hers. "Do you want me?" he whispered.

God, yes. She nodded, almost afraid to speak.

"And do you trust me?"

The question gave her pause. "I-I think so."

His lips tightened. "That's not good enough. You're going to have to trust me completely tonight, baby. It's the only way I'll be able to get you through it."

Her brow furrowed. She didn't understand what he meant and—

"I can give you what you need," he told her, and the fingers of his right hand eased down the front of her dress, pausing in the hollow between her breasts. "Exactly what you need." He pulled the delicate fabric to the side, and stroked the curve of her breast.

Her body trembled.

His fingers moved slowly under the lacy edge of her bra, then rose and circled her nipple.

Yes.

"Do you like that?" His voice was a rumble of sound in the darkness. His eyes glittered down at her.

She nodded, her lips parted. "Jon, I—"

He kissed her. A deep, hard kiss. His tongue plunged inside her mouth, and swirled over hers, taking it, claiming it. And his hand covered her breast. Fondled her, teased and plucked the tight nipple, and the need that was gnawing at her grew.

He freed her chin, and she felt the weight of that hand move instantly to her hip.

She could smell her own arousal in the air. She, the woman who never let a guy to first base until the third date, was moaning, twisting her body against Jon's and wishing they were naked.

The hard, pulsing length of his cock pressed against her stomach. She wanted that cock inside of her. Wanted him thrusting deep, again and again until she screamed—and she'd sure as hell never been the screaming type before.

But with Jon, she wanted to scream. She wanted to bite. To take.

To fuck.

His hand, clenched on the skirt of her dress, began to lift the material.

Sanity tried to fight the fog of lust. She pulled her mouth from his. "S-someone could see." Anyone could glance through the glass doors and see them. Jon's broad frame covered most of her, but. . .

His lips curled, just the briefest bit. "Do you really care?"

No.

She just wanted him to keep touching her.

"I didn't think so." He lifted the skirt, baring her thighs. She hadn't worn panty hose; she'd always hated the feel of nylon. Besides, Richmond's winter nights weren't arctic by any means, and she had planned to be indoors for most of the evening.

She hadn't known Jon would be touching her. Rubbing his fingers over her thigh and squeezing her flesh.

While he kept teasing her nipple.

"You're wet for me."

More like soaked. She lifted her chin, and her hand eased between their bodies. Finding his aroused flesh, she stroked him through the material of his pants. "And you're hard for me." The knowledge made her feel powerful.

She started to smile, then felt the blunt edges of his fingertips push between her legs and grasp the cotton of her panties.

"Let me in," he ordered.

Her breath choked out, but she widened her stance. Voices drifted around her. Murmurs.

His fingers moved under the elastic of the panties, pushing aside the material. Then he was touching her creaming sex. His thumb rubbed over her clit, lightly scraping the sensitive flesh, and Anna gave a sharp moan. Her hand tightened around his shaft.

"Easy, baby, easy." He parted her folds, slowly working one finger into her sex.

Oh, God. Her fingers were moving on him, stroking, feeling the entire thick length from root to tip and—

He freed her breast, then grabbed her hand. "I can't hold on if you touch me."

She didn't want him to hold on. She wanted him wild, desperate—as wild and desperate as she was.

Her hips were moving, her sex rocking against the fingers between her legs. He pushed her hand against the cold wood of the railing. "Hold on," he muttered. Then he lowered his head and took her breast into his mouth, drawing the nipple deep inside, then laving her flesh.

Her other hand rose, wrapped around the thick railing. Her nails dug into the wood, scratching deep.

He pushed a second finger into her, withdrew, then thrust. Again. Again. His thumb worked her clit, and his teeth bit her nipple, not enough to hurt, just enough to make her whimper.

Her sex clenched around his fingers. She could feel a ripple moving through her body. Her thighs were taut, her belly quivering. She was close, so close—

A third finger thrust inside her. She came, gasping his name as the pleasure rocked through her.

As she shuddered and her knees trembled, Jon lifted his head. His lips were glistening. He pulled his hand away from her sex with one last, lingering caress that had aftershocks of release snaking through her. He raised his hand to his mouth and licked away the moisture.

Anna gulped.

"I told you, baby, I can give you what you need tonight."

Could he ever.

She pushed against his chest, feeling overwhelmed. *On a balcony.* She'd just let him—*on a balcony.* Her fingers trembled as she righted her clothes. With the red haze of hunger sated, her common sense was coming back—slowly, but it was coming back. "This isn't me," she told him, her voice too soft. "I don't—" *nearly have sex in public,* "get involved with men I don't know."

"You know me, and by the time dawn gets here, you'll know me a hell of a lot better than just about anyone. Just as I'll know you." The words were a sensual promise.

"I-I don't have one-night stands." Hard to say, considering what she'd just done. Sure, she could fantasize about it, because a fantasy was harmless, but reality—

She'd never been ready for a reality like this.

"Haven't you ever wanted to be bad? To let go of that control you hold so tightly, and just feel?"

He was talking to the secret part of her. The part she'd worked so hard to make certain no one knew.

Yes, she wanted to let go. Wanted to so badly.

But she'd been holding onto her control for too long. The idea of giving up that power to someone else, it scared the hell out of her. "I can't. I—"

"The hunger's going to come back. The lust. Worse than before."

How did he know that? How could he sound so certain?

"I can give you what you need," he repeated again. "All you have to do is trust me to take care of you."

So tempting. Her sex still quivered from his last job of taking care of her.

One night. The words seemed to whisper through her mind. Would giving up control for one night be so bad?

Or would it be too good?

"Anna!"

Jon tensed at the voice.

She squeezed her eyes shut, just for a second. *Steven.*

Jon moved slightly, turning toward the other man, but keeping his body between her and Steven.

The faint light both revealed and concealed Steven's face. It was a handsome face, a little soft around the chin. His eyes were brown—not warm, rather cold really—and they were studying her and Jon now with vague animosity.

"Hello, Steven." Had she really dated him for six months? Jon had just given her more pleasure in two minutes than this guy ever did.

What a waste.

Steven ran a hand through his sandy blond hair. "Can we talk, Anna? Alone?"

Breaking up with him had been hell. The guy kept calling, telling her that she was throwing away a "good thing." "Uh, now isn't a good time for me." She touched Jon's arm, finding the muscles rock hard. "Steven, this is my date, Jon."

She could see his mouth tighten. "I didn't know you were seeing anyone."

Jon grunted. "Now you do." He took a step forward.

Steven's eyes narrowed. "He's not going to be able to get you off any better than I could."

Her face went fiery hot, then ice cold.

"Oh?" Jon drawled. "Well, I didn't seem to have too much trouble a minute ago."

Steven lunged for him.

Jon caught him, wrapping one hand around the smaller man's throat. "You don't want to mess with me," he growled.

Steven froze.

"Let him go," Anna ordered, her hands tightening into fists. Humiliation and rage were pouring through her. Damn. She'd always known Steven was an asshole, but what had gotten into him tonight?

Very slowly, Jon released his hold.

"We're over, Steven," Anna said, moving forward. "We have been for a long time. That means you stay the hell out of my way, and I'll stay out of yours."

She saw his nostrils widen, and then his lips trembled, "Anna, I need you."

What? Since when? What the guy needed was a hard kick in the ass, and if he kept pushing, well, she was feeling just pissed enough to screw the good manners that one of her foster moms, Mrs. Tate, had taught her, and give the guy what he deserved.

He needed her. Right. Anna snorted.

Vaguely, she was aware of Jon muttering, "Oh, shit," beneath his breath. Then he was grabbing her arm, and pulling her past Steven.

"Anna!"

She ignored his plaintive cry. Not that she had much choice in the matter; Jon was practically dragging her back into the house, through the throng of people and—

"Anna!" Jonas Tyler reached for her arm. He was Ronnie's neighbor, a tall, handsome man in his early forties with just a touch of gray near his temples.

She smiled at him. "Hi, Jonas, I—"

He licked his lips. "You look really good, tonight, Anna. *Really* good."

What? She blinked. "Uh, thanks."

"We're leaving." Jon was definite.

She barely had the chance to toss a wave to Ronnie, and then they were outside, moving too fast. "Jon, dammit, slow down!"

"Can't, no time."

Had she stepped into the twilight zone? Anna stumbled to a halt, her high heels scraping against the sidewalk. "Look, I don't understand, what's happening—"

She caught a scent on the wind then. A thick, dank odor. Wild.

The hair on her nape rose.

Her head tilted to the right. Her gaze scanned the dark row of twisted pine trees that lined the edge of the park near Ronnie's house.

"*Sonofabitch.*"

Her gaze jerked to Jon's face. She found him watching the trees, a muscle ticking along his clenched jaw. Her heart began to race.

Someone was in those woods. She was absolutely certain of it.

Someone was out there, watching them, watching *her.* "Jon?"

"The bastard's hunting you."

Every bit of moisture disappeared from her mouth. Anna had to swallow twice before she could speak. "Wh-what?"

His fingers tightened around her wrist. "You're coming home with me."

Well, that had been an option before. Right after their fun on the balcony, she'd given serious thought to indulging in her fantasies and having a wild night with Jon.

But that was before Steven went crazy. Before Jon dragged her through the party. And before some psycho started watching her from the woods.

Now, she just wanted to get home, lock her door, and wait for the relative safety of the New Year's dawn. Alone.

She tried to pull away from Jon, but found his hold unbreakable.

His SUV waited a few feet away. They'd driven separately to the party, with Jon following closely behind her. Her car was down the lane a bit. Closer to the dark lines of trees.

She forced a laugh. "Okay, I think we both need to calm down a bit."

His gaze never left the trees. With his left hand, he pulled out his keys and automatically disengaged the lock. "You don't understand what's happening."

Yes, that had pretty much been the story of her night.

"But you're in danger, baby. Serious danger."

He was scaring her.

For just a second—one wild, horrible second—she thought she heard that damn dog's growls in her ears again.

Not possible.

"Trust me, baby, just trust me—and get in the SUV."

His gaze was on her now. Hard. Determined.

But she hesitated. Just driving off with Jon—well, if she left with him, she knew what would happen. Knew what she wanted to happen.

They'd be naked in less than an hour's time.

She didn't really know if someone was out in those woods or not, but she did *know* that she wanted Jon York. If she left with him, she'd have him.

Trust me.

Every instinct she possessed was screaming at her to get into the Ranger. So she did.

And, as they sped down the street, she could have sworn she heard the howl of a wolf echoing through the night.

The heat built in her veins as they drove. Her skin began to itch, her breath to pant out, and all the while, the fierce need flooded her body.

She forgot about the watcher in the woods. Convinced herself he'd never been there. She hadn't seen anyone, after all—only caught a faint scent on the wind.

So she blocked the fear from her mind, as she always did, and concentrated on Jon.

His scent filled the confines of the Ranger. His strong fingers wrapped around the steering wheel, the same fingers that had plunged inside of her and brought her to a shuddering release.

She licked her lips as she watched him, and her gaze dipped to his thighs. Strong, powerful thighs. She could ride them, ride *him*, for hours.

A harsh groan tore from his throat.

"Jon?"

He didn't look at her. He whipped the SUV around a corner, then spun onto a long, curving dirt drive. "You don't know how fucking good you smell. I swear, I feel like I could devour you."

Oh, that sounded good. Real good. "Promise?" She barely breathed the word.

The SUV slammed to a stop. He faced her then and she could see the lust in his eyes. "That's a damn guarantee."

Her hands were shaking. She balled them into fists and felt the sting of her nails digging into her palms.

"The first time's gonna be fast and hard," he told her, his voice a deep rumble. "I need you that way."

That was just how she wanted him.

"If things get too rough, you tell me to stop, got that?"

Was that what he'd meant when he asked her if she trusted him? Anna nodded.

"Then let's get inside, baby, or our first time will be right here, and this damn gear shift isn't what I want to be feeling against me." His hand lifted, smoothed over her shoulder, then drifted down her arm and brushed the side of her breast. "All I want to feel is you."

No man had ever talked to her this way.

It made her even hotter.

Anna shoved open the passenger-side door and barely paid attention to the sprawling, wood-frame house as she and Jon climbed the porch steps.

His shoulders were tense as he unlocked the door and disabled the alarm. She thought about touching him, but had the vague feeling he'd pounce on her if she did.

Her panties chafed against her sex as she walked, and Anna wanted to rip them off. Her folds were wet, her body eager, and she wondered how long it would take for her to come again.

The instant the alarm was reset and the door closed behind them, Jon seized her. He spun her around and shoved her back against the door frame. He didn't kiss her. She expected him to, had even parted her lips in anticipation of the thrust of his tongue.

His hand slid under her dress and clenched around her thigh. "You're so soft." His fingers rose, caught the crotch of her panties, and ripped. "And so damn wet."

Her skirt was bunched around her waist. She looked down, saw the red curls that shielded her sex, and saw his hand, pushing between her legs.

Yes. She reached for him, wanting to rip his shirt off and feel his muscled chest against her.

His hand jerked away from her sex. He caught her hands, slamming them back against the door on either side of her head. "Too dangerous to touch now." He pinned her wrists together with one hand. Then his right hand, it slid back down her body, and two broad fingers drove into her pussy.

Her head fell back against the door.

He pumped into her, stretching her, spreading the warm cream between her thighs and making her moan and shake.

His mouth locked on her throat. Caught the flesh just over her pulse point and suckled. His tongue laved her, and then she felt the sting of his teeth in a light bite.

She jerked against him, not with fear. No, not fear. . .

Hunger.

The fire in her gut raged higher. Her hips surged against his hand. "I need . . . more . . ." She needed him inside, slamming deep with that thick cock of his.

And she needed him *now.*

His fingers withdrew, giving a parting caress to her hungry flesh. The hiss of a zipper filled the air.

Anna eased open her legs, shifting slightly. She still wore her heels. Jon was pretty much fully dressed.

And they were going to fuck.

With one hand, he slid a condom over his straining shaft. Damn. Where had that come from? Then her gaze found the discarded wallet on the floor.

Ah, she loved a man who was prepared.

She swallowed, watching him as he rolled the thin latex up his cock. She wanted to taste that dark flesh.

He caught her stare, and must have read the intent on her face, because he growled, "Next time."

Oh, yes, next time.

His cock nudged against her sex. His right hand clenched around her hip while his left still imprisoned her wrists.

"*Jon.*" Not enough.

He kissed her, plunging his tongue deep inside her mouth. She tasted his need, knew he tasted hers.

"Lift your legs, wrap 'em around me," he ordered, and she struggled to obey. His right hand held her, helped to brace her back against the door.

He was strong, much stronger than she'd realized.

The head of his penis pushed into her, one inch, two. The condom was a thin barrier, and she wanted to feel every inch of his hot length in her sex.

He was trying to be easy. Gentle.

She'd always wanted that before.

But not tonight. Her legs tightened around him. "Harder."

His pupils were wide and dark, swallowing the blue. He pulled back, just a little, then slammed balls deep into her.

Yes.

Again and again he plunged, pounding into her and pushing his thick flesh over her clit.

Her heartbeat filled her ears. Drumming fast. Too fast. She kissed him, catching his lips and savoring the feel of his tongue just as she savored the thrust of his cock.

Deeper. Faster.

More.

Her release was close. Her sex tightened around him, the muscles quivering as they fought to hold his length.

Close.

She felt him swell even more inside her. His fingers dug into her hips and he choked out her name.

Anna came, bucking and arching against him and, seconds later, she felt the shudder that ripped along his body.

Yes.

More. . .

He was in trouble. Serious trouble.

Jon fought to calm his racing heart and steady the breaths that were jerking out.

Oh, shit.

Anna Summers was the best fuck he'd ever had.

And they'd barely even gotten started with the games they'd play.

Why couldn't he have asked her out before she'd been bitten? Would the sex have been the same?

He had a sinking feeling it would have. Because while the change of the bite was drawing him in—hell, there was no way to fight the pheromones the woman was giving off, those two assholes at the party were proof of that—it was the woman herself who was driving him crazy.

Her legs slowly slid down his body. His cock still nestled between her thighs. He knew he should move, but he wasn't going to, not yet.

One of the side effects of a werewolf bite was a little phenomenon called a heat cycle. In the first twenty-four hours after a person was infected, the individual's body went through a multitude of changes.

And the heat cycle was one of the hardest changes to endure. Lust built, merging with wild need and hunger, until the sensations were literally a fire in the blood. The heat started gradually, it always did, but soon the bitten person was almost mad with need.

Sex. Hard. Fast. Over and over.

After each orgasm, the need abated, just for a bit.

But the hunger soon would come back.

The night ahead of them was going to be long, and hot as hell.

Yet he knew it was time for him to tell Anna the truth. She had to know what was waiting for her in the coming hours.

She deserved the truth. He just hoped she wouldn't be too afraid.

He eased away from her, hating the loss of her creamy warmth. Her sex felt like damn heaven, so warm and wet. And tight. So tight.

Jon swallowed. He needed to ditch the condom and make certain Anna was all right.

She looked okay. Hell, she looked fantastic. A faint flush covered her cheeks. Her green eyes sparkled, and behind her plump red lips, he could see the edge of her teeth.

The canines were a bit sharper than they'd been before.

So were her nails. He loosened his hold on her wrists, letting her hands fall to her sides. Back at her friend's house, Anna's nails had dug into the wood, leaving deep grooves. She hadn't even noticed the marks, but he certainly had.

Anna would never completely change into a werewolf—that wasn't the way for the Bitten—but her body would alter. The teeth. The nails that changed into claws. If she didn't have control of herself, she could hurt someone.

The newly Bitten were often dangerous. Sometimes deadly.

Her fingers rose and traced the curve of his jaw. "That was amazing."

He swallowed. Yeah. "Anna, I—"

The alarm sounded, a high, fast beeping that filled the house.

Jon jerked his pants back in place and ran for the control panel. Shit.

"Jon?" Anna was behind him, her voice tense.

"Property code. Someone's out there." And that someone had tripped one of the sensors he'd installed.

Jon had never been a fan of uninvited guests—and he'd made damn certain he secured his property against intruders.

He had a bad feeling gnawing at his gut, a dark suspicion about his trespasser's identity.

Crossing the room quickly, he opened his desk drawer and pulled out a gun, then loaded the bullets—silver, of course—in an automatic move.

Anna's high heels tapped across the hardwood floor.

He turned and leveled a hard stare at her. "Stay here."

Her lips tightened. "Look, I may not be some kind of security expert like you, but I can help. Whatever's going on, *I can help.*"

No, she couldn't. His sweet little history scholar had no clue how to fight a bad guy, especially the kind of bad guy that was most likely waiting out in the darkness.

Damn, but she was cute. He kissed her again. He had to. Jesus, but he loved the way the woman tasted.

And he'd have more of a taste. Once he got rid of the asshole outside. "Promise me you'll stay inside. No matter what you hear, you'll stay inside."

She shook her head. "No, I'm not. You might need me!"

If she came running out after him, she'd get killed. Plain and simple. "Baby, you don't have any idea what we're dealing with here."

Her chin lifted. "Neither do you. Some kids could have set off your alarm while they were shooting fireworks, some animal could have done it—"

Yeah, that's what he was betting.

"—you don't know and I—"

Something slammed against the front door. Something big. Strong.

Anna spun around. "What in the hell is that?"

His fingers tightened around the butt of the gun. "Our lost little animal."

She grabbed his arm. "You can't go out there!"

Bam. Bam. The door frame shook.

"We need to call the police or—"

Bam.

Anna screamed. He pushed her back. "It's all right, baby, just go upstairs—"

Silence.

Her nails were digging into his arms. "I'm not leaving you," she whispered.

Part of him admired her for that. Another part—a much bigger part—wished she'd run for safety.

But she wasn't budging, despite her fear, and Jon knew it was time to face the big, bad monster.

Time for Anna to see what waited in the darkness.

Jon stepped forward, lifted the gun another inch, and opened the door.

Chapter 4

When Jon wrenched open the door, Anna wasn't quite sure what she expected to see. But she didn't see anything. The porch was empty, littered with shadows.

Glancing down, she noticed that the front of the door was dented. Scraped. *Something* had been there, but it was gone now. She hoped.

Jon stepped forward, and she followed on his heels. Anna's nostrils flared as she moved and, pulling in the scents of the night, she caught a familiar smell.

Raw. Wild. Heavy, with a thick musk.

Her lips began to tremble, even as a growing certainty filled her.

She knew that something very, very bad was happening. She knotted her hands into fists, and gasped at the sting of pain.

Anna glanced down, slowly uncurled her fingers, and saw claws stretching from her fingertips.

Oh, my God.

Her knees started to shake, and suddenly the noises in the forest were loud—too loud.

She could hear the rustle of leaves, the flutter of a bird's wings, and a thumping—a hard, furious thumping.

A heartbeat.

Hers? No, hers was much faster, racing like crazy.

Jon's.

She could hear his heart beating.

Impossible.

As impossible as her being able to see without her trusty glasses?

"Bastard's gone."

And he was. Even now, she could hear the thuds of the intruder's running feet. Far away.

Too far for her to hear.

Anna's knees gave way and she fell onto the porch.

Jon spun around. "Anna!"

She flinched back from him. Her gaze darted to the woods, the woods that she could see perfectly. No, better than perfect. She could see the bark on the pine trees more than a hundred feet away, the nest of a bird, and the delicate movement of its wings.

"What's happening to me?" she whispered, as fear grew in her belly. This wasn't right. She shouldn't see so well; shouldn't be able to hear Jon's heart beating.

She sure as hell shouldn't have claws.

"It's all right," Jon told her softly, reaching for her arm.

The hell it was. She was scared spitless, so afraid her whole body was shaking. But behind the fear, starting to unfurl deep within her, was that dark hunger. *Lust.*

This shit was so not normal.

"Don't touch me." The words were soft, but underlined with a desperate strength. Anna didn't want him touching her—not in any way. Her control was far too tenuous.

He stepped back, casting one last, hard look at the woods. "We should get back inside."

"Who was out here?" Who or *what* had been outside, struggling so hard to get in?

To get to Jon?

Or to get to her?

"I don't know."

He was lying. She'd bet her life on it. He didn't change expression, didn't so much as blink.

But his heart rate picked up. Doubled for a few seconds.

Lie.

Gut instinct guided her. "What's happening to me?"

The pounding of his heart spiked again, even as he smiled at her, showing those dimples that had always made her weak. "I don't know what you're talking about, baby."

Lie.

Anna pushed to her feet. Her hands pressed against the wood of the house for support. "How come I've suddenly got better than twenty-twenty vision? How come I can hear every noise in those woods?" *Your heartbeat?* "And just how is that I've suddenly got a brand new manicure?" She held up one hand, just for a moment. Her claws glinted.

His lips tightened. "We need to go back inside. He could come back."

He. "Who, Jon? Who was here?"

But he just shook his head. "Inside. We'll talk, but not out in the open. I want to make sure we're safe."

Because the man—thing?—who'd been out there was threatening them? Well, it certainly wasn't as if he'd knocked politely at the door.

She eased around the side of the house and crept inside the

doorway. Jon stalked in behind her, slamming the door and re-setting the alarm.

Crossing her arms over her chest, Anna watched him. She was so scared. The last time she'd been this afraid—she'd just watched her parents die in front of her.

But dammit—something was *very* wrong with her.

Jon crossed to her side and stared down at her with eyes that glittered. "You're not going to believe me."

"Try me." Anything would be better than what she was starting to imagine.

A rough sigh blew past his lips. "Earlier, when you were attacked—that wasn't a dog."

Sure it was. Her brows furrowed. "Uh, yes, it was—"

"It was a wolf. Actually, it was a werewolf."

A gurgle of what she sincerely hoped wasn't hysterical laughter bubbled in her throat. *Right.*

"I'm completely serious."

She shook her head. "I hate to break this to you, but werewolves aren't real, Jon. Neither are vampires, or demons, or—

"Lift the bandage off your leg. You'll find the wound's already healed."

Bull. But she did as he asked, mainly to prove him wrong. Her fingers were trembling as she pulled back the white tape and eased the gauze off her leg. Oh, damn, but she hoped it wasn't too bad. It hadn't hurt in the last few hours, but she could still remember the feel of that beast sinking his teeth deep into her and—

There was no mark on her leg. "That's not possible," she whispered, her fingers smoothing over the unmarred skin. She *remembered* the bite. The burn of the teeth.

"It was a werewolf bite. He infected you, and now you've got the power of the moon coursing through your blood."

Infected you. "Wait a minute. Just take a step back." Anna realized she was snarling and took a deep breath, trying to calm down. "Werewolves aren't real, okay? I was bitten by some ugly mutt, not—"

"How big was the creature?"

She shrugged at that. "I don't know. I was running away from him, not trying to make a sketch." When he just stared at her, she muttered, "I think his head came to my chest."

"And his eyes? Do you remember what you told me his eyes were like?"

Glowing silver. A hard swallow. "No, I don't remember."

"Bullshit."

Her chin lifted.

"They seemed to be shining, didn't they? Too bright? That's a sign of the werewolf—a gaze that burns with the moon's power."

She didn't want to believe him. The idea of a werewolf running around Richmond, hanging out in her parking garage, well, it was just ridiculous.

But how had her wound healed? And how could she see and hear so well?

Infected.

"They're in every major city. By day, the *Weres* look just like everybody else, but when the moon rises, those who are Bound, they change."

"Bound?"

"The Bound are chained by the power of the moon from the moment of birth. Linked to the moon and bound by the beast." A pause. "They are the ones who can shape-shift."

"Shape-shift, right." Her gaze darted around the room. *The couch.* Anna stumbled toward it and sat down—hard.

"Werewolves can only transform at night, when the moon rises. The Bitten don't change, not completely. Their senses sharpen—"

Like hers had sharpened.

"Their ability to heal speeds up."

As hers had.

"And, for a while, their sex drive kicks into overdrive."

Her shoulders hunched. Oh, God, was that why she was acting so—so crazy? Why, even now, she couldn't help but notice the way Jon's broad shoulders stretched his shirt and wonder how it would feel to touch that strong chest when he was naked.

His words humiliated her, but the hunger she felt couldn't be banished.

"The Bitten—you—your pheromones have gotten stronger. You're going to have an effect, a sexual effect, on every man and some of the women you meet."

Her eyes closed. "Is that what's happening with you?" *This isn't true. Not a word. I don't need to feel this ache in my heart. It's not true. Jon wants me, me, it's not because of some pheromone-induced lust.*

She'd wanted him before the bite.

And even more after.

"Your scent is drawing me in," he admitted, "but I wanted you before the damn bite."

Her eyes shot open as he seemed to echo her thoughts.

"The Bitten become stronger than normal humans. A hell of a lot stronger. And with the lust that pumps through their blood, well, some of them have been known to hurt their human partners."

Too dangerous to touch now. Jon hadn't been talking about some edge-of-control passion moment when he'd said those words. He was literally afraid she'd hurt him.

"How . . ." Her voice sounded like a frog's croak, so she cleared her throat and tried again, "How do you know all this?"

His lips hitched into the briefest of smiles, a hard, sardonic twist of his mouth. "Because I've been bitten before, too."

Her heart slammed against her breast.

"Don't be scared," he muttered, easing onto the couch beside her. "You don't need to fear me."

She didn't believe him. She knew, by the watchful expression in his eyes, that he heard her thundering heartbeat.

And he must have heard it all the times she was near him in the past when she'd gotten excited, aroused by his presence.

If she could have vanished right then, she would have gladly faded away.

But there was nowhere for her to go, and she needed to hear more of Jon's story—and she needed to determine if he was telling her a horrible truth or an outrageous lie.

"When?" She asked him, taking a quick breath.

"Years ago. Hell, I was just a kid. Barely eighteen. Driving in the wrong place, at the wrong time. My Vette broke down, I tried to fix the engine, and the next thing I knew, I was on the ground and a wolf was going for my throat." He shook his head. "Thought for sure I was dead. Could even taste the blood in my mouth."

She clenched her fingers into a fist so that she wouldn't reach for him. "How—how did you get away?"

"A man came out of the shadows and shot the wolf. Two shots—one in the shoulder to get him off me, the other dead center between the eyes." Jon caught Anna's left hand in his, unfurled her fingers, and traced a light fingertip over the claws that had yet to disappear. "I managed to drag myself a few feet away from the wolf, then I watched the animal change back to a man. That happens when they die; they always shift to human form then."

He stared down at her hand. "I was scared to death. Certain I was dying, sure I'd gone crazy and just imagined the wolf. Then the guy—Travers Smith—he loaded me into his car and started telling me a story about nightmares and werewolves. By the time he pulled up at my folks' place, I knew what I'd seen, and I knew exactly what I'd become."

One of the Bitten.

"This guy—Travers—how did he know what was going to happen?" She asked.

"He was a pack hunter."

Was, not is, she realized.

"His job was to watch the werewolves in the city. To make certain none of them turned on the humans. And if they did, well, then it was up to him to stop the *Weres*, by any means necessary."

Like by putting a gunshot between the wolf's eyes.

Oh, God, she was starting to believe him.

Anna swallowed and wondered just how her life had taken such a deadly turn.

All things considered, Jon thought Anna was handling things pretty well. She wasn't screaming or crying hysterically. She just sat on the couch, watching him with eyes that were a bit too wide and skin a bit too pale.

Travers Smith. If only Jon had realized back then just how much the guy would change his life. A cop who worked the day shift, Travers had taken Jon home, given his parents a bullshit story about a pit bull on the loose, and even managed to convince his folks that he had to stay overnight for "observation"— because the cop had a "soft spot for kids."

Observation. Right. Travers stayed to see if he needed to put a bullet between Jon's eyes. The first twenty-four hours after a bite were critical. Those who couldn't handle the sudden power and needs coursing through them, well, they went crazy.

That night, Jon snuck out of the house just after midnight, his body burning with lust and a hunger he couldn't understand. He went to his girlfriend's and took her hard and fast, but didn't hurt her. He didn't hurt anyone, thank God.

And when he crept out of Bridgette's house, he found Travers waiting for him.

The cop eyed him carefully, then said, "If you'd so much as scratched her, I was gonna have to kill you. Good thing for you, kid, I know the difference between the sound of a woman's pain and her pleasure." Then he put his gun away, the gun he'd been aiming at Jon's chest, and Jon realized just how close he'd come to death.

He also understood that he could control the power within him. So did Travers. From that night on, the cop started training him, preparing him for—

"This is insane!" Anna snapped, standing up in a quick, stiff move. "Werewolves aren't real and I don't even know why I'm listening to a word you're saying!"

He grabbed her wrist, letting his claws stretch and press against the tender skin. "You believe me."

She looked down at his hand. Her lips trembled as she eyed the claws that were at least two inches long—claws that hadn't been there seconds before.

"The longer you live with the bite, the more control you have." He could even partially bank the scent of his pheromones and almost double his enhanced healing speed.

Her gaze rose to his face. He smiled at her, deliberately, and flashed the canines that had burned and lengthened into fangs.

She blanched. "Oh, hell."

Yeah, that had pretty much been his original thought, too. His lips lowered, covering the fangs, and the hand that had imprisoned her relaxed and began to stroke her with slow, soothing movements. "You're not alone in this, baby. I can help you." Guide her, teach her, as he'd been taught.

He didn't think Anna would turn feral. The woman had always struck him as having a deep, tight control over herself. She might give in to the physical lust burning between them, but she wouldn't give in to the greedy power of the moon.

She wouldn't kill.

But the one hunting her just might.

"I'm some kind of . . . monster."

"No." He was definite on that. She was the same beautiful, smart woman she'd always been. Just with a few new . . . enhancements. "You're the woman you were before, baby. Your life *will* go on just as it has before."

"How can it?" A lone tear slid down her cheek. "God, Jon, I'm standing here, talking to you about damn werewolves and death and I'm so scared. But even now," she swallowed and shook her head, "dammit, even now, I want you. My body seems to be burning up. These clothes are too hot and tight and you smell so good and I just . . ." She bit her lip, then finished in a whisper, "want you. It doesn't matter what I am, or what you are. I want you."

He knew how hard the admission was for her. She'd laid her

pride bare before him. He rose slowly, stepped close to her, and breathed in her sweet scent. His cock was already hard; it had been the entire time they'd talked.

He wanted Anna, wanted her with the same raw hunger she felt for him.

Only he didn't have the excuse of a fresh bite.

The woman herself made him ache.

Pheromones or not, he'd have felt the same.

His thumb traced the plump line of her lower lip. "And I want you." He would have her again, very, very soon.

But now that she knew the rules of their new game, he had to make certain she was ready for what would come next.

Her tongue snaked out, pressing against the pad of his thumb. He clenched his teeth and forced himself to tell her the rest. "The roughest time for you will be in the next twenty-four hours or so. After that, things will steady up. The need—it'll ease."

Her teeth caught the skin of his thumb, and she bit lightly. *Damn.*

His cock was twitching with hunger. "I want you again, baby. Want you so bad I can taste the hunger in my throat. But you know the truth about me now," *and about yourself,* "so the choice is yours."

Werewolves. Death. Madness. Need.

She'd said she still wanted him. He could see the desire in her eyes, but he also saw fear.

Which would win? Fear or desire?

Her teeth released their hold on him. She stepped back.

Fear or desire?

She lifted her chin. Her fingers rose to the back of her dress and fumbled with the zipper.

The garment dropped to her feet in a silken, black puddle.

Her heart was racing too fast. Her breath came too quickly. And the smell of her sweet cream filled his nostrils.

"I know what you are, and I know what I am." The lace of her bra pushed against her breasts. The curls of her sex gleamed like fire. "You're a man, I'm a woman, and I want you so badly I ache."

Wanted him, feared him.

Fear and desire.

A heady combination.

Time for the real games to begin.

He took her upstairs, into his darkened bedroom. A massive, king-sized bed with short, thick posts waited in the middle of the room.

Jon's hand slid over the curve of her ass and squeezed. Anna's breath caught in her throat.

"Get on the bed," he ordered, his breath hot on her neck.

She crossed the room, eased onto the mattress, and heard the faint squeak of the bedsprings. The room smelled like him—the same, rich, tempting scent.

He was in the closet now, rummaging around. Her nipples were tight, and her thighs trembled. "Jon?"

He stepped back into the room. Two long, thin strips of rope dangled from his hands.

"I-I've never . . ." Never even *thought* about letting her lover tie her up.

Jon stalked toward her. "This'll make sure you don't give in to the temptation to use those claws of yours on me."

She shook her head. "I-I won't, I—"

"And I want you helpless. Naked. Ready for me."

Anna gulped. Her sex quivered with excitement.

"Lay back."

Her spine brushed against the cool covers.

"Lift your arms."

Her hands rose. He caught her right wrist, looped the rope around her, and tightened it. She expected the material to be rough, to chafe her skin.

But it felt so soft.

He tied the other end of the rope to the post, keeping her arm stretched out.

Then he caught her left wrist, leaned over her body, and secured the rope the same way. "Too tight?"

She shook her head no.

"Good." His head lowered over her chest and he caught one taut nipple and suckled.

Her breath hissed out from between her teeth.

"I told you, baby," he whispered against her flesh. "I'm going to fucking devour you."

And she could hardly wait.

His teeth closed over her nipple. Tugged lightly. Bit. Then his tongue swirled over the peak.

Her hands jerked against the ropes, but they held tight, and she arched her body, pressing her breast harder against his mouth.

His clothes rubbed against her flesh, sending her to an aching sensitivity. His fingers drifted over her stomach, then eased between her legs. When he touched the core of her sex, she shuddered, her hips bucking.

"Easy," he whispered.

But it wasn't easy. Nothing was easy. Not the hunger, the need—

He sucked her breast, pulling it hard into his mouth and making her whimper.

"Jon!"

His head lifted. His mouth gleamed, and behind his lips, she could see the deadly outline of his fangs.

Fear thumped through her, tangling with the lust.

He'd wanted her helpless, and she was. The ropes were secured; they were strong. She wouldn't be able to escape, not unless he untied her.

"You're creaming for me."

She was. The fear was only turning her on more.

Because she trusted him. Deep down, she didn't think he'd hurt her.

Jon had saved her in the parking garage. He'd brought her to the heights of ecstasy.

And she knew he'd have her coming again.

His fingers rubbed against her folds and pressed against her clit. He smiled at her—a dark flash of intent, a wink of dimples— then he took her other breast. Licking, sucking, and biting, while his fingers brought her to a desperate pitch of arousal.

Her legs were spread wide, and he pushed himself between them, settling his legs inside hers and using his hips to anchor his body against hers.

He kissed his way down her stomach, laving his tongue over her flesh and biting the skin below her belly button.

She knew what he was planning. Knew even before he slid down her length what he would do.

His breath was warm against her sex, and when he bent over her, when he put his mouth against her clit, she choked back a scream.

He used his lips and tongue and teeth on her. Carefully, skill- fully. He had her twisting, almost fighting him for release. The rope dug into her wrists, not hurting her—the hemp was too soft for that, but binding her well. Reminding her that she was helpless to fight the surge of pleasure rising within her.

He pushed a finger inside her. Licked her clit. Thrust the finger knuckle deep.

She wanted to grab his head, to clutch his dark mane of hair, and force him to kiss her harder.

A second finger worked inside her. Withdrew. Thrust.

She was going to come. Anna's sex trembled. Telltale shivers worked through her body. She was—

His fingers withdrew and Anna could have snarled in frustration. So close. She'd been—

His tongue drove into her. Again. Again.

Anna came on a long, hot blast of pleasure.

Jon rose over her, licking his lips. "I knew you'd taste good. Fucking delicious." Then he reached over the side of the bed, fumbled with a drawer, and pulled out a small packet.

She was still trembling when he thrust inside her. His cock filled her, stretching the flesh already oversensitized from her climax. He pumped into her, slamming his cock into her body so hard that the thudding of flesh filled the air.

She couldn't move her arms, but she lifted her legs, wrapped them around his hips, and clutched him tight. She arched toward him, meeting him thrust for thrust.

The bed jerked. Rocked. His cock shoved into her. The smell of sex filled the air.

And Anna spiraled into a second climax.

Moments later, Jon stiffened against her and she felt a fierce satisfaction as he cried out her name as he came.

Then he was holding her, his fingers untying the ropes and

stroking her wrists. His shirt—the man was still dressed—rubbed lightly against her breasts. And his cock still rested in her sex.

The. Best. Sex. Ever.

In the distance, she heard the wail of sirens—dozens of them.

Her gaze jerked to the left, and she saw the glowing gold of Jon's beside clock: it was midnight.

Jon touched her cheek, drawing her stare back to him. "Happy New Year," he told her softly, and Anna felt her lips curl.

A strange flutter began in her heart. A soft, warm glow. Oh, damn.

He kissed her lightly. A gentle brush of his lips against hers.

The fluttering grew worse.

Anna was afraid right then, very afraid that she was falling for Jon.

Or maybe she'd already fallen for him—all those months of dreaming, fantasizing.

Her arms wrapped around him and she pulled him tightly to her.

New Year's. And, unlike her Christmas, she wasn't spending the special time alone.

She was spending it with a man right out of her hottest dreams.

And other than the fact that a werewolf—a *freaking* werewolf—was on her tail, well, the new year was looking pretty damn good.

Jon stretched against her and kissed her again.

Oh, yes, pretty damn good indeed.

Anna stopped being afraid of falling and met his eager lips with a passion that was rising fast once again.

*** * ***

When she finally slept—or rather, when her body was too tired for any more pleasure—she thought she'd dream. Perhaps of the wolf who'd attacked her.

Or of her parents. She often dreamed of them.

Nightmares, really. Of the shooting. Of her mother's scream and her father's blood.

But this night, she didn't see her mother and father. She didn't see anything; she just felt the comforting embrace of her lover and the blanket of sleep.

When she opened her eyes to the light of the dawn, she found that Jon was gone. Then she heard the faint mumble of his voice.

"Not a threat . . ."

Silence.

"She's not feral."

Anna pulled the sheet around her and rose from the bed. She didn't hear any other voice, just Jon's. He was probably on the phone with someone.

"I told you, there's no need to worry about Anna."

The mention of her name had every muscle in her body stiffening. Just who would have to worry about her?

She crept closer to the door. Jon was downstairs, yet she could hear him speaking. Sure, the words came like a whisper to her, but she could understand him perfectly. And the words he spoke, they scared her.

"If she'd been dangerous, I would have taken care of her by now."

Her heart iced. *Taken care of her by now.*

She shook her head. No, this wasn't happening. He hadn't—

"Yeah, I can handle Anna."

Her arm knocked into the dresser, and sent the lamp on top of it bumping back against the wall.

The *thump* of the lamp seemed far, far too loud.

The sudden silence from Jon echoed up the stairs. Then, "*Christ.* I've got to go."

He was coming for her.

Her gaze darted around the room and found the crumpled black dress that Jon had brought upstairs some time during the night. She ran to it, and jerked it on as fast as she could, not bothering with her bra, and knowing that her panties had been ripped beyond repair.

I would have taken care of her by now.

His words played through her mind, pounding at her. Their meaning was unmistakable.

He was such a bastard. And she was a stupid, romantic idiot.

The bottom of the dress had just brushed against her knees when he shoved open the bedroom door. His breathing was hard, as if he'd taken the stairs at a run, and he probably had.

Anna stared at him, sick to her stomach and aching in her heart. His chest and feet were bare. A pair of faded jeans hung low on his hips. Damn, but the man was sexy—even when she was furious, he was still too *sexy*.

"Let me explain," he began, and she realized he knew she'd heard everything. That supersensitive hearing—she had to remember that it worked both ways.

"What's to explain?" She asked, dragging a hand through her hair. "I mean, we had a night of great sex, you were planning to kill me, and—"

Jon crossed the room in three steps, and grabbed her arm. "I would never have fucking killed you!"

"Oh, really?" She knew he could hear the frantic drumming of her heart. His was pounding so hard she was surprised the floor wasn't shaking. Damn, but she was stupid. She'd been thinking she finally found her Mr. Right, and he'd been thinking of ways to kill her.

Sometimes, life was such a bitch. She glared at him, refusing to let the churning in her gut cow her. "Then you mind telling me just how else you planned to take care of me?"

Chapter 6

Jon's lips thinned. "There are many ways to handle a feral Bitten."

"So how would you have handled me, then?" A Bitten, was that all she'd been to him? Just another infected human?

"If you'd shown signs of losing control," he gritted, "I'd have sedated you—"

"With what?" She sure didn't like the sound of that. Yes, it was a hundred times better than the threat of a cold, hard killing, but the idea of Jon playing doctor while she'd been tied to the bed scared her—a lot.

He dropped his hands, walked to the dresser, and pulled out a thin vial of clear liquid. "With this."

The man sure believed in being prepared. "So what, you make a habit of keeping drugs like that in your bedroom?" Mr. Right he wasn't.

Time to leave—as fast as she could. Her gaze darted to the door.

A growl rumbled from Jon's throat. "You don't understand what I am."

"Uh, yes, I do." Her own anger shot past the fear. "You're the guy who was thinking about *taking care of me* because I'm some kind of dangerous threat to the world! The guy who had fabulous sex with me even while he was thinking about the prospect of offing me—"

"It was pretty damn fabulous, wasn't it?" he murmured.

Her lips parted, and air rushed out as she floundered.

He put the vial back in the dresser, and pushed the drawer closed. "I didn't tell you everything about myself last night."

No shit. He'd conveniently left out the part about being a killer.

"I'm a hunter, Anna. A pack hunter, just like Travers Smith used to be."

She'd suspected that. The minute she heard his words on the phone, the thought had entered her mind. "And so now I'm one of the creatures you hunt?"

His hands clenched. "No."

She licked her lips. There was a question she had to ask, one that would lance her pride. "Did you spend the night with me— have sex with me—just because you're a hunter and you had to make certain I wasn't some kind of threat?" She felt dangerous right then—furious, enraged. Her claws were out, but her hands were curled into fists, so he couldn't see them.

He cursed, and marched back toward her. He didn't touch her, just glared down at her. "You know the damn answer to that question."

"No, I don't." And it was eating her up inside.

"Then let me clear up a few things for you." He was less than a foot away. "I had sex with you because I wanted to. Because I'd been wanting to get you naked and under me for months. The bite—hell, that didn't have anything to do with it."

"My pheromones—"

"Turned me on, yeah, but I'd been turned on from the minute I met you."

She wanted to believe that, and she might have, if she hadn't heard him talking on the phone so casually about getting rid of her.

Now, she wasn't sure she trusted a word he said. "Then why didn't you do something about it? Why didn't you just ask me out?"

"Why didn't you ask me?" he whispered. His hand lifted then, and brushed down her bare arm. "You wanted me, too, baby. Don't deny it. I could hear the fast beat of your heart when I came close. Could smell the rich flavor of your cream."

She swallowed. "Answer my question."

"I was working on a case, rounding up a rogue wolf. The timing was shit." His fingers tightened around her arm. "Still is, especially with your bite being so fresh and that bastard out there, stalking you."

Like she'd forgotten *him*.

"I swear to you, killing you, hurting you—that was never an option for me, *never*."

Her eyes locked on the dresser. "You would have drugged me though—"

He exhaled. "I'm not going to lie. If you'd gone after me, or any other human, I wouldn't have had a choice. I would have had to disable you, and take you to the Center."

Things just kept getting worse and worse. "The Center?"

"A base in Richmond. It's for the Bitten who can't control their power—a place like—like—"

Anna understood, and wished she didn't. "Some kind of supernatural psych ward?" Her voice was a horrified shriek.

He gave a curt nod.

Oh, hell.

"Well, thanks for not pumping me full of meds and dumping me at the nuthouse." She jerked away from him and headed for the door. *Asshole.* So much for being her knight in shining armor.

"You don't understand." His quiet words stopped her just as she reached the threshold. "You don't know what it's like, to see someone who was perfectly normal one day plunge into insanity the next."

There was an ache in his voice, a remembered pain. She couldn't help it; Anna glanced back at him.

A muscle flexed along his jaw, and memories raged in his blue eyes. "When a Bitten turns feral, it's like nothing you've ever seen or imagined. An animal takes the place of the human. A fierce, brutal animal that attacks any person—hell, it doesn't matter if the victim is a lover, a friend, or even a child. The bloodlust drives the Bitten to destroy, and that's all the creature can do."

Certainty filled her. Jon was talking about someone in particular, she knew it. "Who was it, Jon? Who did the bite destroy?"

His jaw worked. He glared at her.

"Jon?" Someone close to him. She'd bet her life on it.

"A few years after I met him, Travers fell in love with this sweet, pretty little widow. They started planning a wedding, talking about building a house."

This wasn't going to end well. Part of her wanted to stop him, to hold the words back. But a bigger part of her *needed* to hear what he had to say.

Anna still didn't know what she was dealing with. She didn't fully understand the life of a Bitten, and she sure as heck was having a hard time buying the whole werewolf idea. But . . . "What happened to them?"

"Travers was hunting a brutal asshole named Kane—a rogue werewolf who'd attacked members of his own pack before turning on the humans. Kane knew Travers was on his trail, and he had a reputation for playing with hunters."

"Playing how?" Her bare toes curled into the hardwood floor. She'd forgotten to grab her shoes. They were near the bed; she could see them out of the corner of her eye, but she didn't bother to get them. She wanted to hear the rest of the story first.

"He liked to turn the tables on them, make them the hunted. That's what he did with Travers. Started stalking him. Following him during the day and night. Kane saw him with Donna, and being the bastard that he was, he figured out just how to hurt the hunter."

Oh, no. "H-he bit her?"

"Caught her just as she was leaving her shop. Donna used to own a bakery." His lip curled up for a fleeting moment. "Made the best damn cakes I'd ever had." The smile vanished. "But that was before Kane got ahold of her and pushed his poison in her veins."

Anna's eyes closed as the memory of her own attack came flooding back to her—the slashing pain in her leg, the sound of the snarls and growls, the stench of the wolf. "Wh-what happened to her?"

"Travers found her in the street. Took her home, tried to take care of her." Jon's legs shifted slightly and the wood creaked beneath his feet. "Two hours later, I got a call from him. She'd attacked him, slashed his arms, and almost ripped open his throat."

Oh, God.

"When I got there, she was screaming and snarling. Trying to attack with her teeth and claws. Donna wasn't there anymore—not sweet, good Donna. Something else was in her place. Something full of hate and bloodlust."

Her lips trembled as she asked, "So you eliminated her?"

"No! Dammit, listen to me!" He crossed the room in a flash, towering over her. "I wouldn't have hurt Donna. Hell, do you really think Travers would have even let me think about something like that? The guy was broken, Anna. *Broken.* He was the one who came up with the idea for the Center. He wanted a place to help the Bitten, like her. To try and get them back to being the people they *used* to be."

The ache in her chest eased, just a bit. "You didn't kill her?"

"Hell, no! I called in the leaders of the local packs. Not all werewolves are bad, baby, you've got to understand that. They didn't like what was happening to their own kind, either. And every time a *Were* went rogue, they got scared shitless. So when I told them we wanted to start a place to help the Bitten, they poured as much damn money down my throat as they could.

"You see, they didn't want just a place for humans, they wanted a research facility set up to find out *why* some of their own went bad. If we could figure out why some went insane, and if we could help them, the world would be a damn lot safer for humans *and* werewolves."

"Have they," she stopped and cleared her throat, then spoke again, her voice stronger, "have they figured out why some lose control?" Was she still at risk? She'd made it past the first twelve hours, but did she still need to worry that she'd start slipping into madness?

The stronger senses, the hotter sex drive—jeez, it had almost seemed like a fun new beginning for her. But it was actually a very dangerous, dark world, one that was making her stomach clench.

"The scientists believe it's a sort of chemical imbalance. One that makes the functions of the brain go haywire." His eyes narrowed. "Anna, what is it?"

"Will I—could I still turn—" What was the word he liked to use so damn much? "Feral?"

A hard negative shake of his head. "Would have happened by now."

The shoulders she'd been holding ramrod straight relaxed. *Thank you, God.*

"For some, the bite just makes life a hell of a lot better. Their reflexes get stronger, they heal faster, and the sex gets wild." His eyes narrowed. "But for the others, it's like they are stepping into hell."

"And last night, when I was bitten, you didn't know what would happen to me, did you?" *Like they are stepping into hell.* She hadn't understood just how serious the attack had been. She'd thought it was just a dog bite and worried vaguely about rabies and infection, not about insanity.

"I wasn't sure what would happen," he told her, and she knew he was speaking the truth. "I knew I had to stay with you, every minute, to make certain you were safe."

Tears rose in her eyes, but she blinked them away. She'd known that was the reason he'd stayed with her, of course. "Well, looks like I'm all right, so there's no need for you to sacrifice yourself anymore—"

He caught her arms, and pulled her close. "I had sex with you last night because I wanted you more than I've ever wanted anyone or anything."

Oh.

"When you were bitten, I was so damn worried about you. But you're strong, Anna. Damn strong. You had to be, after your parents died and—"

"What?" She'd never told him about her folks. Only Ronnie knew about them. "How do you know about my mom and dad?"

He winced, but admitted, "I ran a background check on you. Right after we started working together."

Well, that was just great. "What, Jon, were you afraid I was some kind of criminal bent on infiltrating the museum and stealing all the old rocks?" *Asshole.*

His fingers tightened around her. "I'm a pack hunter. I can't take chances with anyone. We were working closely together—I had to make sure you weren't a threat."

Like she'd ever been a threat to anyone—well, at least that was true *before* she'd been bitten. "I can't deal with this right now," she muttered. "I just—I need to go." To get away from him; to think about werewolves, and insanity, and men who lied to her.

"Anna, it's not safe. The wolf that bit you—"

"It's daylight, okay? I thought you said these things only shift at night."

A reluctant nod. Then, "But even in human form he could still hurt you."

"Well, then I'll make damn sure to lock my doors, and if some stranger comes a-knocking, I'll call the cops, okay?" Her body was vibrating with tension. "But I. Am. Leaving." Escape. It was all she could think of. "Now, either you take me home or I'll steal your damn car." Okay. Maybe that was a bit extreme, but she was really pissed off. Jon should have come clean with her the moment she awoke in her office.

He didn't have any right to keep secrets like this from her. *It was her damn life.*

Jon studied her in silence for a moment. His jaw worked, but his fingers finally loosened as he read what must have been the obvious intent on her face. "Fine, I'll take you home, but this isn't over between us."

She wanted to deny his words. But she knew if she spoke, she'd lie.

Because as furious as she was with him, she also knew that, yes, things between them were a long, long way from being over.

Her traitorous body and her weak heart wouldn't let her just shut him out. Dammit.

How can I still want him so much?

And why do I need him?

Jon pulled the SUV to a stop at the edge of her driveway. Anna stared up at her house, a white cottage, with dark green shutters. She'd painted those shutters, and planted the flowers that lined the sidewalk and would bloom come the spring.

"I want you to have something."

His words caused her to jerk. She glanced to the left, and saw him reaching under his seat and pulling out—

A gun holster.

"Jon . . ." She'd never liked guns. She was terrified of them because of what happened to her parents.

"It's all right, baby." His voice was soothing, and she realized he knew why she was afraid.

The bastard.

Her chin lifted. "I don't use guns."

"Well, this time, you just might have to." He pulled the weapon from the holster and the metal gleamed. "This is the safety. Just pull here to turn it off. Then all you have to do is aim and fire."

Aim and fire. Like the man who'd killed her parents had done. Her fingers reached for the door handle. Her claws raked over the leather upholstery, gouging the expensive fabric.

"The bullets are made of silver," he continued in that low, nonthreatening voice. "Be careful, if you're loading or unloading 'em, don't let the bullets touch your skin. The silver will burn you."

Another fun side effect. He put the gun back in the holster, secured the weapon, and pushed it toward her. "Take it."

She wanted to refuse it. She *hated* guns—never so much as thought about firing one. But what if the wolf that attacked her came back? She'd sensed him twice now, and if he came after her again, she didn't want to be defenseless.

"You can come back home with me," Jon said, pulling the weapon back. "I'll take care of you, I'll—"

Her left hand reached for the gun.

His jaw clenched. "I-I'm going to put a team of men on you, just to make sure you're safe."

She nodded. She wasn't stupid, and she really didn't have a burning death wish. A team of security agents sounded like a great idea to her.

But being with Jon . . . she just needed some space. Some time to think.

With a soft *snick*, the locks were electronically disengaged. This time, when she tried, Anna was able to open the door. Cool air washed into the SUV.

"Anna."

She met his stare.

"I meant what I said before. Things between us, they aren't over. I still want you like hell on fire, and I'm not about to give you up."

The ache between her legs told her the passion she felt for him hadn't nearly burned out.

And the ache in her heart, well, she'd deal with that, soon enough.

Anna climbed from the SUV. She hesitated, "Jon . . ."

He leaned over the passenger seat.

"Donna. Travers. What happened to them?" They'd been in the back of her mind during the drive—the thought of what could have happened to her stealing her breath away.

His eyes seemed to warm. "Travers has been taking care of her every day for the last three years. And she's doing better, much, much better. The scientists have an experimental drug they're using on the Bitten, one made from the antibodies in the nonferals' blood. It seems to be working, and Donna seems to be returning back to her old self." A smile curled his lips. "She even baked a cake for me last month."

Anna nodded. Good. That was so good. "I-I'm glad." Glad for the woman she'd never met and for the man who loved her so. "Good-bye, Jon."

"No, Anna. It's not good-bye." His eyes were so blue, and so determined. "Take care of yourself, and know that I'll be waiting for you."

She turned from him and forced herself to move, putting one foot in front of the other until she was inside her house. Safe in the home she'd made for herself.

And locked safely away from the temptation of Jon York.

For now.

But he had been right, she realized, as she paced slowly down the hallway. Things weren't over between them.

Not now, and maybe not ever.

Her clothes were too hot. Too tight. Too binding. The fabric rubbed against her flesh, chafing her, and making Anna wish she'd worn another short dress instead of her black suit.

It had been two days since she'd last seen Jon. She'd talked with him on the phone, answering his diligent calls with the quiet response that she was safe.

She'd caught glimpses of the men he'd ordered to protect her.

But she hadn't seen Jon.

That was about to change.

Anna glanced at her clock. In five minutes, Jon was scheduled to meet with her for a last walk-through of the museum's new security system. She tried to tell herself that she wasn't looking forward to seeing him.

Tried, and failed.

She dreamed of him. Every time her eyes closed, she saw him. *Felt him.* And it should have been impossible, but she actually . . . missed him.

She was so screwed up.

And she wasn't wearing panties.

Because she knew she'd be seeing Jon—and she wanted him. He'd know she wasn't wearing the panties, of course. He'd be able to smell her, catch the scent of the arousal she wouldn't be able to hold back.

Was she trying to tempt him? Or herself? Anna really wasn't sure, but she was tired of riding the hard edge of need twenty-four hours a day.

She needed release.

No, she needed *Jon*. Liar. Pack hunter. Protector. The best lover she'd ever had.

She needed—

"Uh, Anna?"

Her eyes lifted from the computer monitor. She'd been staring at the tropical desktop background for the last five minutes. She'd heard the man's approach, but hadn't moved. Since New Year's, she heard every damn thing. But she was getting better at tuning out the louder noises and even the really small, annoying ones—she had to filter them out, otherwise, her head was splitting with constant aches.

Her chair squeaked as she shifted slightly. "Yes, Mike, what is it?" Michael Harris had joined the museum's staff about a month ago. He was one of the grant officers, a good-looking guy with pale blond hair and light gray eyes. He'd asked her out shortly after he started working there, but by then, she was already hooked on Jon.

Mike had asked her out again yesterday, as did three other men at the museum: Larry, one of the members of the security staff, a guy who had to be at least sixty; Bill, a paleontologist with thin glasses and a sweet smile; and Gary, a real ladies' man down in Advertising—a guy she'd been trying to avoid for years.

Were her new high-powered pheromones kicking in? Probably. Or maybe the guys just thought she looked different without her glasses. Either way, it didn't matter. She had the same problem now that she'd had when Mike first asked her out.

Jon York.

Mike flashed her a smile and stepped farther into her office. The scent of his cologne hit her then—cloying, far too strong. Her nose twitched at the smell. She'd noticed the odor yesterday and had sincerely hoped the man would tone it down today.

No such luck.

"I've got some grant applications that need your signature. One's for the Dinosaur Fossil Hall."

Ah, the fossil hall, her pet project. Anna stood and reached eagerly for the paperwork. Her dad had been a paleontologist, and her earliest memories—and some of her happiest—had been of them building tiny dinosaur models together.

"Thanks, Mike, I really appreciate—" He caught her hand. His fingers tightened around hers, as the papers fell onto her desk.

"Anna, have you thought any more about my offer?"

"Uh, your offer?"

Faint lines appeared around his mouth. "I'd like to take you to dinner tonight. I think we could be good together. Very, very good. We've got a lot in common, and I think—"

"I'm seeing someone," she blurted. *A lot in common.* Doubtful, unless the guy had been bitten by a werewolf recently. Besides, she didn't want him. Interesting, really, considering that her sex drive was working overtime. Yet she didn't want him, or Gary, or . . . anyone but Jon.

Now, if she could just stop being so pissed at the guy.

"You—you're what?" Mike looked stunned.

Well, hell. He'd asked her out. Was it really so shocking that another guy had done the same? Anna lifted a brow, tugged her hand free, and slowly and clearly stated, "I'm dating someone."

"Who?" Mike asked, blinking, as if confused.

"Me."

A stab of yearning rocked through her at the sound of that hard, deep voice. Her gaze lifted, met his.

Mike spun around.

Jon smiled at him. Or rather, he bared his teeth—his very sharp teeth.

"Oh. I, uh, see." Mike nodded, his face reddening. "I-I'd better get back to work."

"Yeah," Jon agreed. "You had."

Mike cast Anna one last glance, then pushed past Jon. Jon waited a beat. Two. Then kicked the door closed with his heel and secured the lock with a *click*.

He paced toward her with a slow, measured stride. "So we're dating, huh?" His nostrils widened as he caught her scent.

"Well, we're doing something, wouldn't you say?" She murmured, aware that her heartbeat was speeding up, just as his was.

Oh, damn, but her suit felt stifling.

And her sex felt so wet.

Just from seeing him and imagining all they could do.

He stopped directly in front of her, put his arms on either side of her body, and caged her against the desk. "I've missed you."

Her breasts were aching, the nipples hard and tight, and she wanted his mouth on them. God, the man had just walked into the room less than two minutes ago and she felt like she was about to explode.

No, she wanted to explode, with him inside her.

A growl broke from her lips.

One dark brow rose. "Feeling hungry, baby?"

He had no idea. She'd held back the need for as long as she could—tried to act normal at work and at home, when the lust burned her skin from the inside out and her sex quivered with each breath she drew as she fantasized about him.

But now she knew the reality of the man. And she wanted him even more.

They were alone. The door was locked. Sure, she could hear voices from the hallway, the rustle of papers, the ringing of phones, but she didn't care.

She wasn't going to be the good girl anymore.

She was going to take what she wanted. Power beat through her blood.

Take.

Her hands rose to his shoulders. Her claws were out, but Jon didn't so much as flinch.

He smiled. "God, baby, you're so damn beautiful."

She stood on tiptoe, brushed her lips against his, and tasted the hunger on his mouth. Then she caught his lower lip between her teeth and bit lightly.

It was his turn to growl.

Her hands smoothed over his chest and felt the rock-hard muscles through the barrier of his shirt. Oh, she liked his chest. Liked his strength. But there was something else she liked a heck of a lot more.

Her hands pushed between their bodies. She found his belt, undid the buckle, and eased open the top of his pants, even as she kept kissing him.

His cock sprang into her hands, already swollen, heavy with need. Her fingers curled over that thick length, stroking slowly from balls to tip. Then pumping harder, faster.

His hands were on her breasts. Squeezing, fondling her. Plucking the nipples and making the cream flow between her thighs.

Her right hand stayed curled against his cock, her left splayed over his stomach and pushed back.

Jon's head lifted. "What—"

She eased down in front of him. The desk was behind her, the heavy tip of his cock in front of her. Anna licked her lips, already tasting him.

"Oh, damn, baby, I won't be able to make it—"

Her mouth opened, and she licked the head of his arousal. A slow, swirling lick.

Jon jerked.

The power flooding through her blood drove another growl from her lips.

Her lips widened, and she took his cock into her mouth, pulling him in deep and sucking. Her head moved slowly on him, taking him inside one desperate inch at a time. The fingers of her hand circled the base of his shaft, controlling him.

She could taste the salt of his pre-come on her tongue. And she wanted more.

She wanted everything.

She took him in deeper, stroking her tongue over his flesh and hollowing her cheeks as she pleasured him, and herself.

More, *more*.

Jon was muttering her name, telling her how good her mouth felt. His hands were tangled in her hair. He was trying to move her faster, harder.

But *she* was the one in control, and she raked her teeth over his straining arousal to let him know that the power was hers, and hers alone.

The phone rang somewhere behind her, the shrill cry scraping over her eardrums, but Anna didn't stop. Her hand began to squeeze him as her mouth caressed his flesh and she felt his cock swell even more inside her. He was about to climax, he was—

Jon snarled and pushed her mouth away from him.

"Why did you—"

Her words died in her throat. Jon looked savage. His eyes were glittering, his cheeks dark with passion. His lips were parted, showing the edge of his fangs.

He grabbed her, yanked her up, and shoved her onto the desk. Anna's arms swiped out for balance. The phone hit the floor and the ringing finally stopped.

She kicked off her pumps. Jon jerked down her pants and hissed out a sharp breath when he saw her bare sex.

Then he was pushing her legs apart, spreading her wide. The wood bit into her buttocks, the rough edge of the desk bruising the backs of her thighs. But she didn't care.

The tip of his cock pressed into her. There were no preliminary touches from him. No testing fingers. He stared into her eyes, his face stark, and he shoved deep inside her with one hard thrust.

Finally.

Her sex clamped around him. Her legs rose, wrapped around his hips. Her arms were behind her, braced across the top of the desk.

He plunged into her, again, again.

"Dammit, I'm going to come—" He pulled open her suit top and shoved her bra out of the way. He locked his mouth over her breast and sucked, his mouth ravenous against her flesh.

Then she felt the hard explosion of his release inside her—the warmth of his semen jetting into her.

And still he kept thrusting. Strokes just as hard, just as powerful.

She came seconds after him, squeezing him tight, growling with pleasure.

When the release ended, when the shudders finally stopped rocking her body, his head lifted. His lips glistened, but the fangs were gone.

He stared into her eyes. Silence for a beat or two, then, "Are you protected?"

Anna managed a nod. She'd been on the Pill since Steven.

"I-I'm sorry, baby, I just—" Jon ran his hand over his face, "lost control."

She'd wanted him that way. Beyond control. *Hers.*

"You don't have to worry," he told her, "I'm clean. Hell, I can show you my medical records if you want. I *always* use protection—well, shit, I did before and—"

"I'm clean, too," she whispered. Well, except for the wolf virus, she was clean.

His gaze raked over her face. "Damn, but you felt good." His cock was still inside her. "*Feel* good."

She flexed her body, deliberately squeezing the delicate muscles around him.

His eyes narrowed. "Oh, shit." His cock began to rise again.

"You're clean, I'm clean." She tightened around him again. "Pregnancy isn't an . . . ah, issue."

His mouth closed over her neck, biting lightly.

"So . . . why . . . don't we . . ."

He pulled his cock to the outer edge of her sex, then thrust deeply.

Anna moaned. "Yes, that. Let's . . ." *Hell.* She stopped talking, wrapped her arms tightly around him, and held on for the ride.

* * *

The woman was making him weak, quite literally. After a second climax that left him feeling completely wrung out, Jon managed to crawl off Anna's delectable little body. They'd made it to the couch before they climaxed. That nice, black leather couch he'd fantasized about.

Oh, shit, he was seriously getting hooked on the woman.

Anna disappeared into the small bathroom that connected with her office. He heard the soft sound of running water, then—

A hard, furious knock at her office door.

A quick downward glance assured him that he was once again decently covered. The scent of sex hung in the air, but there were fresh flowers spread around Anna's office, so only someone with enhanced senses would be able to detect the slightly rich, musky smell.

He turned the lock, opened the door, and found Mike glaring at him.

Okay, the guy was starting to get on his nerves.

"I need Anna downstairs," Mike snapped. "I tried calling, but—"

But the phone was broken somewhere on the floor. Jon shrugged. "We were having a meeting." Actually, they really did need to meet about the security, but tasting Anna, having her, well, that had surely taken precedence for him.

Mike's glance darted over his shoulder and landed on the desktop that was still askew. "I bet you were."

Jon's jaw locked.

"She's too good for you," the smaller man snapped. "You don't understand what she can be—"

"Is everything all right?" Anna called out.

Jon glanced back at her. She was fully dressed, her hair loose around her shoulders and her lips swollen from his kisses.

The scent of her pheromones hit him like a punch in the gut, and he heard Mike inhale sharply.

"Don't even fucking think about it," he snarled the warning. Perhaps it was time for a heart-to-heart with old Mike—a nice, stay-the-hell-away talk.

Mike pushed past him. "Two representatives from the Greenbough Corporation are here—they want to talk about the research grant."

A furrow appeared between Anna's brows. "But I thought they weren't coming until tomorrow."

"Well, they're here now." His lips thinned. "Maybe you got the date wrong, *Ms. Summers.*"

"And maybe you need to check the attitude, *Mr. Harris.*" Anna straightened her shoulders and glared at him. "And while you're at it, maybe you need to remember just who the supervisor is here."

Mike swallowed, but said nothing.

"Now, let me finish my meeting with Jon, and I'll be right out." She pointed to the door. "You can wait outside." Frost dripped from her words.

Mike inclined his head, turned, and marched from the room.

Anna exhaled heavily.

"Problem?" Jon asked softly. If so, he'd be more than happy to take care of the situation for her.

But Anna's little chin immediately shot into the air. "Nothing I can't handle." Her hands combed through the mass on her desk and drew out a small black book. "I *do* have the meeting scheduled for tomorrow." She sounded confused. A sigh. "But hell, the way this week's been going, I'm surprised that's the only thing I've screwed up." Her gaze rose to meet his. "Jon, I'm sorry—can we get together later to talk about the last security details?"

"Yeah." He walked toward her, deliberately leaving the door open. He didn't care what Mike heard or saw. "And we can meet tonight for dinner."

Her gaze held his.

"I want to try us," he told her, his voice calm, clear. "But what do you want?" Just sex? Just an outlet for the heat? Or—

"I want to try us, too."

"Good." Jon felt a satisfied smile curve his lips. That was damn—

The sudden flash of a wolf's stench burned his nostrils. *What the hell?*

He spun around and ran to the door.

Mike was talking to a secretary. Both looked up, frowning at his approach.

And just as fast as it had appeared, the scent vanished.

But all of Jon's nerves were on alert.

The bastard was in the building.

"Jon?" Anna approached him slowly.

Shit. Now wasn't the time to talk about this—not with the two in the lobby watching them with wide eyes—but he had to warn her. Jon caught her arm, leaned close to her ear, and whispered, "Baby, do you have that gift I gave you? Is it someplace close to you?"

Her body stiffened. "Y-yes, yes, I do." She pulled away from him, just a bit. Her hand tapped against the purse slung over her shoulder. "It—it's in here."

"Good. You're gonna need to keep that close to you, okay? *Real close.*"

Tension tightened her lips. "What do you know?"

That he'd caught a scent—one that she hadn't. "I know our friend is close. Closer than I realized." Dammit. He'd actually thought the werewolf had fled. Two days and no sign of him. Jon's men had been keeping surveillance on Anna around the clock. If the *Were* had been watching her, they would have known.

But obviously the bastard had just been biding his time. And now, well, now he wanted to play again.

With Anna.

Not going to happen.

"Go to your meeting," he told her. "Then come right back here." She would be safe enough until the moon rose. By then, he'd have her ensconced at his place. "Don't go anywhere alone, and keep your purse with you at all times, got it?" He knew she didn't like the idea of using the gun, but there really wasn't a choice for her. Only silver bullets could take down a werewolf.

Her fingers curled around the purse strap. "I understand."

He kissed her. Hard. Fast. "Go to your meeting, and when you get back—" Well, she wasn't going to like this, but. . .

"What?"

"We're going shooting."

Her face paled.

The meeting went off without a hitch. Other than the day mix-up, everything was as smooth as could be.

Anna stood in front of the elevators, her right foot tapping and her fingers curled around her purse strap. She wanted to get back upstairs as soon as possible and find Jon. His words had scared her, and the thought that the werewolf was running around somewhere in her museum—even in human form—well, it was making her shake.

"Anna, wait up!"

She turned at Mike's cry.

The elevator opened. Anna stepped inside and thought about pushing the "close" button, but Mike jumped inside just as the doors slid closed.

In the close confines of the elevator, the scent of his cologne was even more overpowering.

"I-I wanted to apologize. I was out of line before, and I-I'm sorry."

She nodded. "Fine." Anna wasn't cutting the guy any slack. He'd pissed her off, but at least she could be professional.

"I just—didn't know you were seeing anyone." His mouth curled down into a frown. "And I had such plans."

The elevator was dinging softly as it rose. Two more floors to go.

"Anna, be careful, would you?"

The worry in his voice had her gaze darting back to him. His hands were locked together, twisting in front of his body.

"Why would I need to be careful?" She asked him quietly.

"I-I've heard things about Jon York. Crazy things."

Another soft *ding*. One floor to go.

"I don't think he's the man you believe he is." Mike swallowed. "Some say he's not even a man at all."

Ding.

The doors opened. Her floor.

"If you need me, hell, if you just need someone to talk to, I'll be close by."

She stepped from the elevator and saw Jon waiting for her. Anna glanced over her shoulder. Mike was watching her with worry in his eyes. The doors slowly slid closed and he disappeared.

She turned back to Jon and felt the warmth of his arms wrap around her.

"Everything okay?" He asked.

Her heart was racing. She knew he had to hear the furious beat, but she forced a smile to her lips and lifted her arms to hold him. "Yes. Everything is just . . . yes. Okay."

They both knew she was lying.

They finished the walk-through on the security system, and then Jon took her shooting. Or rather, he took her to a shooting range that one of his friends owned at the edge of the city.

No one else was in the gallery when they arrived. Jon guided her to the last aisle and handed her a pair of ear protectors and a gun.

"It's just like the one you have—that will make it easier for you."

Nothing was going to make it easier for her.

She pulled on the ear protectors, and the sounds around her were immediately muffled. She reached for the gun—

And remembered the night her parents died.

Walking through the park, because the night was so warm. The sky so clear.

The guy with the gun sprang from the bushes—he'd looked so old to her then, but now she knew he had only been in his late teens.

"Here." Jon stepped behind her and put his arms around her. "Aim like this." His voice was slightly muted, but she could understand him.

He wanted money. Her mom's purse. Jewelry. The gun had shaken in his hand. Her dad stepped in front of her and her mom.

The guy, he'd been about to leave, to run away when—

"Safety's off. Pull the trigger. Target the heart."

A car backfired in the distance. The guy jerked back, and an explosion rocked the night.

Her finger squeezed the trigger. The bullet thudded into the target, slamming into the shoulder.

"Good. Again. Remember, aim for the heart. Hold your wrist steady."

Her dad fell. Her mom screamed and ran for the gunman.

Another explosion.

She'd seen his eyes then—wide, burning with fear.

He pointed the gun at her.

Then he turned and fled.

Her finger tightened around the trigger. Fired.

Missed the heart by about two inches.

"Again."

She aimed. Fired.

Blasted a hole straight through the heart.

"Good, baby, real, good. But remember, if he's coming at you, he's gonna be moving, fast. You aim and you shoot the bastard as quick as you can, got that?"

She put the gun down, realizing her hands were rock steady. Anna took off the earmuffs and turned to Jon.

"Anna? Baby, you're crying."

Her hand lifted, and wiped away the moisture. "The man who killed my parents . . . did I ever tell you that he was only seventeen?"

Jon shook his head, staring down at her. "You've never told me anything about him."

Oh, yes. That was right. He'd researched her. Dug up all her little secrets to make certain she wasn't a threat.

"Guess you know what happened to him, don't you?" She muttered.

"I'd like you to tell me." His words neither confirmed nor denied.

Anna swallowed to ease the dryness in her throat. "The police found him a week later. He'd killed himself, with the same gun he used to kill my parents."

Jon said nothing, just watched her with eyes that saw everything.

"I don't think he meant to kill them." The admission was hard, because she'd been so angry, for so long. A child's confused rage. A woman's blind hate. "He was scared. High. When a car backfired, I think he just pulled the trigger without thinking." And he'd killed her family. "I don't think he could live with what he'd done."

"No, I don't think he could," Jon agreed softly.

Anna huffed out a hard breath. "I don't know . . ." Jon had to understand this. "I don't know if I could ever shoot someone."

"Even to save yourself?"

It was a hard question. She stared up at him, her guts in knots.

"If the time comes, Anna, I think you'll do what you have to do." His hand smoothed over her cheek. "I've always known you were strong, and I think you'll fight like hell against anyone or anything that comes after you."

"I didn't fight before." The admission slipped out. That night long ago, she hadn't fought, hadn't helped.

"You were a child. Thrust into a nightmare. There wasn't anything *for* you to do but survive."

She nodded and felt a tear trickle down her cheek. Dammit, she *hated* to cry.

"But now, baby, it's time for you to fight. Time for you to take that fear and use it to make you stronger. This bastard isn't going to get you—and if he makes the mistake of coming after you, we will take him out."

We. God, but she liked the sound of that.

Anna managed a nod. Then she picked up the earmuffs again, steadied the hands that wanted to shake, and finally reached for the gun.

Time to be strong.

As her finger tightened around the trigger, a growl rose in her throat.

* * *

Damn, but his woman was a fighter. Jon walked beside Anna as they approached her house, and a fierce admiration filled him.

The lady had guts. And, he was realizing, a spine of pure steel.

He'd known going to the shooting range would be hard for her. But she'd lifted that chin of hers, taken the weapon, and fired until she was satisfied that she knew just what the hell she was doing.

Anna Summers was someone very, very special.

And it was time he told her so.

"Anna—"

She unlocked her door, and pushed it open. "Oh, my God."

He was inside in a flash.

Sonofabitch. The place had been completely trashed—furniture smashed, pictures broken, cushions and pillows hacked to pieces.

"Shit." He grabbed his phone and punched in the number for the lead investigator who'd been assigned to watch her house. "Myers! What the fuck happened?"

Anna crept forward.

"No! Stay there. Don't touch anything." They couldn't call the police, not on a pack matter, but he could get his team in to start searching for prints.

"What? What are you talking about, boss?" Myers asked in his ear, voice dazed.

"Anna's house is trashed. The bastard's been here."

Myers swore.

"Yeah, my thoughts exactly. Now why the hell didn't we see him?"

"I don't know—but I'll damn well find out."

One of the guys on patrol had probably gone to piss, or to lunch. And the wolf had taken the opportunity. "You do that," Jon snarled, "and get me a team out here to go over every inch of this place."

He ended the call, knowing the guys would be swarming inside any moment and—

Anna's phone rang. Once. Twice.

She glanced at him.

"Let the machine get it," he ordered.

"You think it's even still working?" She asked softly.

His gaze scanned the room, finding the phone and machine on the floor. Not broken like everything else. Odd. . .

The machine picked up. Anna's voice filled the room, then—

"Anna!" Jon knew that voice. It was Anna's friend, Veronica. "Anna, you have to come over here, right away! I've got to talk to you! Dammit, where are you? I *need* you. Hurry—" The line went dead.

Anna ran for the door.

Jon grabbed her arm. "Where the hell are you going?"

One red brow arched. "Where do you think?"

No, the whole thing felt wrong to him. Jon shook his head.

"You don't know Ronnie," Anna told him quietly. "She's had problems in the past, okay? Problems with drugs. She's recovering now, but she knows that when she needs me, I'll be there."

Screw that. "You've got enough problems of your own right now."

Her gaze held his. "She's the closest thing to a sister I've got, and she needs me."

Spine of pure fucking steel. But not necessarily the best common sense. "Fine," he snarled, "but I'm going with you."

Her lips curved in the first smile he'd seen in hours. "Well, of course you are, Jon. You're the one driving."

Ronnie's house was dark. No, not dark, Anna realized. Pitch black.

Jon braked in front of the house. "This isn't good."

No, it wasn't.

He pulled out his phone. The guy seemed to always be doing that. "I'm calling for backup."

Then they heard the scream. Loud. Feminine. *Ronnie.* Anna jumped from the SUV and ran as fast as she could, her purse clutched tight in her left hand.

Jon followed right on her heels.

The front door was open, swinging inward with the breeze— the same breeze that carried the stench of the werewolf.

Oh, God, Ronnie.

She rushed into the house.

"Anna, dammit—"

The lights flashed on, momentarily blinding her. Anna stumbled, ramming her knee into the coffee table. Behind her, she heard Jon swear—

And then the wolf attacked.

Springing from the darkened hallway, the creature launched his body at Jon, taking full advantage of Jon's momentary blindness.

The wolf hit him hard, slashing with claws and teeth, and Jon fell, his head slamming into the granite flooring of the entranceway.

OhGodohGodohGod. "*Jon!*"

He wasn't moving. The wolf was over him, fangs poised to rip Jon's throat wide open.

Anna's hands dug into her purse. She found the leather holster and yanked the gun free. Her fingers caught the safety and released it.

The wolf lowered his head for the kill.

"Get the hell away from him!" Anna screamed, raising the gun. *Aim. Fire. Aim. Fire.*

The beast froze.

"You heard me, you bastard, get away from him!" She wasn't going to think about the fact that Jon was lying too still. No, she wouldn't think about that. She'd go crazy if she did. He was fine. He had to be.

And she had to get the damn werewolf away from him.

The wolf's head lifted and turned. His glowing silver eyes locked on hers.

The gun didn't waver. "Move away from him or I'll shoot you right between the eyes." That was where she was aiming.

The wolf snarled. He was an ugly bastard, with yellow claws and twisted fur.

He rose, moving away from Jon's body and taking slow, cautious steps toward her.

Sweat trickled down Anna's back. Jon still wasn't moving, and where was Ronnie? What had happened to her?

The wolf was stalking Anna. Slowly.

"Stop!" She didn't want the wolf coming any closer to her.

His lips curled back. His head lowered.

"Don't take another step," she ordered.

A snarl rumbled in his throat.

Shit.

He sprang for her, claws outstretched, teeth ready. The stench of his body assaulted her and a familiar, cloying scent filled her nostrils.

Fire shot through her blood and a growl rumbled in her throat. *She wasn't going out like this.* Her finger jerked on the trigger. The bullet exploded from the gun.

Almost instantly, a second, echoing blast shook the room.

The wolf jerked, whimpered, then fell to the floor.

Her shot had caught him high on his front, left leg. A second bullet had slammed into his back.

The beast was bleeding, shaking.

Anna looked past him and saw Jon sitting up, blood trickling down his face and chest. His fingers were tight around a gun, one still aimed at the wolf.

She glanced down. She was still pointing the gun at the beast.

She'd shot him.

A soft moan sounded behind her. Anna spun around to find Ronnie pushing herself slowly up from behind the sofa.

"Ronnie!" She ran to her, terrified that she'd been bitten.

Ronnie shook her head, wincing. Blood trickled from a cut on her forehead. "Where the . . . hell is . . . that bastard? Made me . . . call you . . . then h-hit me with . . . something."

Anna glanced over her shoulder. The bastard in question was currently on the floor, slowly changing from wolf to man.

"Did he bite you?" Anna asked as she hugged her friend.

"Wh-what?" Ronnie pulled back. "No, he—*holy shit.*" She gaped. "What the hell is that?"

That was something that would require one heck of an explanation. But there was one simple way to start. "That's a werewolf, and trust me on this, you're really lucky you didn't get bitten."

"A werewolf," Ronnie repeated, her voice dazed. "A . . . werewolf? Oh, God . . . I think—I think I need to sit down . . ."

The creature's fur had all nearly melted away, revealing his gleaming male flesh. Muscles. Naked skin. The man moaned, turned to the left, and Anna caught a glimpse of his pain-filled face.

Mike. She'd known it was him when he charged at her and she smelled the traces of his cologne. She knew it was him and she fired the gun anyway. Because she wasn't about to let that jerk kill her.

Jon crossed to her side. "Baby, are you all right?" The gun was still in his hand, still trained on Mike.

"Yes, yes, I'm fine." She licked her lips. "But what about him?"

He grunted. "Lucky asshole will live, for now. I'm going to call in the pack—they have a special way of dealing with their rogues."

Oh, she just bet they did.

And if her knees weren't shaking so hard and her mouth wasn't so dry, she'd ask him about that method. But right then, well, the details could wait.

The big, bad wolf had been captured, and she just wanted to get him the hell away from her—the sooner, the better.

Then she wanted to grab Jon, take him to some convenient, comfortable bed, and make damn sure that he was all right.

She'd never forget the fear that raced through her when the wolf crouched over him, fangs and claws ready to kill. Oh, damn.

She grabbed Jon, taking care not to jar the hand with the gun, and kissed him—a hard, fast kiss on the lips.

"What? Anna?"

"Don't ever scare me like that again." She kissed him once more. "If you do, *I'll* kill you."

His eyes gleamed. "Fucking spine of steel."

What?

"Baby, when this asshole is taken off our hands, we're going someplace nice and quiet and you and I are going to—"

"Uh . . . I'm still here you know," Ronnie muttered behind them.

"Talk," he finished softly. "Cause there's a hell of a lot I've got to say to you."

And she had plenty to say to her hunter.

But Anna wasn't planning on just talking, and she knew from the lust lurking in his eyes, that Jon had more sensuous plans in mind, too.

Chapter 9

It seemed to take an eternity before they were alone together. They had to calm Ronnie down with some serious explanations, and then the pack took Mike away.

By the time they got back to Jon's house, Anna was almost desperate to touch him. The fire that always heated her blood these days was rising to the level of an inferno, twining with and feeding off the adrenaline that still pumped in her system.

She'd come too close to death. They both had. She needed Jon, fast, hard, and deep, to reassure her that everything was all right. They'd beaten the bad guy and lived to tell the tale.

He was kissing her as they shoved the front door closed, stripping her as they climbed the stairs. And her hands were all over him, yanking off his shirt, jerking open his belt.

When he kicked open the door to his bedroom, she was clad only in her bra. He was wearing a half-opened pair of pants.

They tumbled onto the bed. Anna landed on top of him, exactly where she wanted to be. Her hands fisted in the soft material of his slacks, pulling them out of the way. She straddled, him, rubbing her sex over the thick bulge of his cock.

Oh, yes. She lifted her hips, rocking against him, riding him.

She was creaming for him; she had been during the long drive back to his house. He'd reached for her, slid his fingers between her legs, rubbed her folds and clit through the fabric of her pants, and had her on the brink of orgasm.

There wouldn't be a slow buildup to release. No long foreplay.

Time for a fast, hard fuck.

Jon's hands were on her breasts, jerking away the bra, squeezing her breasts, and fondling her nipples. Damn, but the man sure knew how to use his hands.

"You smell so damn good," he gritted, pushing up to catch her breast in his mouth. His lips closed over the nipple, and sucked hard.

Pleasure lashed through her.

Anna reached between her legs and caught his thick length in her hands. Her fingers ran over him, pulling, pumping.

A dangerous rumble sounded from his throat. *No time to play.*

She guided his cock to her and coated him with the cream that had built for him. She rose onto her knees, took the head of his erection and pushed it right between the lips of her sex.

Then she shoved down, hard, and took every inch of him inside.

His fingers dug into her hips, but Anna wasn't about to let him take control, not yet.

She rose and fell, moving faster and harder, driving down onto him and impaling that thick cock again and again.

Sweat coated their bodies. Groans filled the air. The bed began to shake.

And her sex tightened as her climax built. *Close. So close. Almost—*

She ground down against Jon, her clitoris pressing hard against him as his cock drove deep. She came, choking out his name.

Jon took control. As the tremors rocked her, he spun her around, forcing her body beneath his. He grabbed her legs, forcing them high and wide as he thrust into her. Deeper. *Deeper.*

She could see his fangs, the hungry desperation in his eyes. His flesh slapped against hers. His cock swelled—and he pressed his mouth to her shoulder. Kissing, licking, then—

Biting.

Anna gasped at the stinging pain, then moaned with pleasure as her sex quivered.

Jon bucked against her, growled, and filled her with the warm wave of his release.

When the climax ended—for both of them—Jon lifted his head. His face looked so intense, his eyes . . . almost afraid.

Anna forced a smile. "You're not . . . about to tell me," she licked her lips, tasting him, "that something bad is gonna happen since you bit me . . . are you?"

He shook his head. No answering smile curved his lips. No tempting dimples flashed. "Doesn't work that way. Only the werewolves spread their power with the bite."

Worry began to whisper through her. His voice . . . the passion had burned so bright, but now he was too solemn. "Jon?"

His hands tightened around her. "I don't want to let you go." Stark.

What? Her hands lifted and cupped the rough angles of his cheeks. "Since when do you have to?" There was no place she wanted to be, other than in his bed and in his arms.

"I've done things in my life, Anna, bad, dangerous things. Hell, I'm not a nice guy, never have been."

She frowned. What was he trying to say?

"I wanted you," he muttered, "from the first minute I saw you. But I didn't take you because I was trying to protect you . . . from me."

She shook her head. "I don't need protecting from you." There was one thing she needed from him, but it sure as heck wasn't protection.

"You deserve better," he whispered.

She stared straight in his eyes. There was no "better" for her. "I deserve you. I *want* you." No more fantasies. No more fears. Just real, wonderful, hot-as-hell reality with Jon. "It took the bite to make me realize, I was spending my life dreaming and fantasizing. I don't want to do that anymore." She wanted passion and fire. *Jon.* "It's a new year, and it's time for me to start a new life."

Jon exhaled slowly. "Be sure, baby. Be very, very sure. I'm possessive as hell, demanding—" He gave a rough laugh, "and I was like that even before the bite."

Well, she'd found that she could be more than a little possessive and demanding, too. The way she figured it, they were a pretty good match. She drew in a deep breath and decided to take a risk. "My house is pretty much totaled right now." Her finger stroked down his chest. "Think you could handle a roommate for a few days?"

He stilled. Then his cock began to harden inside her. "Not a few days." He eased partially out of her, then pushed back inside with a slow, steady pressure.

"O-oh?"

"Forever." Another withdrawal, another leisurely thrust. "Do you know . . . what I like best about you?"

Had the man really said *forever?* Anna shook her head, dazed.

"You're the strongest woman I've ever met . . . and that's fucking sexy as hell." He bent his head to her shoulder, and licked the faint marks his teeth had made in the height of passion.

The feel of his cock was driving her crazy, and the light, teasing thrusts were almost torture.

His breath blew against her skin. The edge of his teeth raked her. "I don't want a few days with you, baby. I want everything that you have, all that you are . . . for keeps."

She squirmed beneath him.

His head lifted. His lips tightened. "But what do *you* want?"

Anna growled, using her enhanced strength to roll him across the bed. As they tumbled, his cock stayed firmly lodged inside her. "What I want," she muttered, as power and joy filled her, "is you." She'd realized the absolute truth of that statement when she saw him on the floor of Ronnie's house. A taunting smile curved her lips as she lowered her head to his shoulder. Her tongue laved his flesh. "And I also want my chance to bite."

Her teeth locked around him, pressing lightly into the flesh, and Jon muttered hoarsely beneath her.

Then they were moving, thrusting, fighting for a release, despite the climax that had come only moments before.

As Anna held him, as she felt the ripples of his muscles and the drive of his cock, she realized that her reality was a hell of a lot better than a fantasy could ever be.

A growl built in her throat.

And she knew she wanted another bite.

CYNTHIA EDEN is an author of paranormal suspense and erotic romance tales. She lives along the Southern Gulf Coast with her husband and son. Cynthia has held a myriad of jobs in the course of her life—she's been a magician (very, very amateur), a recruiter, a college counselor, an editor, and a history teacher. However, her true passion has always been writing. Cynthia loves to create "what if" stories with strong paranormal elements, and equally strong heroes and heroines. To learn more about Cynthia and her writing, please visit her website at: http://www.cynthiaeden.com.

Part 2

Night Resolutions

DIANA MERCURY

She rubbed her wrists. Her arms had been bound a long time, and now they ached from the liberty of movement. She stared up at him with uncertainty.

"You're free to go, Chantal," he said.

She lay beneath him on the bed in the little cabin. He sat, looking down on her, but he wasn't holding her captive anymore.

"You've been teasing me since the moment we met," she said softly. "You've done everything but fuck me the way I know you want to. The way *I* want you to . . . and now you're backing off again?"

"No . . ." he looked confused. "It's nothing to do with . . . I mean, you're *free*. It's all worked out. They'll never come after you again . . ."

She lifted her arms as if they were still cuffed at the wrists and looped them around his neck, pulling him down on top of her, and sliding her fingers through his hair as she reached up a little to meet his mouth with hers. He gently let his weight down on her, and his cock hardened between her thighs as he breathed in the feeling of her breasts cushioned under his chest. He deepened the kiss and his tongue stroked inside her, thrusting and hardening against her tongue. His body moved against hers the same way his tongue stroked her mouth. His hands roamed over her, and hers were all over him now, too. He looked deeply into her eyes, then lowered his head to kiss her throat, her neck, her collarbone, the crevasse between her breasts—

He couldn't help it; it was like diving into her all over again.

"I'll lose control if you let me," he said, beginning to pant.

The first time Chantal saw Jake he was standing on the edge of a cliff with the ocean winds whipping his silky dark hair around his sharp Irish profile. The Celtic wildness went well with the lanky, lean, but muscular proportions of his body. Though he stood slumped and sullen-looking, as if thoroughly bored with the spectacular view, he couldn't conceal his restless, virile energy. She imagined him as a sulky Irish prince, looking out to sea.

I definitely needed this break from my studies, Chantal thought, smiling at the direction of her own thoughts. *An Irish prince!* She was deep in a research project on ancient Ireland, and everything she experienced seemed to come back to that. But she had trouble keeping her gaze down. She wanted to keep looking at him, in his faded jeans, winter coat, and hiking boots with the long laces double-tied, standing with his legs spread, his hands jammed in his pockets, seemingly lost in his own world.

But she pulled in her interest out of respect for Billy, her date, who walked beside her on the stone path. Billy was gorgeous, a tall, shaggy-headed blond with a sweetly crooked front tooth. He was adorable and smart—which was why she had been drawn to him that first morning he came into the coffeehouse where she worked and ordered a double latte.

Billy's body was sleek and muscled in all the right places.

He asked Chantal out for a date the second time he came into the shop, and she met him the next evening for dinner. He was a gentleman, always generous and polite, funny and fun to be with, and she couldn't believe her luck at finding him. He seemed too good to be true. Then again, maybe he was.

He never brought her to his place and he never tried to stay at hers. She began to suspect that he wasn't really interested in her. But he always called again, always asked to see her. She continued to go out with him and, as time went by, she became rather frustrated when the simple good-night kiss they shared each time they parted failed to develop into more.

Well, there *was* that one night in the back of a dimly lit restaurant when they had shared a bottle of good wine. They were playing around, being silly together, and somehow she found herself sliding down below the tablecloth and opening his pants. By then, she was curious to know if he actually had anything going on down there. He did, and it was semierect—growing ever more so the longer she examined it—but in the end, she just couldn't put it in her mouth, not when he'd never even French-kissed her. She fondled his testicles a little, just to demonstrate the potential; but she slithered back up onto her seat before the waiter returned to bring them their check.

He was such a great guy; she kept hoping something would develop. But after a few weeks of this, her mind was beginning to wander. She found the idea of letting him go more and more appealing. She knew herself well enough to know how important passion was to her, and if they hadn't kindled some kind of flame by now, it wasn't likely to just suddenly happen. Not the kind of passion she desired, anyway. The winter holidays were upon them, and Chantal decided that if nothing spectacular happened during Christmas, she would stop seeing him in the new year. In other words, she would put off the inevitable a little longer.

And then he had asked her to go with him to a house party between Christmas and New Year's. They would be guests at an estate on the coast owned by the uncle of a good friend of his. It would be relaxing and romantic, Billy said. Clearly, he was eager that she accompany him.

Chantal was delighted. Any other time it would have been impossible, but she had that week off from both school and her job at the coffeehouse. She had planned to get caught up on her housekeeping and make amends to some long-neglected friends, but what the hell. A week of relaxation and sex? *Hopefully* sex. It was too tempting to pass up.

This invitation meant Billy was about to make his move.
Right?
She was sure things *had* to heat up.

Jake turned at the sound of voices on the wind and saw her—only her—walking toward him, her long, bright hair flowing back off her proud shoulders. The thing he noticed about her first was the way she carried herself. Though she was a little curvier than the current fashion, she had a sense of grace and fluidity about her, as if her body was sculpted of water. Her waist was small and her wrists and ankles were delicate; her breasts were round and full and high; her belly swelled slightly, her arms and thighs were rounded—she was the sort of soft, juicy woman a man could sink into. Tongue and cock and heart.

He shook off the thought. He felt safer with brittle babes who didn't touch him deep enough to penetrate. This one looked dangerous. And she was apparently tight with his best friend.

Very tight, judging from the way Billy slid his arm around her affectionately as the three of them met.

"I told you I'd bring her!" Billy announced in a triumphant voice. "Isn't she beautiful? Just like I promised."

"Mmm," Jake nodded slightly. The girl was looking up at him with eyes the color of the ocean behind him. They could be blue, but they were more of a gray, like the water when the winds drive the clouds in from the west.

God, she seemed so young. But he knew, because he had checked her out, that she was in her early twenties. Not too young for me, he thought. He had just turned twenty-seven.

But why was he thinking *that*? He wasn't here for fun and games. And out of respect to his friend. . .

Forget it, he said to himself. But he couldn't stop stealing looks at her.

Billy introduced them, and they made some small talk about the weather and condition of the roads on the ride out from town. Later, Jake couldn't remember a thing they'd said to each other in those first few minutes, except that she had made sort of a smart-ass remark in response to something he had said to her, and he'd deserved it. An energy sprang up between the two of them, and it surprised him so much it caught him off guard—something he wasn't used to. Suddenly, the little group was silent.

"So when do we get to meet the lord of the castle?" Billy asked, filling in the pause.

Castle was an apt term, though it was really just a big house. But it was quite a house, sprawling over the edge of a cliff above the ocean—stone and timber and glass, flanked by groves of Monterey cypress and pine, accessible from a long, secluded drive down from the main road, and gated, like any proper castle. There was nothing else off the lonely highway for miles in any direction. The silence might have felt oppressive if not for the constant sighing of the waves against the beach below.

"Jake. Wake up," Billy said.

Jake realized he had been staring at Chantal a little too long, lost in her. What was it about this woman? He couldn't figure it out. Her eyes? That cool, stormy color. Or the shape of her mouth? Full and sensual, and somehow childlike.

He turned to Billy. "What?"

"When do we meet Antonio?"

"Right now. Follow me." Jake set off toward the house and they trailed after him obediently.

Chantal wondered why she felt this unexpected sense of foreboding. The day was bright and blue and beautiful, sunny and winter cool. The estate was spectacular, and she was finally cozying up with her beau. She had several days to think of nothing but her own pleasures. So why should she feel this prickly uneasiness? And why should the sudden presence of their host's nephew send her into shivers of a different kind of fear?

Billy took Chantal's hand in his as they walked. "This place is really something, huh?"

It was. The stone pathways, the artistic fences and trellises around the property, the outbuildings, and the main house—everything was crafted of imported stone and high-grade lumber. The hardware was heavy and burnished, as if it had been installed centuries earlier. The windows were leaded glass of intricate design, the roofs slate. The landscaping was natural, in keeping with the setting, but impeccably ordered. Everything oriented to the sea.

Billy dropped Chantal's hand almost as quickly as he'd taken it.

She sighed. Billy was always so tender and gentle and loving with her, but there was nothing in his manner that spoke of possessiveness or need.

She watched Jake, who walked slightly ahead of them with a long stride. Her eyes followed the lines of his body from his sleek, dark hair sweeping down over his collar to the long slope of his back, tapering, narrowing down beneath the hem of his coat at the backs of his muscular thighs.

"So this is your uncle's place?" she asked him, trotting to keep up with his ground-eating gait.

He seemed surprised by the question. He stopped suddenly and turned to her, and she walked right into him. He was so large and solidly made that her body colliding with his probably meant nothing to him.

"Whoops, sorry!" she said with a laugh, blushing for her own clumsiness.

He opened his arms to her protectively, and they were suddenly very close together. His eyes were green and vivid. He felt hot and solid against her body. Unmistakably male. His hands moved over her with gentle authority, steadying her. She caught the scent of him, warm and clean and sexy.

It only lasted a moment, of course, and then they came apart. She didn't think Billy had even noticed. No big thing. But somehow it was one of the hottest physical encounters she'd had in a long time.

Damn! Chantal breathed. *What's going on here?* She dropped back to her own pace, but this time, Jake slowed his to match hers. The three of them went on together. She was so aware of Jake walking beside her that she felt almost uncomfortable, afraid she might stumble again. And then she glanced at Billy, who flashed her such a sweet smile with his crooked tooth and angel lips, she was pierced with guilt for this sudden sexual heat rising in her—for his friend.

The interior of the house was as beautifully crafted as the exterior. They followed Jake down wide corridors hung with imposing abstract paintings on one side and windows looking out to the ocean on the other. They came into an immense open room with raked ceilings and huge expanses of glass on the ocean side. Modern-style couches and chairs had been arranged in small groups. There was a big stone fireplace at one end of the room, and a bar at the other, where a bartender was making drinks.

"Tell Paco what you want to drink and I'll go find Antonio," said Jake.

"Sure thing. What can I get you, baby?" Billy asked Chantal.

She let her gaze trail after Jake as he walked off across the room. "I'm fine for now," she said. "I want to go outside and look at the ocean."

"I'm gonna get a cup of coffee. I'll meet you out there in a minute."

"Okay."

Chantal let herself out through a door that led to a deck outside. She crossed the deck and leaned out over the railing, letting the wind ruffle her hair. It was getting cold, but the day was still bright. Her whole body felt alive and tingly from the beauty of the landscape and the excitement flowing through her blood. She was thinking of Jake, and she couldn't wait to be with him again.

Stop it, she said to herself. *You're here with Billy.*

She heard a low, plaintive moan, and came out of her reverie. She followed the source of the sound curiously, slowly making her way along the railing. She began to think it was only the sound of the sea's murmur, but then she heard it again. A soft moaning. Her eyes darted toward the sound and there, down below, just behind a hedge in a spot of warm sun next to the building, a woman and a man were standing, arms entwined. She moved along the railing to get a better view of the couple. They were probably in their early thirties, both of them strikingly beautiful, the man dark and dashing with long black hair, the woman glamorous and rich-looking with red hair, red lips, and huge smoldering eyes. The woman's blouse was unbuttoned down the front, and she was pressing against his chest two half-clad white breasts that were apparently his for the taking.

Chantal watched, fascinated, as the two lovers caressed one another, the lady undulating her body against the man as he kissed her throat. He slipped his hand into her blouse and cupped one of her breasts in his hand, lifted it, and brought his mouth down on her fat, dark nipple. As he licked and sucked, she rubbed herself against him, squealing and groaning as if in pain.

He drew away from her breast and looked at her reproachfully. "If you're going to make so much noise, Anabelle, my guests will think someone is being murdered. You're so very indiscreet."

"Forgive me, Antonio. I can't help it. I can't be expected to control myself when I am with you."

"Then I shall have to be in control of you." With one hand he held her breast and fed it to his mouth, with the other, he fumbled down at his crotch and opened his trousers.

Chantal watched, wide-eyed. *Antonio*. He must be their host!

She felt herself moistening between her thighs. She knew she should move away, let them have their privacy, but she couldn't help staring.

Anabelle threw back her head and moaned louder than ever, spreading her legs as Antonio pulled up her peasant skirt and began fingering her.

"Oh, God, Antonio, are you going to fuck me, or aren't you?" Anabelle cried.

Chantal began to wonder if they weren't looking for an audience. She suddenly had the feeling that Antonio was aware of her, though he didn't look up. She felt like she had been put under a spell and couldn't back away. She noticed her own breathing was coming on faster, watching them.

From where she stood, Chantal could see Antonio pull his hand out from beneath Anabelle's skirt. He reached into his trousers and extracted his cock—a great, purplish monster— closing his fist around it to guide it between her legs.

The woman grunted as he entered her, her head jerking back; Antonio pushed her hard up against the wall of the building, shoving himself into her violently. He kissed her as he fucked her, and groped her breasts, squeezing them and pinching the tips.

Chantal tried to fight down the delicious ache mounting in her own body. She started to turn away, but couldn't resist another look when the woman began to make a high-pitched, rhythmic yelping sound. Chantal looked back and watched as the redhead collapsed against her lover, who rammed himself into her even harder. Suddenly, he let out a cry, low and guttural, and Chantal feared he would slam the woman into the wall so hard she would break her head.

Just when she thought they had finished, they got going again, the man pumping his hips against the woman as she moaned and arched against him.

Chantal withdrew and went back into the house. Billy joined her with his coffee.

"There you are. Want to go outside?" he asked.

"Uh . . . in here is fine."

They sat down at a table by the fireplace. It occurred to her that perhaps she should have brought him outside. Maybe the show would have inspired him.

Jake appeared and joined them. "Well," he said, "I know Antonio is around here somewhere, but hell if I can find him."

"Don't worry about it," Billy shrugged cheerfully. "Antonio's probably busy. Something must have come up."

Yes, Chantal thought with a smile. Antonio is busy. Busy with Anabelle. And something had definitely come up.

If only she could inspire the kind of response in her man that Anabelle inspired in hers! Chantal sent a wistful look across the table, but Billy was having a friendly argument with Jake and had no inkling of the frustrated heat gathering in her. She moved her focus almost involuntarily, then, onto Jake; she couldn't help it. No wonder the metaphor of magnetism was so often used for sexual attraction. It was just something that happened, like a natural law. That force that snaps two things together as if they *had* to be one thing. She felt the pull toward him, and she felt it stronger the closer she got to him.

Billy appeared oblivious to her, unaware of the gathering ache in her womb and in her breasts, but Jake kept looking at her, with a slightly intrigued, slightly wary expression, as if he could feel the heat shimmering off her. Intellectually, though, she knew there was no way he could be aware of how her mind was full of him.

A man. She needed a man.

God, it's been too long. Chantal took a deep breath. She felt overwhelmed by the desire to be filled with a man's tongue and cock; to have a man's mouth on her breasts, to feel his lips and tongue sucking on her nipples; to be pounded by the force of his body, insistent to enter her, deeply and more deeply . . .

There were thirteen of them at the table for dinner that night.

She met their host formally at last, after the sun had set, when he came into the great room where most of his guests had already gathered. Though there was an assortment of colorful characters milling about, Antonio dominated the company when he made his appearance. His presence was larger-than-life, dramatic, and darkly handsome. He had a long, prominent face, a narrow nose, sensual lips, and great caramel-colored eyes set apart and fringed with thick black lashes. His skin was brown; his hair was shiny black, smoothly crimped, tight on his sleek head, and tied back in a ponytail. He wore a loose pair of trousers in taupe silk, and a torso-fitting black silk shirt opened down to reveal a darkly tanned, smooth chest adorned with a single, heavy gold chain.

The muscles of his arms were well developed, like those of a weight lifter. But then, everything about him was well developed, and he commanded the room when he walked in. He was not quite six feet tall, as Chantal noticed later when she stood close to him, though she would have sworn he was taller. He had great public charisma, but individually, he was soft-spoken and smiled shyly at people, which was his charm.

He crossed the room to her at once, as if she were the guest of honor. Once again, she felt as if she were in the presence of a powerful sorcerer who could easily put her under a spell with his penetrating attention. As Jake introduced them, he took her hand and lifted it to his lips. She felt his mouth lingering warm on the back of her hand—the mouth that had been feeding off Anabelle's breasts less than an hour before.

"I'm pleased to have you here, Chantal," Antonio said, his deep voice caressing her name. "Your beauty graces my home." His voice was the sonic version of the warm caramel coloring of his skin. She felt a strange aversion mixed with a sensual thrill at his touch. He was so suave and elegant, as well as compellingly attractive, that she suddenly started feeling very sophisticated and worldly just for being his guest. She was definitely enjoying herself; but the sense of foreboding she'd had earlier suddenly returned, and she noticed it there uneasily, beneath it all.

They had chatted easily for ten or fifteen minutes, with Billy adding his witty and pointed comments to the conversation, when she noticed Jake wasn't there. She cast her eyes around the room, searching the various knots of people to see where he could be. There was Antonio's lover, the striking redhead. She had traded her unbuttoned blouse and peasant skirt for a little black dress, freshened up her lipstick, and was now discussing world politics with a Kenyan runner, who was there with his wife, a small blond Swedish woman. Chantal was fascinated by the contrast made by the lofty athlete, the color of his skin almost pure black, and the delicate woman with porcelain skin and hair so blond it was nearly white.

There was a young British diplomat of Indian descent and her date, a Welsh journalist. In another corner sat a woman in a sari with thick blond hair braided down her back. She was talking to a handsome young man with a short blue Mohawk, skinny black pants, a pierced brow, and tattooed arms.

But Chantal didn't see Jake anywhere in the room.

She sighed. When he was present, everything was more in-teresting. Even Antonio seemed to lose a bit of his luster with-out Jake around.

I can't be with Billy, Chantal thought, suddenly certain that their relationship was going nowhere. The way she was obsess-ing on Jake made that pretty clear.

She was relieved to finally face up to it so firmly, but exasper-ated with herself for letting things go on this long.

I need to tell him. Now.

But obviously *now* wasn't the time.

Jake shivered, but not because he was cold. He stood near the railing at the edge of the deck, overlooking the ocean. The fog was coming in, swirling around the posts and columns of the house. It was night, and winter, but he hardly noticed the tem-perature. He could feel only her—the awareness of her, the memory of her, as if he had left her long ago, missed her dread-fully, and didn't even realize it until now. He had never believed in love at first sight, but suddenly he was beginning to wonder. He certainly had a mad crush on sight. No doubt of that. And no doubt it would amount to nothing, when he got to know her. Falling in love with a woman based on her looks was just plain stupid. And that's all it could be, since he didn't know her at all. But it was weird. He knew lots of women, women more beauti-ful than her. Was she actually beautiful? He wasn't sure. And yet . . . to him, her allure blew away that of any other woman he could remember. And it wasn't just her looks that struck him. It was something indefinable in her expression, in the lilt of her voice.

Still, that was just scratching the surface. It was a deep, sen-sual, sexual chord she was pulling in him, and maybe that's all it was about. Too bad he couldn't just try it out and see. But there was no way he was going there. The situation did not lend itself.

"Hey."

He turned, startled to see her, as if she had materialized out of the potency of his fantasies. She moved to the railing beside him and rested her arms on the top rail. She had a tomboyish way of inhabiting a very womanly body. "Wow," she said. "It's really something, isn't it? We're so lucky to be able to hang out here."

The glance of her grayish-blue eyes nearly undid him. He looked away and mumbled, "Yeah."

There was an awkward pause.

"So . . . you don't like epic views, or you just don't do small talk?" She leaned against the railing, looking at him with a saucy expression.

"I'm . . . probably just out of practice," he said.

"Out of practice with small talk? Or epic views?"

"Both, I guess."

"Anything else you're out of practice with?"

"Well, I haven't been in prison lately." He shot her a grin.

"Well, I hear you can stay in practice, even in prison."

"Uh—yeah. Maybe. If you're into certain practices."

She laughed, deep and hearty, and he felt oddly complimented. He loved making a woman laugh. Was she beautiful? Yes, definitely. When she smiled like that.

"So what *are* you into then?" she asked, cocking her head slightly, teasing him.

I'd like to be into you, he thought, casting his gaze down over her throat, the swell of her breasts, the long sweep of her midriff and her belly, and the soft cleft between her legs, where the denim of her jeans darkened.

"Are you asking about my hobbies?" he murmured. "Or my sexual predilections?"

"They could be one and the same, for all I know," she said.

"You got that right." He moved closer to her, close enough that he could reach down with his hand and stroke the shadow of that cleft with his finger. And her breasts, warm and soft, he could dip his head and bury his face between them—wet them with his tongue through the cotton of her T-shirt, and suck on them until the nipples stood out hard through the wet material. And that was just for an appetizer. He would undress her, scooping her naked breasts out of her bra, taking the hot, heavy fruit into his mouth. . .

And he would fuck her, God would he fuck her, but that would come later.

He was rock hard, thinking about what he wanted to do to her. He knew it would be obvious if she happened to look down; his cock was straining painfully against his fly. He was torn between a desire to turn away and hide it from her, and wanting her to notice.

"Well?" she was teasing him now, waiting for an answer. "Are you going to tell me?"

"You wanna know what I'm into?" He drew even closer. "Do you really want to know?"

She suddenly looked a little scared. "I don't know." She dropped her gaze.

When she looked up at him again, her eyes were huge. He knew she had seen the enormous erection in his jeans. He was embarrassed and proud at the same time, knowing it had to be an impressive sight to a little thing like her.

She took a step away, but he reached out and took her arm, grasping her gently but firmly, and he pulled her against him.

He brushed his mouth over her ear and whispered, "Let me know when you do." And then he let go of her arm.

Paco's soft voice at the door had them turning their heads in unison.

"Dinner is served," he said.

Chantal was panting. Her breasts ached to give suck. She took a moment to get hold of herself before joining the others in the dining room. She had no appetite for food; all she could think of was Jake. She was wickedly thrilled to think that enormous column of stone in his jeans was all for her. For a moment he had held her close and she had felt the huge, hard cock through his clothes and hers, pressing against her belly; she felt the insistent power in it, and felt her own body heat up and melt and open. Her tongue watered, remembering the sensations. She wanted to kiss him and suck his tongue, and she wanted to taste his skin. She wanted him . . . wanted him to open her blouse the way Antonio had opened Anabelle's. She wanted Jake to suckle her breasts that way, hungrily. She wanted him to fall on his knees and open her jeans, yank them down over her hips, pull aside the silk of her panties, and seek out her clit with his lips. To gently press open her thighs with teasing fingers, to fuck her deeply with his tongue, strong and swirling, tearing her panties aside in his frenzy. Licking her, thrusting his tongue deep inside her, then bringing her to shuddering orgasm while she ground herself against his mouth. Then he would pull her down on the floor and mount her, impaling her, fucking her deeply, strongly, with long, swordlike strokes, kissing her and suckling her breasts, crying out her name as she came again with an enormous shudder and he ejaculated explosively, the hot white creamy product of his culmination oozing out of her and down over her legs. And he would stay semihard in her for a long time, and they would lie together, and then he would slowly begin to kiss her again, moving inside her, and he would grow hard again, so hard she could feel him swelling inside her, and he would start fucking her again. . .

"Is the meal not to your taste, Chantal?" Antonio, who was sitting beside her at the dining room table, noticed she wasn't eating.

She glanced at Jake, who sat across the table. His head was slightly turned toward Anabelle, who sat to his right, but his eyes glanced sideways, meeting Chantal's. He wasn't eating much, either.

"No, it's delicious," Chantal said. "I'm just savoring every bite."

"Do try the clam chowder. It's like velvet, the way my cook does it."

"I'd love to try it," she replied, "but unfortunately I'm allergic to shellfish."

"Are you sure you can't try it, not just a little?" Anabelle crooned from across the table. "It's *so* delicious."

"You really don't want me going into anaphylactic shock here at the dinner table," Chantal replied dryly. But then she wondered if that was true. Anabelle didn't seem to like her much.

"And *you* haven't touched your plate, young man," Anabelle crooned in Jake's ear. Chantal felt a whip of jealousy as the other woman's beautiful fingers ran up and down Jake's arm. She wondered if Antonio felt jealous, seeing Anabelle carry on this way with Jake, but she noticed uneasily that Antonio seemed far more interested in *her* than in what Anabelle and Jake were doing.

Antonio lavished Chantal with attention; he told her funny stories and took every opportunity to touch her, his fingers on her arm, his hand pressing her hand, his thigh brushing against hers beneath the tablecloth. She found it somehow sexy, but repulsive at the same time. She wished he would stop.

Funny, she thought. If it was Jake, she would welcome it.

Billy sat on her other side, busy talking about dirt bikes to the guy with the Mohawk. Mohawk was sweet and handsome, with beautiful bones and soulful eyes, but he seemed interested only in motocross and sex, and lapsed silent when the conversation turned to any other topic.

They had just finished the first course when another guest arrived—a rough, good-looking guy with a shaved head, a silver hoop in one ear, and a goatee.

Anabelle waved. "Hello, baby," she cooed. "Everybody, this is my hubby, Derek."

This guy was Anabelle's husband?

From the leather chaps over his jeans and the thick black leather motorcycle jacket, not to mention the helmet he carried under his arm, Chantal surmised that Derek had arrived on a bike. He appeared to be a little younger than his wife, and he looked mean.

Chantal wondered if Derek had any idea what his wife had been up to with Antonio. She shuddered to think of it. Then again, maybe he *did* know. Maybe they had some kind of arrangement. An *agreement*. Chantal hoped so; she wouldn't want to see this guy, Derek, get mad. He was big. And from the tattoo coverage on his heavily muscled frame, she guessed he had a high threshold for pain.

Anabelle and her husband made a scene in the great room after dinner. Derek's voice echoed through the lofty space.

"Did he have you? Answer me, woman!"

It was like a scene from a movie.

Everyone turned to look at them and, for a moment, it was completely silent in the room.

"Who?" Anabelle looked innocent. "What are you talking about, dear?"

"Did Antonio fuck you?" Derek's tone sent an ominous chill through the atmosphere.

Anabelle ran her hands down over her own body, very sensually. Her voice was soft. "Yes," she said.

"Yeah?"

"Yeah."

"Yeah? Say it. Tell me he fucked you."

She said dreamily, "He fucked me. He fucked me *hard*."

Derek stood looking at Anabelle with what appeared to Chantal as murderous wrath. He slowly turned and shouted across the room at his host. "Antonio de la Court, you must account for your actions with my wife!"

Antonio had been standing off in a corner, engaged in some flirty conversation with several ladies; now he slowly advanced toward Anabelle's husband. "You call *me* to account?" he asked disdainfully.

"I do. I consider it a great insult that you have ravished my wife . . ." Derek stepped up to meet Antonio.

Chantal watched in horror as the two men met, eye to eye, close enough now to come to blows.

"For the love of God," roared the husband. "Couldn't you two have managed to wait a fucking hour until *I* got here?"

The two men broke out into laughter and went into an embrace, a manly, strong hug, which was concluded by an aggressive meeting of the mouths.

Chantal let out a breath, which quickly caught again. She

had never seen two men kissing before, not like that. For about three seconds they kissed, mouths exchanging a violent tussle of tongues. Then they broke apart.

"I will have my revenge on you, you know," Derek cried.

"I shall gird my loins in preparation," Antonio shouted back with a roguish smile.

The party had moved to the game room. Chantal was watching Billy and Mohawk play pool. Mohawk had a cute ass and some sexy moves.

"I've had your things moved to another suite." Antonio had taken her aside with a subtle touch of his hand on her arm.

She was aware of Jake, sitting alone in a corner, watching her with Antonio.

"It's rather nicer than the one Paco gave you," Antonio was saying. "When you are ready, I will take you there."

"Nicer!" She laughed, shaking her head. "But the room I was given *was* very nice!"

"*This* one has a view of the sea. I think you'll find it more to your liking. And please don't worry about your friend, Billy," he added in a soft voice. "He'll still be close by."

Chantal had thought it quaint that they had been given separate rooms when they arrived at the estate, but now she was thinking it really was best. She had gone from wondering if Billy would visit her that night to hoping that he wouldn't. But Antonio didn't have to know that. Though she had decided to call it quits with Billy, she was glad to have him as an excuse to ward off Antonio. If she needed such an excuse—and she had the feeling she did. The untoward attentions of her host made her feel uneasy. Why should she, of all the guests there, be treated differently?

Her new quarters were indeed spectacular and quite private and hidden away from the rest of the house. Antonio showed her through a door at the end of the hallway on the second floor, and through an arched passageway to a curved staircase that rose to a gracious third-floor suite. French doors opened up to a private balcony high above the cliffs.

"I feel like a princess in a tower," Chantal said.

"You like it here, don't you?" Antonio smiled with satisfaction at her dazzled expression. He moved beside her, swept his hand over hers and took possession of it. "Come, look at the view."

He led her outside. The way the balcony was situated, nobody looking up from the decks below would be able to see them. Only from one small section of beach would this lofty nest be visible.

Chantal felt deliciously uneasy with this exotic, potent man at her side. His touch was formal and elegant, yet snapping with sensuality. She might have felt afraid of him if he did not seem so genteel. But the fact that she didn't feel afraid did not make her any less wary of him. In fact, it put her on her guard.

"Why did you give this suite to me?" she asked bluntly, turning to face him head-on. "Any one of your other guests would have wanted it."

"Why do you think?" he answered, with a trace of accent she hadn't heard before.

She looked up at him; he moved closer and took her in his arms as if to dance.

His body seemed to hunger for her through his polished decorum. She felt the way he leaned into her, subtly. She found her own body thrilling to the sexuality of his close presence, even as she felt more certain she didn't really like the man.

"What about Billy?" she asked. "And—what about Anabelle?"

"Ah . . . lovely Anabelle," he said smoothly. He pulled Chantal closer. "But, you see, Anabelle is preoccupied now, and I need to be needed, for me alone." His arms were strong, obviously expert in managing a female body, and very difficult to resist. As were his lips, which were now searching out her neck.

She shivered. "So you make a pass at me, when I am here with my date, the good friend of your nephew?" Chantal pressed her hands against his chest, pushing him away, but her heart was pounding and she was breathing very fast.

"You are harsh," he said reproachfully, and let her go with a reluctant slowness. "Are you really so bound to him, then?"

Chantal laughed. She couldn't figure out if this guy was for real. "Thank you for the suite. I really appreciate it. But I can't take it with any strings attached."

"You are increasingly charming," Antonio murmured. "God, what a delightful challenge."

"Shall I take my things back down to the other room?"

"Of course not. You will stay here; I insist. And if it makes you feel . . . safer, you should know the doors lock from the inside. But you needn't worry."

He slipped his arms around her again, and for a moment she felt his body fully against hers as he whispered, hot against her ear: "I promise you, I will not take you until you beg me to take you, with all your body and soul."

"Okay, great. Then we have an understanding."

He snapped his head back and fixed her with his black, penetrating eyes. "But you must understand. Sooner or later, you *will* desire me to take you." He let go of her, but he kept his gaze on her, and didn't break it off until he passed through the door and out of the room.

"Damn," Chantal thought. It was flattering, if nothing else. And admittedly, he was sexy as hell. She rejoined the party, wondering if the others noticed her bright eyes and flushed skin.

Later in the evening, Chantal went to look for Billy, who had disappeared. When she didn't find him in any of the common areas, she went upstairs to his room. Maybe this would be a good time for them to have a talk.

His door was slightly ajar. She pushed it open and peeked inside, not wanting to disturb him if he was asleep.

He wasn't in the bed.

She entered the room quietly, looking around.

She was about to withdraw when she noticed a movement out on the little dark patio off the room. She walked noiselessly across the carpet to the door and peered outside. Billy was sitting slumped in a chair, naked, with his eyes closed, and his long, well-muscled legs slightly spread. He was holding his thick pink cock, sliding his hand up and down in fast, rhythmic strokes.

He's aroused, she thought. *But not by me.*

She tried not to feel hurt that he didn't want to be with her, that he was getting off without her, and found she really didn't feel too badly about it. It only confirmed her feelings that it was time to do something about the situation. She didn't belong with this guy.

As she tiptoed away, she heard him utter a soft cry, and she turned her head in time to see his hard stomach muscles contracting in a graceful spasm. He held his penis away from himself as if it were a water hose, and a spurt of beautiful white liquid jetted out from the tip. Another spurt, then another. Chantal could practically see the steam from the tip of his hot cock.

She slipped through the door and went up to her own room.

She locked her door, undressed, and went to bed—half-fearing, half-hoping that Antonio would somehow slip in and ravish her. Better yet, Jake. . .

"I have some meetings this morning that I must attend," Antonio told them all at breakfast. "So you must amuse yourselves. I command you."

He got the chuckle from his audience that he had expected, and went on: "I have a stable full of excellent horses, if you would like a ride on the beach. There are many excellent hiking trails, and swimming in the pool, or in the ocean if you're daring. We have surfboards and wet suits and other water equipment in the boathouse. Inside, we have the game room, of course, or the library if you're the literary sort . . . I have a theater with all the latest movies and video games. But, of course, I encourage you to indulge in the most pleasurable pastime of all—making love. My entire estate is at your disposal for that purpose!"

A round of applause broke out in the room. Chantal couldn't bring herself to join in, leery of encouraging her host. She glanced at Jake, who wasn't clapping either. He was staring at her. The jolt of electric sex that zapped between them when their eyes met was so high-powered she had to look down at once.

When Antonio was suggesting activities for his guests that

morning, Chantal never would have expected to find herself alone with Jake later that day, just the two of them, deep in a silent wood.

She had expressed enthusiasm for hiking, and Antonio had encouraged a group of them to go, describing the best views and most pleasant walks. Billy begged off, claiming laziness, and that left her with the British couple. Jake fell into stride beside her as they set off, so it was the four of them.

Chantal was thrilled to be walking alongside Jake, but at the same time, she was glad for the presence of the other people. The weather was perfect for hiking, cool and sunny. The trail followed the bluffs for a while, then turned inland and cut through sloping wooded hillsides above the ocean. But the Brits were clearly more interested in each other than in the beauties of nature, and when the group paused to admire a particularly stunning vista, those two settled down beneath a huge Monterey cypress tree, nestling together in the sandy cleft between its large, leglike roots. With one look, Chantal and Jake continued on together, leaving the lovers behind without a word.

They walked along together, laughing and talking about what they were seeing, slipping off easily into various subjects; it was all light banter, but with some edge underneath, like they weren't sure they liked each other.

She was pretty sure they liked the *look* of each other, though. There was the indefinable, unmistakable urge toward each other physically—it was undeniable. She felt it in the way he stared at her, so hungrily, as if he would eat her, and in the way he moved beside her and made her feel his presence—like Antonio, but earthier.

"So what are you doing here?" she asked him as they walked.

"What?" he didn't understand the question.

"I think you always look like you'd rather be anywhere else but here."

"Here?"

"Here, on your uncle's estate."

He flashed his cynical grin. "You're very perceptive," he said. "I'm only here because I have to be."

"You *have* to be? Who is making you?"

"I came here to meet someone on a matter of business. My *uncle* graciously offered me his place for the meeting. I'm beginning to think it was a mistake to have accepted that offer."

"Why? Is it really so awful here?" she stopped on the trail and frowned at him. "I mean, look at the ocean. It's so beautiful." She waved her hand out toward the immense sea, which lay in a long blue ribbon below the windswept hill they had mounted.

"I like it out here," he said. "With you."

She blushed. "But back there in that house you're like a tiger pacing in a cage."

He threw back his head and laughed, genuine, heartfelt laughter, so different from his usual cynically ironic grin.

God, he was beautiful, she thought.

He wore a dark green T-shirt that fit his long body with a slight drape, rippling over lean muscles down to his faded jeans, which he wore slightly loose, so that his little ass just barely showed off; but as he walked and moved, she could see the flex of his thighs beneath the denim, and his strong forearms, bare and tanned from the winter sun. She would be cold, she thought, dressed in so little. She wore a big sweatshirt and black jeans.

"I am like a tiger in some sense," he said. "Pacing. Waiting for my chance."

"To escape?"

"No. To pounce."

"On what?"

"My prey, of course."

They walked on, bumping into each other on the trail. He brushed his hand over her arm to warn her of some minor hazard along the way. She flicked a leaf off his hair.

The day grew warmer, and he watched her peel off her sweatshirt and tie it around her hips. Now her full breasts were outlined under her thin blouse, and he drank in their roundness that seemed to obsess him.

"So what do you do?" she asked.

"What?" He felt so dazed by her, unable to think straight. God, she must think he was an idiot.

"Your business. What kind is it?"

For a moment, he could think of absolutely nothing to say. It was as if she had bewitched him, stolen his tongue—his silver tongue, that had saved him so much ugly violence in his line of work.

"My business is my business," he said smoothly, flashing his lady-killing grin.

"Oh. Excuse me." She attempted a tone of lighthearted nonchalance, but he sensed that his response to her question had killed any developing regard she might have had for him. *Now she's sure I'm an asshole*, he thought.

"Well, at least we've established that you're a predator," she said.

"Actually," he said enigmatically, "predators are my prey."

"Then I guess *I* have nothing to worry about."

He clamped his hand on her arm and spun her to face him. "Are you so sure of that?"

He pulled her closer and felt her breasts softly pressing into his chest. His penis hardened instantly as it came into contact with her warm body through their clothes.

God, he wanted to fuck her.

He wanted to push her down on the ground and mount her, right there in the grass. She'd probably fight him at first, but in the end, they'd be fucking gloriously. He could tell by the way she caught her breath when he touched her that she wanted it—wanted him to fill her with his wet tongue and his hard cock.

If only he could.

But, of course, there was the problem of Billy.

Maybe just one kiss, he thought, staring down into her eyes.

She'd probably slap his face. Or kill him. What the hell, he would risk it.

If he could.

But, of course, he couldn't, and the reason was obvious. It's a no-brainer, he told himself. You don't pull shit like that if you're any kind of man. . .

He wanted her, but he wasn't going there.

He let her slip out of his arms.

Later that afternoon, she paced the corridors, admiring the art, looking out at the ocean, trying to distract herself—trying to think of anything but Jake. But Jake was all she could think of.

She found Billy alone in the library, sitting on a leather couch, working on his laptop.

"Billy . . . I need to talk with you about something."

He set the computer on a side table and patted the seat beside him. "Sure. You can talk with me about anything, Chantal."

She sat down on the couch with him, wondering how best to say it. "Well . . . I mean, it's not like you've ever really indicated you wanted anything *else* with me, but I thought I should tell you that I think we should just be friends."

She watched his face carefully. He looked sad and a little surprised. "Okay," he said slowly.

"That's kind of what I thought you were about, anyway," she said. "Was I wrong?"

"It's funny. It started out just something that I—but then I think I really started feeling close to you. I didn't expect that. I think you're super cool, Chantal. And thank you for being straight with me."

"You're welcome. So are we okay?"

He eyed her warily. "What do you mean—okay?"

"Like, okay with staying here at this place together for the rest of the week as planned, with your friends . . ."

"I don't know." He shrugged. "Since you've dumped me, can I go after other people?"

"You got someone in mind?" She nudged him, teasingly. Who had he been thinking about while he was masturbating on his balcony last night? "Never mind, I don't want to know. Just don't disgrace me. It has to be someone fabulous."

"Don't worry, baby. It always is. And I'm always discreet."

They leaned into each other on the bed. He kissed her mouth softly and they shared a sweet hug. Chantal looked over Billy's shoulder to see Antonio in the doorway, looking down on them with a gleaming expression.

"Glad to see you two are taking my advice to pursue the pleasures of passion," he murmured.

Instead of retreating, as Chantal would have expected, Antonio came further into the room. Nervously, Chantal and Billy stood up, but Antonio came straight to them and put his hands on their shoulders. He pulled them together into a three-way embrace. Chantal felt the sensual pleasure of two male bodies pressing warmly against her.

Antonio started kissing her, as if it was the most natural thing in the world, pulling her more tightly into his arms, right in front of Billy. It happened so fast she couldn't stop it, his tongue slipping expertly over her lips and thrusting into her mouth. But in the next moment, he had turned to Billy and was kissing *him* the same way.

Antonio quickly ended the kiss, smiled at them both and said, "The simple pleasures in life are the most sublime, and they are best shared, don't you think?"

He released them from his embrace, then turned and went out of the room.

"Wow," said Chantal. "That was intense."

"He's quite a character, isn't he?" Billy said.

"He's daring. Some men would have punched out a guy who tried that."

"Yeah, I still might have to."

"I'm thinking about slapping him, myself."

"But you enjoyed it, didn't you?"

"I guess I did, in a weird way. How about you?"

"No comment."

Chantal was happy to have made a clean break with Billy, but that didn't solve all her problems. All she could think of was sex. It was all around her, pressing in from all sides. But she wasn't getting any. Not from the one she wanted.

Feeling restless that night, Chantal left her room to walk outside on the terrace. Her nipples brushed against her silk teddy as she walked, and she felt the tips of her breasts tingling. It was cold. Soon she would have to run inside, but first she wanted to feel the wind on her skin, on her arms, and on her inner thighs. Her long legs were bare up to the silken swatch of her panties. She lifted the teddy and leaned over the railing to let the wind lick her breasts.

"Very nice," came the voice—a deep, sexy voice.

It was Mohawk. In the darkness, he looked lithe and masculine, with wide shoulders and narrow hips. His hair was slicked down and he looked like a warrior come to claim his bounty. Chantal covered herself, but slowly. *Let him see*, she thought. There was something compelling about the way he seemed to eat her up with his eyes. And he was a fine-looking male, vital in his movements. There were others in the room behind him: Antonio, Anabelle and her husband, Derek, and Beth, the girl who had worn the sari last night. Tonight she wore a strapless gown that showed off enormous breasts. She had taken the braid out of her hair and now it streamed, kinkily, down over her shoulders.

"We've come to give you a massage, Chantal," said one of the women. "Get your ass in here and lay down on this bed."

Chantal came into the bedroom and let Beth take her hand and lead her to the bed.

"It's okay. Lie down. You want a massage, don't you? Don't worry, we're all having them. Who else is going to go first? There's plenty of room here on the bed, or you can use the floor if you want. That carpet looks soft."

"Oh, but the bed is huge," someone said. "We can all fit."

Anabelle and Beth shed their clothes without inhibition. "Don't mind us!" Anabelle said. "We're just free spirits."

Antonio sloughed off his jacket and his shirt, leaving only his pants on, but Mohawk cast off everything but his studded leather vest. Only Chantal was fully dressed, if barely, in her teddy top and panties.

People quickly paired off, all on the bed together.

Chantal didn't have to do a thing. She was gently made to lie on her belly. She felt a pair of strong, gentle hands on her back, sliding up under the silk of her teddy.

Mohawk was rubbing her back, rubbing warm oil into her skin as he straddled her, his thighs flexing as he held himself just above her, his cock hanging down between his legs. When he had unbuttoned his jeans, Chantal had seen that his penis was like a battering ram, thick and long, with a wide, smooth head. Now, as she lay there with her eyes closed, she felt it brush against her ass as he straddled her.

Beth was rubbing Anabelle, and Antonio was doing Anabelle's young husband, Derek, who grunted appreciatively at the touch of the other man's hands on his generous muscles. Naked to his waist, his skin gleamed with the oil Antonio had drizzled on him.

Chantal opened her eyes now and then to watch the others, as Mohawk's strong hands worked oil into her skin, melting her muscles. He gradually sank down on her as he worked, and she craved the weight of his body on hers, the hard pressure of his erect cock digging into her almost-naked ass, and the sensitive, skillful fingers kneading her flesh, her neck, her back, sliding suggestively alongside her breasts. The physical pleasures he was inflicting upon her, combined with what she was seeing beside her on the bed, made her pant with lust.

She watched as Anabelle turned Beth over on her back and rubbed warm oil over her thighs and belly. Then Anabelle slid herself over Beth's body, stretching out on top of her, moving up from her belly to her breasts, running her mouth over the oil-slick skin. When her lips slid over one of Beth's big breasts, Anabelle took it into her mouth and began to suck it.

Beth moaned. The women wrapped their arms around each other, taking turns suckling each other.

Chantal looked up at Antonio. She couldn't help but admire his body, more muscular than she really liked, but flawless, male, and admittedly impressive. He sat on the other man like a horse, his arms flexing as he grabbed the tight flesh of Derek's shoulders in his hands, massaging him. Antonio caught her watching him, and he narrowed his eyes.

As Anabelle sucked Beth's breasts, Antonio climbed off Derek, insinuated himself between Beth and Anabelle, and mounted Beth. He slowly pulled his cock out of his pants and made sure everyone got a good look at its purple girth before he shoved it into Beth. He fucked her, very showy, with hard, long strokes, making her cry out. Anabelle continued to suckle Beth's bosom as Antonio fucked her. Beth looked like she would swoon with bliss. Then Antonio suddenly pulled out of Beth and climbed on Anabelle and started fucking *her*; all the while staring down at Chantal.

Chantal had the feeling that Antonio had decided to show her he was some kind of superfucker.

Beth and Derek began kissing. Beth reached down and touched him through his pants, opening his fly and letting his cock out. Derek kissed Beth's mouth, her throat, and her collarbone, dipping his head down even further and getting a taste of those "big scoops of vanilla ice cream with a cherry on top" breasts. He had one of them in his mouth, and Anabelle was nursing the other. They were a pile of writhing bodies.

Chantal felt Mohawk's cock nudging aside the thin strip of silk between the cheeks of her ass. She couldn't see him behind her, but she could feel his cock pushing up between her thighs, rock hard, thick, and dull; he thrust it against her ass, gently but insistently, sliding it back and forth between her thighs toward her cunt, picking up her juices and growing slick, easier. Doing it again.

She felt him pull her panties away from her wet slit. His body was on top of hers, his lips tickling her shoulder and her neck. His hands slid under her and took her breasts, his fingers lightly pinching the tips of her nipples.

The room was filled with moaning and gasping and groaning.

Some back rub, Chantal thought. She was in the middle of an orgy.

She felt Mohawk's movements become more insistent, his breathing hard. He was holding her tightly.

He entered her.

She felt him suddenly full and hard and hot inside her. With her panties still on, he fucked her from behind. He brought his hand down between her legs in front and fingered her while he fucked her. Of course, the others were watching them fuck, but she didn't care. Or maybe it added to the thrill. She felt his mouth on the back of her neck, biting her just hard enough to send her into paroxysms of painful pleasure.

He turned her body slightly and exposed her cunt to the others, with his fingers lifting the furred lips a little to open them, to display them.

Beth crawled away from Derek and Anabelle, and brought her mouth down between Chantal's legs, opening her thighs wider with soft hands. With little nibbling and sucking motions of her mouth, she played with Chantal's clit while Mohawk's cock slid in and out of her from behind.

Antonio, watching Chantal, pulled out of Anabelle, and he hardly seemed to notice as Derek leaned down and took his wet cock in his mouth. Antonio was intently focused on Chantal, who was crying out and rubbing herself all over Beth's mouth and lips. She thrust herself against Beth's tongue, which bathed and licked both Mohawk's cock and Chantal's clit as they slid together, tongue, clit, and cock.

Chantal was so overcome by the sensations she nearly passed out. She shuddered and orgasmed violently, convulsing with massive waves of pleasure, crying out without knowing it. Mohawk pumped her harder, and by the sudden stiffening of his body, the cries in her ear, and the sensation of hot jets going off inside her, she knew he was coming along with her.

The orgasms lasted for a long time, and he kept humping her as Beth kept licking and eating her. Chantal could have continued on, taking even more, but the release cleared her mind and suddenly she came to her senses, aghast at what she was doing and with whom. She eased herself away from Beth's mouth and let Mohawk's half-hard cock slide out of her.

But suddenly Antonio was rearing above her, presenting his great purplish penis, so long and thick it hung down between his legs from the sheer weight of it, though it had to be fully erect. Clearly, he meant to have his turn on Chantal.

There's no way, she thought wildly. But how could she get out of this gracefully?

Forget graceful.

"God, you guys," she laughed, rolling off the bed and throwing her robe over her disheveled teddy. "That was quite a back rub. But I think that's all I can take for now. Please, continue making yourselves at home in here. I gotta go get something to eat. I'm starved."

She ran out of the room and down the hall, stopping at Billy's door, trying to catch her breath. She would see if she could spend the night with him. Just friends.

She opened the door and saw them in the bed, sixty-nining.

Chantal couldn't believe it. *All these weeks with me and noth-ing, now he's fucking frantically, only hours after I break up with him?*

And then she noticed that the person in bed with Billy was a guy. A young man with shaggy black hair; Chantal had seen him around the estate and knew he worked for Antonio.

Ah, she thought. Now *that* makes sense.

They didn't notice her standing there, or if they did, they didn't care.

She went out, shut the door quietly, and continued down the hallway. She came to Jake's room.

She knocked on the door and heard him say, "Yeah."

She opened the door and poked her head in. "Hi," she said.

"Hi."

"Can I come in?"

"That's up to you."

"You're always so suave and debonair in your speech and manner," she said mockingly, letting the door shut behind her as she came into the room.

"I never pull any punches."

"Jake, I need to ask you for a favor—"

The Kenyan runner was sitting on the couch with his shirt off and the top of his pants undone. Jake was sitting back in a recliner with a bottle of beer in his hand. As she came in closer, Chantal caught a full view of the Kenyan's Swedish wife on her knees between Jake's legs. Jake was fully dressed, but his jeans were unbuttoned and the little blonde was running her mouth up and down the shaft of his ample cock, which jutted high and hard from his fly.

"Excuse me. You might have said you were busy." Chantal turned on her heel and went out.

Her heart was pounding. She walked along the corridor, not knowing where to go. And she wondered why seeing Jake with another woman on him should disturb her so much more than anything else she had seen tonight. She felt like crying.

She let herself outdoors and pulled her robe tightly around her. The night was misty and beautiful. The beach was nearly gone; the tide was high tonight.

Suddenly, she felt his hands on her, his arms warming her briefly, then vanishing again. She turned. There he was, close enough to embrace. He was looking down on her with concern.

"What's going on?" Jake asked gruffly.

She glanced involuntarily at his groin, wondering if the big cock that filled out that fly so well was still hard or if it had found its release.

To think she had relished the idea that *she* was the one who made it so big and hard, and come to find she shared that pleasure with at least one hot Swedish blonde—and probably many others.

She turned away, haughtily. "Nothing," she said.

"Don't give me that bullshit," he said. "What's going on?"

"I can't sleep in my room," she said.

"Why not?"

"There are others using it at the moment. I wondered if I could sleep on your floor. But I see you are entertaining guests."

"They're gone now. Come on. You're freezing." He slipped his arm around her and led her back inside. They heard voices down the corridor—Antonio and the others, coming their way. Chantal shied back from the sound, and Jake seemed to understand—he grabbed her hand and they quickly ducked into his room, which was now empty of the Swedish woman and her husband. It was just the two of them in there, alone, and he locked the door.

"Thanks, Jake."

"No problem."

"I'll just lie down here—" She indicated the floor.

"Give me a break," Jake said. "This bed is huge. And I promise not to touch you." He grinned at her, but she didn't smile back.

"That's not necessary," she said in a soft voice. *Because you're the one I want to touch me.*

"Yes it is," he said quickly.

She was surprised at her own flirtatious words, and she felt rejected and hurt by his response.

What am I thinking? Still wearing her robe, she got into bed and snuggled into the blankets. *How in the hell can I relax, with him so near?* Fortunately, she'd been rather well-satisfied just recently, which helped. Finally, she slept.

Unfortunately, Jake had not been similarly satisfied. He lay beside her, awake almost all night long, fully clothed, tortured by her nearness. He squeezed himself through his jeans, but it wasn't enough. It wasn't what he wanted. He wanted *her*. But he had promised himself he wouldn't touch her. It was a question of honor, he reminded himself.

But the real reason Jake wouldn't touch her was one he wouldn't even admit to himself—he was scared. He was scared to let go and touch her the way every cell in his body was screaming to touch her. Because for some reason, he was pretty sure that if he did, it would matter. It would matter way too much.

Billy and Chantal had talked about hanging out and doing something together Wednesday morning, but Chantal couldn't find Billy anywhere when she looked for him after breakfast. She was relieved that Antonio seemed to be busy every morning with business matters. She found herself alone, naturally, with Jake.

Over the next few days, Chantal found herself more and more in Jake's company. She was in a sort of dance between Jake and Antonio, both of whom seemed to want her sexually, but only one of them seemed willing to do anything about it—and that was Antonio, not Jake. She wasn't sure why Jake held back, but she figured it was because of his friendship with Billy. She wanted to let him know that she and Billy were just platonic friends, but she didn't know how to communicate that gracefully. Jake was Billy's good friend, and he would have to come to her if they were to be together. She still wasn't sure if he *really* wanted her all that badly, anyway.

But *she* was smitten. She could think of nothing but Jake and the times they escaped alone together, usually in the evenings, when the others were playing games and she had evaded Antonio's latest attempt at seduction. She would happen to run into

Jake on the terrace, and they would walk together in the moonlight, just the two of them, in the woods or around the estate.

"Let's swim," said Jake one night when their walk had taken them to the edge of the swimming pool on the southern terrace. The surface of the water was still, and steam wafted up into the chilled air.

Chantal nodded.

She watched as Jake slowly peeled off his clothes. She drank in his lean, tightly muscled torso as he stripped off his coat and his shirt. He unbuttoned his jeans and let them fall down over his narrow hips. He wore nothing else, and his cock jutted out the way she remembered it, the way it looked when the Swedish woman was licking and sucking it. He had large testicles that hung from the base of his penis in a tight sack.

Her heart began to pound harder. He gave her a long, meaningful look as she feasted her eyes on his naked body, and then he dove almost noiselessly into the pool.

Chantal slipped out of her jeans, took off her coat, and unbuttoned her blouse. She slipped into the water wearing her bikini panties and her lace bra. The water was warm.

She swam a little, then turned over on her back and floated. She felt him swim up beside her. She felt his hands, under the water, on her body.

He pulled her into his arms. She was startled, surprised. He had kept her at a distance, physically, since the night they had slept together in the same bed. But in the water he seemed to be someone else. Suddenly, it was as if nothing could hold him back from her.

He had frustrated her. Unlike Billy, she was certain Jake desired her. But like Billy, he had made only ambiguous moves, until now. . .

In the water, as she floated, he kissed her, his mouth coming down on her mouth, soft and feathery at first, but quickly gaining hunger, his tongue thrusting into her mouth. He sucked her tongue and then his mouth was traveling over her throat, sucking and biting her neck. His hands moved over her body and squeezed her breasts through the wet lace of her bra. She felt his erect penis bump into her belly.

He was tall enough to stand. She wasn't, but she floated and he held her in his arms.

He opened the back of her bra and let the straps down over her arms. Her breasts bobbed round and full in the water, and he dipped his head to take one in his mouth. The feel of him sucking her nipple almost drove her insane. She reached down and closed her hand around the thick shaft of his cock. He surged against her with a grunt, and she slid her hand up and down his big, thick cock, and then slipped her palm beneath his testicles, holding them. They were full and heavy, even in the water.

His mouth was on hers again, and the kiss they shared was endless, mind-blowing, and as much like fucking as a kiss can be.

He swam away for a moment, and she cried out for him to return to her. He lifted her, his hands on her ass. She lay back in the warm water as he stripped off her wet panties. She cried out and began to shudder when he brought her cunt to his mouth, his lips and tongue teasing her clit, swirling and sucking, then jabbing and thrusting deep inside her.

Jake made her moan, and she cried out, forgetting who might hear her. But they were alone, and it was a wild, moonlit night, with nothing but the sound of their passion on the misty air and the crash of the waves beyond the terrace.

She floated in the water as he fucked her with his tongue, and with his fingers.

He laid her on the steps of the pool and drove her to orgasm, his fingers inside her, his eyes locked on hers, and she gasped and called out his name, and he kissed her deeply. He made her come again and again. She was full of him, and senseless from the onslaught of him, but she became aware that he withheld himself, that he had yet to penetrate her with his cock.

He propped himself up over her on the steps at the edge of the pool, kissing her more, and she rubbed up against him, both of them naked. His cock was engorged with blood and absolutely enormous. She bent her head and took it in her mouth, savoring the smoothness, the hard bonelike strength of it, the way it trembled against her tongue. She teased the tip of it with her lips, running her wet tongue around the rim of the head, thrusting the tip of her tongue into the little hole. She teased and sucked it, and gradually he pushed it deeper and deeper into her mouth, and she took every bit of it until she was sucking it gently as he pushed it in and out, his fingers fisted in her hair as he fucked her mouth.

She sensed he was about to erupt, and her mouth watered to drink of him, to taste his salty hot liquor. But panting, he slowly eased the swollen cock out of her wet mouth. He seemed to be trying to get control of himself.

She climbed up onto the edge of the pool and laid back, opening her thighs to him. "Come," she said softly. "Come in me, Jake."

He moved to obey her with glazed eyes, like one hypnotized. He climbed up the last of the steps, dripping with water, steam rising off his slick skin, staring down on her. He mounted her, his belly contracting, rippling with muscle, his stiff cock homing in to her.

She spread her legs wider to receive him.

He dropped his mouth to hers and kissed her, tenderly and hungrily at the same time, and she felt the head of his cock sliding over her clit, pushing aside the lips to enter her——

But he stopped, holding himself just above her, and he broke off the kiss, breathing fast, looking intently into her eyes.

He gave his head a shake, and lifted himself off her. "I can't, Chantal," he panted. "I can't do this."

"If it's about Billy, you should know that we—that we aren't like this, Jake."

His expression was one of such heartbreaking tenderness, she didn't think she could stand it. He kissed her softly and then drew away with a groan.

Well, she thought. He's heard it from me. I'm not with Billy. But maybe it wasn't enough. Maybe he was scared of offending his friend. Perhaps he needed to hear it from Billy himself.

Or maybe there was something else going on.

The next day, Jake seemed to avoid her, and when she did encounter him, he seemed cool and distant.

He regrets getting intimate with me, she thought, trying not to feel too crushed.

But it was too much to bear. Billy was nowhere to be found, but Mohawk cornered her in the game room.

"Let me fuck you again, Mamacita," he murmured, grabbing her hand and closing her fingers over his crotch. "Remember this? I'd like to jam it between your tits and fuck them until I come all over your nipples, then lick them clean."

But she could only think of Jake, and wonder why he was avoiding her. She slipped out of Mohawk's embrace and ran back to her room.

I can't stand it any longer, she thought. *If Jake's not for me, I can't be near him.*

She packed her bags and looked for Billy, but he was still nowhere to be found. No matter. He was obviously having a good time and she didn't want to take him away from that. She would thank her host and ask him to call her a taxi.

"Do you know where Antonio is?" she asked Beth, meeting up with the other woman in the hall outside their rooms. "I want to say good-bye. I'm going home."

"His rooms are up that stairway," Beth said. "Are you sure you have to go?"

"Yeah."

The two women exchanged a long, soulful kiss. Chantal felt herself tingling between her legs, remembering Beth's mouth on her cunt, and how delicious she was, how luscious her breasts were to suck.

After they parted, Chantal climbed the stairs, looking for Antonio. She went to his room and knocked on his door. He opened it and stood there, staring down at her.

"You've come to me at last," he breathed, his voice a low rumble. He lunged at her and gathered her in his arms.

"I've come to say good-bye," she said.

"You're not leaving," he said with a laugh.

"Yes. I have to." She slipped out of his embrace. "I was wondering if I could use your phone to call a taxi. My cell doesn't seem to work out here."

"Please, Chantal, don't leave," he said softly.

"I'm sorry. I have to go."

"No. You don't seem to understand. I can't let you go."

He reached for a button on the wall beside the light switch and pressed it.

"I made a promise," he said. "Do you remember?" He grabbed her hands up in his. "I told you that you will beg for it, you will beg for *me*. I am a patient man, but I *will* have my way in the end."

"You're crazy," Chantal said.

"Perhaps."

She pulled her hands out of his grasp and turned to leave the room, but she found herself face-to-face with two huge, muscle-bound blond men who blocked her way.

"Take care of her," Antonio said to the two men. "Secure her to the bed. Make sure she is comfortable, but also make sure she cannot get away."

She squirmed, trying to free herself. Antonio watched impassively as his henchmen tied Chantal's legs together and strapped her to his big, four-poster bed.

When they were finished securing her, he sat down beside her on the bed, and he ran his hands over her body, lingering on her breasts and between her legs, feeling the heat of her cunt beneath her clothing.

"You're such a wildcat, aren't you?" he murmured. "How sweet your final surrender will be."

Allowing his goons to watch, he slowly undressed her. He called for a towel, a bowl of hot water, soap, and a razor. He slowly shaved her pussy. Now she lay naked on the bed, and he couldn't stop staring at her, touching her, and rubbing himself against her. She tried to fight off his caressing hands, and then his kisses, his mouth on her skin. He kissed her all over her body, his lips lingering on the freshly shaved mounds of her pubis. She was powerless against him.

She could tell he was growing more aroused as he touched her, and licked her, pressing his own body against hers to ease the ache in the enormous erection in his pants. He remained fully dressed. She felt his mouth on her neck, running over her body, sucking her nipples, tonguing her belly. He pushed his head down between her thighs and she felt his tongue between the cheeks of her ass, felt it warm and moist, pressing into her deeply.

"You test my self-control, woman," he growled, suddenly shoving off her. "But you *will* beg for me, and soon."

He draped a shawl over her naked body, left her there on the bed, and slammed out of the room. His helpers followed reluctantly.

She lay there, heart pounding, panting, and whimpering with the need he had stirred up in her with his mouth, his fingers, and the pressure of his hard cock rubbing all over her. She closed her eyes tightly and thought of Jake. It was all his fault. If he hadn't shunned her, she wouldn't have tried to run from him. God, how she longed for him. To save her. To love her. To fuck her.

God just get me out of here, she prayed. *Before I go out of my mind.*

Antonio came back in an hour or so and repeated his earlier sensual teasing, working them both up into a frenzy of sexual need.

"Tell me how much you want me to fuck you," he murmured in her ear.

But she refused, and after a while he left her again.

And then he came back, and did it all over again.

* * *

Jake couldn't find her anywhere. All day he had been skulking around the estate, pacing up and down corridors, beaches, woods, trying to avoid her, hoping to run into her. He knew he had hurt her, stopping their lovemaking when he did. *No shit.* He was driving them both crazy. For him, something had snapped in that swimming pool, when he had seen her body gliding through the water. He suddenly could not keep his hands off her. His mouth, his cock, he had barely been able to stop himself in time. He hadn't intended to let things go so far. Even now, he couldn't figure out if he had been insane, not to give in to his own lust for her. But his self-respect and honor had a strong hold on him. How strong, in the face of growing temptation, he had no idea.

So maybe it was best he stayed away from her, just temporarily, until he got a grip. Let *her* come looking for him. He knew she would. She was as drawn to him as he was to her.

So he stopped looking for her. And waited.

But she didn't come.

Finally, late the next morning, he grew desperate enough to ask Paco if he had seen her.

"No, not since yesterday or the day before," Paco replied. "I think I heard she left the estate. Had to get home to work, or something."

Jake was floored. "She *left?* Are you sure? Did Billy go with her?"

Paco shrugged. "No, I think he stayed on."

She was gone.

He couldn't believe he hadn't seen *that* coming.

Jake knew the very reason Chantal had been able to slip through his fingers was, ironically, because he was so fascinated and fixated on her. He wasn't paying attention to the essentials.

He went to his room and put together his few belongings in a duffel bag. He looked for Billy, but couldn't find him. *He's been awfully busy and preoccupied lately,* Jake thought, annoyed. What the hell's going on with him?

Billy was probably with Chantal. That made sense. They had come together; they would leave together, right? But it didn't make sense that Billy would just suddenly leave without saying anything to Jake. Not unless something was wrong.

Jake slung his bag over his shoulder and walked downstairs, intent on finding Antonio. Antonio would know if Chantal was really gone. And if she was, Jake could thank his host and be off—to find her.

He searched the common area and the terraces, but found only Mohawk and Beth, lounging in the sun.

"Yeah, Chantal told me this morning she was leaving, and last I saw Antonio was this morning, too. He was going to the kitchen to plan the New Year's Eve menu with his cook," said Beth, answering Jake's questions. "Are you leaving us, big Jake?" she asked, noticing his duffel bag.

"Could be," he said absently.

"Well, have a good one," said Mohawk.

Jake thanked them and made his way to the kitchen to see if he could catch Antonio there. He found the cook, preparing a tray with a plate of luscious-looking food he was just covering with a silver dome. Yes, the cook replied, he had met with Antonio earlier, but hadn't seen him for the last couple of hours. Didn't know where he was now.

The cook's assistant came in from the garden with flowers to put in a little vase on the tray beside the linen-wrapped silverware.

"Who is this for?" Jake nodded at the tray.

The cook shrugged. "Paco ordered it and said he would come and take it personally. It's for a guest."

Jake nodded. A guest. Not much of a clue. That could mean most of the people on the estate. "Well, thanks," he said. "You guys do some kick-ass meals. Antonio's a lucky guy."

The cook and his assistant smiled, looking almost uncomfortable with the praise. They turned to finish their work.

Jake was almost out of the kitchen when he heard the cook rebuke his helper:

"But I *told* you, no shrimp on the salad. No shellfish, remember? Those were the orders. You need to learn to listen better, or you'll make someone sick someday."

Her legs were tied together and strapped to the bottom of the bed. Her hands were tied separately to the bedposts. A thin silk shawl barely covered her from her breasts to her thighs.

"Thank God it's you," she said, looking up from the bed at Jake with tears in her eyes.

It had been simple enough to follow Paco up the stairs after he had come to fetch the tray, and then to wait until he delivered the meal to the prisoner.

"Take it away, I don't want it," Jake had heard her say, and he smiled in spite of himself. Paco came out presently, carrying the tray, and locking the door behind him. He didn't notice Jake waiting in the shadows.

When Jake was sure she was alone in the room again, he had entered easily enough, despite the locks. It was one of his talents.

She was aware of how she must look, her body naked, draped with the shawl, tied to the bed. Jake stood above her, looking down on her with a harsh expression. Her relief and gladness at seeing him suddenly fled and she realized something was terribly wrong.

She stared up at him, blinking. "What's this all about?" she demanded. "Are you in on this with him?"

"No." He shook his head and moved closer. "Not my style. But this just might make things easier for me. He's got you right where I want you." He reached down and stroked his finger along the edge of her jaw.

"Jake," she said. "Are you going to help me?"

"Yeah, I'd love to help you out. *Jessica*."

She looked at him long and hard, frowning. "Why are you calling me Jessica?"

"Isn't that your name?"

"Once upon a time. It was. Does it matter?"

"I don't know. Does it? Apparently, it does to *some* people."

She felt a stab of fear. "Who? Who cares?"

"Some people who have a vested interest in you, it seems."

"Some people? People like RJ Calhoun, right? Did he hire you to track me down? Who the hell *are* you, Jake?" She tried to sound tough, but it was difficult in this awkward position, tied up, so vulnerable. "What's your stake in all this?"

"An excellent fee when I bring you in, quite frankly," he said.

"Bring me *in*? What are you talking about?"

"Please. Show me some respect. Don't pretend you don't know."

"What are you saying, Jake?"

"I'm saying I'm here to apprehend you, Chantal. Or should I say, *Jessica*?"

"Apprehend me?" she was incredulous. "You mean *I'm* the one you've been planning to . . . to meet here?"

"Yeah. I came here to meet you. So I can arrest you."

"You can't arrest me! You have no right."

"I have every right."

"You're not a cop. Are you?"

"No, I'm not a cop. I'm a fugitive recovery agent. A bounty hunter. I work for the bond company, and that gives me the right to arrest you."

"What about my rights?"

"You signed your rights away when you put your name on that piece of paper."

"What paper? Are you talking about that bail bond thing? *That's* what this is about? For that paltry—but that was a long time ago!" She was laughing now. "You're not serious."

"Ah, so the lady is beginning to remember, eh?"

"Well, it's pretty ridiculous. If it's just about the money, I'll—Jake, untie me. Please."

Jake lowered himself down on the mattress, bracing himself on his powerful arms, holding himself above her. He dipped his mouth down to her ear and whispered, "The kind of money we're talking about ain't ridiculous, baby. Not to most people."

"What kind of money?" Chantal looked up at him, frowning. He was looking into her eyes.

He sat up, letting his weight down on her so that she felt the pressure of him through her pelvis. "Enough with the questions."

"So this was all—"

"Yeah. It was all a setup. To get you into custody."

"Is Antonio really your uncle?"

"Antonio is a crazy bastard. I think that much is obvious. A guy Billy knows in law enforcement recommended him. Said he'd be willing to help us out. He was more helpful than he needed to be."

"*Us?* You and Billy?"

"Yes, Billy is my associate."

"Your gay associate."

"That's right."

"So you knew all along he and I didn't have anything . . . going."

"Yeah. I asked him to meet you, get a fix on you. See how easy you would be to get close to, so to speak."

"Why didn't you just do the dirty work yourself?"

Jake shrugged. "It's the way we do business. Billy's a sure thing. Women love him."

"So you *knew* he and I weren't together, that night in the pool." She closed her eyes. "I thought you'd had an attack of conscience out of loyalty to your friend."

"Yeah, well, I did have an attack of conscience. But it wasn't about Billy. It was about the job. It seemed really unprofessional of me, if I were to fuck you and then arrest you."

"So you did everything but fuck me. Couldn't help yourself, huh?"

He frowned, wincing at her words.

"Or was that all an act, too?"

"What?" he said.

"All that hot and heavy stuff. I have to say, you're more convincing than your buddy, but maybe you just have better acting skills. Was all that lust for me just feigned?"

Even as she shot off these comments, they were both quite aware that he had grown an enormous erection while sitting atop her.

"I'll let you wonder," he said.

"Jake," she said softly. "Let me go."

"I can't," he said. "You're in *my* custody now."

His voice was hoarse. He leaned forward, bracing himself on his powerful arms, staring down into her eyes, letting the full bulk of his groin settle into her. If her legs had not been tied together like the tail of a mermaid, he would have pressed them apart with one thrust of his knee.

"What are you going to do to me?" she asked in a whisper.

"First, I have to see if you're packing a weapon," he said. He slowly lifted the shawl from her breasts. "Oh yeah, definitely armed . . . and dangerous."

She shuddered as he revealed her nakedness. She felt him press the bulge of his erection down into the valley of her thighs. She forgot her desire to be free, and instead found herself feeling an insane gratitude to the bonds that kept her vulnerable to him.

He swept his eyes over her plump breasts with the nipples growing hard and erect.

His mouth watered to taste them. He slipped the shawl further down over her body, revealing her rounded belly with the tiny dimple of a belly button. His tongue ached to fuck that little dimple, but he restrained himself. He slid the shawl down further. Now she lay naked beneath him, sweet and soft, her arms tied open wide, as if welcoming him.

Her thighs sheltered a nude mound of Venus, and he knew Antonio had shaved her.

Fucking bastard. He couldn't stand the thought of the other man touching her. *She's mine.*

But he couldn't stop his gaze from lingering, fascinated, over the naked lips of her cunt. He wanted to trace the slit with his finger, then slip his tongue inside . . . and when she was wet and ready, he would replace his tongue with his cock. . .

What am I thinking? For a moment, Jake realized he was seriously thinking of fucking the girl, right then and there, taking advantage of her inability to stop him, heedless of Antonio or anybody else. Her legs were tied tightly together, but he could have them open in a moment. Though he was fully clothed, in a split second, he could release his throbbing cock from his jeans and have it buried inside her.

Damn, Antonio! Jake cursed him wildly. *I'm not thinking clearly already. And now I'm dealing with some kind of twisted fun-and-games stuff that's making it even worse.*

He eyed the cuffs that held her wrists. Not a big deal, but if he let her go, then what? He'd just have to cuff her again. He felt unaccountably inept. She made him question his own methods.

He lingered a moment, unable to keep his gaze off her naked body.

"Oh yeah," he murmured again. "A *deadly* weapon."

"What are you going to do about it, Jake?" she said in a low voice.

"I may have to do a full body search," he replied. "To see if I've missed anything."

He leaned over her and slipped his finger into her mouth. He thought she might bite him; she seemed to be trying to push his finger away with her tongue, but then he felt her sucking it.

He pulled his wet finger from her mouth and trailed it down over her body, between her breasts. He dipped his finger into her belly button dimple, and then continued moving his hand down, down over her belly, his finger sliding between the hairless smooth slit of her sex at the top of her thighs.

She gasped as his finger entered the slit, penetrating the slick, wet insides of her. He lingered on the sensitive knob of her clit, then slowly sank his finger down deep into her. With a whimper, she arched to let him in deeper. He slid his finger in and out of her, flicking her clit with his thumb. She moaned, shaking her head back and forth, as if he was hurting her. But he didn't stop, and she bucked against his hand. He felt her desperation.

"What have we here?" Jake's voice was soft and cajoling. "Contraband." He pulled his finger out of her and tasted it. "Mmm. Ah, yes. High grade and uncut."

She lay writhing beneath him, panting and sweaty, whimpering. "Please, Jake. Please."

He was no longer sure what she was asking for.

He pushed himself off her, and climbed off the bed. His cock was so hard it was painful. He realized he had almost completely lost his wits.

"Jake," she moaned. "Don't leave me. Please."

Her vulnerability struck at his heart. He wanted to drop to his knees beside her and kiss her sweetly on the mouth, like Prince Charming kissed Sleeping Beauty. *One kiss and you're awakened, you are free. . .*

No, goddamn it, he thought. He didn't want to feel this way about her. It was bad enough, this all-consuming lust. He was compromising his professionalism in a big way. He didn't want it all mixed up with emotions. Not when he had to see her brought to justice.

Without answering, he left her there and slammed out of the room.

I can't fucking believe I just left her in there like that.

He knew it was a mistake. But if he had stayed with her, secured her with his own set of handcuffs, he didn't trust himself not to do something terrible . . . something wonderful . . . something terrible and wonderful, taking them both to a place they'd never been before. And, quite possibly, would never be able to return from . . .

He ran down the back stairs and into the hallway that led to the terrace—he intended to get some fresh air, feeling like he was going to pass out—when he rounded a corner and came face-to-face with Billy, who was letting himself in through the door at the end of the corridor.

"Where the fuck have you been?"

Billy blinked. "Well, I—"

"Never mind. I need you to find out who RJ Calhoun is."

"Who?"

"That's what I want to know."

"Calhoun. That's not an uncommon name, my friend."

"Go back over the file, see if we missed something. But I doubt it. I have a feeling some crucial background info on this case was deliberately left out. So we'll start with her hometown, and take it from there."

"Her? Her being—"

"Chantal Brown, aka Jessica Tamerlane."

Billy winked. "Gotcha."

"But first we get out of here. I need you to get your shit together, then meet me with your car in the woods behind the house. I'm gonna go get the girl, and then we're outta here."

Jake slowly pushed the door open. It was unlocked, just as he'd left it. He took in the room with the sweep of his glance, and his guts felt like someone had suddenly dropped a rock on them. Chantal had vanished and only Antonio occupied the room. He sat with his legs crossed on the edge of the neatly made bed, looking dangerously effeminate. He looked up at Jake with a raised brow.

"Nephew! Well, this *is* a surprise."

"Cut the 'nephew' crap."

"But I get off on it. Don't you? Really, Jake, I would not have expected *you* to visit me in my private quarters. Not that you aren't welcome, anytime, you know." He smiled in a sinister, sexual way that had Jake wanting to smash his face in just to wipe off his expression.

"Where is she?"

Antonio cocked his head.

"You are speaking of Chantal, I presume?"

Jake stepped forward menacingly.

Antonio remained seated, apparently unconcerned. "She's gone."

"Where is she?"

"She left, actually. I believe she's off in a taxicab even as we speak."

He motioned to the parted curtains. Jake moved cautiously to the window, not taking his eyes from Antonio. Then he caught the movement of the vehicle from the corner of his eye and he had to look out. There was indeed a taxi speeding away from the estate, down the long drive.

Jake turned to Antonio, who had laid back on the bed, his cock swollen in his pants, showing it off as if to taunt Jake.

"She's a little ruffian, that one," Antonio said. "She likes it kinky, you know. Likes to be tied up and humiliated a little. Fun, fun. But I finally had enough of her."

"You sonofabitch. What have you done with her?"

Two large, pale goons suddenly appeared in the room.

"I've had enough of *you*, too, Jake," Antonio said in a bored voice. "Good day."

Jake, a little roughed up and a little dazed, found himself on the beach road about three miles from the estate—three miles, if he was calculating correctly in his condition. He wondered how long he had been passed out. It was dark now. He remembered, incongruously, that it was New Year's Eve.

"Fuck," he said out loud, appalled at himself. Hell, never mind the voice, which came out like a squawk. He was one messed-up motherfucker. In many, many ways.

His body hurt like hell and his brain hurt worse. Or maybe it was his heart. He ached inside so badly for her. He wanted her back, he wanted her not to be hurt, or—

He could not believe he had been so stupid as to let this happen. He knew he was losing his grip, knew it almost from day one, hour one, moment one, when this whole thing started with the girl. The second he met her, it had begun. He had started acting out of character, doing things he would never have imagined himself doing. He'd made a major misstep. And it was because of her. No, this was beyond a misstep. He'd fucked up. Big time. Because of his feelings for her. Because of the way he felt about her, he had endangered her—possibly had gotten her killed. The woman he was supposed to apprehend, take into custody, and collect a bounty for. The woman he had totally, completely fallen for.

Get a grip, man. . .

He scraped his hands through his hair. "Now," he said aloud, summoning strength enough to stand up straight. "Must think. Now. How best to go about getting the lady back?"

He didn't know what to do, and he wasn't sure if that was because he was too fucked up to think of anything at the moment. He reminded himself that in his line of work, he was often called upon to improvise.

He started plodding through the woods in the direction of the estate.

"Are you crazy, man? What are you doing?"

"I gotta get her back, Billy."

"Yeah, but what the hell are you doing stumbling along the edge of the ditch like a drunken hobo? Don't you realize if Antonio's goons find you out here, you're persona non grata?"

"The sonofabitch let me know—I mean *go*. He let me go. They let me go."

"That's just because he didn't want to knock you off in his own home. Too risky, even for Antonio. But if they see you fucking around again, they'll put you out of your misery. Get in the car. Come *on*, dude. Hey, do I have to open the damn door for you? Jesus. You *are* in bad shape, aren't you?"

"I gotta get her back."

"Yeah, well, we're workin' on that. Put your seat belt on. Look, man, I'm not putting the seat belt on you."

"Relax. I can put on my own goddamn seat belt."

Billy pulled the car onto the road. "Okay," he said. "Turns out, this guy, RJ Calhoun, is—ta-dah!—her *stepfather*."

"Okay. Hmm. That was impressively fast work."

"I guess you don't realize how much time has transpired since last we spoke. We're missing a helluva New Year's Eve party, dude."

"Yeah. Well anyway, good use of time."

"So Calhoun is also very high up in the local DA's office and appears to be tight with his state senator—shitloads-of-money-every-election sort of tight."

"So he's got bucks."

"Right."

"And he's got power. And influence."

"Right. Influence that reaches right down into my law-enforcement connections, apparently—hence, our dubious connection to Antonio. Sorry about that. Anyway, Calhoun had to pull some strings to get the girl brought back for some relatively lightweight charge, something she did back when she was just barely legal. The bond wasn't more than a grand or so. Apparently, she stole some money and ran away from home. She had just turned eighteen and her stepdaddy got the powers-that-be to come down hard on her. They found her about to cross the border into another state and brought her in. She was released on bond to go home to stepdaddy, but she disappeared before the trial, this time for good. Until *you* found her."

"A grand!" Jake shook his head. "Then it doesn't even make sense. My fee is a lot larger than that."

"Right. It's all very fishy. And rather disappointing, actually. I had thought she was some sort of big-time criminal."

Jake laughed. "No, I think she's exactly what she appears to be—a sexy little runaway from a bad home scene, who took on an alias and spent the next several years getting her shit together in faraway California."

Damn, he thought. Now he had to admire the bitch, along with being charmed by her and wanting to fuck the hell out of her. "And what part do mom and biological dad play in this sordid soap opera?" he asked in a repressed, Sherlock Holmes sort of voice.

"Daddy died before she was born. Mom was a boozer, had several short-lived marriages over the years. Calhoun happened to be the current husband when mommy finally used up her nine lives. That left Chantal with him at the age of sixteen."

"Right."

"Now, I'm not saying stepdaddy was necessarily a child molester at heart. God knows, sixteen-year-olds these days often have a very adult appeal. But, buried in the records, I found a one-sentence statement Jessica made to a school counselor that her stepfather was 'pressuring her to become involved with him romantically.' No charges were ever filed against the guy."

"I wonder why he's trying to get her back?" Jake mused. He was beginning to wake up, forgetting about the pain he was in. His mind was busy now, working. "You would think if he got off without a real accusation, he'd be relieved to see her go."

"Maybe he's cocky. Maybe he's that sure of his position. Maybe he wants to reclaim his power over her. Maybe he's obsessed. She *is* lovely, in a voluptuous, womanly way. If you're into that sort of thing." He grinned at Jake. "Maybe he's in *love*."

Maybe. Jake pondered. He knew it wasn't that crazy a theory. She had affected *him* in that way. Why not someone else?

Jake had become obsessed by this beautiful, womanly girl. He had fallen in love. He had let her down and delivered her into the clutches of a madman. And he would do anything to get her back.

Maybe he had a rival who felt exactly the same way.

"God!" he roared out the window of the car. "What am I gonna do? I gotta get her back, but I've fucked everything up and I have no idea what that sonofabitch did with her. "She could be on her way to Mexico by now."

"Jake, my friend, relax. I've got everything under control."

Jake looked at Billy suspiciously. "Do you, now," he said.

"Yes, I do."

"You got her? You know where she is?"

"Not yet. But I know someone who knows where she is."

"Who?"

"Antonio's night watchman."

"Antonio's what?"

"His night watchman. That's what the dear boy calls himself. His name is Mauricio Andalante and he takes care of security for Antonio. He's assured me the girl is fine, she is still on the estate, and he will lead us to her."

"How did you get him to agree to that?" Jake's voice held a note of doubt.

"It's rather easy to persuade a man when you have his cock in your mouth. Who do you think it is I've been so busy balling the past few days?"

Jake nodded slowly, taking in this new understanding. "Excellent work," he said.

"Now," Billy said, his eyes searching the edges of the road. "I think here's about where we find a place to stash the car for later. We need to reenter the hot zone by stealth."

"Agreed," said Jake. "But you know he's got an electric fence."

"Mauricio has taken care of that problem for us."

"That must have been quite the blow job."

"Yes, it was—and then there's the promise of more to come. That's the secret to my success."

"I'm in awe of the power you wield."

"Tempted to test it?"

"Not in the least."

"Had to ask."

"As you've done once a year since we were twenty."

"Well, I've always figured as long as you haven't found the *one*, I still stand a chance."

"That I'd turn gay?"

"No, just get hard up enough to let me suck you off."

"Ain't gonna happen, dude."

"It seems so unfair. I'm your best friend, after all. And you, having been in prison and all. You can't tell me you're untested."

"Well, it's true I once experienced a man's cock, shoved into my mouth. And it *was* in prison."

"I knew it. You let another man come in your mouth. But never me. Your best friend." Billy feigned hurt.

"No, I did *not* let another man come in my mouth. It was prison, see? I had a knife at my throat and two other dudes holding me down at the time. The guy stuck it in my mouth for a second, just for kicks, but the real plan was to do my ass. They started turning me over and . . . I guess the idea of being a rape victim pissed me off so much—I became so enraged—that I somehow managed to shove the knife into the skull of the guy who was trying to do me. I killed him instantly and seriously hurt one of the others. I got the crap beat out of me and solitary confinement for a long time, but I didn't get raped. And nobody ever tried that shit with me again."

"Thanks for the warning."

Billy pulled the car off the road where it would be shielded from view by a thicket of trees. He was silent. Jake had never told him anything so personal in so much detail. He had always wondered about the time Jake spent in prison. It was long ago, when they were young. They'd both been equally involved in the crime, a youthful indiscretion involving a gun Billy had found under his father's bed and a convenience store cash register. Somehow, Jake had been apprehended with the gun, and he was the only one who served hard time for it. He could have said more to implicate his friend, but he kept his mouth shut. Billy had never forgotten that.

Years later, they ran into each other on the street again, both of them dangerously aimless, and started hanging out, like the old days. They were both aware of their own tendencies toward the seedier side of society—it was what they knew, where they came from. But Jake was determined not to go back. He began to look for a legal pastime that would take advantage of the skills he had developed on the streets and in prison.

It had all led to this moment.

Mauricio was waiting for them at the back gate of the estate. He led them to a secluded outbuilding made of stone with steps leading up to a small tower room.

"He's got her in there," Mauricio said, indicating a door at the top of the steps.

"I'll go in. You stay here with him," Jake said to Billy in a low voice. "Make sure he isn't going to alert his boss."

* * *

Antonio was growing increasingly impatient with Chantal. His taunting was becoming more hostile, his sexual needs more demanding. Now when he visited her, he shed his clothes so that they were both naked on the bed that filled most of the small cell where he kept her prisoner. Still, he held himself off her, waiting for her to break. He knew she was close.

He wasn't surprised when Jake showed up. In fact, it was what he was waiting for. Jake's presence would add an extra layer of spicy drama to the situation. Antonio needed an audience to attain his peak experience, and an unwilling audience excited him most of all. He had designed this sensual cell with just this sort of scenario in mind. The barred door between the vestibule and the room where Chantal lay would ensure that Jake witnessed everything Antonio did to her, yet he would remain an outsider, and the locked, barred door would prevent him from interfering. Antonio figured Jake was good at picking locks, but these locks were custom made, and he knew that Jake didn't have the time or tools necessary to deal with them just now.

"Ah, your hero has returned," Antonio said to Chantal. "I knew he wouldn't be able to stay away—because he's as hot for you as I am. And I must admit, your preference for him has caused me some painful moments over this past week. But now, my dear, it is payback time. And the big bounty hunter is here just in time to watch. Shall we give him a good show?"

Naked, her legs and arms tied so that she was splayed open and exposed, Chantal writhed with the mixture of sensations coursing through her body. The insane sexual need that Antonio had been continuously arousing in her—and never fulfilling—warred with the horrifying fear she felt, for herself, and now for Jake. She'd had no idea how many emotions and desires could coexist inside her.

"Did you know? He's actually famous in tough-guy circles," Antonio said, for Chantal's benefit. "I am rather ashamed to confess I spent hours on his website, staring at his picture. His crotch makes me hungry. Did you know he's known for not ever using a gun? Yes it's true. Isn't that quaint? Big bad PI never uses firearms."

Antonio sucked her ear and pressed his purple cock against the tight, naked lips of her pussy. "So when I fuck you, he won't be able to do anything about it. Because he only uses those martial arts moves they do in the movies. Very sexy. But he can't reach us. He can't do anything. Even if he threw a knife through the bars, he'd risk cutting *you*. Hmm. That's an interesting idea, isn't it?" He reached beneath one of the pillows at the top of the bed and brought out a long knife with a thick blade. "Maybe *I* should cut you, you little bitch. Bleed out some of your spirit."

The feeling of his cock nudging her hairless clit left her gasping. Involuntarily, she opened her legs to him a little more. She felt the head of his penis slip just between the naked lips of her cunt. In a moment he could be shoving the big purple monster deep inside her. She cried out, appealing to Jake, who was across the room, staring through the bars of the cage with a furious expression.

Antonio was breathing hard and trembling. He pulled the head of his cock away from the honeyed opening of her cunt. It was obvious his self-control was frayed and weakening. "He'll be helpless while I'm fucking you," Antonio said hoarsely. "Which I will now do. Because you're ready to beg for it, aren't you? I told you, I would only take you when you begged me for it." He pushed the blade of the knife against her throat tenderly, delicately. A thin red bead appeared on the surface of her skin.

He lifted the knife blade to show her it was wet with her

blood. He bent his head and suckled the wound, grunting, as he slid his cock against her, pushing it between her legs, sliding it up and down from her clit to her anus.

"Beg for it!" he commanded. "Beg me for it."

She felt the knife pressing into her throat again and she could no longer hold back. "Yes," she cried, "*Yes*. Fuck me. Oh, God, just *fuck* me." And, in the moment, she wasn't sure if she was crying out the words because she had a knife to her throat or because she was so desperate to be filled with cock. Any cock. It was Jake's cock she wanted, but she was so far gone that it almost didn't matter if it was Antonio who fucked her. She almost didn't care.

Antonio laughed delightedly and pulled one of her breasts into his mouth. He sucked it, still rubbing his cock against her pussy, fucking the cleft between her clenched thighs. Then he let go of her breast with a wet smack of his lips and smiled down on her. "Say it again. I love hearing you say it. Loud enough so that he can hear you. And he'll be completely helpless, watching me have you. Penetrating you so deeply and thoroughly. First your cunt, then your mouth, then your ass. I'll fuck you and fuck you, and he won't be able to do anything. Except watch. Because he's behind bars, and he hasn't got a gun. How do I know that? Because it's his trademark, if you will. He doesn't use one. He doesn't even own one—"

"True." Billy stepped into the doorway behind Jake and lifted a gun. "But *I* do."

"Allow me," said Jake.

Antonio was so startled for a moment that he forgot his grip on Chantal. She rolled away from him, as far as she could manage with her legs shackled and her hands cuffed to the bed.

Jake pulled the trigger.

Chantal lay curled up in the backseat of the parked squad car, her hands cuffed in her lap. She heard the men talking, but couldn't make out what they were saying.

She was still naked, but someone—was it Jake?—had wrapped the shawl around her. Antonio had been taken away in another squad car, shaken, but unhurt. Jake had only shot out the lock on the barred door. After that, it was no contest between him and Antonio. Jake, with Billy looking on, had quickly subdued Antonio and secured him with his own handcuffs. The police were there in what seemed like minutes.

And now, after what seemed like hours, she heard the voices come nearer.

"Okay, Jake. She said she doesn't want to go to a hospital. I guess he never actually raped her. So she's all yours."

Chantal opened her eyes. A uniformed police officer was looking through the window at her with lust glistening in his expression.

"Yeah," Jake murmured. "I'll take it from here."

She was helped out of the car by a couple of eager policemen, and transferred to another vehicle, a high-off-the-ground, no-

nonsense SUV cluttered with empty paper coffee cups, blues and rock CDs, and smelling of leather—and something else. It smelled of *him*.

Jake slid in beside her and took the wheel. "You're all mine now, baby," he said to her in an odd, humorless voice.

She looked at him without answering. For some reason, she felt contented to be his captive, happy he was in control—happy to be at his mercy. She was ashamed of it, but it was true. She settled back against the big leather seat and closed her eyes.

I could just curl up here and travel through the night with you forever.

She opened her eyes to see what was going on. Why didn't he start the car?

He was staring at her, holding the keys absently on his knee.

"Jake, take the cuffs off me."

He shook his head.

"Please? They hurt."

"No way."

"Why?" Her voice was plaintive.

Because I want to so much. So you can put your arms around me and hold me and I can hold you and comfort you after all you've been through.

"Shut up," he said softly. "I ought to chain you to the seat."

They drove for half an hour up the coast.

"Where are you taking me?" she finally asked him.

"Where do you think I'm taking you?"

"To jail, I guess."

"Do you deserve to be in jail?"

"Do you deserve to be in jail?" she shot back at him, mockingly.

He laughed, surprised at how she was able to uplift him even as she was castigating him.

"So what did you do?" he asked.

"What did *you* do?"

"What are you, a mimic? I asked you first."

"You mean, what crime did I commit? I'll show you mine if you show me yours. I mean—" she broke off with a smile. "Trade you tit for tat. Uh . . . that didn't come out the way I meant, either—"

"I know what you meant." He let a beat go by. "Armed robbery."

She blinked. "Oh. Did you kill anybody?"

"Not that day."

She began to cry softly. He pulled the car into a side road, aimed for a sheltered cove of trees, and parked. He pulled her into his arms awkwardly, her hands joined together at the wrists by the handcuffs.

He kissed her temple. Her hair was slightly damp. She smelled like a sweet young animal, rather than anything perfumey, and it stirred him. His cock leaped up inside his jeans. He realized that just a moment earlier he hadn't been thinking of her sexually at all; he had been thinking of her, just *being* with her, with love. And now he was thinking of her with love and with sex. Love and sex, together. And he was holding her in his arms. He could hardly believe it was happening to him. It was something he had never experienced before.

He wondered if she could feel his cock growing hard against her soft little ass. He didn't want her to. He didn't want her to think he was after anything, because he wasn't. He wanted her badly, hell yeah, but not now. Not like this.

She moaned softly and rubbed her cheek against his chest. She was no longer complaining about the cuffs, which was weird.

She lifted her head and looked up at him. Her eyes seemed to see right through him—cliché, but it was like that. With her wrists cuffed, her breasts were pressed into full cleavage. And the shawl seemed to be slipping lower and lower so that now her nipples were barely covered. And she didn't seem to mind. She seemed to want him to enjoy the sight.

And, God, how he enjoyed the sight. He couldn't think of anything else he wanted to do more than to pull the shawl away from those magnificent breasts, and take them into his mouth, one at a time, and suck them and lick them . . . except to kiss her, which he wanted to do most of all, even more than he wanted to fuck her, which he wanted to do as badly as anything else he'd ever wanted to do. . .

Jesus, he was absolutely loco for this girl.

He slowly let her out of his arms. He took off his coat and draped it around her shoulders. He straightened himself up and turned the key in the ignition, but he didn't start it up.

"Jake . . ."

"What?"

"Will you fuck me? Please?"

The sudden wrench of his heart startled him. Her voice was so soft, but what the hell was she asking of him?

"Please. I need you to." She was still crying.

"Hey." He nervously patted her knee. Then he realized his hand was on her knee and he pulled it away. "It's gonna be okay. You've been through a lot, but it's almost over now. Let's get out of here. Okay?"

***

They drove on up the coast, then turned inland. She began to recognize the neighborhoods. It was three-thirty, nearly morning. He switched on the windshield wipers as large drops of rain began to smack the glass.

"I thought you wanted to," she said after a while.

"I do. But not like this."

"Like how, then?" She sounded bewildered.

"Like . . . didn't I tell you to shut up?" He reached over and gently flicked her under the chin.

She began to talk in a soft, broken voice. Pouring her heart out, he thought. It nearly killed him.

"The worst thing is . . . it was like I . . . it was like I wanted him to do it to me. I didn't, but yet I did. By the end, I really did. He was right. By the time he was holding that knife to my throat, I was glad to have a reason to say yes. I wanted him to do it to me and I wanted you to watch. Thank God you and Billy got there when you did, and he never actually . . . but if you hadn't come, he *would* have. And by the time it happened, I would have let him. I would have encouraged him. And it would have been *my* choice."

"No." Jake's voice was firm. "That was never your choice, Chantal. And your physical and emotional responses in that situation aren't anything you can hold yourself accountable for."

Jake was thinking about a cold, gray prison and the taste of a man's cock in his mouth. Sometimes he thought about it, and sometimes it made him hard, thinking about it. He was grateful as hell that he hadn't had to go through with it. But sometimes it actually aroused him to fantasize about what it might have been like if he had. It wasn't something he wanted to try in real life, unfortunately for Billy, but sometimes he masturbated himself to orgasm, thinking about it.

Maybe someday he'd tell her about that. Maybe it would help her understand that she wasn't alone.

But not now. Right now it was all about her. He needed to take care of this girl.

"You know I wanted it to be you," she said in the same soft, broken voice. "From the first moment I saw you. Not Billy. Not anybody else. Only you."

She didn't know if he heard that last bit or not; she had said it so quietly, and the rain was hard on the windshield. She tucked her chin to her breast and nestled into his warm coat.

She realized she had dozed off when she felt the car slow, and then come to a stop. Jake cut the engine. He came around to help her out.

"Are we at the jail?"

"Yeah. I'm gonna process you now."

"Okay."

But where was the concrete, the bright lights, the cinder-block walls, the bars?

The only building she could see through the darkness of the night was a small wooden structure that looked like a garage.

With his arm around her, Jake brought her along a path skirting some dark shaggy pines, through a small garden, and up a short flight of stone steps. A little house came into view, painted dark like the surrounding woods, trimmed in white. He helped her up a few more steps to the porch. Now he was opening the door with a key and letting her in. She felt bewildered.

Inside, the little cabin was cozy, clean, and spare—a few pieces of comfortable, functional furniture, a desk, a bookcase, and one large impressionistic painting of the ocean.

"Where are we, Jake?"

"We're home."

"This is your place?"

"Uh-huh. Listen, I have to make a few phone calls, okay? Sit down in here for a few minutes. I'll get you something to eat or drink if you want, in a minute."

He went into the bedroom and pushed the door partway closed. She could tell he was keeping an eye on her, but he didn't want her to hear his telephone conversation.

She was pissed off that he was ignoring her and sore that she was still cuffed, wearing nothing but the shawl and his jacket. She didn't sit down as he had suggested, but paced the small living room, studying his habitat.

Finally he came out of the bedroom, without his phone. He reached out to the wall switch beside him and turned off the bright overhead light. Now the room was dim and illuminated only by the mellow light of a single shaded lamp.

His attention was fixed on her, and he walked up to her directly. She held out her cuffed arms, to stop his further movement toward her, and to offer her arms to be freed.

He ignored her outstretched arms, pushed her against the wall, and kissed her mouth, forcefully, his hands on her, running up and down over the curve of her hips, her cuffed arms between them. The jacket fell off her shoulders. The shawl slipped down over her breasts and fell to the floor. She was naked except for the handcuffs.

He snaked his tongue between her lips and she felt the muscle of his tongue against hers, licking and stroking. As he drew her tongue into his own mouth, she felt a tremendous pull, deep down inside her, as he sucked.

"Jake," she gasped, when finally she was able to break off the kiss. "What are you doing?"

"Processing you," he said innocently.

She stared at him, dumbfounded.

"First, I have to take your fingerprints," he said. He grabbed her cuffed hands and lifted them to his mouth. He ran his tongue over her fingertips and pressed her palms to his cheek.

"You're strange," she said, wonderingly.

"The more fingerprints you give me the better," he said.

"Take all you want."

He did not take the cuffs off her. She realized, later, that this was deliberate. He seemed to know exactly what she needed, which was for him to fulfill the role of captor. He became all men for her, the ones in her past who had threatened her, held her prisoner, and wounded her. He did it in a way that somehow transmuted the pain, distilling the damning desire into pure and profound pleasure, shattering the chrysalis that had enclosed all the horrible memories, and liberating them like butterflies that fluttered away into the clouds. He continued until only *he* was left there with her, only the two of them remained, and a healing took place. She felt it, amazed, and he seemed to feel it, too.

At that moment of emotional release, he slid a key into the cuffs, they fell away, and she was naked of everything now. Her arms suddenly felt very light.

"You're free to go," he said.

With the cuffs still on her, he had driven her to orgasm with his mouth while she was tied up in the shower. Still in his clothing, dripping wet, he had pushed her down on the kitchen floor and pumped her mouth with his enormous cock, amazed at how eagerly and deeply she took it in. He'd almost lost it then.

He'd hauled her into the bedroom, thrown her on the bed,

oiled her body, and used his fingers on her, in her, every way he could think of.

He let her rest, then brought her to orgasm again, in several different ways, getting to know her, how she responded physically, always keeping her cuffed, bound, captive—always at his mercy, always his prisoner.

And when he was certain he could stand it no longer, that he would have to spread her legs open and plunge his cock deep inside her or he would go crazy, explode—he knew it was time.

He had unlocked the cuffs and lifted himself up off her. Told her she was free.

Now she lay on the mattress, looking up at him curiously. "You've been teasing me since the moment we met." Her voice was like velvet. "You've done everything but fuck me the way I know you want to. The way *I* want you to . . . and now you're backing off again?"

"No . . ." He stammered. Didn't she realize what he was telling her? "It's nothing to do with . . . I mean, you're *free*. It's all worked out. They'll never come after you again . . ."

Holding her soft, slender arms as if her wrists were still cuffed, she pulled him down on top of her, sliding her fingers through his hair as they kissed.

He felt her body beneath him, felt his cock growing even harder between her thighs. He loved the smell of her, loved the softness of her breasts cushioned under his hard chest. He began to fuck her mouth with his tongue the way he wanted to fuck her cunt with his cock. He made her know his need with his whole body, with his hands on her, his mouth wandering all over her.

"I'll lose control if you let me," he said in a raspy voice.

With her fingers threaded through his silky hair, she pushed his head down, gasping as he greedily pulled her breast into his mouth and began sucking it.

The sensation of his teeth and tongue on her nipple had her arching and opening against him. She loved feeling him finally in her arms. She wanted so badly for him to be completely inside her. The ache between her legs had been assuaged many times in the last few hours, with his tongue, his lips, his fingers . . . but never with his cock. And he had never let himself go with her. She had never seen him come, never felt that liquid heat inside her.

"So I'm free, right?" she whispered. "I'm no longer your responsibility, right?"

"What do you—" He lifted up from her breast, and was breathing hard. "What?"

"So you can finally, freely fuck me." She smiled at the irony. *As if we haven't been going at it, hot and heavy, for hours. For days. Even when we weren't touching each other, all we could think about was touching each other. Since the moment we met.* It felt like a lifetime, since she had met him. "We're both free, consenting adults. It's all very ethical. You can make love to me. And I can make love to you."

"And it *will* be lovemaking, won't it?" he said fiercely.

She nodded, burying her face in his shoulder to suppress a smile. The words he spoke seemed so at odds with his gruff, bounty-hunter personality.

He peeled off his damp shirt and unbuckled his jeans.

She watched him reveal his body—the long sleek muscles, wide strong shoulders, long flat torso, and the big hard cock, erect and cradled by his powerful thighs. She tried to help him undress, but he did it so quickly her assistance wasn't necessary.

* * *

Then he was with her on the bed, on top of her, stretched out on her, feeling her beneath him. Now that he was about to come inside her, he was suddenly afraid again. God, she felt so good under him. They were both naked, like that night in the swimming pool. And he was finally going to fuck her.

"My Irish prince," she whispered.

He kissed her and sucked on her neck, her lips, and tongue, and he moved his hips against hers, the particulars of their bodies finding each other so easily. He lingered with the smooth head of his cock playing with her slippery cleft, teasing it, teasing himself, dipping between the moist lips. He nearly went ballistic when she brought her hands down to handle his balls, circling the shaft of his cock with her fingers, guiding him closer, deeper, yet still teasing him with her thighs, squeezing against him as if forbidding him entrance.

They played like that a while, then suddenly he grabbed her hands and pinned her arms down on the mattress, and with a roar of what sounded like pain, he plunged his cock deep inside her. They cried out together as he felt himself gaining entrance to the hot, wet sheath between her legs. He pushed her partway up the mattress, he rammed her so hard. He rammed her again, and again. He kept pumping it into her, faster and harder. Her head was thrown back with a faraway smile as she closed her thighs around him and pulled him into her deeper with her hands on his buttocks. He kissed her mouth and sucked her nipples as he fucked her. She was crying out with every thrust.

Her body was a mass of sensation, so intense and momentous she lost track of herself as a being inside a body; no longer was she something separate from him and everything else. She didn't know where she began, or where she ended. Or where he began or ended. They were one and the same, and they were everything.

To hold off his release a little longer, Jake pulled out of her and moved down between her legs, licking as he traveled down her body to take her swollen cunt into his mouth. She moved against him wildly, moaning and crying out as he nibbled at her clit and fucked her with his tongue.

She twisted around, pulled his hips down to her head, and began licking the head of his penis. He shuddered and pushed it deeper into her mouth.

She loved the feel of his cock moving in and out of her mouth, while his mouth did such wondrous things between her legs. And so did he, apparently, judging from the way his thighs were beginning to tremble, and his groans were deepening along with his thrusts. It was almost too good to bear, and almost too close to heaven to stop, but she sensed his determination that this time—this time, he would hold her cheek to cheek, loin to loin, heart to heart. . .

They moved into each other's arms and he entered her again, with desperation and force. After only a few deep strokes of his cock, she felt him detonate inside her. She knew from the change in his cry, the way his whole body hardened, and the sudden hot wash inside her. He resumed his plunging and brought her over the edge with him as he rode out the waves of his orgasm.

Jake could hardly believe the joy of having her in his arms as they lay together in bed after sex. This feeling of peaceful bliss was every bit as pleasurable, in its own way, as the massive pleasure of finally getting off in her. And that was strange to him.

Yeah, he noticed the fear. It came on again, and he was aware of it. But he was no stranger to fear. He could deal with it. He had a feeling she was worth it.

"What are you thinking, Jake?" Her voice was warm and playful, but wondering, too.

He tousled her hair. "What am I thinking? Hmm . . ." How could he explain the jumbled knot of things he was thinking about? Mostly, he was thinking of the conversation he'd had with Billy right before they parted, hours earlier. After they had finished sorting things out with the local police, Billy had come up to Jake, put his hand on his shoulder and said, "Jake, good buddy, I am no longer going to hit on you, ever again."

"Why not?" Jake asked drolly. "Did I suddenly become un-attractive to you?"

"No, you're as hot as ever; I just don't want you to kill me."

Jake laughed. "You know, Billy, I can't say it hasn't been a little weird for me over the years when you periodically offer to suck my dick, though I suppose it *is* kind of flattering. I'm not going to kill you, okay?"

"I know. But I'm giving up on you anyway. You want to know why?"

"Uh . . . I guess."

"Remember how I told you that I figured until you found the *one*, it didn't hurt to ask?"

"Uh-huh."

"Well, I think you've found the *one*." He nodded at the squad car where Chantal was sitting. They could see her profile through the glass. Jake's heart almost broke, just looking at her.

I'm in love, Billy, he wanted to say. But, of course, he didn't. That's what Jake was thinking about when she asked.

"I'm thinking . . ." Jake wasn't sure how to answer her question. He wanted to tell her that he hoped Billy was right. That she was the one.

But I don't want to scare her, he thought. Give it time. *Someday I'll tell her about that conversation I had with Billy.*

Someday, when he was sure that she was as hooked on him as he was on her.

But for now . . . He glanced out the window of the little bedroom, where dawn was beginning to lighten the sky. He tightened his arms around her. "I was thinking . . . I was thinking I'd like to make of habit of this."

"This?" she asked archly.

"Waking up with you."

"We never slept," she pointed out.

"All right. Let's just say, I'd like to make a habit of being in bed with you like this—at five a.m. I'll make you coffee every morning before you leave for school."

"Okay," she nodded, laughing. "I'm cool with that."

"Then let's make it our New Year's resolution."

"Oh my God, *is* it? New Year's Day? It *is*. I didn't even realize it."

"It is." He kissed her deeply, feeling his cock hardening again. "Happy New Year, my little runaway."

Diana Mercury

DIANA MERCURY is a writer living in northern California.

Part 3

Snow Blind

VIRGINIA REEDE

Chapter 1

"*This* is a ski villa?" Gerry made another exaggerated turn to scan the exposed log walls. His back was turned to me, and I took the opportunity to perform a really world-class eye roll. Gerry had been bitching since I picked him up at the airport, and it was starting to get on my nerves. Well, not really. We always bantered like this.

"I never said it was a villa," I replied, when his gaze made it back around to me. "You made some kind of mental leap while you were talking Maggie into coming." Gerry's girlfriend thought staying anyplace without a five-star restaurant downstairs was roughing it.

"Jules, you led me to believe—"

"I told you it was a cabin with all the amenities—which it is. You're just letting the décor put you off."

"It looks like it was decorated by Attila the Hun," he said, and I tried to take an objective look at the place. It *was* a little heavy on antlers and other dead animal parts. "Good God," he went on, "is that an actual bear rug?"

"It has a certain barbaric charm," I coaxed. "Come on, doesn't all this evidence of bloodshed bring out your testosterone? Or are you too much of a metrosexual for this ubermacho stuff?" Gerry was a city boy from London, and had little experience with the great outdoors.

"A man can be masculine and still appreciate the finer things." His face lit up, and I saw he had spotted the bar. He strode over to investigate, and I watched him while he pulled out bottles and read labels, occasionally grunting in approval. He certainly looked masculine enough. His workout schedule, which was far more disciplined than my own haphazard efforts, kept his body honed to perfection. The well-weathered jeans fit him to a tee, and the brand-new sweater, bought mail-order just for this trip, showed off his broad shoulders perfectly.

"At least someone knows how to stock a bar," he said, sniffing appreciatively at a brandy bottle he had just opened. "Shall we start our weekend with a toast?"

"Why not?" I peeked out the windows as he took snifters down from a hanging rack and poured two generous helpings of whatever was in the bottle. I sighed—the snow covering every surface was beautiful, glittering in the bright sunshine. It coated almost everything, but one roughly octagonal surface was bare, and steam escaped from vents underneath.

"Oh, *excellent!*" I exclaimed, as Gerry handed me a glass. "They remembered to turn on the hot tub."

"Where is it?" He peered through the window next to me and I pointed. "So, we just sit in a tub of hot water, with no walls, surrounded by subzero air?" He sounded more interested than skeptical. Finding the brandy must have improved his outlook.

"Hardly subzero. It's . . ." I squinted at the thermometer attached to the outside of the window frame, "almost twenty degrees out. And the heat rising off the water means the air above the tub is a lot warmer than the surrounding area." I grinned at him and winked in a parody of a come-on. "Wanna try it out?"

"Now?"

I shrugged. "Maggie and Joe won't be here for three hours at least. We don't really have time to go out on the trail or drive up to the slopes and get back in time. But we could sit out there and drink our brandy surrounded by snow." *And it might improve your mood before the others show up, so you and Joe don't end up in yet another argument.*

"What the hell, we're on vacation." He looked around for his bag. "Just let me get my shorts on."

"You brought *shorts* to Colorado in the middle of winter?"

"You said there was a hot tub. Didn't you bring a bathing suit?"

"I figured we'd all get in there naked," I lied, enjoying his scandalized look. I was just teasing him—my bathing suit was tucked into my suitcase.

"Maybe after dark," he said. "I'm not showing you my naughty bits in daylight. You'd be unable to control yourself."

"Oh, in your dreams." I smiled, feeling much better now that he was teasing back. Gerry was my best friend, and I had been worried that he wouldn't enjoy the weekend. "I'm joking. I've got a suit. Here, take my brandy outside. I'll meet you in the tub in three minutes."

"Where are the bedrooms?" he asked.

"Downstairs, I guess." The cabin was built into the side of a mountain, so that the main floor was on a level with the driveway, with the bedrooms below, each room having a view across to the next ridge.

I humped my suitcase down the stairs to one of the suites and pulled out my bathing suit, wishing I had brought one of my conservative one-pieces instead of the tiny bikini. I put it on and gave myself a critical once-over in the mirror. Not too bad. Good breasts, better-than-average ass. But nothing like what silicone-meets-supermodel Maggie would look like in whatever designer postage stamp she showed up with.

Why do you care what you look like in front of Gerry? I reminded myself that he and I were buddies and that was all. It had never been anything more, and it never would be. "Gerry wouldn't care if you put on eighty pounds and started wearing Hefty bags for dresses," I muttered under my breath as I headed down the stairs. There were several sets of rubber clogs next to the French doors that led to the cedar tub, and I slipped into a pair to cross the snowy deck. Gerry had removed the tub's cover and was already in the water.

"I see you have your customary Miami moon burn," he said, as I settled into the water and he passed me my brandy snifter. "You're almost as white as the snow."

"I'll have the last laugh in twenty years, when you have skin like an alligator and people still think I'm twenty-seven," I retorted. I finally took a sip of the brandy. "Hey, this *is* good." I could feel the warmth as the fiery liquid rolled down my throat and into my stomach.

"I have to admit, it goes exceedingly well with a hot tub in the snow," he concurred, stretching. I watched the muscles of his well-tanned chest flex and ripple above the water. He really *had* been working out. "It's good you invited us, Jules."

I looked beyond the deck railings at the farther vista. It was breathtaking—right out of an adventure magazine or a ski resort brochure. The outside deck where the tub was located looked out to where lines of mountains, each higher than the previous, marched away west toward the Continental Divide.

I saw that Gerry was looking at the view, as well. "I've always thought the word 'awesome' was overused," he said. "But it's really the only thing to call this view. Again, thanks for thinking of us."

"We always celebrate New Year's together, Gerr. And, besides, it seemed silly having this enormous place with just two people."

"Especially since once Joe arrives, the two of you probably won't leave the bedroom."

I splashed hot water at him for that comment, and he pretended outrage. "Hey, be careful. You might get water in the cognac, and that would be a crime."

"Good point." I took another sip, and it tasted even better than the first. I was starting to get a warm feeling. The hot water and the brandy were combining to give me a languorous, sexy outlook. I closed my eyes and tried to imagine spending the remainder of the weekend holed up in the suite downstairs with Joe.

The image wouldn't come.

Why wouldn't it? Spending a weekend playing in the snow by day and fucking like rabbits by night had been my original vision when I put this thing together. I had won the accommodations in a company contest, and it seemed like the perfect opportunity to get Joe away from his endlessly ringing phone for a while. I had already checked my own phone, and found to my delight that cellular reception up here was virtually nonexistent. Joe was an energetic and inventive lover, and had a body as good as Gerry's. Well, almost as good as Gerry's. He just always seemed to have to rush off somewhere before we could have an encore. Or he had to get up early for a business meeting.

"Dreaming of the Cuban Casanova?" Gerry's voice didn't hold any real rancor. Although he and Joe hadn't exactly bonded, they got along well enough as long as a couple of hot topics were avoided. "You can start ignoring me once he gets here. In the meantime, let's talk about the rest of the weekend."

"Oh, and you're not planning to ignore me once Miss South Beach arrives?" I smiled to take the bite out of my words. I was really trying to like Maggie. Really. We just didn't have a lot in common.

"I thought the four of us could do *some* things together. I've been using the cross-country ski machine at the gym to get all the right muscles ready." He lifted a leg out of the water and flexed his calf muscle in demonstration.

I snorted. "I'll bet you fifty dollars right now that you aren't going to get Maggie anywhere near a pair of cross-country skis."

"She skis."

"She wears designer ski outfits and goes to resorts," I replied. At his pained expression, I added, "Okay, so maybe she has gotten out on a downhill slope or two. With the best instructors, of course. But cross-country skiing isn't anywhere near glamorous enough for her."

"And your Latin lover is going to tear himself away from his BlackBerry long enough to do a lap around the mountain?" He reached behind the edge of the tub, where he had stashed the brandy bottle. Pouring me another generous helping, he continued, "Maybe I should bet *you* fifty dollars that *he* won't go with us."

"You'll lose," I said good-naturedly. "Joe's really been looking forward to it. He wouldn't miss cross-country skiing for the world." *Wouldn't miss a chance to show everyone up,* I added silently. Joe was the most competitive guy I had ever dated. If Gerry and I were planning to go out on a ski trail, Joe would come along just so he could arrive back at the cabin five minutes ahead of everyone else, then race to change clothes and pour himself a drink so that he could pretend to have arrived at least half an hour earlier.

Where did that thought come from? Joe's drive was one of the things that had attracted me to him. Wasn't it?

My thoughts were interrupted by the ring of a telephone, loud enough to be heard through the windows. "I'll get it." Gerry leaped out of the tub like he had been electrocuted. "It's probably Maggie. I gave her the landline number on the chance my cell wouldn't work up here."

As he hoisted himself over the side of the tub, I was treated to a view of the front of his wet shorts. They clung to his package like cellophane, and I suppressed a gasp. Did Gerry have a *hard-on*? The tantalizing vision slipped out of sight before I could fully grasp it. No pun intended.

As he slipped into the clogs, grabbed a towel and dashed for the ringing phone, I felt a clenching in my nether regions. Oh, *great.* I can't conjure up a sexual fantasy about my boyfriend, and I'm practically having an orgasm after one glimpse of Gerry's willy. Correction, the *outline* of Gerry's willy. I'd never actually seen the genuine article.

I watched him through the French doors, trying to wrap the towel around his waist with one hand and hold the phone with the other. He looked magnificent, but that was nothing new. Over the course of the last five years, I had watched him sculpt his good-but-nothing-to-write-home-about body into an ad for gym equipment. I had seen him on the beach, in his pool, across a tennis court, and even in his pajamas a time or two. Now, all of the sudden, why was the thought of his erect cock making me want to. . .

To pull off those shorts and wrap my lips around it. To tilt back my head and let the head slide into my throat. To run my tongue along the silky skin on the underside until he groaned in ecstasy. To. . .

"The plane just arrived at the airport." I jumped, spilling some of my brandy. I hadn't even realized that I had closed my eyes until he spoke. Or that my left hand had slipped inside my bikini bottoms and my finger was edging toward my clit.

"O-oh?" I replied, unsure of my voice. "Was it early?" I wondered if he noticed my hastily withdrawn hand.

"No, it's almost four." He slipped out of his clogs and climbed back into the tub. I tried—unsuccessfully—not to look at the bulge in his shorts as he did so. It had gotten smaller. So, talking with Maggie had taken away his hard-on. Interesting.

"Did she find Joe?" The two of them were on the same flight, and had met a few times.

"They were able to change seats and sit together."

"That's nice." I wondered if my face was red. Probably. Oh, well, he would think it was from the steam.

"What's even nicer is that Joe ordered a limousine, so they won't have to share a shuttle," he went on. "Maggie wasn't too keen at the prospect of jamming into a van with strangers." His grin was rueful.

"No, I don't imagine she was." *And ordering a limo gave Joe the opportunity to show off a little.* Oh, great, another uncharitable thought about my boyfriend.

"Anyway, they'll be here in about two hours."

"Perfect. They'll make it in time for the sunset," I said. "I think we're facing due west here."

But it wasn't perfect. I didn't want to share the sunset with

Joe and Maggie. I wanted to sit here, sip brandy, and watch the sun go down over the ridge with my best friend—just the two of us.

"So, what were we talking about before I got out of this lovely hot water to freeze my ass off on the way to the telephone?"

"The plan for the weekend—cross-country skiing tomorrow, and then?" We'd gone over this before, but after weeks of looking at brochures and Web sites, I was too excited to mind reviewing our plans. It felt so much more real now that we were surrounded by snow. Snow!

"Then snowmobiling the following day, which is New Year's Eve; so, we'll all come back here and put together a really spectacular meal and drink gallons of champagne. It'll be a night to remember." A breeze lifted across the deck, and we both sank a little lower to get our shoulders under the hot water. "Not that last year wasn't fun."

It had been—sort of. Gerry had just started dating Maggie, and she'd secured tickets for a much-sought-after South Beach nightclub's party, with the requisite celebrities and paparazzi buzz. Actually, she'd just managed the reservations—Gerry and I had paid for the tickets. I'd even bought one for my date, because I didn't think it was fair to expect him to shell out the outlandish sum when the evening wasn't his idea.

Then there had been the stretch limousine—Maggie had insisted it was crazy to try to drive in South Beach on New Year's Eve, and the rest of us agreed, although I secretly thought Maggie's motives had more to do with making an entrance than driver safety.

The club itself was everything that had been promised. The music was excellent, I had to admit, even if it was playing at a volume that precluded any conversation that wasn't shouted directly into someone's ear. The celebrities were everywhere, as were the photographers. Maggie proved adroit at being in the frame when the bulbs flashed without looking like she was working at it.

Our table was about the size of a postage stamp, and liquor was only sold by the bottle—at $150 a pop—but the atmosphere was festive and we all danced. And since we hadn't arrived until 11:00 p.m.—actually early for a typical night out in South Beach—there hadn't been too long to wait until the big countdown and kiss moment.

My date and I had shared a fairly chaste kiss—we hadn't been dating long and, in fact, stopped seeing each other very soon after—but Maggie and Gerry had performed a really world-class face suck. A picture of them had even made it into a local paper, and you could just make me out in the background. I'm sure the look of disapproval on my face was just a trick of the camera. *Of course it hadn't bothered me to watch Gerry kiss his girlfriend. What a ridiculous idea.*

"I was a little surprised Maggie agreed to come here for a weekend that includes New Year's Eve," I said.

"Oh?"

"Well, doesn't she usually like to be seen at—" I amended my words. "I mean doesn't she prefer to be at one of the big parties? I know she's always meeting celebrities—isn't Rosie or P. Diddy or one of them having a New Year's Eve bash this year?"

Gerry shrugged. "It took a little persuading, but she agreed. Of course, she might have been under the impression we would be at a resort where there might be a party."

"I never said—"

"I know, I know. I made the leap, like you said." He grinned, wickedly. "Do you want to know why I really think she agreed to come?"

"Why?" This was good. Gerry never dished about Maggie.

"I think she wasn't able to get an invite to any of the really prestigious events. This way, if someone asks her why she wasn't at J. Lo and Marc Anthony's party, she can say she turned it down because she had a ski trip planned."

I started to laugh, then sobered. *I wonder if Joe agreed for the very same reason.* He would be more interested in the political A-list than the beautiful people of South Beach, but hadn't he said something about the mayor having a party? I tried to remember. Not at the mayor's house, but there *was* something with a lot of Miami bigwigs at a mansion on Tahiti Beach. He had mentioned it a month or so back, but never said anything more about it.

"Say, have your boobs gotten bigger?"

I almost choked on the brandy I had just started to swallow. "Wha-at?"

He laughed at my reaction. "Maybe they're just buoyant because you're in the water. Or it's the way your bikini top fits. They just look bigger to me."

I looked down, as if I expected my own familiar breasts to have suddenly swollen into footballs. "Well, the bikini top *is* a little small for me. It may be pushing them up." I put down my glass and tried to rearrange myself more securely into the tiny bits of fabric. "It's not very comfortable."

"Take it off, if you want," he said. I looked quickly at his face for signs of lasciviousness. I saw none. "I've seen them before."

"You have not!" I laughed. "When?"

"When we were in Key West. You were changing. I peeked." He gave me a naughty-little-boy grin.

"*What?*" I splashed him, pretending outrage. But the thought of him watching me undress caused a small tingle between my legs. "You pervert! Why didn't you tell me?"

"It was an accident and I am not a pervert. You didn't have the door closed all the way and I was getting something out of the closet. It didn't seem important at the time."

"Well, you should have told me." I pretended to pout. "I could have demanded equal time. As you so recently pointed out, I've never seen your . . ." I tried to remember his phrase, "naughty bits. I'm at a disadvantage."

"Fair enough." Gerry took another swig of the brandy, and I looked carefully at his eyes. Was he getting a little merry with drink? "I'll strike a bargain with you. You take off your bathing suit and I'll take off mine. As you pointed out, one is really supposed to be naked while drinking cognac in a hot tub behind a snow-covered cabin."

"You're not afraid I won't be able to control myself?" I kept my tone light, but the tingle between my legs turned into a throb. *What is going on here?*

"I'll risk it." He put down his glass and reached down to remove his shorts. He lifted them out of the water with a flourish. "Ta-dah! Your turn." He wiggled his eyebrows dramatically, and I couldn't help but laugh.

"Okay, okay." I untied the string top and pulled it off, tossing it to him. "There. So, was it the bikini, or do you still think they've grown?" I arched my back a little so that my nipples just cleared the surface of the water. It was strange showing Gerry my breasts, especially when he was watching them so intently.

"I'm not sure," he said slowly. "The water may be helping you defy gravity. You'll have to stand up for me to make a proper assessment."

"As you wish," I said with mock solemnity. In order to stand, I had to put my feet into the well at the center of the round tub, which brought me about two feet closer to him. When I stood, my breasts cleared the water by a full two inches.

"Very nice, indeed," he said, still staring. "I've always thought you had nice tits, darling. They're standing up quite well without any artificial support."

I knew that "darling" was Gerry's very British way of addressing any member of the opposite sex, including his mother, but I had always liked it.

"I would think that anyone who got to see Maggie's fabulous tits on a regular basis would be unimpressed by a little gravity defiance."

He made a dismissive gesture. "Hers are supposed to sit up straight—she picked them from a catalog."

"That's not a very nice thing to say about your girlfriend." I was starting to feel very self-conscious under his regard.

"She's the first one to admit it. She's gotten so many referrals for her cosmetic surgeon that he does her lip collagen for free."

"Wherever she got them, they're nice."

"They are. But they don't feel the same as natural breasts. And I don't think . . ." He finally looked away, seemingly embarrassed by what he was about to say.

"You don't think what?"

"I don't think she has much sensation in her nipples since the operation." He glanced back, just in time to see my reaction. As soon as he had mentioned nipples, mine had both started to harden. Probably just the breeze, which had picked up again.

"Mine definitely don't have that problem."

His gaze flickered from my breast to my eyes, and I thought I could see a question. Taking a chance, I answered it. "Go ahead. See for yourself."

He reached out both hands and placed them on my breasts so that his fingers cupped the outside and his thumbs brushed across the still-hardening pink tips. A shudder ran through my body, but I didn't move. This felt too good. He rotated his thumbs, and I tried not to moan.

"Very nice, indeed," he repeated, this time almost in a whisper. "Do you mind if I . . ." He trailed off.

"What?" I breathed in response, but he didn't finish, or wait for a response. He leaned forward and put his mouth over one nipple and grasped it lightly in his teeth. He flicked his tongue over the end, and this time I did moan aloud. I felt warmth growing between my legs that had nothing to do with the hot water. He withdrew his tongue and sucked hard. At my gasp, he looked up, releasing me.

"Sorry," he said, not backing up. "I got a little carried away. I really enjoy teasing a woman's breasts, and it's nice when someone appreciates it."

"Oh," I said, a little unsteadily, "I appreciated it all right. But . . ."

"But what?"

"But I still haven't seen anything new. You're hiding all the good stuff way down under the water. I thought you were going to show it to me." I tried to sound casual and mocking, but I really wanted to see it. Really.

"You're right. As I said before, fair is fair. Now, how can I do this without freezing my balls off?" He pulled his legs under him and crouched on the underwater seat. He stood up slowly, his back to me. I laughed.

"Gerry, don't get me wrong, the view is great. You have a terrific ass. But if you don't turn around I'm going to smack you on it."

"It's just that I'm a bit . . . well, what do you expect after I was sucking on your tits?" He turned around and I caught my breath.

"Holy shit!" I said before I could stop myself. "Where have you been hiding that thing? It's huge!"

"Stop, you're making me blush." I looked up at his face. His cheeks really were pink.

I returned my attention to the matter at hand. "Can I touch it?"

"Jules . . ."

"Hey, you got to touch mine," I reminded him, unable to take my eyes off the sight before me. I had thought he was aroused when he got out of the tub before. Maybe he had been, a little. But now he was fully erect, and I wondered how I could have known him for five years and never known he was carrying a concealed weapon. "Well?"

He paused. "Go ahead." I saw his leg muscles tense and knew he was preparing himself.

Tentatively, I reached out and ran one finger along the smooth skin of the shaft. The whole thing twitched, and for the first time, I noticed his balls. They were perfect—large and round and surprisingly smooth. I had never thought testicles could be pretty, but his were. I cupped them in my other hand.

He gasped. "Jules, what are you—"

"Shhhh." I interrupted. "I'm trying to concentrate." I wrapped my fingers around him, trying to get an idea of his full girth. It was a good thing I had long fingers. I stroked up and down, measuring the distance between the root and the head. "Impressive."

"Julie, if you don't stop I'm going to—"

"What? 'Cause I'm not ready to stop yet." Before he could speak again, I leaned forward and took the head in my mouth. I was gratified to hear his deep groan. *Fair is fair, Gerry,* I thought to myself. *You got to squeeze, nibble, lick, and suck. So do I.*

It was perfectly smooth and firm. I found the opening at the tip and teased it with my tongue, then explored all around the edges. I wondered how much of the shaft I could get into my mouth. I had certainly never given a blow job to anyone with a cock this big before, and I wondered if I could get it all the way in. There was only one way to find out.

I crouched a little lower to optimize my angle and tilted my head. Within a moment, the head of Gerry's cock was pressed against the top of my throat, and I willed the muscles to relax as I prepared to take him in. *This is exactly what I was just fantasizing about. Now, if I can just loosen my throat—*

Suddenly, he pulled back. "My God, Jules, you have to stop!" Startled, I looked up at his face, which was contorted with something. Anger? I didn't think so. Awkwardly, he got down from the seat so that he stood at my level, hiding the object of my recent attention under the water. "I said you could see it. I didn't mean we should . . . I didn't think that you would—"

I should have felt ashamed, but I didn't. Joe would be here in a little more than an hour and a half. I should get out of the tub, take a shower, and wait for him to arrive. *He's the one I came up here to have sex with, after all.*

But I wasn't ashamed. And I wasn't finished. "I know we were just playing show-and-tell, Gerry." I tried to laugh lightly, but it sounded pretty weak. "But I didn't know you had so much to show."

He picked up on my halfhearted attempt at humor. "I tried to warn you."

"Yes, you did. But Gerry . . ." I moved forward and reached below the water's surface. I grasped his cock firmly, delighted it was still diamond-hard. "I need to know one more thing before you . . . before we stop." I looked him very straight in the eye so that he couldn't look away. But then, it's easy to keep a man's attention when you have his cock in your hand.

"What do you need to know?" His breathing was a little uneven.

"I need to know what a cock this big feels like . . . inside me." I held his gaze. As seconds ticked by, I realized I was holding my breath and let it out in a whoosh. I felt his organ twitch in my grip.

"Okay," he said finally. "Okay, let's do this." His hands snaked around my ass and found the bikini bottom I was still wearing. He grasped the ties on the sides and pulled them free. "How do you want to—"

"Sit back," I instructed. "Let me climb on top of you." I wanted to control how far and fast he went inside me. I wasn't sure I could take in his full length.

Wordlessly, he complied. I slid onto his lap, resting my knees on the wooden bench on either side of his thighs. His shaft stood between us, and I realized I was going to have to let myself float up a few inches in order to fit the head inside me. Doing so positioned my breasts directly in front of Gerry's face.

"I think I missed one of these earlier," he said, as I carefully positioned the head of his cock between the soft lips of my cunt. As I eased myself down, my body resisted the widest part of the head. But I was wet and ready and throbbing with desire, and the resistance gave way with a feeling like a puzzle piece suddenly popping into place, and I gave a great internal squeeze just as Gerry's teeth bit down on my swollen nipple.

"Aaaaahhhh." He was so big. My cunt spasmed and shuddered, and Gerry's breath grew ragged.

"Take me in," he said around my nipple, which he now sucked and licked. One of his hands reached around and supported my ass. "Take me all the way inside you."

Using the side of the tub for leverage, I pushed myself down a couple of inches, feeling the amazing pressure as his shaft slide deeper into my body. "Oooohhh." I could not be silent, not with this incredible feeling filling me up.

"Oh, God, Gerry, you're so big." Not very original, but true. I slid down another couple of inches. *God, where does it end?* I felt with my hand and gasped. There were still at least two inches of cock extending beyond my swollen lips. I leaned into him, trying a different angle and, summoning my courage, pushed myself the rest of the way down.

Pleasure exploded through me like a Fourth of July fireworks display. I was completely filled, not a millimeter to spare, and the inside of my cunt quivered and thrummed like the bass strings on a grand piano. Groaning, Gerry took my ass in both of his hands and lifted. Taking his cue, I slid up the endless shaft of his cock and then thrust myself back down again. I almost shrieked aloud. *Why not?* I thought vaguely. *We're in the middle of the woods. I can yell all I want.*

"Yes!" we said in unison, and I finished a second slide up and down. As I moved up for a third, he rose to meet me and we banged together with a force that threatened to start an earthquake. Water splashed from the tub and onto the snowy deck as we found our rhythm.

We hadn't completed our tenth stroke when I felt the gathering heat of my orgasm spiking from my groin to my belly. "Ay-eeeeee!" I didn't even try to be quiet, but I lost my grip on the edge of the tub.

"Not yet," said Gerry through gritted teeth. Before we could slip apart, he got to his feet, my body still deeply impaled on the spear of his cock. He pushed me diagonally across the tub to where the steps led down from the edge. He positioned me on a high step and stood on a lower one, then pulled my legs up over his shoulders. Now he had all the leverage, and he drove into me like a pump.

"Oh, GOD!" I screamed, as even more water slopped over the tub's edge. "Oh, YES, Gerry! FUCK me!" I clung to the sides of the tub, as his pelvis slammed against mine, forcing his huge tool all the way to the back of my cunt. "FUCK ME!" He obeyed.

Orgasm after orgasm shook me until one blended into another. The sounds I made were no longer words, just inarticulate gasps and cries. *I can't stand any more. I'm going to explode.* The thoughts had no more formed than I felt Gerry stiffen and his rhythm quicken. "Jules! Oh God, Jules!" I felt his cock give a huge, throbbing pulse and then was filled with warmth as his seed jetted into me.

I squeezed with all my strength, wanting to milk every drop from him. He shuddered, his face contorted, then collapsed against me. As our breathing became more even, the only sound in the woods was the quiet hum of the pump refilling the tub. Oh, and the pounding of my heart.

From the cabin's front porch, I could hear the limousine a long way off in the silent woods. Such a vehicle wasn't designed to navigate unpaved driveways, and besides the engine, I could hear the occasional scrape of the oil pan on the frozen ground. I winced, glad I had taken Gerry's suggestion and upgraded my rental car to a Range Rover.

Gerry. A ribbon of heat spread from my groin to my face. *Did I really just have sex with my best friend?* I shivered from a combination of cold and guilt, and tried to get a glimpse of the limo between the trees. Joe was in that car. Not to mention Maggie. I groaned inwardly at the thought of trying to face both of them without guilt written largely upon my features.

I had only seconds to compose myself, because the limousine, gleaming above and splattered with icy slush below, rounded the final corner and emerged from the trees. The driver pulled it directly in front of the steps, and I stood up from the porch swing, my nerves tingling.

The driver stepped out and opened the rear door, and a fur-clad leg emerged, followed by the rest of Maggie. She was wearing thigh-high boots covered in something that looked like the pelt of an endangered species over skintight black pants. Her jacket matched the boots, which I noticed had spike heels about five inches high. As soon as she stood, she started to slip, and only the driver's grip on her arm prevented her from landing on her perfect, size-two ass. Long blond hair fell from a fur hat, not a single strand out of place. Her eyes were hidden by Versace sunglasses, and her enormous lips—she must have visited her buddy the surgeon this week—wore their customary pout.

"Darling!" she called to me. She had picked up the word from Gerry, and I privately thought it sounded ridiculous coming from her too-plump lips. "So glad to finally be here." She walked unsteadily up the icy walk and air-kissed both of my cheeks before pulling off her glasses and scanning the front of the cabin with a jaundiced eye. "Wherever 'here' is. I swear we've been driving through woods for centuries."

"I thought the ride went pretty quickly," said a smoothly accented voice, and I looked up to see Joe. He flashed his veneered smile and leaned to kiss me lightly on the lips. "At least we were in good company."

"Yes, I don't know what I would have done if Joe hadn't been on the same flight," she replied. "My phone stopped working three mountains ago. Where's Gerry?"

"Making dinner," I said, horrified to feel a flush rise to my cheeks. "He would have come out to greet you, but there were timing issues with the cuisine."

"I'll go see if he needs help." I resisted the urge to snort as Maggie tottered through the door on her ridiculous heels. Her idea of helping with dinner was to demand that Gerry interrupt his preparations to fix her a mojíto cocktail. I turned to Joe, who was signing something on a clipboard proffered by the limousine driver.

"Thank you, sir," said the man, taking his clipboard back. "I'll bring the luggage in. Do you need help with that?" he asked, indicating the battered leather case next to Joe's ankle—he must have put it down to sign the credit card slip. Recognizing it, I groaned.

"You did *not* bring your notebook computer with you. No working this weekend—you promised."

"I just brought it to check my e-mail," he protested. "I went online and saw that my cell service might not work here." He waived the driver away and picked the case up himself.

"It won't," I confirmed. "And there's no high-speed Internet, either."

"You mean I have to use *dial-up?*" His voice rose in disbelief.

"You don't *have* to use anything," I said, a little more tartly than I intended. "You *could* just let your e-mail messages wait until Monday. The world will not stop turning if the great José Vargas skips two days of e-mail."

He put his free arm around me and nuzzled the side of my face. I resisted the temptation to pull away in annoyance. "Someone's in a crabby mood. Did you and Gerry have some kind of a fight up here?"

"No, of course not," I replied, flustered. "Gerry and I don't fight."

"It seems to me like you're always giving each other a hard time," he said, taking his arm from my shoulders in order to open the door.

"Just normal friend stuff. Don't you joke around with your friends?" I went into the cabin and Joe followed. The warmth was welcome—I hadn't really been dressed warmly enough to be sitting still on the porch—and a delicious scent wafted from where Gerry stood in the open kitchen at the opposite side of the cabin's main room.

Joe scanned the interior. He didn't look any more enthusiastic than Gerry had been at first perusal, but he wasn't as quick to tell me his first impression. *Gerry is always completely honest with me,* I thought. *He doesn't weigh his words before coming out with them.*

"It looks very . . . comfortable," said Joe, and I winced inwardly at how carefully diplomatic his words were. "It has rustic charm."

"*I* think it's dreadful," said Maggie. "Take a look at the size of that moose head over the dining table. I could put my fist inside its nostril." She fluttered a graceful hand. "I'm sure I'll lose my appetite with it staring at me."

"Here's your martini," said Gerry, handing her a drink. "I'm sorry I forgot to order mint for mojítos." The cabin's kitchen had been stocked to order by a nameless employee of the management company—Gerry and I had filled out an online form to select groceries. We both liked to cook, and generally did it together. Tonight I had left him to his own devices rather than spend time with him in the close quarters of the kitchen.

The door opened and the driver started setting suitcases inside the doorway. *How much stuff did she bring?* I thought idly, as the stack of animal-print leather cases grew. Tipping his hat, the driver exited.

"Can I get you a drink?" I asked Joe. I had brewed a pot of coffee for myself after Gerry and I self-consciously emerged from the hot tub, and he had immediately fled for the shower. Although I didn't blame what happened on the brandy, I had wanted a clear head when Joe arrived.

"Sure," said Joe. "Is there any Crown?"

"Yes, I made sure there was a bottle here." I took ice cubes out of the small freezer by the bar and dropped them into a heavy tumbler, then looked for the familiar shape of the Crown Royal bottle.

"Oh, *shit!*" Maggie jumped off the stool from where she had been watching Gerry cook and skittered in her heels across the pine floorboards toward the front door. "I left my cell phone in the limo." As she flung the heavy door open, I heard the sound of the limousine's engine. Apparently, it was still idling in the driveway. "Wait, driver! Don't leave! I need to get my—"

The rest of Maggie's words were cut off by a bloodcurdling shriek, followed by a *thumk*. Dropping a wooden spoon, Gerry ran around the counter and headed for the door, where he and Joe spent a second competing to get their broad shoulders through the frame. I abandoned my cocktail-making activities and followed them. By the time I reached the porch, Maggie was sitting propped up between them, holding her lower leg in both hands and wailing.

"I think I b-broke it," she sobbed. "I slipped on the stupid ice on the stupid porch."

"We need to get this boot off," said Joe, always Mr. Take Charge.

"Let's get her inside first," said Gerry, and the two of them lifted a whimpering Maggie and carried her through the door I held open. They placed her on the couch, and Gerry fumbled with the zipper on the long boot.

"Ow!" squeaked Maggie. "Be careful! That hurts, you know."

"I know, darling, and I'm trying to be careful. But if this is as far down as the zipper will go, I may have to cut it off."

"Don't you dare! They're Balenciaga."

Well, of course they are. "Let me try." I elbowed between the two men and took the foot of the boot in my hands. "Maggie, I can take it off without cutting it, but I'm going to have to do this in one quick movement, and it might hurt. Ready?"

"Ye—" she started, then yelped as I yanked off the boot before she could finish the word. "OUCH! That really hurt." Her eyes, surrounded by impossibly full lashes—*implants?*—turned toward me with a sullen expression. "You didn't say it would hurt *that* much."

"Sorry," I said, meaning it. "But at least it's over, and I saved your boot." We all examined Maggie's ankle, which was beginning to swell noticeably.

"I think we had better take you to the emergency room, darling. To get it x-rayed," said Gerry, and I couldn't argue.

"Excuse me, but would you like me to drive?" It was the limousine driver, who had apparently followed us back into the house and was hovering near the door.

I shook my head. "No, we should take her in the rental car. We might have to be there a while."

"I'll take her," said Gerry. "You stay here with Joe."

Again I shook my head. "I didn't get your name on the rental agreement, which means you're not insured to drive. I'll have to go. You can sit in the back and Maggie can put her foot on your lap."

"Wait a minute!" said Maggie to the driver, who was heading out the door again. "I left my cell phone in your car."

"I put it on the cases." He nodded toward the stack of luggage and, sure enough, the tiny phone was perched on top.

Joe and Gerry carried Maggie to the back seat of the Range Rover, where she was propped up with several bed pillows and an ice pack.

"Joe, you can sit up front with me."

"Actually, I thought perhaps I would stay here and get un-packed and settled. You don't mind, do you?" Joe came up next to me and massaged the back of my neck while he spoke, which I had come to recognize as a persuasion tactic. I shrugged his hand off.

"Going to give that dial-up a shot, aren't you?" I said aloud, then winced. I had not intended to voice that thought—at least not with so much acid in my tone.

"You can hardly accuse me of neglecting you when you're not even here," he replied smoothly. "I just got out of a car. I don't want to get back into one."

"Are you sure you don't want me to stay with you, darling?"

Ensconced on the sofa and surrounded by pillows, drinks, magazines, and snacks, Maggie had somehow managed to apply all her makeup and style her hair. She looked like an ad for ski resort wear in *Vogue* magazine—cast, crutches, and all. She had even talked Gerry into painting the toenails that poked from the end of the plaster.

Maggie sighed theatrically. "I don't want my little accident to spoil your entire weekend. I'm just so disappointed I can't go with you. I was so looking forward to it."

Like hell, I thought uncharitably. I wasn't in a charitable mood. I had listened to her whimper all the way to the emer-gency room and whine all the way back. She had convinced Gerry that her mishap was his fault, for "bringing her to the fucking North Pole" when they could have taken a nice Medi-terranean cruise, with a New Year's Eve port of call somewhere "civilized," like Monaco.

I had wanted to tell her that a child would have known better than to wear spike-heeled boots in icy weather, but I held my tongue. Luckily, she had zoned out from the painkillers before we made it back to the cabin, although I wasn't sure the awkward silence between Gerry and me was much of an improvement.

To put the icing on the cake, Joe was sound asleep by the time we returned, his notebook computer still open on the dining table. He had resisted my admittedly halfhearted attempts to awaken him, and he was awake and dressed before I woke up in the morning—so much for my sex-fest weekend. *But you already had mind-numbing sex this weekend, remember?*

Did I mention I wasn't in the best of moods?

"How do I look?" I looked up to see Joe coming down the stairs in full designer outdoorsman regalia.

"You look amazing!" piped Maggie from the sofa, and I had to admit she was right. How he had found that outfit in Miami—it fit too well to be mail order—was beyond me. As he reached me, I put my fingers up to stroke the collar of his heather gray turtleneck.

"This is so soft. What's it made of?"

He shrugged. "Silk and cashmere, I think the guy said. I told him I wanted something that would be warm without being too bulky."

I self-consciously touched my Old Navy fleece hoodie. It was about as sexy as a potato sack, but I would be warm.

"Ready to go?" Gerry was zipping up his own jacket.

"Sure. Where's the equipment?" Joe was starting to get that "I'm a winner" glint in his eye. Great. I would spend all morning trying to keep up with these two. Gerry didn't usually care about coming in first, but Joe brought out the mostly dormant competitor in him.

"I laid it all out on the back deck. The trail passes by the cabin just a few hundred yards through the trees to the north. It's an intermediate level, but we're all in pretty good shape. The guidebook says it should take two to three hours." This last comment was intended for Maggie, but I could see the wheels turning in Joe's head as he no doubt resolved to finish in less than two hours. We headed out to examine the equipment.

"Did you wax them?" asked Joe. Gerry looked surprised.

"No, they're waxless skis. They're supposed to be easier for beginners."

"But waxed skis are faster," said Joe.

"I thought you'd never been cross-country skiing," I said to Joe.

"I haven't. But I didn't want to be a drag on the group, so I did a little online research while you guys were at the hospital." He turned his attention to Gerry. "Which is how I know you can still put glide wax on a waxless ski. Do we have any?"

"Sure, there was some wax with the equipment, but I don't think—"

"Where is it?" Joe cut off Gerry's objections, and I saw Gerry's jaw tighten ever so slightly.

"Suit yourself." With just the trace of a shrug, Gerry pointed through the glass doors toward the closet that held the equipment, and Joe went to retrieve the wax.

Both Gerry and I declined Joe's offer to wax our skis, and we were soon moving awkwardly through the woods in the direction of the trail. I had done this once, years before, and the motion was beginning to come back to me by the time we saw the bright blazes and tracks from other skiers that indicated we had reached the trail. Gerry was a first-timer, but his training at the gym must have worked because he seemed to be getting the hang of it very rapidly.

Joe was swearing creatively in Spanish.

"I think these skis are broken," he told Gerry. "Look, it's bending in the middle."

"It's supposed to," said Gerry. "That's the camber."

"Yeah, I read about that, but I didn't think they'd bend *this* much. Besides, the less camber, the faster the ski. Maybe we should go back for a stiffer pair. Didn't they have any in that equipment closet?"

"Yes, but the guidebook said inexperienced skiers shouldn't try to use them until they learn not to slip backward on hills. It didn't seem like a good idea on our first time out."

Joe looked like he was about to argue, but we were on a slight upgrade and he was indeed slipping backward. I managed not to laugh as he regained his grip on the snow and made some forward progress.

"Okay, let's go this way." I indicated a trail that Gerry and I had tentatively decided on while pouring over the guidebook before we left Miami. "It should take us around the side of a hill and then we should see a lake. It's sort of a big counterclockwise loop—we'll end up back here."

"We'll have to go single file most of the way," Gerry said. "Shall I take the lead?"

Joe looked like he wanted to protest, but he was still having trouble getting the basic forward motion, and probably did not want to be in front where we could see him struggle. He nodded, and Gerry moved onto the track, skiing with increasing grace. I followed and Joe brought up the rear. Within five minutes, I had forgotten all about the tension between us, Maggie's theatrics, and Joe's computer.

The woods were incredibly beautiful. The air was crisp and cold and smelled delicious, and the sun shone between the trees and made a pattern of alternating shadows and dazzling shafts that sparkled on the ice and snow. Every now and then, the trees thinned and we got a tantalizing glimpse of mountain vistas. The sound of the skis sliding over the snow fell into a pleasant rhythm, and the single-file configuration mostly precluded conversation.

I could still hear the occasional "*coño!*" drifting up from Joe. We came to a wide spot in the trail and I pulled aside and turned to see how he was doing.

As he came up the slight grade toward me, I could see the strain of effort on his face. He was moving quickly up the hill, but it seemed more out of sheer determination than because he had gotten the hang of the smooth strokes Gerry and I were employing. His face was red from exertion and his mouth was open.

"Do you want to stop and rest for a few minutes?" I asked him. "If I remember the map correctly, there's a clearing ten minutes or so ahead. Gerry will know to wait for us there once he realizes he's left us behind."

He shook his head determinedly. "No, I don't want him to have to do that."

"He won't mind."

"I said no."

"Come on, Joe, you don't have to prove anything to me. You've never done this before. It's not as easy as it looks." I noted his labored breathing. "I would much rather you went at a slower pace and enjoyed yourself."

"I *am* enjoying myself!" He forced a big smile, showing very white teeth. I'd never quite had the nerve to ask whether they were capped. "I'm really getting the hang of it now. Come on, let's catch up with old Gerr." So saying, he passed me on the trail, making determined if not graceful strides. I could see the muscles in his legs bunch and knew he was working very hard to look as if this wasn't absolutely killing him. I sighed and followed.

Gerry was waiting in the clearing, and the moment we emerged from the tree line, he started to wave. His smile was huge, and he was gesturing at the vista opening before us. "Joe! Jules! Just look at this view!"

The trail had opened onto a clearing that overlooked a small mountain lake. It was partially frozen, but a light breeze rippled the open sections and created a sparkle like thousands of diamonds caught in the light. I caught my breath—it was the most beautiful thing I had ever seen.

Joe, moving more confidently now, waited for me to catch up.

"Oh, Joe," I said, "isn't that amazing?"

"Impressive," he agreed, but his attention was on Gerry, not the lake. "Hey, Gerr, according to that map you had, it's all more or less downhill from here back to the cabin, am I right?"

"It should be." Gerry was as mesmerized by the lake as I was.

"Well, now that I've gotten used to these skis, why don't I take the lead?"

Uh-oh, I thought. Now the race begins.

Gerry frowned. "I certainly don't mind, but the books all say that going downhill on cross-country skis is a lot trickier than you would think. It takes time to learn how to glide properly. You want to be careful—we've already got one broken leg in the group."

Joe waved off the warning. "I'll be careful. We're not talking about the Olympic slalom course here. Just a little less climbing."

Seeing trouble ahead, I tried to intervene. "Look, Joe, are you sure you want to—"

"I'm sure. See you guys back at the cabin!" Without another glance at the lake—or me—he whooshed past us and into the woods beyond the clearing.

"I *guess* I hope he doesn't break his neck," I muttered under my breath, but I had forgotten how quiet it was, and Gerry overheard me. He laughed. It was as if the tension between us had broken.

"Look, Jules, we need to talk about what happened yesterday afternoon."

"Yes, we do."

Now that it was out in the open, we were both reluctant to start. Finally, Gerry spoke.

"It was just one of those things. I'm not saying I'm sorry it happened, but we need to keep it our secret."

"I'm not sorry either. But, yes, we should just keep it between us."

"And it can never happen again, Jules. Never."

Ouch. I was a little surprised at how much it hurt to hear Gerry say that. I mean, it was exactly what I had intended to say to him. Wasn't it?

"Agreed." We looked solemnly at each other, then Gerry stuck out his gloved hand. Laughing, I shook it. "Now that we've got *that* out of the way, are we going to stand here all day or get back to the cabin and spend some time with our significant others?"

He smiled, and my heart squeezed just a tiny bit. "In a bit. It's early yet and, if you don't mind, I'd like to enjoy the view a little. In fact, why don't we detour around the lake? Unless . . ."

"Unless what?"

"Unless you're in a huge hurry to get back to Joe."

I laughed. "No, it'll give him time to change and set the scene. You know he's going to be sitting with his feet propped up, pretending he's been back for hours and asking where we've been."

"Maggie will rat him out," replied Gerry. "Unless he bribes her."

"He just might." We laughed, and I reflected on how good it felt to have my best friend back. And how funny he sounded pronouncing an oh-so-American expression like "rat him out" in his London accent. "Okay, let's do it. This day is too perfect to be inside."

There was no trail, but we didn't need one. It was wonderful to glide over untouched snow, and I was comfortable enough that the slight downhill path to the side of the lake was easy to negotiate. I went first, and Gerry followed.

The line of fur trees—Aspen, I thought, but I wasn't sure—stopped about forty feet back from the edge of the open water, leaving a level expanse of snow that led like a path to the other side of the lake. I was just about to start across when I heard a muffled curse behind me.

I turned and immediately laughed aloud. Gerry must have lost his balance on the downhill glide, because he was sitting in a most ungraceful position, largely imbedded in a snow bank.

"Evil bitch, laughing at a man in distress," he said, but he was smiling. There was snow on his face.

"I can't help it—you look so funny. Do you need help getting up?" I started to move back up the slope.

He groaned theatrically. "No, leave me with a little of my dignity, darling, for pity's sake. You go along, and I'll extricate myself and be right behind you." He started to maneuver out of the pile of snow, then saw that I was still watching.

"Get going! Don't stand there and gloat at my distress." He was laughing now, too, and I inclined my head in an exaggerated gesture of ascent, then did as he instructed.

Using my poles to gain momentum on the level ground, I pushed myself out onto the flat expanse of snow. I took a deep breath of the crisp air—it seemed even cleaner here next to the sparkling water—and lengthened my strides as I moved toward the opposite side of the lake.

A loud, sharp "c-c-crack" rent the air and I looked around, startled. It sounded as if someone had fired a gun. *Do they hunt near here?* I thought, vaguely, as I scanned the surrounding forest.

"*Jules!*" I looked to where Gerry was now standing, free of the snow bank, and saw that he was gesturing wildly. "It's the ice! *Move!*"

"Huh?" I looked over at the lake edge, a good twenty feet away from where I stood. There was some ice on the lake, but it was over against the opposite side. What was he talking about? "What about the ice?" I shouted back at him.

"*You're standing on ice!*" He said, and I finally caught his meaning.

The reason the ground was so level here was that *it wasn't ground*. It was ice, and I'd been fooled by the thick covering of snow. The tree line didn't end forty feet from the lake's edge, the tree line *was* the lake's edge.

Another "crack" rent the air, and this time I felt the ice shift slightly under my skis. A surge of adrenaline made every nerve in my body tingle, and I felt panic brush against me like the wings of a frightened bird.

I turned on my skis and prepared to head back in the direction from which I had come. I saw Gerry heading toward me, but I barely had time to move in his direction when another one of those gunshot sounds assaulted my ears and the world around me tilted alarmingly. My gaze tried to dart everywhere at once, and I slipped fully into panic when I realized that I was surrounded by fissures.

I saw the tops of the Aspen trees slant suddenly toward me and simultaneously felt cold water on my legs and feet. I looked down to see a chasm opening before me, and I slid hip-deep into icy water.

"Gerry!" I realized I was still clinging to my poles and flung them away, trying to pull myself up from the water by grabbing the ice around me. This turned out to be a bad move, as the ice, now broken into small slabs, merely teetered and moved farther apart. Instantly, I was chest deep.

"DON'T MOVE!" Gerry's voice broke through my panic, and I realized he had never stopped shouting. *"Dammit,* Jules, hold still until I can get to you."

Something in his tone caught my attention and allowed me to focus through my terror. My fear-blurred vision cleared and I looked across the ice and directly into his face.

He had stripped off his skis and was crawling toward me across the ice.

"Hurry," I breathed. I moved my legs experimentally and felt no sign of the lake bottom. The movement made me slip a few inches farther into the water.

"Be *still,*" Gerry hissed. "I'm almost there."

He was. I could see the part of the ice he was sliding across had not yet cracked and, by lying on his stomach, he was distributing his weight in order to prevent the ice from breaking beneath him. Or at least I hoped so.

I slowed my breathing and stared straight into his face. Suddenly, I knew I would be all right. Gerry's expression left no doubt. The determination I saw there was nothing like the way Joe looked when he was set on a goal. It wasn't a desire to win, it was an absolute certainty that he *must* succeed.

Gerry's gloved hand grasped one of the abandoned ski poles, still resting on the ice about a foot from my reach. He pulled it over so that it was directly in front of him, then pushed it forward so that it was aimed at me.

"Julie, you need to reach out *slowly* and grab the end of the pole. Try not to shift your weight against the ice, okay?"

I had one elbow on a relatively stable slap of ice, and the other arm stretched out flat on a less-steady chunk. As I tried to slide the extended arm toward the ski pole, the ice around me all started to shift.

"*Freeze!*" said Gerry.

"Not the best choice of words, Gerr," I said, surprised at the steadiness of my voice. But I obeyed him, waiting for the ice to still before starting again.

"That's my girl." He gave me a grim smile. "Now, come on."

This time, I moved more slowly and got my hand all the way to the end of the ski pole, grasping it.

"Now, get a good grip on it before moving your other arm," he said, and I nodded. I understood what he was trying to get me to do. My sodden glove still offered some help, with the textured grips designed to help hold pole handles. I wrapped my fingers tightly around the shaft, ignoring the pain in my frigid joints.

"That's it," encouraged Gerry. "Now, hang on tight and bring your other hand around. Don't worry if you drop back a little, I won't let go."

It took every ounce of will I had to forsake the support of my elbow on the ice slab, but when I looked at Gerry, I knew that I trusted him completely. I took a deep breath, which was growing harder to do in the icy water, and swung my other hand around to grab the pole.

I did slip farther into the water, but Gerry's tug on the other end of the ski pole was reassuring.

"Okay, Jules," said Gerry when I had stabilized. "I don't have anything to use for leverage, so I'm going to have to do this a little at a time. You just hang on with everything you've got, okay?"

I nodded, saving my breath, and then watched as Gerry, closing his eyes with effort, pulled the pole toward his chin. Even through the thickness of his fleece jacked, I could see the great muscles in his shoulders expand. Veins stood out in his forehead.

Nothing happened at first, then there was a tug, and then I felt my chest lift as I slid higher, a few inches of ice now supporting my chest.

"Okay," said Gerry, now out of breath. "I'm going to slide back a few inches and do that again. You doing okay?" he asked.

"Okay," I managed to gasp, and I watched as he shifted his weight from side to side, slithering backward on the ice like a snake in order to move without releasing his grip on the pole.

"Now," he said, and again he pulled back on the pole. I gained a few more inches of ice, and the pull of the water on my lower extremities lost some of its menace. *It was working!*

"One . . . more . . . time . . . should do it." Gerry was gasping now, and I marveled at the Herculean effort he was making to pull my not-insubstantial weight across thin, slippery ice using nothing but his own strength. He finished his backward slide and with a nod, pulled back with even more force than the previous two times.

The bulk of my weight slid forward onto the ice, which didn't break. I let go of the pole and put my arms on the ice. There was nothing to grip, but I was able to wriggle away from the hole I had made. Gerry flung the pole aside and slid toward me, and I felt strong hands grip me under the arms and haul me forward.

We slithered and wriggled until a roughness under the ice told us we'd reach the edge—the real edge—of the lake. He pulled me into his arms and we lay there, panting, too exhausted to speak or even feel the cold.

"I can't believe I was so stupid," I finally managed to gasp. "It was so obvious that the part of the lake sheltered from the wind would be covered with snow. I blundered on out there like an idiot."

"I thought it was solid ground, too, Jules. If I hadn't fallen on my ass, I would have been right there with you, and we'd have gone through together and probably both drowned."

"Or frozen to death." I shivered, feeling the cold now that my adrenaline was returning to a normal level.

"You must have been terrified," said Gerry, stroking my hair. "When I heard the ice breaking, and realized you didn't know where the sound was coming from . . ." His shudder had nothing to do with the cold.

"I wasn't, not really," I said. "I mean, I panicked a little bit at the beginning, but once I saw you coming toward me, I *knew* you'd get me out of there. I was absolutely certain."

"That's good, because I wasn't. I couldn't be sure the ice

would hold my weight, never mind be strong enough to hold both of us once I pulled you up."

There was an awkward silence as we both considered what had nearly happened. "I don't think I'm going to die of hypothermia today, but we really need to get moving. The only problem is that my skis are at the bottom of the lake."

"You can take mine." Gerry stood up. "I barely got wet at all. In fact, you should strip that off—" he indicated my sodden hoodie, "and put on my jacket. I'll be warm enough with just the sweater, once I'm hiking."

I was too cold to protest, so we made the switch and left my bright red sweatshirt hanging on a branch like a flag. I wondered who would find it and what they would think about how it might have gotten there.

"I feel bad skiing off without you," I said, but my wet pants were starting to freeze and my feet were ice cubes, and I knew Gerry was right about sending me ahead. He'd given me his dry gloves, too.

"Just hurry back and get in a warm shower," he said. "I'll be fine—it's a perfect day for a hike and the snow's not that deep. Now, go."

My heart squeezed. Had anyone ever had a better friend?

"No, baby, I'm too sore." Joe groaned from where he lay with his back to me on the bed. "I can barely move."

"If you hadn't had to prove you were Mr. Macho, you wouldn't be in this condition." I was pissed. Here I was, wearing my brand-new nasty underwear—purchased at the most exclusive lingerie shop in Coral Gables—surrounded by scented candles, and with sexy jazz playing on the little stereo in the corner, and Joe just wanted to sleep.

"Give me a break, wouldja? I never even cross-country skied before, and I beat both of you back to the cabin by forty-five minutes."

"It wasn't a race!" I considered smothering him with a pillow. "And if I can recover from falling through the ice and nearly getting hypothermia or frostbite, and still feel like making love, you could certainly rise to the occasion."

I was still smoldering about Joe's reaction when I had arrived at the cabin, half-frozen and alone. As I had predicted, he was sitting on the sofa with his feet up, sipping a glass of brandy, and looking determinedly casual.

"I was wondering if you two would ever show up," he said, then frowned when he realized Gerry wasn't with me. "Where's your buddy? Lagging behind?"

I explained what happened, and Joe finally noticed my pants were soaked and I was wearing Gerry's jacket. He made a few concerned noises, but I wasn't fooled. I'd seen his initial look of annoyance when he realized that my accident had robbed him of his little victory.

Gerry was back by the time I got out of a very long, hot shower, his cheeks pink from the wind, but insisting he hadn't been overly cold on his hike.

"So, what are you cooking me for dinner?" Maggie had asked from the sofa, where she still sat enthroned. She'd hobbled around a little, but said the crutches hurt her underarms too much, so she only got up when it was absolutely necessary. *Like to change clothes. Twice.*

"After preventing me from becoming a Popsicle, Gerry deserves a break from kitchen duty." I was finding Maggie's voice more annoying than usual.

"Well *I* certainly can't cook," she said, gesturing at her cast.

I suppressed a snort—Maggie's ineptitude in the kitchen had nothing to do with her current handicap.

"I'll do it," I said. "Joe can help me."

Joe looked doubtful. "I don't know much about cooking," he said, and I knew it was true. Like most Cuban men, his mother had waited on him hand and foot until he left home, by which time he made enough money to eat most meals at restaurants, except for the several times a week he still sat in attendance at his mother's table.

"You can follow instructions, can't you?" I was being more snappish that I usually was with Joe, and he looked momentarily surprised, but he conceded to my wishes, if not precisely with good grace, and between the two of us, we managed to put together a reasonable meal.

Nevertheless, dinner hadn't gone well. Maggie was pouting, Gerry was uncharacteristically quiet, and everything Joe said seemed to get on my nerves. After the meal was over, I decided that I needed to make a serious effort to mend fences and change the mood. So I put on my naughty lingerie and set up the mood lighting and music in the bedroom.

One place Joe and I had always gotten along was in bed. He had a strong sex drive, and it was easy to get him in the mood. Usually.

Tonight was, for some reason, another matter.

"Look, Jules, I'll make it up to you in the morning, I promise. But for now, can you *please* just let me rest, for God's sake?"

"Aaaargh!" I growled like the bear that had once inhabited the skin stretched out in front of the living room fireplace. "Fine. But I'm going upstairs for another drink." I dug through my suitcase and found my less-than-sexy terry cloth robe. As I stomped toward the door, making more noise than necessary, Joe's voice rose weakly from the bed.

"Could you turn off the music on your way out? And blow out the candles—they're giving me a headache."

I had to take several deep breaths before I could comply without resorting to violence, but managed to do so.

Upstairs, the fire had died to embers but still cast a little glow, along with light from the moon reflecting off the snow and through the glass doors. Not bothering to turn on a lamp, I rummaged through the bar, looking for vodka. I found a half-full bottle and some ice, and made myself a drink. I decided to drink it in front of the fireplace, and stepped barefoot onto old Smokey's furry coat, feeling a little foolish. Why would someone want to turn a living, breathing animal into a rug? It was just too weird.

I settled next to the fire and took a sip of the drink.

"Trouble in paradise?"

I nearly jumped out my own skin, then I saw Gerry. He was lying on one of the facing couches, and with no lamp on, he was almost completely hidden by shadow.

"Mr. Competitive wore himself out proving he's faster than us. He's exhausted, and I wasn't ready to go to sleep." I gestured with my glass at his blanket and pillows—he was obviously set up to spend the night. "What about you? Miss South Beach give you the boot?"

"No, I volunteered to leave. She said I was moving around too much and making her leg uncomfortable."

"Didn't the painkillers knock her out?"

"She seems to be developing a resistance." Gerry sat up and looked at my glass. "Is there any more of that vodka left?"

"A little. Here, take this one. I'll pour myself another." I tried to hand him the glass, but he was already up and at the bar. In a few moments, he came back and sat on the floor next to me.

"Some romantic weekend this is turning out to be," he said as we clinked glasses. "Doesn't look like either of us is getting laid."

"We already *got* laid, if you recall. Quite satisfactorily."

"Oh, I remember." He smiled ruefully. "But don't forget we agreed that was an isolated incident."

"Absolutely." We drank in silence, watching the remains of the fire. I felt something tickling my nether regions and shifted uncomfortably.

"A bit twitchy, darling?"

"No, it's this damned rug." I pulled my robe around so that it was between my ass and the prickly surface. "I put on this stupid thong thingy to entice Sleeping Beauty . . ." I gestured with my glass toward the staircase, "and I was too pissed to change into something comfortable before I came upstairs to pout."

"New lingerie? Let me see."

"No way, bucko. The last time we played 'I'll show you mine,' we ended up . . . well, you know." I drained my drink and got up to make another one.

"You have a point," said Gerry, "But a week ago, you wouldn't have hesitated to show me new undies. I hope we aren't going to have to go through the rest of our lives being cautious with each other. Doesn't seem natural."

I considered what he said as I poured another vodka. "This is the last of it. Top off your glass?" He held up the tumbler and I poured the last drops of the vodka into it, then returned to my position.

"You're right, it doesn't seem natural. One of the things that's always been great about our friendship is that it's uncensored. We just say or do whatever we want. We don't . . . we don't pretend that we like something that we hate. If you're saying something that annoys me, I tell you to shut up."

"*Me* annoy *you?* Isn't it usually the other way around?"

I punched him for that comment, and he feigned injury. Again, we were laughing.

"So," he said, "What has Joe said or done that you hate, and haven't said anything about? That's what's really going on here, isn't it?"

I sighed. "Not any one thing. It's just the whole 'I'm the master of the universe and must always win' thing. I used to tell myself that it was just healthy ambition. Now I'm starting to think . . ."

"What?"

"I'm starting to think he's trying to make up for some kind of insecurity or something. I just get tired of competing all the time."

"I know what you mean. I've got the same issue with Maggie."

"Surely you don't compete with *her*. She's always telling everyone how fabulous you are, how much money you make, how nice your condo is—"

"Exactly. I'm not competing with her, I'm completing against everyone she knows. She thought my Mercedes was fabulous until we valet parked at a restaurant and it got parked in the second row, because the first row was full of Bentleys and Ferraris. My condo was great until her ex-boyfriend moved into a penthouse at that new high-rise on the southeastern tip of South Beach."

"You can't afford a Bentley. They cost more than my house."

He shook his head. "I wouldn't buy one if I could afford it. Spending a quarter of a million dollars on a car seems insane to me. I'd get a nice Lexus and give the difference to charity or something. But . . ." he took a big swig of the drink.

"But what?"

He scratched his head. "But I know that eventually she'll leave me for someone who has different priorities."

He looked so glum. "Jeez, Gerr, I'm sorry. I know you really care about her."

"I'll get over it." He grinned at me. "Now, are you going to show me your damned underwear or not?"

I hesitated. We'd agreed the incident in the hot tub was an aberration and would not happen again. So why did I flush with heat at the thought of showing him my black-with-red-lace-trim underwear?

"I need another drink first," I said, mostly because the bar was outside the circle of dim light cast by the fire. I didn't want Gerry to see my blush. He might misinterpret it. "Is there an unopened bottle of vodka in the back?"

"I don't think so," he said. "And quit stalling. Off with the robe, woman!" He looked me up and down. "And speaking of that robe, where on earth did you get the tatty thing? Salvation Army?"

"It was nice when it was new," I protested. "I've just had it for a while." I continued to shuffle bottles around on the bar.

He got to his feet and came over to help me. "If Joe's seen you in that thing, it explains why he's avoiding sex."

I swatted at him and he ducked, laughing. He found a light switch on the side of the bar and turned it on, then perused the stock carefully. "As I thought, no vodka." He turned to face me and, quick as a snake, reached out and snatched the end of the tie that held the robe together. "But there's gin, and I'll make you a lovely martini as soon as you show me your damned lingerie."

I held the edges of the robe together. "I don't want to. It's too . . ."

"Too what?" He tugged playfully at the belt.

"Too . . . nasty." I had been surprised the upscale boutique even carried brassieres with cutout nipples, but had thought Joe would like the surprise. And, when I'd tried the bra on in the fitting room, the sensation of having my nipples poke out of the lacy holes had been a turn-on, even with no one to see me.

Gerry let go of the belt and folded his arms. "Jules, now you *have* to show me. You're blushing. If the underwear is so naughty that it's actually embarrassing for you to think about it, there's not a chance in hell you're getting out of this room without letting me see it. Now *strip!*"

I raised my eyebrows and made a mock salute. "Yes, *sir!*" I found I wanted to show him—at least someone would appreciate how sexy it was. I turned my back and untied the robe, allowing it to drop below my shoulders. I turned my head and looked back at him with what I hoped was a theatrically coquettish expression. "Ready? Stand back—this may be more than your heart can take."

"I'm ready," he said, taking a step back. I dropped the robe, but didn't turn.

"Oh, darling, the thong is *perfect.*" I glanced back again and saw that he was staring at my ass, grinning.

"You like it?" Thongs were hardly a novelty to someone who lived in Miami, where they were as common on the beach as conventional bikinis.

"The little red bow is a great touch," he said. "But I wouldn't really call it nasty."

"No? Well, get a load of *this*." Steeling myself, I turned around, hands on hips. I was gratified to see his jaw actually drop.

"Wow!" he said after a moment's recovery, almost in a whisper. "Now, that *is* nasty. But I love it."

"Do you?" I knew my nipples were already hard, teased by the lace of the bra, but mostly stimulated by the excitement of being seen in this outfit. "I can tell you where I bought it. You could get one like it for Maggie."

He shook his head. "No, I don't think Maggie would go for it. She'd rather go completely topless, and I'd never get her to wear something just for my entertainment."

"But it's for my entertainment, too," I told him. "It feels really hot. Like I should be swinging around a pole in a strip club or something."

He nodded slowly. "Yes, yes I can see that. You've just taken off your tear-away business suit and fedora hat . . ."

". . . and now I'm dancing in nothing but this outfit and some high heels."

I thought he actually gulped. "Have you got any with you? High heels, I mean?"

"No," I said, thinking of Maggie's boots. "They didn't seem appropriate in the Colorado woods. But I did bring a CD with some sexy music. I thought I might do a little dance for Joe, but . . ." I shrugged.

"Where is it?" Gerry's voice had taken on some huskiness, if I wasn't imagining things. "The CD, I mean."

"In the player in the bedroom," I told him. "Which has been turned off because it was annoying Joe."

He was still staring at my breasts and I was feeling more and more self-conscious. I leaned over and picked up the robe, ready to put it back on.

"Don't," said Gerry. "Not yet."

I held it in front of me but didn't put it on. "Why not?"

He hesitated, looking at my face now. He seemed to be formulating an answer.

"I think . . . I think you were really looking forward to having someone appreciate how beautiful you look in that outfit, and to doing something fun and sexy. Like dancing for your man." He walked over to the sofa and sat down, facing me. "I know I'm not the man you imagined doing it for, but I would be honored if you would consider dancing for me."

I was aghast. Gerry thought I was going to put on some kind of exotic show for him? But the idea was . . . interesting.

"I don't have any music. And you'll laugh at me."

"There's a perfectly good stereo in the corner, and I'm sure I can find a station. And I promise not to laugh."

"What if Joe or Maggie wakes up?"

"Maggie took enough painkillers to knock out a moose. And you just said Joe was exhausted."

"But I'll be . . ." I felt another flush warm my face.

"You'll be what?" Gerry's tone was gentle.

"I'll be embarrassed!" I still held the bathrobe in front of my exposed nipples, and I gripped it more tightly. "You go to all those trendy clubs where gorgeous girls dance in cages or on the dance floor. I've seen the pictures. I don't look anything like those women."

"Jules, you are every bit as attractive as the club girls, and a hell of a lot more interesting. You could put any of them to shame. And . . ." He walked over to the stereo and pushed a button. Jazz came from a speaker, and he lowered the volume, "the most important reason for you to dance is because you want to. I can tell."

"You can?"

He gave me a mock-solemn look. "I can."

"And you won't laugh?"

"I already said I wouldn't." He returned to the sofa.

The music had a steady, pulsing beat, and the saxophone had a sensual feel. The terry cloth rubbed against my nipples. *Oh, what the hell.*

Lifting the robe in front of me like a matador's cape, I held it so that it just barely hid my nipples from view. I did an experimental hip roll to the music, cocked a shoulder, and tossed my head back. I gave Gerry an exaggerated come-hither look. He grinned, but shook his head.

"Come on, Jules, you're clowning, not dancing. Listen to the music and give it a real go. If you're going to do it, do it right."

He had a point.

I closed my eyes and listened to the counterpoint of the saxophone against the thrumming base. With a conscious effort, I released all the tension in my body, and started to sway with the beat. As the soloist's tune danced a slow circle, so did I, ending up with my back to Gerry. Almost unconsciously, I dropped the robe and began to move my arms and hands.

"That's better," said Gerry. "Now you're getting into it." I must have slowed at the sound of his voice, because he went on, "No, don't stop. Pretend I'm not here. Or, even better, pretend I'm your dream man, and I'm spying on you, and I don't know you're aware that I'm watching."

I felt a smile curve my lips. *Dancing for my dream man.* I tried to imagine the movie stars who sometimes populated my more sensual fantasies—George Clooney, Gerard Butler.

But the image wouldn't come. It was Gerry watching me, and that was sexy enough.

I turned to face him, my hands over my breasts, and opened my eyes. His gaze was intent, and he was holding very still. I did another hip roll, but I knew there was nothing clowning about this one. It was pure seduction.

"Very nice," he breathed. Emboldened by his encouragement, I moved my hands so that instead of hiding my breasts, I was caressing them. I pushed them up in their lace enclosure, then encircled the exposed nipples with my fingertips.

Turning my back again, I pushed the straps down from my shoulders and ran my hands along them. Then, reaching behind me, unhooked my bra. I pulled it free and let it drop.

Did I hear a quiet groan?

I spun to face the sofa, hands over my breasts. Gerry was leaning forward now, and the teasing expression was gone, replaced by something more intense than I was used to seeing on his face. I pressed my breasts together, rubbing them in circles, then released them and ran my hands down my stomach to the lace strings of the thong.

Definitely a groan this time.

"I didn't know you were going to do a real striptease," said Gerry, his voice even but revealing just the slightest strain.

"Maybe I'll make it a lap dance," I teased, and I saw his gaze sharpen.

"If you want to," he said, "I wouldn't object."

Taking this as an invitation, I stalked over to the sofa, trying to move with a feline grace and, I thought, succeeding. I leaned forward and put my hands on his shoulders, then did a slow grind. My nipples came within inches of his face, and he

pretended to try to catch one in his mouth. At least I thought he
was pretending.

I lifted one hand to shake a finger at him. "No, no, no, mister.
Lookie, no touchie!"

"Whatever you say," he breathed. "Are you sure you haven't
done this before?"

"Maybe I have and maybe I haven't." I released him and
turned my back, bending in order to sway my ass back and forth
in front of him, just barely above his lap. "This *is* why they call
it a lap dance, isn't it?"

"Uh-huh." He answered in the affirmative, but this time I
could definitely make out the strain in his voice. I slipped my
fingers under the lace at the sides of the thong and caressed the
smooth cheeks of my ass as I swung it from side to side.

I did another big roll, moving back farther toward his lap,
but I must have bent a little lower than I intended, because I felt
something brush the underside of one cheek.

"Is that a hard-on?" I asked, already knowing the answer.

"Just means you're doing it right," he replied. It sounded like
he was gritting his teeth. "No worries—I have my sweatpants
on."

I shivered a little at the thought. Now that I knew what
Gerry's hard-on looked like—and felt like—the thought of his
engorged cock just centimeters from my pussy was enough to
make me tingle. I made another circle with my ass and unin-
tentionally brushed against him again. Well, it was probably
unintentional.

"Be careful, Jules," he said. "This is turning into a hotter
dance than I expected."

"Oh, really?" I could hear the purring quality of my own
voice, and the tingle in my cunt was turning into a throb. "You

think that was hot? How about *this?*" I bent forward and pushed my thong down to my ankles, knowing the position was spreading my pussy open right in front of his face.

"Jesus!" Suddenly, he had his hands on either side of my ass and was pulling me toward him. I almost lost my balance and fell on his lap. I reached behind to steady myself and my hand landed on his cock, still covered by the soft fabric of his pajamas, but clearly rock hard.

Without thinking, I reached under the waistband and pulled the fabric down, allowing it to spring free. He rocked me back and I was instantly impaled, his full shaft sliding easily into my now-soaked pussy, even though the fit was wonderfully, impossibly tight.

"God, Jules, you feel so *good.*" He leaned back, pushing his hips upward, and I writhed and clenched my muscles. He pumped again, and even though it seemed impossible for him to go deeper, I pressed hard into him, savoring every centimeter.

"Your cock is soooo nice," I moaned.

"And your ass is perfect," he replied in the same tone. "I just want to drive myself into you."

"Then do it." I pulled forward, squeezing, and bringing him with me. He understood what I wanted, and we eased off the sofa and onto the thick fur rug, settling with me on my knees and him locked behind me.

The position made it feel as if he was even bigger. As he pulled back and drove deeply into me, I could feel my pussy stretching and contracting. I was so wet and slick that sucking sounds could be heard above the throbbing beat of the jazz.

Gerry was fucking me. Again. My best friend was slamming into me doggy-style, while my boyfriend snored away in the bedroom below. It was surreal, and I should have felt guilty, but all I could think about was his cock and the way it felt driving into me like a jackhammer.

"Aaaaaagh!" I pressed my face into the fur of the rug, muffling the sounds I could not completely hold back. There was a slapping sound as his groin slammed against my ass, and I could hear his jagged breathing.

"Oh-God-Gerry-that's-so-good," I said, the staccato of his thrusts accenting my words. "I'm-going-to-come!"

"Me, too," he managed to growl.

And then we did. Like a freight train.

"Do you want me to take you to the emergency room?" I asked Joe as he tried, unsuccessfully, to rise from the side of the bed.

"No, it's just my—my back." He grimaced as he made a third and, this time, successful attempt to get to his feet. "Pulled it, I guess. It's happened before. It'll be fine by tonight. Or in a day or two."

"I knew you were sore last night, but you didn't seem crippled." He was hobbling toward the bathroom like an arthritic octogenarian.

"Well, I fell. A couple of times." He closed the bathroom door and I heard a tremendous groan. He must be trying to lower himself onto the toilet seat.

"Gee, I guess Gerry was right about the glide wax," I said under my breath.

"What was that?" came through the bathroom door.

"I guess I'd better call and cancel the snowmobile reservations," I said more loudly. "Between Maggie's leg and your back, it doesn't sound like a good idea."

"No, you should go," said Joe, coming back through the door, still moving like he needed a walker. "It's New Year's Eve.

Someone should have a little fun. Just because Mags and I are laid up, it doesn't mean you and Gerry have to stay inside and entertain us."

"Mags?"

He shrugged. "She said I could call her that."

Two hours later, Gerry and I were seated on two bright-red Yamaha "sleds," which, we had quickly learned, was how an experienced snowmobiler refers to the vehicles. Gerry revved his engine, and I knew today wasn't going to much resemble the Zen-like experience of cross-country skiing on a nearly silent trail. *Zen-like until my little swim*, I reminded myself.

During our twenty-minute lesson, our instructor had informed us that these were the new "quiet" models, with engine noise toned down after some wilderness areas had established noise regulations. You could have fooled me.

I had been afraid we would be traveling on tourist-crowded tracks, but the instructor assured us there were plenty of trails to go around, and gave us a map that rated trails based on grade, narrowness, and how heavily treed they were. After observing most of the riders heading toward wide, smooth trails that would not restrict their speed, we selected a slower trail that would take us to the top of a mountain.

When we finally pulled into a small clearing at the top, there was no one else around. Gerry cut his engine and I did the same.

"That was fantastic!" he said. "Don't you think that was fun?" He pushed back his goggles. His face was flushed from the cold and his eyes sparkled. Smiling from ear to ear, he looked like a little boy, and my heart did a flip-flop. I realized my smile was just as big.

"It was exhilarating," I laughed. "Kind of sexy, too, straddling that big engine."

"Naughty wench," he said, climbing off the sled. "Come on, let's check out the view."

An observation platform had been built at the edge of the ridge with guardrails and a plaque that displayed the elevation and other pertinent information. Like yesterday at the lake, it was peaceful, although the far-off sound of other snowmobile engines could occasionally be heard. The view was even more spectacular than the one from the deck.

"I'm glad we decided to come up here," said Gerry. "I thought about staying in and keeping Maggie company, but with Joe laid up too, I knew you wouldn't go out by yourself."

"And you knew that sitting around the cabin with Maggie and Joe might result in a homicide?" I laughed. "This weekend sure didn't turn out like I planned."

"No." Gerry's response was especially quiet, and I turned to see that his expression had become pensive.

"Is something wrong, Gerry?"

"No. Yes." He turned to me, his eyes intense. "Jules, I wish it was just you and me up here. I wish Joe and Maggie had never come." He pushed back his ski hat, then pulled it off entirely. "Hell, I wish I had never *met* Maggie and Joe."

"What are you talking about?" I think my heart had actually stopped.

"Oh, hell, Jules. It's all . . . I'm all mixed up." He ran his hand through the usually tame thatch of blond hair, tousled into curls by the winter wind. "I thought I knew what I wanted, and it all looked good on paper, but now . . ."

"Now *what*?" My heart hadn't stopped after all, because each beat felt like someone was squeezing my chest in a vise.

He didn't answer me. Instead, he grabbed me by both shoulders and kissed me.

My knees almost went out from under me. I was paralyzed for a moment, and then I was kissing him back. It was perfect, exactly right. His mouth was hot and sweet and tasted like . . . like home. I wrapped my arms around him and gave myself over to it completely.

I don't know who pulled away first, but it was good that one of us did because I seriously needed to breathe.

"Gerry," I said as soon as I could speak. "Jeez, Gerry, we never did *that* before. Not even . . . you know. Day before yesterday. Or last night."

"This is more intimate than day before yesterday." He brushed his lips along my temple and pulled me close to him. "Or last night. I've thought about kissing you before, but the time never seemed right."

"You have?" I was surprised. "But we've never thought about each other as anything but friends. At least not until . . ."

"Is that really true for you?" asked Gerry. "Because if I'm being one hundred percent honest with myself, it's not true for me." He linked his arm through mine, and we strolled along the fence that prevented visitors from getting too close to the edge of the ravine.

He went on. "And then yesterday, when you fell through the ice, my heart almost stopped. I realized that if I were to lose you, I'd . . . I don't know what I'd do. I can't imagine not seeing you, not being able to call you up and talk about my day. Jules . . ." He pulled me around to look at him. "Before this weekend, have you *really* never thought of me as something more than a friend? Never?"

I thought about it. Hard. "Well," I finally said, "I sometimes thought about it a little. Remember when you broke up with Sheila?" He nodded. "There were a few weeks there when we were spending almost all our time together. I wasn't really dating anyone, and I started to feel . . ." I trailed off, trying to remember how it had been. "Then, I called your condo one morning to tell you about something I'd read in the paper—a street fair I thought we might go to. And Maggie answered the phone."

I pulled back so he could see my face. "That's when I realized I'd been thinking of you as more than a friend. Because when I heard her voice, my stomach just knotted up into a giant ball. I went on autopilot, and managed to leave a message. Then I hung up and tried to tell myself that maybe she was a— a neighbor or some other female friend you had never mentioned. But I knew better."

"I remember that," he said softly. "Maggie asked a lot of questions about you when she gave me the message."

"Yeah, well, after that, I told myself I was being ridiculous, and that I'd been imagining there was more between us than friendship. And then I met Joe."

"I definitely remember *that*." He grinned, but it wasn't a particularly humorous expression. "I had been thinking that maybe being with Maggie wasn't such a good idea, and that I had missed a chance with you. And then suddenly there you were, head over heels with this tall, good-looking, rich guy. And you seemed so happy."

"I was working hard at it. Being happy, I mean." I looked up at him. "But it shouldn't be hard work to love someone. Should it?"

"No," he said. Then he kissed me again, and I realized it wasn't hard to love someone. Not at all.

"Jules," he said a moment later. "Jules, we have to make love."

"We already have. Twice, if you recall."

He shook his head. "No, we've had sex. Fantastic sex, but once two people have . . . have realized they love each other," he paused, as if savoring what he had just said. "Once that happens, it's different. Jules, I am dying to make love to you."

"I . . . me, too. But . . ." The edges of harsh reality threatened to burst my happy bubble. "Where?"

Therein lay the problem. We had a lovely, warm cabin, complete with two king-sized beds, an enormous fireplace, a hot tub, and a bearskin rug—and, unfortunately, Joe and Maggie.

Gerry groaned. "Where, indeed." He hugged me, and we both laughed.

"Look, Gerry, as much as I hate to say it, I think we have to break up with Joe and Maggie before we can make love. I mean, I would happily risk frostbite and jump you right here, but it would be wrong."

"And it wasn't wrong to fuck in the hot tub two days ago? Or to rut like wild moose last night?" He didn't really sound annoyed.

"Not as wrong as this would be. Like you said, that was just sex. This would be a breach of something or other."

He sighed. "Yeah. Yes, I guess it would be." He looked out at the view again, and then back to me. "But I'm kissing you again, first."

He did—right there on the mountain, and again at the snowmobile rental shop, and again in the Range Rover when we pulled up in front of the cabin, as we marshaled our courage for what lay ahead.

"Isn't there some special place in hell reserved for people who break up with their lovers on holidays?" I tried to keep my tone light, but dread was beginning to circle my stomach like a restless animal.

"If there is, at least we'll be there together. Come on, darling, one last kiss for luck."

It was sure difficult to feel guilty when Gerry kissed me.

"Ready?" he asked as he withdrew his lips.

"No. But let's do it." I got out of the car and together we walked unenthusiastically to the door. "We haven't planned what to say."

"Probably better to just take it as it comes," he said, and opened the door. Trance music blared out, incongruous with the rustic surroundings.

"Joe?" I called, although the music drowned my words. "Where are . . ." I stopped, frozen in my tracks.

"Jules, what—" Gerry's words came to an abrupt halt when he saw what had stopped me.

Maggie lay on the bearskin rug, right where we'd been the night before, naked except for the cast on her ankle and some kind of fur bra. Her ass was propped up with one of the sofa pillows, her legs were splayed, and Joe was between them, one hand on each tanned thigh and his faced buried in the cleft of her pussy. Which, I couldn't help but notice, was completely shaved.

Gerry walked over and switched off the stereo. Maggie stiffened, and Joe lifted his head, his eyes round.

I took one look at his face and started to laugh. He looked exactly like a little kid who had been caught doing something very, very naughty. His expression darkened. As Maggie reached around frantically for something to cover herself, he got to his feet. He was wearing a pair of silk boxer shorts that I had bought for him, and was sporting a rapidly vanishing hard-on.

"What's so funny?" he said. He sounded pissed, which struck me as even funnier.

I tried to speak, but only managed to point and squeak. "You . . . her . . . that stupid r-rug . . ." Hysterics overcame me and I collapsed onto the facing sofa. Maggie was on her knees now, crawling around bare-assed and looking for something. Next to the bear's head, I spotted the lighter-colored fur of the thong that matched her bra and tried to point it out to her, but she found it herself and flipped over to shimmy into it.

Gerry was standing with his arms folded, looking more bemused than angry. "I suppose we can stop feeling guilty about leaving you two to your own devices."

"It's *your* fault," said Maggie, who had reached her crutches and was pulling herself up into a standing position. "You invited me to this . . . this *dump* and then spent the whole weekend with *her*." She used one crutch to point accusingly at me.

"I wish I *had* spent the whole weekend with her," said Gerry. "It would have been a good deal more enjoyable." He seemed to notice her outfit for the first time. "Good God, Maggie, do you own *anything* an animal didn't have to die for?"

"Just what the hell is that supposed to mean?" thundered Joe. "You think you two would have had a better time without us, is that it?"

"I'll hand it to you, Joe, you have balls," I managed between gasps. "We walk in and find you with your tongue in Maggie's cunt—" Joe winced at the harshness of the word, "and *you* get mad at *us*. That's rich."

"We didn't think you'd be back so soon," said Maggie, who had maneuvered herself onto the other couch. She pulled up the Indian-print throw to cover herself. "You said you'd be gone all day."

"Oh, well, that makes it perfectly all right," said Gerry. "I suppose if we'd arrived an hour later, you would both have behaved as if nothing had happened."

I winced. Hadn't he and I done just that—twice?

"Actually," said Joe, "I've already called for the limousine. Between Maggie's ankle and my back, and being a million miles from civilization, neither of us wanted to spend another night up here, let alone New Year's Eve. We called and moved our flights to this evening."

"We were going to leave a note," said Maggie, sounding like a petulant child. "We already packed."

"Your back seems to be okay now, Joe," I said. I wasn't feeling angry at all, but I couldn't resist twisting the knife just a little. "Or at least it was okay while you had your head between Maggie's legs." The last vestige of the hard-on disappeared.

"Should we get out and wave good-bye?"

Gerry and I were back in the hot tub. I had thought it would be a good idea to stay out of the way while Joe and Maggie cleared out and, for one reason or another, we still hadn't seen the sunset from the west-facing deck. We had heard the limo pull into the drive a few minutes before, followed by the sound of slamming doors and the trunk.

"Nah," I replied. "We'd miss the last of the sunset. And I still have half a drink."

We hadn't bothered with bathing suits this time—we just walked out and stripped, then climbed naked into the tub. I had no idea what Maggie and Joe thought of this—we didn't look back, and neither of them came outside. They hadn't left yet, though. I could still faintly hear the rumbling of the limousine's big engine.

"I want to ask you something, Gerry." We weren't touching above the water, but had been idly playing footsie while we sipped our drinks.

"Shoot."

"Do you prefer shaved pussies? Because mine isn't. It's neatly trimmed, but not hairless."

"I caught a couple of glimpses," he replied, then grinned. "I don't mind a little hair in my pie."

I splashed him and he ducked his head, holding his drink out of the way. I heard two successive car-door slams, then the rev of the engine as the limo pulled away.

"Gee," I said. "I guess they aren't going to say good-bye." I gazed out at the horizon. "Look—it's almost gone." A tiny wedge of the sun appeared above the outline of the mountains, then vanished.

"It's official," said Gerry. He drained his glass, then stood up. "Come into the cabin, Jules. It is now morally, ethically, and legally possible for us to make love." He hoisted himself onto the deck and held out a hand to me. "Shall we start in the shower?"

As I came out of the water, I landed in his arms. The cold breeze against my wet body made me shiver, but not as much as feeling his body, solid and right, pressed against me. I tilted my face and his lips found mine, and I shuddered as another of those soul-wrenching kisses pulled me out of time. This time, I drew away first.

"If we don't get inside," I said, "you are going to freeze off some body parts. And you are going to need all of them."

"Sounds good." We left our clothes on the deck and ran into the cabin and up the stairs naked. "Here, let's shower in my bathroom. It's enormous."

"It certainly is," I said, not talking about the shower. He was already erect, and I couldn't wait to get my hands on his incredible cock again. Not just my hands.

The shower had jets on three walls, and we turned them all on. We were barely inside when we were kissing again, water washing over us from all directions like warm rain. Gerry pulled me against him and I felt his hands slide down and around my ass. There was a shelf around the edge of the stall and he lifted me up so I rested against it. The fingers from one of his hands slipped under my thigh and started to tease my clit.

"You're slippery," he said around a kiss. He demonstrated by sliding a finger inside me. I moaned. "Oh, you like that?" He moved the finger in and out, then found my clit and squeezed it lightly between his thumb and forefinger.

"Oh!" I exclaimed. "That feels so—"

"Good?" he inquired. The fingers of his other hand found the crack in my ass, and rocked me forward. "How about this?" One of his fingers slid into my anus.

"Ayeee!" I squealed a little. "How did you—" I couldn't talk. He was moving the fingers of both hands in concert—teasing my ass and clit at the same time, sliding in and out.

"How did I know you'd like to feel something in your ass?" He nibbled on my ear and his hands continued to move. "I didn't. I just fantasized that you might." He withdrew the hand in front and crouched before me. "But I didn't get that hair pie yet!"

So saying, he spread my legs and plunged his tongue between the lips of my cunt. Simultaneously, he pushed the teasing finger deep into my ass. I shrieked with pleasure, a sudden orgasm wracking my body. He licked and probed and my orgasm went on and on, until I started to laugh between cries.

"What's so funny?" He paused to look up at me.

"The limo hasn't even reached the bottom of the hill, and

I've already had an orgasm. Ohhh!" Gerry was back on his feet, lifting my ass with his finger still inside it.

"One of many, darling. Just one of many." He lifted me up and set the head of his cock where his tongue had been. "You're a tall girl. Let's see if I can carry you." He pulled me down so that he slid all the way inside me, and I wrapped my legs around him. "Ahhh, there we go, love." He kissed me deeply, pressing me against the side of the shower. Then, his cock still deep within me, he turned and pushed the shower door open and carried me to the bed.

It was an old-fashioned, four-poster, and he didn't need to crouch down to drive into me. "Fuck me," I panted, and he obliged. Within moments, I was in the throes of another orgasm. "Oh God, I'm coming again!"

To my dismay, he withdrew abruptly. "Turn over," he said huskily. "I want to see that magnificent ass of yours." I didn't argue.

Again, he plunged his enormous cock into me. In this position it felt even bigger, but I was so wet and slick that it slid in and out like he was steel and I was warm Jell-O. I wanted more—more friction, more pressure.

"Gerry," I gasped, "Do you want to—to take me—oooh!"

"Take you in the ass?" he asked, almost as breathless as me. "God, yes. But if I do, I'm going to come fast and hard."

"Then hurry!" I panted. "Hurry."

He pulled his cock out and I felt the head pressing against my anus. It felt impossibly big, and I willed my muscles to relinquish their tight grip and relax. He must have felt the resistance, because he breathed, "Are you sure?"

"Yes, I'm sure. Just go"—gasp—"slow and steady"—gasp—"and I'll let you in."

The pressure increased, and for a moment I thought I was going to have to tell him to stop, but then there was an easing, a relaxation of the tight muscles, and I could feel him sliding into me. "OOOOH!" I screamed. He started to move forward and then to slide backward—gradually, not letting his entire length in. *Could* his entire length fit into me? I rocked back and forth, and he matched my rhythm. With each stroke, he pushed a little farther. "Ah, ah, ah, ahhhhh." Yet another orgasm rocked me.

"Can't . . . hold . . . back . . . much longer," he said, and I could tell his throat was constricted with the effort.

"Then don't," I managed to wheeze, and he plunged all the way into me.

Starbursts filled my head and I heard screaming. It was me, I realized. No, it was Gerry. It was both of us, and our bodies bucked and writhed and then I felt the great, hot jet of his come shooting into me like it was expelled from a fire hose. I gripped one of the big bedposts and hung on as he clung to my back, his face pressed between my shoulder blades.

"Jules," he gasped, "Oh my God, Jules." He withdrew, and we collapsed in the middle of the bed, spoon-fashion.

It took a long time for our breathing to return to normal, and then Gerry started to chuckle.

"What," I asked, echoing his question in the shower, "is so funny?"

"You stupid cow," he said. "We could have been doing this for the last five years."

"Who are you calling a cow?" I sat up and looked for a pillow, then stuffed it over his face. He kicked his legs in mock suffocation, and I removed it and planted a kiss on his lips. He grabbed my face in both hands and kissed me, long and soulfully. When he was done, I snuggled up happily next to him.

"I have an idea," I said.

"Oh really? One I'll like?" He did the eyebrow wiggle and my heart gave a nearly audible throb. *How long have I been in love with him?* I wondered.

"Maybe. I was just thinking. Maggie and Joe called and changed their flight reservations, right?"

"Right."

"So, we could do the same thing. I mean, the cabin is mine until next Friday, if I want it. I had only booked the weekend because I knew Joe couldn't take the whole week off from work. But I have plenty of vacation time accumulated."

"And I *am* self-employed," he replied.

"So . . . you'll do it?"

He propped himself on one elbow and looked at me. "Julie, darling, I can't think of anything better than to spend the week up here, just the two of us."

I sat up, excited. "Excellent. There's still so much we haven't done! Like snowboarding and hiking and . . ."

"And sixty-nine and mutual masturbation . . ."

I fell back against the pillows, laughing. "We'll find a way to work everything in." I sighed contentedly.

"Jules?" Gerry's hand reached up to stroke my breast.

"Yes?"

"Will you teach me how to make a snowman?"

I laughed again. "Of course. Let's make one—no, two—that are anatomically correct and leave them for whoever rents the cabin next week."

Suddenly, he sat up, looking around the room. "What time is it?"

I located the clock on the dresser opposite. "It's almost seven. Why?"

"I have just over five hours left to make love to you this calendar year. Now, assuming we want to have a simultaneous orgasm precisely at midnight . . ."

"We do?"

"We do. Which means we both need to reserve our stamina. *But*, considering how long I've waited to make love to you, I'm quite sure we can still do it one more time now, and, with your complete cooperation, of course, I'll still have sufficient recovery time before the big event."

I snorted. "Pretty sure of yourself, aren't you?"

He pulled me close. "No, I'm pretty sure of *us.*"

We timed everything perfectly. It was one of those magical evenings when nothing could go wrong—when the universe had no choice but to bend to our will. We made love again, gently this time, and rested for a while in each other's arms before rousing ourselves to make dinner.

The steaks were perfect, the wine delicious. Even cleaning up the kitchen was fun.

About eleven, I found myself staring out the glass door. "Gerry, before we go back downstairs, there's something I want to do."

He came up and stood behind me, slipping his arms around my waist and laying his chin on my shoulder. "What's that, Jules?"

"I want to go outside and look at the stars. You can't really see them in Miami, but we're a long way from a city. I'll bet there are millions."

He let go of me and retrieved our parkas from the hall closet. "Okay, but let's not wander too far. Remember—midnight exactly."

"I won't forget."

We slipped out onto the deck and, even though we were far from where anyone could hear us, we kept silent as though through an unspoken agreement. The moon had not yet risen, and the stars were so thick they almost seemed to blend together. For the first time, I understood what was meant by the "Milky Way."

Gerry broke the silence, his voice low and tinged with awe. "You're wrong, Jules, there aren't millions. There have to be billions. I don't think I've ever seen them so bright."

"I know I haven't." I lowered my chin to look at him. Even with no moon, I could see his face clearly in starlight reflecting off snow. "I think I was blind, before. But I can see now."

His gaze lowered to meet mine, and I knew he had perceived my meaning. "So can I." He took my hand. "Come on, darling, it's time to go inside. We have champagne to open and candles to light."

I felt myself smiling. "Let the countdown begin!"

Ten . . . nine . . . eight . . .

"Aaaah!" I moaned. We'd left the television on so we could hear the countdown, but neither of us had glanced at it. We were much too busy.

Seven . . . six . . . five . . .

"Ah, God, Jules." Gerry spoke into my neck. He was sitting on the bed, with me on his lap and impaled deeply by his cock, my legs wrapped around his back as he lifted me up and down, up and down.

"Almost, Gerry. Just . . . aaaahhh!" The inside of my pussy was thrumming at about twice the rate of the countdown. I wasn't going to make it.

Four . . . three . . .

"Now, Jules! *Now!*" I felt his cock give a great throb and suddenly I was right there with him, about to come.

Two . . . ONE . . .

My orgasm burst like the popping of a champagne cork, and I felt Gerry's come jet into me like the froth from a shaken bottle. I threw back my head to scream, but my mouth was covered by his.

"*Happy New Year!*" Cheers erupted from the television, as our kiss and my orgasm went on and on. Finally, at about the time the TV revelers were starting the second verse of *Auld Lang Syne,* he gently broke away.

"Happy New Year, darling." This time, the word didn't sound like something he would call his mother.

"Happy New Year, Gerry."

"It's going to be, you know. A very happy new year." He lay down against the pillows and pulled me onto his shoulder. I snuggled there, contentedly.

"Let's spend all our New Year's Eves exactly like this. And Valentine's Day, and Presidents' Day, and Saint Patrick's Day . . ."

"Okay. Oh, and Jules?"

"Yes?"

"Did I mention that I'm in love with you?"

My heart leaped. "Not in so many words."

"Oh. Well, I'm in love with you."

I sat back up. I could feel tears welling in my eyes. I reached over and pushed the hair out of his forehead. His smile was serene. "I'm in love with you too, Gerry."

"About bloody time." He pulled me down for a kiss.

Oh, yes. About bloody time.

Virginia Reede

VIRGINIA REEDE likes to say it's easier to list the jobs she *hasn't* tried. From lifeguard to lounge singer, bartender to bill collector, door-to-door salesperson to corporate business analyst—Virginia has been there and done that. Then, she decided that what she *really* wanted to be was a writer. After fifteen years in Southern California and seven in Miami, Virginia has recently returned to the lakeside cottage in Connecticut where she spent her childhood summers.

You may contact Virginia through her website: http://www.virginiareede.com.

Part 4

Coming on Strong

DENISE ROSSETTI

Heck, it wasn't supposed to be this hard. Collect one elderly Australian from the airport and drive him to his hotel.

Except. . . . Where *was* Professor Jones?

From behind the security wall of toughened glass, Gina peered at the baggage/customs area. An elderly couple stood quietly with their shoulders touching, so obviously *together*. Nope, the man she was looking for would be alone. She skipped the families with small children and the phalanx of Japanese businessmen.

Lord, it was a jungle down there. She had to smile. The bags and suitcases circulating on the endless loop of the carousel looked lumpy and somehow vulnerable, while the passengers milled and prowled like weary lions at the end of a long day on the veldt, almost too tired to pounce, but too hungry not to.

Her gaze moved on. Uh-huh, there were more professor prospects near the wall.

Whoa.

A lean, compact-looking man in jeans and a battered leather jacket bent his head attentively as he spoke with a frail, elderly woman. She laid a veined hand on his strong forearm and smiled up into his face. Lucky Grandma.

A fiery tingle ran up the side of Gina's neck, just under the skin. Irritably, she tugged at the turned-up collar of her sweatshirt. Not now, dammit! She pulled in a breath, concentrating fiercely—then another and another, until the heat subsided. She had a scarf in her bag as a last resort, but she hated having to use it to conceal her, her . . . The train of thought hitched on the word, as it always did.

Her deformity? God, she *hated* the word! Her . . . disability. She could control the problem with the strength of her will, the power of her mind. That she *would* control.

Fine. Good. Casually, she ran exploring fingertips along her jaw and around to the nape of her neck. Cool, nothing but cool, smooth skin.

Forget Grandson Guy.

She blew out a gusty breath and shook her head. Back to her professor.

Luc had called to ask the favor, and there wasn't much she wouldn't do for the big cousin she'd adored as a child. Professor Jones was coming to Miami all the way from Down Under for Luc's wedding on New Year's Day. Wasn't that nice? Especially at his age.

"How will I know him?" she'd asked Luc when he called.

"The Sydney flight, the day after Boxing Day? It's sure to be packed," rumbled Luc. "Make one of those signs and hold it up. Like a limousine driver."

"Okay." She dug out her PDA. "What's his full name?"

A chuckle. "Sam Jones, but we called him Indy at college."

"*Indy*? As in Indiana? An Australian? But why?"

His voice had a grin in it. "You'll see." Above the background hum of traffic at Luc's end, she heard Maeve's laugh, contralto-clear. Gorgeous, redheaded Maeve, Luc's fiancée.

"He looks like Harrison Ford?"

"It's . . . joke . . . blue eyes . . . shorter than me . . ."

Yeah, that figured. Most of the world was shorter than Luc, including the Hulk. "Luc? Luc, you're breaking up!"

" . . . glasses . . . wire rims . . ."

"Speak up!"

" . . . poor old prof . . . gave him hell . . . lectures . . ."

"*Luc!*"

" . . . north . . . tunnel . . . you later, honey . . ." The connection cut out.

Recalled to the present, Gina extracted the sign from her bag and surveyed it doubtfully. "INDIANA JONES," it said, printed in huge, square capitals with a red permanent marker. With a sigh, she raised it to chest level and stepped out of the shadows.

Grandson Guy waded in and snaffled a red duffel bag for Grandma. He followed that up with two big black suitcases and a small one, all without any discernable fuss or effort. He loaded the lot onto a trolley, and settled a battered camera bag and a laptop case on his hip. Then he put an arm around the old lady and shepherded her toward the waiting customs officers.

With an effort of will, Gina tore her eyes from the pair. Ah, that must be Professor Jones at last, emerging from the security area, all gray-haired and distinguished—every inch the scholar. Gina nodded and smiled in the man's direction, but he frowned and glanced away, avoiding her eye. She felt the flush stain her cheeks. Damn!

A moment later, Grandson Guy sauntered into sight, pushing the trolley, and shortening his long strides to match Grandma's hobbling gait. He was taller than she'd first thought, but he moved with such easy grace that the size of him had escaped her. The old lady was chatting away, her lined face animated with pleasure.

Reaching the exit doors, Grandson Guy glanced over his shoulder. His eyes met Gina's, taking in her face, the sign, and her chest in a single comprehensive glance. One corner of his mouth tipped up and he raised his forefinger in a casual salute. Bending, he murmured something into Grandma's ear. A peck on the cheek, and he'd grabbed the red duffel and was striding back into the building, directly toward her.

The sign dropped from Gina's nerveless fingers. Ignoring it, she ripped open her bag and fumbled for her scarf.

Sam's lips quirked. Trust Luc to send a female. God, it was going to be good to see the big bastard again. So who was this? Not Maeve. Luc had e-mailed photos.

This woman was dark-haired and full-figured, lush even, though . . . he frowned as he took in the baggy sweatshirt that came almost to her knees, the jeans, and sneakers. At first glance, she'd registered so high on his internal fuck-o-meter that he'd damn near heard the hammer hit the bell. But now. . .

He wasn't particularly proud of the fuck-o-meter, but shit, he was male, wasn't he? Adam had the prototype in the Garden of Eden, he'd bet his balls on it. The snake probably gave it to him, disguised as an apple. Bloody snakes . . .

He flexed his toes inside his snakeskin boots and smiled down at the woman. "G'day," he said, offering his hand. "Sam Jones."

She hesitated, then reached out and brushed his palm with hers. "Georgina McBride. I'm Luc's cousin."

Before she could retreat, he grasped her fingers in his, squeezed once firmly, and let go. "Yes," he said slowly, making no bones about examining her features, one by one. Why was she so tense? "You have the look of him." She had his friend's broad Slavic cheekbones and fierce hazel eyes, but feminized in a delightfully kittenish way.

"Where are your glasses?" she asked abruptly.

"In my pocket. Only need 'em for reading." He tilted his head. "Why?"

"You're not a professor?"

He patted the camera bag. "Photographer. Why?"

"So that wasn't your grandmother?" The tension increased. One hand crept up to clutch at the scarf around her neck.

Strange girl. "Nah, she just needed a hand to the cab rank, poor old duck."

Georgina shut her eyes and shook her head, a torrent of dark curls bouncing on her shoulders and swinging forward over her cheeks. "Idiot!" she muttered, but the way she spoke gave the word a strange reverberation. He didn't think she meant him.

"Where's your luggage?" she asked.

Sam hefted the duffel. "I travel light." As they walked toward the exit, he added, "I'll rent a tux for the wedding."

For some reason, that seemed to annoy her. She pressed her lips together and increased the pace. Strolling beside her, Sam enjoyed the hint of a jiggle beneath the sweatshirt—two perfect handfuls and a demi-cup bra, if he wasn't mistaken.

She shot him a sideways glance as they negotiated the parking lot. "Better get your hair trimmed while you're at it."

Prickly little thing. Sam raked a hand through his hair, letting the shaggy ends drop against his collar. "I've been out in the bush," he said. "Got back and hopped straight on the plane.

What's wrong with my bloody hair?" he demanded, testing her. How would she react? She was kind of cute, all flushed and ruffled, though he was damned if he could work out what was setting her off.

To his delight, the color rose in her face, a wave running up under the clear skin of her cheek, though she didn't answer. His interest sharpened. Sam counted himself a patient, observant man. He had to be, in his line of business. Wildlife photography was all about stealth, waits so long they numbed the brain as well as the backside, alert to a rustle in the grass, the sound of the birds, or a change in the wind.

The hunt.

This one was as tense, as wary, as any shy bush creature— poised to flee. The instinctive response hit him low in the gut, the predator's urge to slam down a big paw, devour the struggling prey.

But that would never do. He rasped a hand over the stubble on his cheek. It plain wasn't right. Luc would kill him for a start, not that he couldn't handle anything the big bloke could dish out. A grin tugged his lips. The three years he'd spent at college in the States, earning his journalism degree, he'd been on a Track and Field scholarship. Luc would have to catch him first.

Sam waited patiently as Georgina came to a halt by a small red sedan and rummaged in the cavernous depths of her bag. Something was decidedly wrong with Luc's little cousin. The clothes were protective camouflage; that much was obvious. The sweatshirt made her look blocky, as though she didn't have a waist, but she did—a set of sweet, plump curves. When she finally fumbled the door open and swung around to toss her bag onto the backseat, her shirt rode up, exposing a length of slim thigh, and pulling the baggy jeans taut in a decidedly pleasing way over the rounded curve of hip and buttock.

Intriguing. Very.

Clenching her jaw, Gina jammed the key in the ignition. Her heart hammered. She could feel the frantic pulse tripping in her throat, and—damn it all to hell—here came the burning sensation, sliding around her rib cage and under her bra to cradle her breasts. The heat made her nipples stiffen, pushing against the filmy fabric. Somehow, Sam Jones took up all the psychic space in the car and there was none left for her. Every time she breathed in, she inhaled Essence of Man, a blend of leather, warm skin, and healthy male.

This was stupid—some kind of aberrant reaction. He had to be pumping out more pheromones than a cologne factory. Talk about sex appeal. No wonder they'd christened him Indy at college! Take that indifference to his own good looks, combine it with the rugged Aussie persona, and every female freshman would have fallen at his feet.

Well, she simply wouldn't permit herself to be affected, that's all.

The only way to keep her peculiar problem under control was to banish all excitement from her existence—zilch, zip, nada. Boring job, boring clothes, boring existence. It was why she did her yoga postures every morning without fail. The blessed calm saved her sanity and made the loneliness bearable. Lowering the window, she filled her lungs—twice, three times. Oh, yes, she could do this.

On a burst of concentration, she managed to say, coolly enough, "Luc's got a houseful of relatives. He said to call him from the hotel." She indicated the glove box with her chin. "There are tourist brochures with information in there."

"Thanks." He leaned forward to open the compartment, shoving a lock of hair out of his eyes with an irritated grunt.

He'd wanted to know what was wrong with his hair. Sheesh! Everything about him was wrong, that's what! Because he was perfect.

From the long, powerful thighs encased in snug denim, to the shadow of stubble on his hard cheek, he'd been designed by a cruel god to torment her.

No, not a god—a goddess, and a horny one at that.

She supposed his hair was just brown, but the kind of brown the sun can't resist. Streaked with blond, it curled over his ears and flopped over his forehead.

Her trembling fingers closed hard on the wheel as she set the car in motion.

Everything about him was more than it seemed. Luc had said his eyes were blue, which was a purely male description—functional, but barely adequate. Indoors they'd been a cool blue-gray, but in the weak winter sun, they shone such an intense blue-green that she hardly dared to look him full in the face.

Clothe him in the severity of a tuxedo, and he'd be devastating. She'd die.

The sooner she unloaded him the better—twenty minutes max of yoga breathing to get to the hotel. Starting now.

Steadying, she slowed to pay the parking attendant, but a long arm in brown leather stretched across her chest and over the upper swell of her breasts. Sam leaned right into her shoulder, his breath hot on her cheek. "Sorry, love," he murmured, as he handed a folded note past her. "My shout. Least I can do."

Without haste, he withdrew. Gina turned to stare. Her breasts tingled. "Shout?" she asked weakly. "Why do you want to shout?"

For the first time, Sam grinned, the lines at the corners of his eyes crinkling attractively. "Aussie slang. Means it's my turn to pay. As in, 'I'll shout you a beer.' Okay?"

"Oh."

"Relax, Georgina." Reaching out, he wound one long finger in the curl falling over her shoulder, and tugged it gently. "I don't bite."

I might. "It's Gina."

He chuckled. "Gina, I owe you a beer. At the first opportunity. All right?"

She cast him a narrow-eyed glance. So much laid-back charm was positively blinding. Sam Jones projected an air of complete masculine confidence; the slow, cheerful drawl and the set of his broad shoulders suggested he could fix anything, solve any problem. She'd bet he was terrific at repairing engines with rubber bands and bits of chewing gum, not to mention rescuing kittens from tall trees and soothing fractious infants. She already knew he was a dab hand at little old ladies.

God, what a dangerous man!

"Tell me how you met Luc," she said, desperate for a diversion.

Obligingly, he settled back, his eyes half-closing with memory. His voice washed over her like a soothing balm. He was a born storyteller, Sam Jones, but he didn't waste words. In a few laconic sentences, he drew a picture of a wide-eyed kid from the bush on his first real adventure away from home. His humor was self-deprecating, and so bone-dry he kept her in a constant bubble of amusement.

As she navigated the downtown traffic, a smile on her lips, she realized with a sense of wonder what he'd accomplished. First he'd unsettled her, yes, but then he'd soothed her down. Beneath her skin, the heat still simmered, but it was stimulating now, rather than unbearable. Energy coursed through her. She felt alert, poised, ready for anything. Pulling up at a red light, she flicked Sam a sideways glance only to find him stifling a jaw-cracking yawn.

Unabashed, he grinned, stretching his arms behind his head to press his palms against the car roof and roll his shoulders. The action made his jacket fall open and his hips surge up-ward, but she refused to look at the denim that pulled tight across his thighs, the healthy bulge behind his fly. "Sorry, darl. Nothing to do with the company." Another yawn. "I'd kill for eight hours horizontal, a shower, and a shave. In that order."

"It's only another couple of blocks. Don't go to sleep yet. What about football? Were you on the team like Luc?"

"Nah. The gear drove me crazy, especially the helmet." He shuddered theatrically. "Played backup quarterback for half a season though. Luc and the other linebackers scared me shitless."

"Somehow, I doubt that." Gina smiled. "What was the real reason?"

"Track coach said if I got damaged, he'd wait till they fixed me up, then kill me himself. Couldn't risk it."

"Really?" She swung the car into the forecourt of the modest hotel. "Here we are."

"Well, no, he was a good bloke." Sam unbuckled his seat belt. "And his missus made a mean pot roast. They used to have me over for Sunday lunch."

Without warning, he swiveled, leaning between the seats to snag his camera bag and laptop from the back. His shoulder brushed Gina's, and his hair whispered past her cheek. Inadvertently, she inhaled, filling her lungs with the unique smell the most primitive part of her brain already associated with Sam Jones.

Gina stiffened as a tingling wave surged up her spine and soft, dark heat bloomed in her pelvis. Gritting her teeth, she pressed her thighs together against the sweet, liquid ache, while heat slid over her rib cage and her breasts like the fiery clasp of hard, masculine palms.

Sam patted her knee as if he'd been doing it all his life, and she nearly bit her tongue. "Hang on a sec." In the unruffled way that characterized all he did, he retrieved his duffel bag from the trunk and came around to the driver's side. Gina forced a smile and waggled her fingers in a weak little wave, but she didn't lower the window. His brows drew together in a frown and he rapped sharply, insisting.

Reluctantly, she pressed the button and the glass slid down. Immediately, Sam leaned into the car, his face so close she could see the stubble on his cheek; she could have turned her head and brushed her lips over it, discovered whether it was abrasive or silky.

"Bye, then." Staring straight ahead, she half-raised her hand from the wheel, then let it drop.

"Thanks, Gina. For everything." His breath stirred her hair. "Next time, it's my shout, remember?"

He took half a dozen steps toward the hotel while she watched out of the corner of her eye. The quintessential athlete—the broad back tapering to a trim waist, the taut ass flexing against faded denim. Helpless against her hormones, she imagined him naked, knowing whose body she'd see in her mind's eye as she eased a vibrator deep into her aching, empty flesh. Abruptly, her fantasy spun on his heel and came striding back toward the car. Caught staring, Gina shut her mouth with a snap, feeling the warm color flood over her cheeks. Her skin drew tight and hot, too small for her body.

Control, control. But Sam had moved so quickly, he was on her before she could do more than gulp for air. Heck, she must look like a goldfish in a face-off with the family cat.

He dropped the bag to brace his forearms on the door.

Clutching the wheel with both hands, she met his gaze full-on for the first time. The ocean—that was it—he had ocean eyes, as beautiful and changeable as the sea. Right now, they sparkled like the high, reaching curve of a surfer's favorite wave in the noonday sun.

She swallowed.

"It's not that bad, you know," he said gently.

"What isn't?" she whispered through numb lips.

"Whatever it is that's got you in such a grip," he shrugged, "or whatever you're holding onto."

Yes it is. She was almost sure she hadn't spoken aloud—almost.

But Sam Jones had to be a mind reader because he grunted a negative, one side of his mouth quirking.

"I'm fine." She cleared her throat and said with more emphasis, "Fine." No one could help her. *No one.*

Sam's smile disappeared. "Mind my own bloody business, in other words."

Gina raised her chin and held his eye. "That's right." She slammed her palm on the window control. "See you at the wedding." *But not if I see you first.*

He had to jerk backward or risk decapitation. Irritation flashed across his face. Then he shrugged, shot her a long considering look, and walked out of her life and into the hotel.

Sweet Jesus! Gina slumped, resting her forehead between the fists that gripped the wheel. Less than an hour in his company, and Sam Jones had *seen* more about her than anyone in her life—more than her father, more than Luc.

Her skin still burned; a spot on her neck was particularly annoying. Grumbling, Gina slipped the stick shift into gear and slid the fingers of her other hand under the scarf to scratch. The hot, stretchy sensation traveled to the difficult spot between her shoulder blades. Setting the hand brake, she wriggled against the back of the seat, cursing.

Between one breath and the next, her guts congealed into a solid, icy ball of apprehension. Tears rose in her eyes.

No. Oh, no. Please, please not now.

She'd thought she had at least another two months, thought she'd be safe for the wedding. Shit! She glared at the gold lettering on the hotel doors. The cause of her current troubles would be signing the register, grinning that come-to-bed grin at the woman on the desk, heading upstairs. He'd drop his bag the moment the door closed behind him, shrug out of his jacket, rip the shirt off over his head—

Double, triple shit!

His presence had brought it on early—the part of her problem she loathed more than any other.

The molt. She'd never been able to think of another word for it.

Gina clamped her jaw shut, suppressing the urge to let loose a bloodcurdling roar of rage. The wheel creaked under the merciless strength of her fingers. One at a time, she loosened them. How could she explain it to a mechanic—a crushed steering wheel inside an undamaged car?

There'd be two or three days of that prickling sensation; it made her so insanely sensitive that the movement of air over her skin became a sensual torture she could barely withstand. Inexorably, the pattern would tighten its grip, ramping up her discomfort, her arousal, until she couldn't see straight for wanting.

It hadn't really been difficult to deal with until she'd reached puberty, but the moment her breasts had begun to blossom, the moment she'd glanced at Tommy O'Hara from under her lashes and found him looking back, she'd had a battle on her hands—a fight to the death with her own nature.

Adrenaline did it, every time. She'd learned there was a definite threshold of stimulation. If she exceeded it, the symptoms appeared—the rash that wasn't a rash, first on the sides of her neck, then moving down over her ribs, cupping the undersides of her breasts like some beautiful, bizarre corset. Sometimes though, temptation became overwhelming and she'd abandon her discipline. Her baser self would whisper, *You're all alone, Gina. Just this once, it's just this once . . .*

Naked before the mirror, she'd rasp her thumbs over rosy-brown nipples till they stood proud and long. Then she'd pull a chair up close so she could sit and spread her thighs. With her favorite vibrator, she'd tease the lips of her sex, watching the milky dew pearl and spread, inserting just the tip, delaying the moment before penetration until her clit peeped out of its hood, hard and pink, like a tiny strawberry.

With every stroke, every panting breath, the sensation of being encased in a burning net of fire increased, but it was never painful, only pleasurable. She'd watch the woman in the mirror through eyes glazed with urgency, the regular, overlapping pattern blooming on her body, in shades of lavender deepening to a purple so dark it was spiced with burnished green-bronze.

Each section was about the size of her thumbnail—for all the world, like scales shining under her smooth flesh.

If only she had the nerve to pass it off as a tattoo. But who had a tattoo that came and went, that shimmered soft and lustrous *beneath* the skin?

No, Mom had been right.

It was weird. They'd say she was sick; they'd poke and probe, slice and cut. The child inside the woman shuddered with terror. Perhaps they'd decide it was psychosomatic—all in her mind—and give her drugs, numb her out. She'd wake up somewhere with padded walls, her brain foggy and pliant.

Because that wasn't all, not by a long chalk.

She had to be careful when she climaxed, so careful not to moan, not to cry out. Because if she did, the sound emerged as a bass reverberation deep in her chest, a muted roar no man could have bettered.

Blinking furiously, Gina gripped the steering wheel. *Get over the pity party, just get over it.* Unseeing, she gazed at the palm trees whipping in the wind.

The first time had been the worst. It had happened out of the blue, and she'd gone so crazy she'd practically raped Tommy O'Hara in the backseat of his old junk car after their prom.

Luckily, his shock had morphed almost instantly into a young man's eager compliance. He'd done the best he could, poor Tom, but his hands had shaken uncontrollably as he drove her home afterward. He'd barely been able to keep up, and she'd been the virgin. Oh, God!

She squeezed her eyes shut, wrestling with the memory. Because what she'd done to Tom had only been the beginning . . .

When she'd let herself into the apartment that night, everything had been dim and quiet, her father out of town at yet another business conference. Trembling, she'd locked herself in the bathroom, kicked off the heels that hurt her feet, and wriggled out of the gown she'd chosen all by herself. Thinking back now, she winced at the glitter, the frills, the whole wedding-cake effect, but Mom had been gone more than ten years. She wasn't coming back from God knew where to shop and giggle with her only child, to fuss over her on the most important night of her life—or to help her cope with a father more defined by his absence than his presence.

She'd expected the blood on her thighs, but not the rest of it. Warm water pelting over her body, she'd looked down at the shifting, glowing colors, hating them, wanting them gone so badly she shook. As she watched, the skin over her torso shimmered, a rivulet of sensation traveling up and over her left breast. She caught her breath, the tingle becoming hotter, harder, until it was a shaft of pain that had her collapsing in a fetal ball on the floor of the tub. After a few seconds, the skin split in a long, wavering line and peeled back. The process accelerated, across her back, her ribs, her neck. But when she screamed, the sound came out like a sonic boom, rattling the light fitting and echoing around the apartment, loud enough to wake the whole building, so she bit her lip, holding the moans inside with a shaking hand clamped over her mouth—and sheer willpower.

In the end, the pain dulled, receding like an outgoing tide, and she could breathe again. Shuddering with distaste, she'd crawled out of the bath, averting her eyes from the strips of patterned skin lying there, only to catch a glimpse of her body in the mirror.

The towel slid from her lax fingers as she stared, openmouthed.

Why, she looked almost beautiful! Like an otherworldly being, something from an art house movie about fairy creatures from another dimension. The pattern glowed as never before, clean and clear and iridescent, in the most luscious shades of amethyst and violet.

Marveling, she twisted to look over her shoulder, and a ghost of phosphorescence followed the movement. No, that couldn't be right. She squeezed her eyes shut, then opened them again. The verticality of the design enhanced her curvy, hourglass figure, her breasts tight and full, crowned with broad rosy nipples, standing taut and proud. The colors trailed off over her rounded belly and she followed them with her eyes, down to the springy thatch of curls between her thighs. Heart thudding, she'd widened her stance, watching the gleam of moisture trickling over her thighs, the pink puffiness of the lips of her sex. Even her tongue tingled, as though beautiful lips caressed and sucked it.

God, Tommy hadn't been able to make her feel like this. Not even close.

Luxuriously, she cupped her breasts, ran her palms down over her sides.

And came.

The orgasm was so violent, so unexpected, she'd screamed again, collapsing to the tiled floor.

When the dark spots in her vision cleared, she ran exploring fingertips over the new skin, whimpering with pleasure. It was as soft as a newborn's, so hypersensitive that every touch sent lightning twists of sensation spiraling down to her clitoris, stiffening her nipples and engorging her sex all over again.

Without ceremony, she'd climbed back into the bath, scooped up the discarded skin, and dropped it over the side. Then she grabbed the showerhead and pleasured herself until she couldn't see straight.

Finally, she rose on shaky legs and wobbled off to bed. But as she passed the wardrobe mirror, she couldn't resist one last glance.

In the dimly lit room, the whisper had come out of the dark of childhood memory.

You mustn't tell, sweetie. You can't *tell.* Her mother's voice. *We're weird, different.*

A horrible, greasy void had blossomed behind her breastbone. All the joy and the beauty of it drained out of her, as if they'd never been. And once again, she was seven, not truly comprehending the hurt to come, but knowing enough to brace herself for it as best she could.

Mom's fingers, trembling as she shook another cigarette from the packet. "I'll only be gone a little while, darling. Just long enough to put myself back together, you know?" She'd leaned forward, her clothes smelling of stale tobacco, a hint of whisky. "Promise me you won't let anyone see, not even Daddy."

"But Mommy—"

Her mother had overridden her. "You're a weirdo, honey. Like me. If they find out, they'll take you away, poke you with needles, cut you up in the hospital."

Her lower lip trembling, she'd tried to climb onto her mother's lap, but the woman had held her off, peering into her face. Thin fingers wrapped around her small wrist like a manacle. "*Do you understand, Gina? It'll hurt, real bad. Don't let anyone see.*"

"Yes, Mommy," she'd whispered, tears spilling down her chubby cheeks. "I'm a big girl, I'm brave. I understand."

And she was still brave, wasn't she? Gripping the wheel, she stared straight ahead at the hotel parking lot, blinking back the tears. The whole thing was gross and humiliating—not only the discoloration when she got excited, but the molt every six months. It so wasn't fair! Why couldn't she be normal? She'd bet every carefully hoarded dollar in her bank account Sam Jones only dated normal women.

"Where's your cell phone?" Sam opened the door and slid in beside her. "In here?" He rummaged in the glove box.

Gina whipped around so fast she practically dislocated a vertebra in her neck. She gaped. "Wha—? What happened?"

"They won't do an early check-in, the stupid buggers, not until three. And that's another four hours. I'm beat. I need somewhere to crash right now."

Wordlessly, she pulled her cell out of her pocket and handed it over.

"Good. Luc's number in here?"

No prizes for guessing how that would go, what Luc would suggest. Oh no, no, Sam couldn't stay with her! Gina leaped out of the car and sprinted into the hotel foyer.

Five minutes of fruitless expostulation later, she stomped out again. No wonder Sam's charm hadn't gotten him anywhere.

The desk clerk was a man in his forties, bald, desiccated, and obviously immune to the Jones allure.

"Well?" she growled, yanking the driver's door open so hard the metal creaked.

Blinking, Sam favored her with a calm, sunny smile from the passenger seat. "Luc said you'd give me a bed for a few hours, specially since you're living in Maeve's cabin." She was conscious of his gaze on her fingers as she tightened the scarf into a stranglehold around her neck. "That's not a problem, is it?" The sea-blue eyes focused on her face, all innocence.

"Not at all." She pulled into the traffic.

Prana breathing. Slow and deep, right from the base of the belly. Feel the chi at the base of the spine. In—one, two. Pause. Out—one, two. Sam Jones in a bed. In—one, two. Sam Jones naked in a bed. *Her* bed.

Better breathe out, sometime soon.

Double, triple shit!

"That's a red light, darl," said Sam mildly. "You going to stop?"

Sam dumped his bag on the bed in Gina's spare room, then sat, bouncing experimentally. Nice, firm mattress. No rattle.

Grinning, he leaned down to yank off a boot.

Strewth, she was a funny little bundle, all fire and passion one moment, all rigid control the next. Keeping a wary eye on the hotel doors, he'd asked Luc about her, but the other man's answers hadn't made much sense.

The second boot hit the floor and he yawned. Must be the jet lag—women didn't usually muddle him up this much.

"We Kaminskis are a strange family, Indy." Luc's deep voice had been grim. "And Gina's mom was particularly strange, even for One of Us."

Sam had taken the phone from his ear and stared at it. For a moment there, he could have sworn his old friend was talking in Capital Letters, like a Victorian novelist. He shook his head and put it back.

"Yeah, mate, I know. We go way back, remember?"

"Actually, *mate*, you have no idea. But hurt her and I'll break your fucking neck."

Sam had stiffened. "Well fuck you! As if I'd—"

"You don't do it on purpose, Indy, I know, but I remember all those coeds with broken hearts. Be careful, okay?" Luc's voice softened. "Uncle Col died a few months ago, and she's only just come home again. After her mother disappeared, he took Gina away from us, all the way to New York, the unfeeling bastard, so I haven't seen her since she was a kid."

"All big eyes and pigtails?"

"Yeah, pretty much. She drove me nuts, the little pest, but heck she was gutsy. Now, did you get my e-mail about the bachelor party?"

And the conversation had moved on to other things.

Sam tossed his clothes over the back of the upholstered armchair near the window, ripped the covers off the bed, and dived headfirst into the pillows. Georgina McBride still had big, dark eyes a man could drown in, but it was the pouty mouth and luscious tits that had kept him half-hard with carnal possibilities since the first moment he'd seen her, holding up that silly bloody sign. Good old fuck-o-meter. Never failed.

So what was it that bothered her so much she couldn't relax in his presence? Hell, he *liked* women, adored them; he was endlessly fascinated by the female mind—and body. He chuckled to himself. Most women enjoyed his company, his calm good humor, his innate courtesy and concern, he knew that. But not Gina. Curiosity, lust, and that plain old male urge to *fix* surged within him. A heady mix.

Later, bugger it, later. A huge yawn smothered his train of thought. With his last scrap of consciousness, he twitched a fold of the sheet over his naked body.

Three o'clock. Gina paced from the kitchen to the spare room and back again. Maeve's cabin was nestled in the woods on the outskirts of town and it was very quiet, save for the wind in the trees and the low burbling of the stream that ran through the bottom of the garden. So very different from the neat sterility of Dad's New York apartment. She loved it.

She pressed her ear to the bedroom door. Nothing, not even a snore. She tapped restless fingers against her thigh and rubbed the itch on her neck. Should she wake him? He'd want to return to the hotel, wouldn't he? And she couldn't wait to be rid of him.

Putting her lips to the keyhole, she called softly, "Sam? Sam, are you awake?"

Nothing.

Her heart thundering, she eased the door open the merest fraction and applied one eye to the crack.

Every physical process slowed down, as though a great hand had reached out and stopped the world spinning. All she could see, think about, was the naked man sprawled across the single bed. He'd fallen facedown like a toppled tree, one big, bare foot dangling over the end. His head was turned away from her, the golden brown hair all mussed and tangled. The rays of the afternoon sun streamed in the window, making the pale sheets glow, caressing Sam's skin with adoring fingers.

And there was plenty of it to love, because in his sleep, he'd kicked the sheet almost completely off. It still clung to the curve of one muscular buttock, but the other was entirely exposed, together with a length of brawny thigh and muscled calf. He'd shoved one hand up under the pillow and draped the other arm over the top of it, creating a gorgeous harmony of bone and muscle and sinew, a long fluid line, all the way from broad square shoulders to the dimples in the smooth rise of his ass.

Lord, that ass! Because of the tantalizing way the sheet was disposed, the taut muscled curve was showcased in a way that was nothing short of intensely erotic, almost as if this part of his body was an exotic fruit, covered with downy, blushing skin—warm, smooth, resilient. There for the taking.

Biteable.

Scarcely daring to breathe, Gina clamped a hand over her mouth. The growls jostling for room in her chest threatened to explode. She wanted to roar her lust, her hunger, like some great carnivorous beast—a lion, a tiger, a dragon even.

Sam Jones in her bed looked almost too beautiful to be real, like a Michelangelo sculpture of a sleeping David, wrought in golden, living flesh. Her gaze snagged on his left forearm, and she gasped. Oh God, what had happened? A wide, lumpy scar snaked all the way from elbow to wrist, shockingly white against the tan. Jesus, whatever it was, it must have hurt so much. Sam was real, all too human and vulnerable.

Her reaction to the thought of his pain was immediate and physical, jolting down her nerves, making her stomach lurch, and recalling her to where she was, what she was doing.

Shaking, Gina took one last look, imprinting Sam Jones on her retinas, in her heart, knowing the image was all she would ever have of him. Quietly, she eased back, pulling the door closed behind her. Then she leaned her forehead against the wall, counting the breaths, putting herself back together.

Maeve's cabin was too small, way too small, though she'd never noticed it before. Her whole body was on fire, prickling, her breast flesh tight and stretched, the nipples aching for a touch, the hard, suckling pull of a strong mouth. She pressed the heel of her hand so hard over her clit it almost hurt, sending herself into a spasm that had her hunching over, stifling the moans behind clenched teeth. But it wasn't enough, not even close. The damn pattern had her poised on the brink of orgasm, unable to go over the edge.

Air, she needed cool air. And ordinary people, men who didn't send her insane with wanting. The mall! That was it! The idea came to her like a gift. She'd drive down to the mall, where everything was as mundane as it could possibly be.

Stumbling to the kitchen, Gina scrabbled through the drawers until she found a pen and paper. She scribbled a note to Sam, snatched up her bag and keys, and barreled out onto the front porch.

Where she came to a dead halt.

Heck, not another one!

The snake lying on the top step raised its head, round black eyes staring into hers. Prudently, Gina remained motionless, but she smiled, thinking the gleaming bands and splotches of its scales were beautiful. It would certainly be more scared than she was and strangely enough, she wasn't frightened at all. It was probably a harmless garter snake, anyway, and not a very big one at that, not much wider than her thumb. She'd only been at the cabin a month, but in that time, she reckoned she must have tripped over almost every snake in the district. The critters were everywhere, all kinds, shapes and sizes, almost as though they sought her out.

Strangely enough, they all did much the same thing once they'd found her. After a few tense seconds during which the snake appeared to be checking her out, it would move its head up and down several times, a sinuous nod for all the world like an obeisance to some higher power. Then it would slither off, going about its snaky business without further ado.

Gina didn't know where the words came from, but it seemed

only courteous to acknowledge the greeting. "Why thank you, little one," she murmured, "and a good day to you too."

The flicker of a tongue, the twitch of a tail, and the reptile undulated off the steps and disappeared into the grass.

As she drove carefully down the narrow road, Gina's lips curved, remembering Sam's snakeskin boots. She wasn't at all sure her scaly friends would approve.

It was fully dark by the time she returned, a couple of beers and a bag of Chinese takeout on the seat beside her. Sam had switched the light on over the porch and others, inside the cabin. Gina exhaled in a gusty rush, clawing after her hard-won calm.

She trotted up the steps, mercifully reptile-free, though she heard a receding rustle in the grass. "I'm back!" she called, opening the door. "Do you like Chinese?"

Silence.

"Sam? Where are—"

The bathroom door opened and Sam Jones appeared out of a billow of steam, wearing a towel knotted about his hips, and nothing else. The takeout hit the floor with a soggy thud, followed closely by the beer.

The view from the bedroom door had been stunning enough, but this was even more so, because now Gina received the full brunt of his personality, the intensity of the blue eyes, the flashing grin—along with a chest a mile wide, decorated with a silky mat of hair that dived happily beneath the towel.

"Nngh," she said eloquently.

"Bugger!" Sam's brow creased as his gaze dropped. "That's no way to treat beer. Lucky they didn't break. Here, let me—"

He bent to scoop up the bottles and the bag, giving her the

best view possible of the fluid play of muscle and sinew, the strong knobs of his spine. Gina swallowed.

God knew how far her tongue was hanging out, but when Sam straightened, his cheekbones were stained with pink. "I'll put these in the kitchen, shall I?"

Wordlessly, she nodded, and he edged past her, smelling of soap, shaving cream, and masculinity. His bare chest grazed her arm and she had to suppress the startled twitch. Unable to help herself, she swiveled to watch his ass flex under the towel as he padded down the passageway, so that she was standing in the same place when he returned.

His composure regained, he paused when he reached her, looking down into her face, his blue eyes dark as dusk on the water. He tapped her nose with a long forefinger and Gina gurgled. "Guess I'd better dress for dinner?" She nodded. That slow smile broke over his face. "Don't start without me, okay?" She nodded again.

Sam had taken two steps toward the spare room, when something near the back door made a sizzling noise and the lights went out.

"Shit!" They spoke simultaneously.

The darkness was as thick as a blanket, the cabin so isolated there were no streetlights.

"It's probably a fuse." Sam's voice came deep and reassuring. "Find me a torch and I'll fix it."

"Yes." Gina licked her lips. "I think . . . Maybe there's one in the kitchen."

"Good-oh."

She sensed his body heat as he took a step closer. "Sorry," she muttered, moving to the right.

Sam grunted an acknowledgment and took a step to his left,

just as she attempted to shift out of his way in the same direction. Abruptly, they were standing breast to breast, thigh to thigh. Nudged off balance, Gina reached out in a panic, clutching at skin and chest hair.

"Ow." Sam took her hand in his big one and transferred it to the smooth, hard swell of his biceps. "Hang on to me here, if you're scared, darl. Doesn't hurt as much."

Oh, God, she was going to die! Self-combust, right here in the dark! "I'm not scared," she husked. *But you should be*. Each scale of the pattern burned individually beneath her skin and the fire flowered deep in her empty, weeping core, all the flesh there throbbing like a jungle drum in tune with the hammering of her heart.

"Don't give me that, Gina, you're shaking." A big warm hand rubbed soothingly between her shoulder blades, clasped the nape of her neck. It paused. "Crikey, you're hot! You're not sick? Do you have a thermometer?"

"No, but I remember . . ." Gina had to stop, clear her throat, and relax her death grip on his hard biceps. "When I was ill, my mom used to bend down and put her cheek against my forehead. Did yours do that?"

"Yeah, when I was a little fella." His voice came softly out of the gloom. "Hold still."

His hands slid up her arms to rest on her shoulders, pressing her into a wall of warm, hard muscle. Soft, silky hair still damp from the shower brushed her cheek and she tilted her chin. Slowly, oh so slowly, Sam bent his head until his clean-shaven cheek rested against her forehead. His skin was cool and smooth, with a hint of the underlying heat of his blood. Gina closed her eyes, luxuriating, sensing the soft whisper of his breath, and blessing the complete absence of light. All she had to do was rise on tiptoes and turn her head the slightest bit to bury her nose in his neck.

"Gina, you're burning!" She felt his throat vibrate as he spoke.

"I know," she said. "Don't worry about it." Almost gladly, she stopped fighting, let the fire roar right over her, incinerating every particle of common sense she'd ever possessed. He was so wonderful, Sam Jones, so perfect. The fates had conspired to give her this man, and the concealing dark. She'd be mad to pass the opportunity by, regardless of the consequences on the morrow. There'd never be another chance like it.

"Yes, but shouldn't we—"

She nipped the smooth skin below his ear, then soothed the spot with her tongue. Sam's whole body went rigid against her. "Christ!"

"You can say no," she breathed into his neck, trailing small, stinging nibbles along his jaw. God, he tasted fabulous, like salty, honeyed sin.

"No?" he croaked. One hand slid up and under her hair, cradling her skull. "You think I'm crazy?"

The other palm cupped her cheek, holding her steady. Firm, cool lips traced her eyebrow, whispered over her eyelid. A thumb stroked across her lower lip, pressing gently. She scraped it with her teeth, bit. Sam made an unintelligible noise, deep in his throat, as if something had snapped inside him. His fingers tightened against her cheek and his mouth came down hard on hers.

Why on earth had she thought his lips were cool? They were furnace hot, his tongue a searing brand that slid into her mouth like a marauder, a conquering king. Her head spinning, Gina strained upward, her breasts mashed against his unyielding chest, accepting the invader, loving it, letting it do as it willed. Oh, God, yes, *yes!* The pattern writhed, turning her universe into a soft dark space of wet and warmth in which nothing existed except the urgent dance of lips and tongues and hard desire.

It took her long, drugged moments to realize Sam was withdrawing, very slowly and gently, but nonetheless. . . . His arms were still banded about her, one big hand splayed over her ass, pressing what felt like a long, thick bar of molten metal into her belly. From neck to knee, there wasn't room to slip a piece of paper between their bodies, but now his lips were featherlight on hers, no more than the merest brush. Instinctively, she slid her arms around his neck and raised her head, seeking, chasing more of that addictive taste. Feeling the towel begin to slip, she wiggled her hips against it, delighted.

"Gina." It was no more than a rasp in the blackness. "Love, stop." His chest rose and fell against hers, the breath sawing out of him. He sank his fingers into her hair, tugging gently. "*Stop,* I said!"

He might as well have dunked her in cold, greasy, washing-up water. Ah, *shit!* Tears of humiliation welled in her eyes. Abruptly, she jerked back, very nearly succeeding in tearing herself out of his arms. Reflexively, they tightened around her. "No," he said. "No, that's not what I meant. Strewth, I can't see a fucking thing!"

"I said you could say no." Gina braced herself on the hard slabs of his pectorals and shoved backward, feeling the silky hair tickle her palms. "Let me *go!*"

"Nu-uh." He stepped forward, one thigh coming up firmly between her legs, so that she rode him, the thick seam of her jeans catching her quivering clit fair and square. As he backed her into the wall, the towel slid off completely, flopping softly over her feet, and her core released a slick gush of fluid. Oh, God, she could smell her own arousal! What must Sam be thinking? She moaned her distress.

"Gina, listen." He lowered his head, his nose brushing hers, and she caught the gleam of his eyes. "Don't push me." His voice dropped an octave, the Aussie drawl very pronounced. "I'm within a hairsbreadth of shoving you against the wall and fucking your brains out."

She froze, allowing herself to feel the bulky throb of his cock pressing into her stomach, the way he was crowding her, looming above her, so she felt small and helpless and oh-so-female. Surging up from the depths, her spirits rose so high, so quickly, the roller coaster of emotions made her dizzy. Digging her fingers into Sam's shoulders, she flicked out her tongue, licking his upper lip.

He groaned, the sexiest sound she'd ever heard. "Darl, it's darker than the devil's armpit in here. Tell me I haven't got it wrong." She sensed him run a hand through his hair. "Shit, Gina, you don't know me from a bar of soap." He swiveled his hips against her and she whimpered. "Jesus, I reckon I've got two seconds left—talk quick."

"Suppose I . . ." She couldn't catch her breath, couldn't hear herself think over the pounding of her blood. Something about the dark interfered with her inhibitions, made it an erotic dream, a fantasy in which all things were possible. In which she was bold and beautiful and impossibly sexy. "Suppose I tell you what I want. Explicitly."

A woman who talked dirty. For chrissake, his balls were going to explode past his ears any second. Sam slid a hand up under the stupid sweatshirt, over satin skin so fever-hot it damn near scorched his fingers. "Go on," he managed, his hands shaking so hard he fumbled the catch on her bra. Fuck, if her skin was this hot, this smooth, what would it be like to be buried to the hilt inside her heated, honeyed flesh, rammed as high as he could go?

Gina writhed, giving that sexy little growl in her throat. God, what a turn-on! He'd never had a woman growl at him before.

"I want you . . . to do it, do everything."

Everything? Holy hell.

"Like what?" He pushed her bra out of the way, filling his hands with creamy, heavy breast flesh. Ah, what gorgeous tits, crowned with nipples that beaded up immediately, all furled and velvety under the rasp of his thumbs. His mouth watered. If only he could see!

"Like fucking me," she breathed.

Jee-sus! Driven, Sam swooped, wrapping his lips around a nipple, sucking hard, no mercy.

"Aargh!" Her fingers gripped his hair and she arched her back, pushing into the sensation. He had to pin her against the wall with his hips to keep her still. Crikey, she was strong for her size.

"Fuck me senseless, Sam." Her voice dropped, echoing off the walls. "Oh, Sam."

His mouth full of her breast, he tugged at her jeans, but she nudged his hands aside and unzipped them herself, shoving them down to her knees. And fuck it, when his eager fingers followed, he discovered she'd taken her panties with them.

He'd love to be able to see what he was doing, watch the reactions flit over her expressive features, but the dark was fucking sexy too, magnifying all the other senses—the crisp curls tickling his knuckles; the slick, searing satin of her vulnerable sex, wide open to his exploring fingers; the husky cries that spilled out of her mouth. Jesus, she was like fire in his arms, the smell of her sweet and tart at once, with a strange smoky undertone. He couldn't wait.

Without preamble, Sam slid a finger in deep, then two. Crooking them, he massaged the soft pad of flesh behind her clitoris, driving her up and up. Panting, he released her nipple with a final lick and blew on the wet flesh. "Touch me," he demanded. "Christ, touch me before I bloody die." Then he switched breasts, working nipple and G-spot together, trying to coordinate the rhythm, make it good for her before he lost it completely and slammed himself into her like an animal, up against the wall.

Grab it, he wanted to say, but he could no longer think, let alone speak. *Pump my cock with those hot little hands, squeeze, stroke—*

Too late. He *was* going to die. His thighs iron-hard with tension, Sam spread his legs to give her room, her fingers barely closing around his girth. Holy shit, she was working him hand over hand, pausing on the upstroke to smear his own moisture over the head with her thumbs. Fire streaked up and down his length, her grip so hot it hovered on the borderline between pleasure and pain.

All the blood had left his brain. With his last scrap of sanity, Sam croaked, "Condom?"

A long silence.

"Oh, *noooo*." She sounded close to tears.

"In the bathroom," he paused for breath. "I have." Too desperate for finesse, Sam pried her fingers loose. Then he bent and hoisted Gina over his shoulder in a fireman's lift, her jeans still caught around her knees, his arm clamped across the delectable arse he had yet to explore.

"Nearest bed?"

"Left. No, shit, that's me. Your right. Two steps." He heard her nails scrabble along the wall, and felt a draft as they went through an open door. "Bed's straight ahead. Hurry, *hurry*."

Three steps and the bed hit him at the knee. Without ceremony, he tumbled Gina onto the mattress, grabbed her foot and ripped one shoe off. Then the other. If he didn't get her bare and spread this instant, he was going to spurt all over her, like a kid with his first girl.

Condom. Fuck. Right.

"Don't. Move." Barely able to speak, Sam left her jeans dangling from one ankle and fumbled his way the few steps to the bathroom, bouncing off the walls as he went. Locating his shaving kit by feel, he upended it in the sink, scrabbling through the contents until he felt the blessed crinkle of foil under his fingertips.

Desire made him deft. Sheathed and rampant, he felt his way back to the bedroom, climbed onto the bed, and kneeled over her, her face no more than a pale oval framed in the inky torrents of her hair. "Ready?"

For answer, she kicked the jeans away, threw her arms around his neck and drew him down with surprising strength. Her ankles rose to lock in the small of his back. Gritting his teeth, he surged forward, his broad tip nuzzling the pouty little mouth of her sex. Tilting her hips, Gina took the first inch with a wriggle and a squirm that had him seeing stars. Desperately, he tried to hold back, to go slow, to make it easy for her. She was so fucking narrow, so luscious, so searingly hot and slick, his head spun. He was going to blow the moment he hilted all the way, he knew it.

But she dug her nails into his shoulders. "More," she demanded, her voice so rough with passion, it sounded as deep as his.

He managed a hoarse chuckle as he sank another inch. "Wildcat."

She arched, taking him deep. "Yesssss," she hissed. On the word, her body went completely still beneath him. Her hand came up to fumble at her mouth, as if something had taken her by surprise.

Sam hauled in a breath and slid the rest of the way without hindrance, a long solid glide into gloving heat. Glorious. His groan was lost in Gina's full-throated bellow. "Don't sstop! Pleasse!" The windows rattled.

Startled, he froze. But then it began, the most amazing sensation he'd ever experienced. Her internal muscles *rippled*, up and down his length, the fiery, resilient walls of her sheath massaging him from root to tip and back again. It was magnificent, ruthless. Unbelievable. The seed boiled against the tender skin of his balls.

No, not yet, not yet. "Fuck, oh *fuck!*" Sam threw caution to the wind, flexed his hips, and hammered into her with long, pounding strokes.

She clung to his shoulders, growling on a low, continuous rumble, her grip so hard he knew he'd have bruises in the morning, not that it mattered. He slid one hand between their bodies and found the prominent, slippery bud of her clitoris. When he rasped it with his thumb, Gina arched up and nipped his shoulder, openmouthed, her tongue flickering across his skin in the strangest, most erotic way. God, she drove him crazy, the little devil.

"Oh, oh, *oh!*" She threw her head back. "Aaaaargh!"

Something—a picture?—slid off the wall and crashed to the floor, but Sam was barely conscious of it. The force of Gina's orgasm tightened her on him to a deliciously excruciating degree—a slick, fiery vise that kick-started the flood in his balls, the ecstatic surge the length of his cock, jets so violent they made his vision haze.

The room, the shadow of her dark hair against the pale linen of the pillow, it all went away. For a few ecstatic moments, he wasn't sure whether he'd simply closed his eyes or passed out in sheer gratitude, but he came back to himself sprawled all over her, comfortably ensconced in the cradle of her thighs.

Dropping his forehead to rest against hers, he eased his weight away, enough to let her breathe. "Holy hell, darl," he murmured, his chest heaving. "Where did that come from?"

She brushed the hair out of her eyes with trembling fingers. "I guess I had it stored up." He thought her face twisted, it was hard to be certain in the dark, but echoes of remembered pain strained her voice. "Sorry if I . . ." she cleared her throat, "came on a little strong. It's been a while." He caught the gleam of something shining on her cheek.

"Hey, hey." Resting his elbows on the pillow on either side of her head, he wiped the tears away with his thumbs. "Sweetheart, you were incredible. What the hell sort of gym work do you do?"

"Nothing unusual." Her teeth flashed in a shaky smile. "Guess it was just me."

"Gina." Gently, he disengaged himself. "You fucked me like there was no tomorrow. I've never—"

Gina watched Sam's dim shape as he shook his head, searching for words. The only man she'd ever had who was still there with her at the end, and it looked like he'd be leaving any minute. Her legs felt like wet noodles, her sex replete and pleasantly pummeled, but her stomach was all knotted up again, aching with tension.

Thoughts whirled about in her head, colliding at random. The fabulous girth of him, powering her flesh aside, slamming into her with the exact, ferocious rhythm she needed, the one he seemed to know by instinct. The way his shoulders and arms had turned to stone under her clawing fingers, the taste of his skin, his mouth—sweet and fiery as sugared brandy.

Oh, God, his mouth. *Her* mouth. Her *tongue*. What had happened—? She pressed trembling fingers to her lips.

Sam peeled himself away and rose. "Back in a sec."

Back? He was coming back?

She must have made some kind of noise, because he bent and brushed his lips across hers. "You stay . . ." He licked her right nipple, "right here . . ." moved to her other breast for a quick, pulling suck, "don't move . . ." and swirled a wet tongue around the tiny cup of her navel, "okay?" On the last word, he spread the lips of her sex with his fingers and thumb. Warm lips sucked her clit, the sensuous tugging exquisitely gentle, and released it, leaving her shaking, tears prickling behind her eyes. In his own way, he'd paid her homage, as if she'd been some pagan sex goddess.

With a final pat, he moved out of the room, trailing a hand along the wall as he went. She heard the passage creak, the bathroom door open and close.

Immediately, Gina rolled over and fumbled in the drawer of the bedside table. Where was that perfumed candle? Ah, there. Her fingers closed over it. And the lighter? Another frantic scrabble and she had a flame. The candle flared and she stood, panting, to weave her way over to the full-length mirror on the wardrobe.

Her tongue still tingled. She stuck it out, not caring how stupid it looked, and peered in the buttery glow of the candlelight. A faint, purplish line was visible, bisecting it, running back from the tip. The moment Sam had entered her body, her arousal had built to insane levels, levels she'd obviously never reached before.

Because her tongue had prickled and burned. And then it had simply divided—*forked*. Jesus! Just as well she'd grown accustomed to the majorly weird. It hadn't hurt—in fact, it made her feel erotic, naughty, all-powerful. And when she'd flicked it over his chest, across a tight, male nipple, she'd learned his taste, tracked the frantic thudding of his heart, inhaled him with every sense she possessed.

What would it feel like to kiss him deeply, wrapping that forked tongue around his, or to lick his cock from root to head, while he shuddered and shook with the sensual torture of it?

"Cool tattoo," said Sam from the door. "Thought you had one. Who did it?"

Gina squeaked, nearly swallowing the tongue in question. In a single movement, she snatched her sleep shirt from under the pillow and hauled it on.

Gloriously nude, Sam leaned against the door frame, his hands full of Chinese takeout, beer, and condoms. "Dressing for dinner after all?" He grinned like a boy. "And me without my tux."

She relaxed, a long breath of relief whispering out of her. "You're, um, excused," she said with a twinkle, climbing onto the bed. "Just this once." All of a sudden, she wanted to laugh aloud, let the fun and joy of it bubble out of her.

Sam handed her the food and placed half a dozen condoms on the bedside table, chuckling when he noted Gina's eyes widen. Settling next to her against the pillows, he wrapped a heavy arm about her shoulders and tugged her close. "You know what's for dessert, don't you?" He nibbled her earlobe, sending hot and cold chills coursing down her spine.

Mutely, she shook her head.

"You." His voice went husky with greed. "And I'm starving for every fuckable inch, from your gorgeous tits to your pretty pink pussy. Eat up, sweetheart; you're going to need your strength."

Sam made short work of the takeout, barely tasting it, all his concentration on Gina, anticipation a gleeful fever in his blood. She looked so pretty in the wavering light of the candle, so edible. His mouth watered, and his fingers itched to strip the sleep shirt off her. The uptight little number who'd picked him up from the airport had vanished. This woman was a temptress, all flushed and tousled, her flashing eyes darting over his body, from the breadth of his chest to his hungry cock, already swelling in the most gratifying fashion.

He was dying to inspect the tattoo showing clearly on her neck—with his tongue.

God, he'd just let go of every inhibition he'd ever had with a woman. He'd always taken such care, not to crush, not to ram and rut, like the male animal he was, aware of the slick delicacy of female flesh, his own bruising strength.

But Georgina McBride had relished everything he had to give. He'd never had a woman match him that way before, thrust for thrust, giving as good as she got. And those sexy growls rumbling in her throat, as if she wanted to eat him alive. She'd set him free to do as he willed. Satisfaction broadened his smile, and he leaned forward to trail a finger down her forearm. As she'd tumbled over the crest, it was his name she'd shouted, the sound echoing around the room. She had the cutest lisp when she was worked up. "Ssam," she'd cried, "Oh, Ssam!"

Bloody perfect, that's what she was, and he couldn't wait for more.

Sam scooped everything back into the takeout bag and rose to put it out of the way on the dresser. He was conscious of Gina's gaze on his backside, feeling the kick of it deep inside his pelvis, his balls lifting hard into his body. She'd been telling him about the shaky tree house she and Luc had built together as kids, laughing at the memory, but now her voice trailed away.

Cradling his cock in one hand, he turned and paced back to the bed, a predatory grin curving his lips. "Lie back for me, sweetheart," he said.

Her eyes gone wide and dark, she obeyed, but slowly.

The blood pounded in his temples, his cock. Hardly able to

string the words together, he said, "Grab the headboard and don't let go." He climbed onto the bed, between her knees.

A pause, but she did it.

Sam didn't take his gaze from hers, wanting to see the shudders of arousal she couldn't quite control, *needing* to see them. He ran his palms up her thighs, savoring the tender, satin skin, the tremors and gasps. He'd meant to shove the shirt way up high, exposing all of her lush little body, but the glimpse of pink glistening in her dark curls lassoed his attention, and drew him down to nuzzle and lick. The musky, smoky smell of her, wet and female, bypassed every civilized, rational faculty and streaked straight to the animal hindbrain.

Ruthlessly, he spread her wide, and lifted her legs over his shoulders.

"Oh!" A startled, breathless squeak.

Gorgeous. Each lip all pinkly engorged and ruffled; her clit sitting up right out of its hood, begging for a kiss; the dark, intriguing entrance to her body; the sweet little pucker of her arsehole. His, all his.

Thirstily, he sealed his mouth over all that tender flesh, and Gina reared up with a desperate cry and blew the candle out.

Bugger! But he was too far gone to stop and light it again, his head spinning with the intoxicating flavor of a woman aroused especially for him. By him.

He'd always loved this, feeling a lover come apart under the lash of his tongue. Already, he was as hard as he'd ever been in his life. If he wanted to last more than a single instant inside her, she had to come, preferably in the next ten seconds. Sam began a relentless rhythm—flick, suck, flick, suck. Simultaneously, he impaled her on one finger, then two, and finally three.

Gina's thighs clamped around his ears and her panting cries

dropped to the deep, lusty moans he'd come to crave. *Soon*, he thought dizzily, *make it soon, darl. I can't take much—*

She arched into his mouth, demanding, and he responded, sucking harder, flexing his fingers.

"Ssam!" Her whole body tensed in a ferocious spasm, then another and another, until he could barely keep a grip on her. Her growls of completion reverberated off the walls.

Sam snagged a condom from the bedside table. "Off!" he demanded, tugging at the sleep shirt. Anything approaching a coherent sentence had become impossible.

"Yess." Gina flung it away, a vague white shape billowing to the floor. But then she grabbed him by the shoulders and tried to press him down to the mattress.

"Hey!" She was amazingly strong for such a little bit of a thing, but no stronger than he was. Sam held her off.

"Ssam, your turn." A hot whisper in the dark.

"Love, I'm dying, don't—"

"Pleasse, Ssam, let me!" Her fingers closed around him, pulling up in a long, dragging stroke. Her head dipped and she flicked her tongue out, lashing one nipple. God, how did she do it? He'd had no idea his nipples were that sensitive. The breath whistled out from between his teeth, he fell back, and the torture began.

Chapter 5

By the time Gina reached his groin, Sam was clutching hand-fuls of sheet, gritting his teeth. Fuck, it was hard to know which turned him on more—the happy, hungry noises she made deep in her throat, or that mouth.

Oh Christ, it was hot, hot, *hot*. She nibbled his belly, delved into his navel, licked a trail down the notch between hip and thigh, while his cock jerked and leaked in anticipation.

And when her mouth closed over the broad head, enclosing it in surging bliss, his hips arched off the bed, a groan stran-gling in his throat. Her tongue flickered up and down his length, now wrapping around his girth, licking over the collar under the glans, digging into the weeping slit, fluttering back over his balls. She might as well have had two tongues, the little witch.

Quite distinctly, Sam felt his eyes roll back, the searing flood forcing its way out of his balls. He groaned with dismay as much as with pleasure, and she stopped.

Fuck it, she stopped!

With a wicked chuckle, she drew back, blowing a stream of warm air across his screamingly sensitive skin.

He reached down, sinking his fingers into her hair, and she

peeped up at him, her teeth flashing in a naughty grin. "It'ss good?"

"Too good. Gina, I—"

"You tasste . . ." she inhaled, and that diabolical tongue danced lightly over his aching flesh, "wonderful. I've never— Jusst a few more sseconds?"

"Hell." He squeezed his eyes shut, struggling with the concept of *never*, something in his chest doing the strangest flip-flops. "Then I fuck your brains out."

"Yess." One small hand fumbled up his body, coming to rest over his heart, and Sam clamped it there with both of his, desperate for an anchor, a reference point in the erotic maelstrom of his senses.

He'd take the next sixty seconds with him to the grave, he was sure. Gina's mouth was a miracle, a superlative redefinition of what sensual torture could be. He wished for it never to end and for it to be over. *Now!*

A final, strong pulling suck, deep in her throat, and she released him. Their sighs spiraled together in the shadows. One at a time, Sam unwound his fingers from hers, hoping he hadn't cut off her circulation. But she grabbed a condom easily enough, ripping it open and sheathing him with hands that trembled.

Sam reared up, grabbed her by the waist, and lifted. As if it was an erotic ballet they'd danced together for years, Gina reached down and guided his rampant cock where it longed to go. A deep breath for the initial resistance and she sank down, gloving him in her internal furnace, all gripping, muscular satin. Her breath coming as if she'd been running, she braced her palms on his chest while they both shuddered with delicious sensations.

Greedily, Sam opened his mouth over one beautiful breast,

the velvet flesh taut against his tongue, the nipple stiff with desire. His hands gripped, guiding her in the age-old rhythm, while his hips surged up in counterpoint, giving her every fat inch, so each thrust was a collision that thrilled along the nerves.

Gina's hair flew in a dark cloud, her moans dropping to that astonishing bass register. The unbelievable pulses started again, milking him, a fierce clutch each time she hilted, a tight fist when she rose. But this time, he was almost prepared. Recognizing the signs of her imminent climax, Sam looped an arm behind her neck and tugged her down, needing that hot mouth on his, needing to take her scream down his throat.

But at the last moment, she turned her head aside and sank her teeth into his shoulder as the orgasm stiffened her limbs. The double lash of pain and pleasure a sensory overload he couldn't withstand, Sam released, in scalding jets of mind-blowing intensity.

With a long, shuddering sigh, Gina relaxed on top of him, a limp weight snuggled into his shoulder.

"Next time," he murmured, nuzzling her cheek with his nose. "Next time, we do it slow, I swear."

"Next time?" she whispered. A shudder ran the length of her body.

"Sure." Sam caressed the luscious bottom he had yet to see. "I want to watch it go in, do you from behind."

She lifted her head, pressing a swift kiss to his lips, an air of finality about the action, shy and bittersweet. "I don't believe in next times."

Sam frowned. "Well, I do," he said firmly, rubbing soothing circles between her shoulder blades. "It was bloody fantastic, *you* were fantastic."

"Not . . . too much?"

"Are you kidding?"

"Mm. Good." She stifled a yawn.

"Have a snooze, darl, and I'll show you how much is too much later." With a last kiss, he rolled out of bed and felt his way back to the bathroom.

By the time he returned, she'd put the bloody sleep shirt back on, but when he settled back beside her, she snuggled into his shoulder as if she owned it, one palm resting over his heart, a slim calf hooked over his knee. Her voice floated sleepily out of the darkness, no trace of the lisp apparent. "Why does Luc . . ." A yawn like a satisfied kitten, "call you Indy?"

Sam grinned. "Silly bugger thinks it's funny. I can do a lot of things he can't—drive a tractor, fly a plane, crack a whip, ride a stock horse."

"Pretty impressive."

He shrugged. "I'm a country boy." He walked his fingers over her hip, nudging soft fabric aside. "My family runs a big property out West, beef cattle. Skills like that are essential. One day—" The words died in his throat and his fingers stilled on her skin. Good God Almighty, he'd been about to say he'd show her, one day.

Rattled, he hurried into speech. "It was the whip that clinched it. That and the snakes."

She raised her head. "Snakes?"

"Hate the bastards. Give me the creeps. Like Indiana Jones, see?"

"Oh." Her hand wandered back and forth across his chest, petting. "Why's that?"

Just the memory of his dad's face, pale and clammy, the sweat pouring off him, was enough to kill the mood. It was beyond him to speak of it, how close they'd come to losing his father. His guts clenched.

"Never mind," she murmured with another yawn. "You're not a rancher?"

"Wildlife photographer. I do calendars, stuff like that." He skated inquiring fingertips over the curve of her pretty bottom, drawing gentle circles. "I'll show you in the morning."

"Uh-huh." Such a long silence, he thought she'd drifted off. "What happened to your arm?"

An even bigger mood killer than a snake on the pillow.

"I was stupid." He kissed her brow. "Go to sleep, sweetheart. Round three in the morning."

A noncommittal noise. "Maybe."

"No maybe about it, Gina. You hear me?"

But she'd gone this time, draped trustingly over his chest like a scarf.

Gina's sleeping head on his shoulder, Sam waited for dawn to creep into the quiet room. Outside, trees whispered in the wind, and a frog croaked an amphibian love song from the creek at the bottom of the garden. *Hope you get lucky, mate. I sure did.* With gentle fingers, he took a swathe of her hair and spread it across his naked chest. Unlike the rest of her, it was cool to the touch, and goose bumps paraded across his skin, his nipples crinkling hard. His cock gave a reminiscent twitch, and he pressed his cheek against the top of her curly head, smiling.

God, she'd been incredible. Abso-fucking-lutely incredible. Even now, an hour later, his eyes threatened to cross at the very thought of what she'd done to him.

So now he lay in the cool quiet, arms full of his sweet little Yank, staring into the shadows. With his sleep patterns all messed up, he was wide awake, his brain whirring. Because she *was* sweet—sweet and funny and strong and sexy.

So what the fuck was wrong with her?

If he didn't know there was no such thing, he would have pegged her as a vampire; she changed so completely once the lights were out. Sam worried at the puzzle, trying to reconcile the rigid control of the daylight Gina with the passion of the wildcat in the dark. The first held everything back; the second had given it all. If he could persuade her to tell him. . .

Abruptly, he realized he was massaging the scar on his forearm, pressing it with the heel of his hand. *Careful, you fool,* he thought. *You can't rescue everyone, make it all better. Didn't work for Yasser, did it?*

The impulse had damn near cost him his life two years ago in Iraq. He had to stop doing it, courtesies to little old ladies notwithstanding. He'd left college intent on a career in photojournalism. Persistence, gall, and sheer competence had gotten him there, earned him good money, and made the nickname Indiana stick. But fifteen miles south of Baghdad, the convoy he'd been traveling with had been attacked by AK–47s with armor-piercing rounds. Instead of scrambling to the floor, he'd lunged across the cabin to push the translator down, and a bullet had gouged through the flesh of his forearm and smashed both bones. Two operations and a metal plate later, he was pretty well whole again. Fine for him. A pity Yasser hadn't made it.

So much for a decade of work as a photojournalist. His mother had finally gotten her way. Besides, he had to agree. There wasn't a more terrifying animal in the world than a fanatic with a 50-caliber machine gun. Not even a fucking snake.

But still. . .

Curiosity moved in him, as strong as lust, one of his beset-
ting sins. He had a whole month in the States. He'd find out,
after he'd fucked her again, just to be sure the best sex of his life
hadn't been some kind of wild and wonderful dream. And then
he'd take a good look at that exotic tattoo, the one that seemed
to come and go.

The yawn caught him unawares, and he relaxed into the pillows, spooning around Gina's warm body.

Gina cupped her hands around the coffee mug and inhaled
gratefully. She'd left Sam Jones slumbering peacefully in her
bed, an exercise in self-discipline of which she was immensely
proud. Sighing, she rose to rummage in the pantry for bread to
toast.

"What happened to round three?"

She whirled around. Sam stood in the doorway wearing jeans
and a T-shirt, his hair endearingly mussed and his feet bare.

"You change your mind, darl?"

Gina's heart sprang into her throat and attempted to strangle
her. "Yes," she croaked. "Ah, no. Luc called. There's a rehearsal
at ten and he wants you there because you're a groomsman."

"Sure." Sam sauntered closer, slung a casual arm around her
waist, and planted a kiss under her ear, just above the turtleneck
of her sweater.

The pattern tightened and burned, apparently unappeased.
Gina jerked away. *"Don't!"*

"Why?" he asked reasonably, eyes all innocent and blue and
calm. "After what we did last night . . ." The broad shoulders
shrugged and a brow rose. His mouth kicked up at the corners.

Her nipples stiffened, a silvery twist of lust riding low in her
pelvis. "That was a one-time-only deal."

"Really?" Both brows went up this time, and his lips compressed.

Gina's stomach knotted. Deep breaths. In, pause, out. She wet her lips. "I left you to sleep," she said, feeling the reminiscent blush heat her cheeks. "So there's not much time. Five minutes, okay?" It wasn't precisely the truth, but she couldn't take much more of Sam Jones in daylight, not without losing her mind.

Oh, lord, now he looked pissed. He loomed over her, grasping her chin in strong fingers and tilting it. All the chill of an arctic storm looked out of his beautiful eyes. She shivered. "Don't take me for a fool, Gina," he said, the accent very marked. "I know you're hiding something."

Panic flaring, she jerked her head aside, unable to meet his hard stare. Why on earth had she thought him amiable, easygoing? This Sam Jones was like flint, as tough as his namesake. "No," she whispered. "No."

The uncompromising line of his mouth softened. "You can tell me, you know. I'm safe." He brushed her cheek with his knuckles.

Grief clogged so hard in her throat, she was unable to speak. She shook her head and turned away to gaze at the trees framed by the window.

"Fine." Sam stepped away from her, and she felt the loss as if he'd taken a soul-shaped piece of her with him. "I'll get my things then."

Gina made sure she was seated in the car, all buckled up, when he emerged. Without a word, Sam slung his gear in the back and climbed in beside her. The trip to Luc's was accomplished in such a suffocating silence, that after ten minutes she felt compelled to slide a CD into the player. Defiantly, she warbled along with the Dixie Chicks. "Goodbye Earl," she sang, fortissimo, ignoring his body heat and the ominous tightness of the skin over her ribs.

Sam jammed on a pair of sunglasses, hiding his ocean eyes.

But when they pulled up at the beautiful old house Luc was restoring for Maeve, she couldn't control the tremble of her lips, watching him bound out of the car for the reunion, the back-slapping, the broad grins, the rough affection.

"Hell mate, it's good to see you," said Sam, his whole face alight with pleasure. His blue gaze swung to Maeve. "Wow." He cranked up the wattage on the grin. "You too, love."

He swooped on Maeve, bundling her up in a rough hug, until Luc growled and hauled him off. "Find your own woman, dick-head." Maeve just laughed, her cheeks pink. The Jones effect, thought Gina sourly.

Sam grinned, unruffled. "No problem."

Of course not.

The pattern chose that moment to flex, sending licks of fire over her skin. Gina couldn't hold back the gasp of arousal and discomfort. She turned away, her breath coming short and fast.

A gentle touch on her elbow. "Gina, are you all right?" asked Maeve.

A huge hand closed over the back of her neck, and she squeaked with shock. "Yeah, little cuz," rumbled Luc, his hazel eyes uncomfortably keen, "you okay?"

"Just . . . j-just a cold," she stammered, conscious of Sam's thoughtful blue gaze.

"Hmm." Luc didn't sound convinced. He ushered them in-side. "Honey," he said to his fiancée, "why don't you and Sam put the coffee on? I want a word with Gina."

As Luc shut the study door, Gina heard Sam's plaintive voice, "and no bloody breakfast either!"

"Will you be all right for the wedding?" said Luc abruptly.

She frowned. "It's only a cold."

"No, it's not." Luc patted her hand awkwardly. The action was so unlike him, she gaped. "Here, sit down, honey." He pressed her into an enormous leather chair, obviously fashioned for his huge frame. Her feet dangled like a child's. "You forget, Gina, I knew your mom. It's okay if you have to miss it. I'll understand."

Gina's stomach tried to climb out of her throat. She forced it back down. "Luc," she managed through numb lips, "I have no idea what you're talking about."

Luc pushed a laptop and a pile of papers aside so he could perch his hip on one corner of the massive desk. His dark brows drew together as he stared at her. He examined her face in silence, feature by feature, and gradually, his expression grew thunderous. "Lying won't work, little cuz. I'm a Kaminski too, remember?"

"Lie? Why would I lie?"

Luc reached out and jerked down one side of the turtleneck. "Don't tell me you don't know what this is," he growled.

Automatically, she slapped his hand away. *Cut you up in the hospital.* Black spots danced in her vision. *It'll hurt real bad, baby, real bad.*

"Gina? Gina, honey!"

Reluctantly, she opened her eyes. Luc was kneeling on the floor in front of her, both her hands clasped in his. On his face was the most extraordinary expression, an amalgam of fury, surprise, and horrified concern. "Jesus," he said. "She never told you, did she? *You don't know.*"

"Know what?" She wasn't sure the words actually came out of her mouth, but Luc understood.

"About being a Kaminski. About your heritage."

Gina simply stared, shock freezing all capacity for coherent thought. "Uh," she said. "No."

"Luc!" called Maeve's husky voice. "If we don't leave soon, we'll be late."

Her big cousin rose, a faint flush on his cheekbones. "God, that voice," he muttered. "Gets me every time."

Gina's brain creaked back into gear. "What heritage?"

"We Kaminskis are Different." The way Luc spoke invested the last word with special significance. "There's Magic in our family tree, Gina, old Magic, out of central Europe."

"What? But—"

The door opened. "Darling, have you finished?" asked Maeve. "We really need to go."

"Come here, gorgeous." Luc held out his arms. "Come and kiss me. I want to show Gina."

"Show her—? You sure?" A throaty giggle when Luc nodded. "Well, if it's all in the family—"

Gina's eyes widened as Luc swept Maeve into a wet kiss, full of passion and tongues. She squirmed, embarrassed, staring at the fingers clasped in her lap.

"Look at me, Gina," said Luc, his tone so authoritative she really had no choice.

She raised her eyes. No, surely not . . . Quickly, she squeezed them shut again. Not possible. Cranking one eye open, she squinted. God! Her jaw dropped. Her cousin's eyes flickered with deep red lights, like flames, and pushing through his thick dark hair were—

"Shit, Luc!" she squeaked. "You've got horns!"

"Aren't they cute?" purred Maeve, rubbing one. "And that's not all." She grinned and nudged Luc with her hip.

"Adrenaline brings on the Manifestation," said Luc. "Mine's courtesy of great-grandmamma Kaminski. She was a real devil, the old girl." He frowned down at Gina. "You're not going to faint, are you?"

"No-oo." Though a little downtime certainly sounded tempting.

Voices drifted from the kitchen, the unmistakable cadence of Sam's Aussie drawl rumbling beneath other, more feminine tones.

"That's Mom and the bridesmaids." Luc ran an irritated hand through his hair, now hornless. "We have to go, honey, I'm sorry. Here." He reached up with a long arm to the top of a tall bookcase and retrieved a fat book with plushy covers in a particularly virulent purple. "This is Aunt Lili's family history project. She, uh, scrapbooked it."

He laid the book in Gina's lap, as carefully as if it was a grenade. "It's all there, everything you've ever wanted to know about your Manifestation, but were afraid to ask."

The silence became glutinous.

"Luc . . ." said Maeve eventually, tugging at his arm.

"Okay, darling. Coming." Luc's hand brushed Gina's hair. "Don't worry, little one. I'll answer your questions when we get back."

"Uh," she said, but the room was empty.

Except for Gina and Aunt Lili's scrapbook.

The sounds of animated conversation receded, the front door opened and closed, and the house settled into silence.

Slowly, Gina rose and set the book down precisely on the center of the desk. It was heavy, very heavy. Her brain seemed to have turned to fog. She couldn't think properly.

Breathe, that was it. Breathe.

Sucking in a lungful of air, she walked to the door. Then back again to the desk. The book of her fate looked so innocent, lying there, lavished with every kitschy cutout shape known to craft persons. Aunt Lili must have enjoyed the heck out of her scrapbooking class. Gina sank her fingers into her hair and tugged.

Make a decision, Gina.

Moving at a panicky trot, she headed to the kitchen and poured a glass of water. She rapped her knuckles against the fridge, listening to the motor hum. Real, definitely real. Not dreaming, not crazy. Drifting into the living room, she ran her palm over the back of the sofa, trailed a fingertip over the silver frame of the photograph on the wall. An informal family portrait. Oh, yes. She smiled with quivering lips. The engagement party. That had almost been fun, though she'd spent most of it hiding in the kitchen.

Wait a minute! What the—?

Gina grabbed the photo off the wall and peered, her nose so

close her breath misted the glass. She rubbed it clear with her fist.

Whoever was behind the camera hadn't been very good. Half the people in the picture had a shocking case of red-eye. Oh, hell. Every one of the afflicted was a Kaminski, including Luc.

God.

The photo slipped from her nerveless fingers and bounced across the carpet.

Gina fled back to the study as though demons were on her heels. Flinging the door back, she pounced on the book and sank to the floor, hugging it to her chest. It took her three tries to get it open, her hands shook so badly.

A heart-shaped frame of cherubs and curlicues, a sepia-toned photograph of a handsome woman wearing an Edwardian gown, fastened high to her neck with a cameo brooch—great-grandmamma Kaminski.

But out of her carefully coiffed hair rose . . . horns, like Luc's! Curved and wicked, like a devil's. And from beneath her skirts, a forked tail snaked out to coil neatly around her buttoned-up boots.

Oh God, oh God!

The book slipped from Gina's lax fingers to the rug, falling open at the middle to reveal a long sheet of paper, carefully folded many times to fit.

Swallowing, she spread it out, smoothing it with trembling fingers. The family tree. With a fingertip, she traced the line back to great-grandmamma Kaminski. Already, she knew there must be other—she could scarcely form the word, even in her head—M-Manifestations, because she and her mom were nothing like Luc, nothing at all.

Back another two generations, back to—

Gina ceased to think, even though her mind took in the familiar shapes and translated them into words.

Georgi Kaminski, b. 17??, d. 1796, the Dragon Djinn (See p. 24).

Very, very carefully, Gina stretched out flat on her back, next to the book. She stared blankly at the light fixture until she was certain she wasn't going to pass out or throw up.

Then she rolled onto one elbow and turned to page 24.

Aunt Lili's careful calligraphy, in purple ink, decorated with a cheerful dusting of tiny pink starbursts. *Little is known of our distant ancestor, Georgi Kaminski, the Dragon Djinn. Sadly, there are no portraits of him. Family legend has it that he worked in a circus as a roustabout and a strongman. He was renowned for his sense of honor, the wealth he accumulated, and his success with the ladies. No one has any idea how his Manifestation came about. It just was.*

Dragon. *Dragon.*

With a series of almost discernable clicks, things fell into place—the pattern, the molt, the extraordinary strength, the fire in her blood. Gina shivered. The forked tongue.

Not that it made her life much better. All it did was make some weird kind of sense. But at least she had someone she could talk to now, given that her mother— She squeezed the tears back and sat up slowly. A clock ticked in the silence, the swish of traffic muted by distance. The old house settled around her, as it waited for the love and laughter to return.

She pressed the heel of her hand to her chest, to the ache.

Now that she'd had him, had Sam, she could name her need. She only had to think of Luc and Maeve to know it was possible after all.

Stiffly, Gina rose to place the book back on the desk, thinking of him—the power of that lean, muscular body, the imperious demand of his cock thrusting her flesh aside, the tenderness of his hands, his lips. She'd slumbered through the hours before dawn as if his shoulder was her special place in the world, her own personal refuge. Her heart began to knock against her ribs, the beats so hard and heavy, they actually hurt.

What if—? Please God, oh *please*.

Without thinking, she reached up under the sweater to scratch at a tight spot in the small of her back. A flake of skin fluttered to the floor—then another.

Hell.

Disappointment swept over her in a wave so dark it was indistinguishable from grief. She had to brace herself against the edge of the desk until the faintness passed.

Too weird, too disgusting. Not normal. Shit, he'd think she was insane.

There wasn't a man born who'd put up with it. With a woman who was part—she stumbled over the thought—part reptile, for God's sake. Shit, no wonder every snake in the district had come to pay its respects.

And Sam *hated* snakes.

Funny, the room didn't look any different, even though something had just died there. Hopes and dreams were such quiet, inward things, so fragile, so easily snuffed.

Nothing to be done except go on with living, one step at a time.

Gina found a pen and paper easily enough. Possessed by an odd, eerie calm, as though she were enclosed in a bubble, she wrote Luc a note, saying she hoped to be well enough to attend the wedding, but knowing she wouldn't. She let herself out, locking the door carefully behind her, and drove sedately home.

* * *

The following afternoon, Gina sat at the computer, dressed in the soft flannelette shirt and track pants that were all she could bear next to her hypersensitive skin at this premolt stage. Methodically, she checked her bank account, her share portfolio, and the prices at the local realtors. Yes, she had enough to make Maeve a fair offer for the cabin. A sour smile tugged her lips. A true dragon, counting her hoard.

She rubbed her shoulder blades against the back of the chair, even as her breasts swelled another excruciating fraction. This one was going to be a doozy, she could tell. With her mouse-free hand, she cupped her mons, pressing hard into her clit, biting her lip against the sensations. There, but not quite. She'd already masturbated ferociously today, three sessions, and she'd barely taken the edge off.

Forget it.

Determinedly, she ran a search for jobs in the area. Ah, this one looked monumentally boring, exactly what she needed. As she reached to turn on the printer, a car pulled up outside. Gina froze, her hand outstretched.

A door snicking shut, the crisp tap of booted heels on the steps.

Her heart ricocheted off her rib cage, and her stomach completed a reverse somersault with forward pike.

I can't, I just can't. Not again, not when I've dealt with it and let it go.

The footsteps stopped. "Oh, fuck." Sam's voice, the merest whisper, threaded through with sick horror.

An instant's silence, then the strangest whirring noise, one she'd never heard before. What on earth—?

A split second later, she was leaping for the door as though she'd been catapulted from her seat.

Sam Jones stood three feet away, utterly still, his attention on something at the far end of the porch. He had a leather folder in one hand and two beer bottles dangling from the fingers of the other.

The broad, brutal head of a rattlesnake reared out from the nest of its coils, an S shape of deadly menace. Its dark, unwinking gaze was fixed on Sam, the tongue flickering with agitation. Its bone-chilling rattle filled the air.

Sam's whole body was rigid, his face not merely pale, but a ghastly grayish green. "Gina?" he said, without moving his lips or taking his eyes from the snake.

"Yes?" she whispered, frozen with shock.

"Go in," a shallow breath, "Shut . . . the door."

The upper third of the snake began to sway. God knew exactly how long it was, but its body was thicker around than her upper arm.

"No," she husked, and this time, the reptile turned its head to look her full in the face.

And she knew.

Sweet Jesus, it had come for her! To greet her, the way all the others had done. Not only that, but somehow it became clear to her that the snake was pissed, irritated at being drawn from its winter hibernation by an imperative it didn't understand. And Sam stood foursquare between the rattlesnake and its objective.

All her fault, her responsibility.

"In three seconds . . . I'm going to . . . throw these bottles." A huge drop of sweat rolled down Sam's cheek. *"Go inside."*

All the unresolved tension of the last two days gathered in a hard ball in her belly. It was no longer necessary to think. For the first time in her life, Gina *summoned* the pattern, deliberately stoking the fire. The scales tightened their heated grasp on her torso, snapping her spine up straight.

"That would be a waste," she said in a normal tone, releasing her death grip on the door frame and stepping forward.

An arm like an iron bar halted her progress. "No," gritted Sam, and the snake hissed, its head following his movement. The rattle grew ominously loud.

Gina looked deep into the snake's cold, flat eyes. "I see you, little sister," she said. "You may go now." The reptile's head lowered a fraction and the noise decreased.

Sam didn't speak, but he pressed Gina remorselessly backward, his arm across her breasts. A sheet of paper fluttered out of the folder in his hand and the snake struck at it, blindingly fast.

Exerting all her dragon's strength, Gina rammed her shoulder into Sam's, pushing him aside. Rage ignited the pattern on her skin, burned in her heart, filmed her vision with red. "NO!" she roared, and the sound reverberated off the surrounding hills.

Rattling furiously, the snake rose, almost as high as her head.

Ruthlessly, Gina ripped open the flannelette shirt and flung it away, buttons pinging on the wooden boards. Without looking, she knew the scales would be gleaming, the bright hues broadcasting Nature's warning. *Beware. I am dangerous.*

Peripherally, she was aware of Sam's mutter of "*Jesus!*," the bruising grip of his hands trying to haul her back, but her entire being was concentrated on her adversary.

"Behold," she said, the strange words coming easily to her

tongue, "I am the daughter of the Dragon Djinn, and this man is MINE!" The last word boomed and echoed.

Silence, save for her breath and Sam's, rasping in his throat.

Gradually, the rattler's head dropped. Then it dipped, once, twice, and slithered off the side of the porch with a ripple of sinuous muscle and dun-colored scales, disappearing with a last flick of its tail.

From behind, Sam said, "What the fuck *are* you?"

For the first time since she'd stepped onto the porch, she noticed the chill in the air. Gina shivered. She didn't want to face him, but it wasn't as if she had a choice. Turning, she stared him in the eye. "Exactly what I said I am—a descendant of Georgi Kaminski, the Dragon Djinn."

Sam's lips opened and closed, but nothing came out. He hadn't regained his color and his eyes were blank with shock.

"Want to see the forked tongue?" she said bitterly.

"Shit!" Sam clapped a hand over his mouth, stumbled from the porch, and disappeared around the corner of the house. As Gina bent wearily to gather up her shirt, she heard the unmistakable sound of retching. Terrific, she'd made him sick.

She was on her knees, chasing buttons, when he spoke again. "So you think you're a dragon?" He was leaning against the bottom post, tucking a handkerchief back into his pocket.

She had to smile. "Only a very little bit."

"Gina, is this some kind of joke? Shit, it's . . . crazy."

She shrugged, feeling the hot bite of tears in her throat. "Ask Luc, if you don't believe me."

Sam's lip curled. "Because he's a dragon too?"

Gina gave up on the buttons. She rose, holding the shirt together with one hand. "Do you want coffee?"

"No." He shook his head, his fingers flexing by his sides. "I brought beer." He gestured vaguely toward the bottles lying on the porch. "My shout. But I, uh, dropped them."

"That's no way to treat beer." Her feeble attempt at a smile went flat. She cleared her throat. "And the folder?"

"Huh?" He'd been running a hand through his hair, over and over. "Oh. A few prints from my calendar portfolio. I thought you'd like to . . ." The sentence trailed away.

"I have to think," he said abruptly. "I thought . . . your eyes went red. Jesus." Without another word, he turned and strode toward the rental car.

Gina wanted to keen out loud, to wail and writhe in her distress, but pride kept her upright, her hands gripping the rail. "Sam?"

He looked back with his hand on the car door, wariness and discomfort in every line of his body. "Yeah?"

She dashed away a tear with the back of her fist. "Thank you for trying to save me." Swallowing, she tried to smile. "You were very brave."

"Likewise." His face didn't change. "See you, Gina." He climbed into the car and drove away, his features still pale and set.

Ignoring the chilly breeze, Gina watched until the vehicle was no more than a moving dot in the distance. Then she went back to the kitchen, made cocoa, and dumped a slug of Maeve's brandy in it. She locked all the doors and windows, drew a warm bath, then stripped and climbed in.

The scales beneath her skin gleamed mockingly under the water, and she clutched her cocoa as the tears welled. In the end, she had to set the mug aside because the storm of sobs wracked her body to such a degree she was in danger of dropping it. But by the time the water cooled and night had closed in, she felt much calmer. Slightly buzzed from the alcohol, she dried off and found the painkillers in the medicine cabinet. She took them to bed with her.

It was going to be a very long night.

Jesus, this had to be the longest night of his life. Sam woke what seemed to be every hour, on the hour, alternately hot and cold. He punched his pillow, swore luridly, pushed the blankets off, pulled them up. The sterile air of his hotel room smelled flat and stuffy. He missed the crisp, green odors of trees in the wind, the warm, exotic scent of female flesh, the smoky undertone of Gina's skin, the flicker of her forked tongue as she ate him alive.

His breath caught, even as his balls swelled with the memory of pleasure. *Eat him alive.* He'd damn near passed out, but God, it had been good.

He'd never considered himself a particularly imaginative man. The world was a strange place, full of mystery and wonder. Still, nothing humans could do would surprise him, or so he'd thought. But this—! It had to be the most original mental aberration he'd ever come across.

Jesus, she thought she was descended from a dragon! It couldn't be true. It *couldn't.*

What she'd done with that fucking snake had been the stupidest, bravest— Sam pinched the bridge of his nose, feeling the sweat chill between his shoulder blades. She'd saved his life, no doubt about it.

But *how*? How had she faced down a rattlesnake that was longer than she was tall?

The digital clock glowed 3:47. With a grunt, Sam snapped on the light and threw off the covers. All right then, bugger it, he'd work it out. He'd been a journalist, he'd spent years piecing together stray scraps of information to make a story. He could do this.

Barefoot, in his boxers, he began to pace. Thinking.

He was still thinking when he met Luc for breakfast in the city. Using the muddled soup that now passed for his brain, he'd been able to discern only two things. It didn't matter if Gina was as mad as a meat axe, he still wanted her. What was more, he wanted the whole package, contradictions and all—the funny little crease between her brows when she was thinking, the shy sweetness coupled with that ferocious self-discipline, the wanton promise, the courage . . . The sheer guts.

He could still see her, standing tall and proud like some bloody warrior woman, trying to shield him with her body, the vivid colors shimmering under her skin, deepening as she grew angrier, defining the luscious curve from her ribs to her waist, cupping the jut of those bare, creamy tits. Her nipples had puckered with cold and tension, a velvety, lickable rosy-brown.

Fuck, Georgina McBride was something else!

Above her shoulder blades, the skin was unmarked, except for the sides of her throat. He wanted to nibble his way up the little knobs of her spine, sweep her hair aside, and press his lips to the nape of her neck where she was pale and vulnerable, snuff at the life running hot beneath the skin. Breathe her in.

"What?" said Luc, stirring his coffee.

"Huh?" Sam's cock filled and swelled, fighting with his zipper, wanting out.

"You're pulling faces. Got a problem, Indy?"

Ask Luc, she'd said, but when it came to it, he found he couldn't even begin to frame the question. Suddenly, fiercely, he knew he couldn't bear to expose her. Whatever there was between them, it was too fragile to betray the trust she'd put in him. Not if he wanted to keep it.

"I need fresh air," he said, and God knew that was the truth. His head hurt. "Where can I do a bit of bush walking, take some pictures?"

He spent the next two days in the national park Luc had recommended, thinking as he tramped along the muddy trails, squeezing off a series of random shots—two frogs perched on a wet rock, a 'gator sliding into the dark water. He didn't see any snakes.

By the time he'd driven back to the city, showered, and changed for the bachelor party, Sam was sick and tired of bloody thinking. Logic wasn't achieving a damn thing. The unexplainable kept butting him right between the eyes and giving him a bitch of a headache. Grimly, he pulled on his favorite snakeskin boots.

Luc had chosen a sophisticated option for his last New Year's Eve as a single man—drinks and dinner at the casino, followed by a special floor show. Normally, Sam would have enjoyed the hell out of it, but he couldn't settle. Moodily, he nursed a scotch, drumming his fingers on the bar, fretting.

Finally, Luc leaned over. "You're beginning to bug me, Indy. Relax, will you?"

Sam said, "About Gina—"

Luc's eyes narrowed. "What about her?"

"She, uh, all right?"

"She's fine." Luc appeared to be choosing his words with particular care. "She has occasional . . . episodes, that's all."

The uneasiness in Sam's gut coalesced into a single nasty lump. "I thought she had a cold."

"Yeah," said Luc. "That's it, that's right. A cold."

"Give me your phone."

Luc's brow arched. "Why?"

"I want to check on her."

"Indy . . ."

"Give. Me. The. Fucking. Phone."

"Jesus, all right. Here." Luc handed it over. "Don't blame me if she bites your head off." That seemed to amuse him so much his eyes gleamed red, but it could have been the warm lighting in the bar.

It rang and rang. No answer.

Shit!

Sam stood. Then he sat. He ate a peanut. He called again. No answer.

The mental picture sprang to the front of his mind, as clearly as if it was painted on the inside of his eyelids. Gina, on the porch, thanking him for being a hero—some hero! Her hands had gripped the rail so hard, her knuckles shone white, but she'd raised her chin and tried to keep her voice steady, the little darling. Game to the end.

And he'd abandoned her.

Fuck.

"I have to go," he said.

Luc frowned. "You'll miss the New Year's Eve cabaret."

Sam really had to concentrate to get him in focus. "Sorry,

mate." He pressed the big man's shoulder as he walked past. "Happy New Year and all that."

Luc's huge hand clamped over his biceps, pulling him back. His hazel eyes were so fierce, Sam could have sworn flames flickered in their depths. "You serious about her?" The grip tightened. "You'd better be."

Sam froze. *Was he serious?*

"Hell, yeah," he said, prying himself loose. "She's . . ." He couldn't think of the right words, "really something."

As he reached the door, he thought he heard his friend say, "She sure is." Then Luc laughed.

Light spilled from the front windows of the cabin when Sam pulled up. Good, he'd check the porch for lurking rattlesnakes. The night air was chilly, the only sounds the burbling of water and the wind soughing in the trees.

What was that?

He tilted his head, listening as he climbed the steps.

Jesus Christ! His guts turned over. Someone was moaning, small wrenching sounds of pain and desolation.

"Gina!" Sam thundered at the front door. "Gina, open up!"

The sounds ceased. A long pause. "Go away." Her voice was clogged with tears.

"No." He rattled the doorknob. Bugger. Locked. "Come on, love, let me help you."

"Can't. Can't help." Silence. "Go away. Pleasse, Ssam!"

The lisp did it.

Sam leaped down the stairs two at a time and ran around to the back of the cabin. Wasn't there a laundry near the back door, with a window? Yes there was, and a handy flowerpot, too. Without compunction, he heaved the pot, shattering the glass.

Then he wrapped his leather jacket over his fist and punched out the rest of it.

Ten seconds later, he was charging down the passage toward Gina's bedroom. No lights, but the room was pleasantly warm. All he could see was the outline of her body curled in a fetal position in the center of the bed. Her harsh breathing rattled in the dark. He flipped on the light.

All the air punched out of his lungs.

Gina lay nude, her arms clamped over her head. The colors that had been so vibrant, so vivid, when she faced the snake were dulled, opaque, and her skin had an unhealthy grayish cast to it, as if she were deathly ill.

He had her cradled in his arms before he even realized he'd moved. "Sweetheart, what is it? What's wrong?"

"Ssam?" All the life had fled from her beautiful eyes. They were flat with misery. "Don't touch. Pleasse."

"Am I hurting you?"

When she shook her head, he tightened his grip. "You should be in the hospital."

At that, an expression of utter horror crossed her face. "No," she hissed. "Promisse me, no."

"Then what is it?" When she didn't answer, he said, "I'm not leaving, Gina. You may as well tell me."

She pushed the hair out of her face and shrugged, but tension thrummed though her body. "You didn't believe me yesterday. Why would you believe me now?"

Sam dragged in a shuddering breath. "Try me."

"Mmm." She made a skeptical noise, but she did close her eyes and lean back against his supporting arm. "I call it the molt. Happens about every ssix months." She got it out in a single breath.

"The *molt?*"

Gina flinched, and her eyes flew open. "My sskin peelss off, all right? It'ss dissgussting."

After what he'd been imagining, that didn't sound so bad. His racing heart slowed. "Does it hurt?"

"Yess, but it'ss over pretty quickly. I can put up with that. It'ss the rest of it, it makess me—" Suddenly, she flushed scarlet and turned her head away.

"Makes you what, darl?"

"Hot," she whispered into his shirt.

Sam's heart picked up speed, a hard, slamming beat. He cupped her chin in gentle fingers and raised her head. "Gina," he said, "open your mouth."

When she pressed her lips together instead, he bent his head and licked her bottom lip in a slow, thorough sweep, luxuriating in the flavor. God, he'd missed her! As he kissed one corner of her mouth, then the other, she moaned, her hands clenching on his shoulders. Enjoying the hell out of the entire process, Sam made a production out of seducing her mouth, lick by lick, nibble by nibble.

Her head fell back against his arm and her lips parted so he could swoop inside. A hot little tongue flickered against his in that erotic way that drove him insane. It took all his willpower to wrench himself away so he could take a good look.

The cutest fork, just at the tip. "Strewth, that's sexy," he muttered, before sucking it back in for an endless mating of wet and hot and smooth and delicately pointed.

By the time he finally let her up for air, Sam was lying full-length on the bed, Gina's supple body sprawled over his, his hands fully occupied with stroking her back, featherlight fingertips only. The skin rasped against his touch, like paper.

He nibbled her earlobe and she gasped. "What did you mean, it makes you hot?"

When she blushed, he grinned, delighted. "C'mon, darl, say the words." He chuckled aloud.

"I get so . . . so horny, I can hardly stand it," Gina whispered into the curve between his neck and his shoulder. "It feels like I'll die if I can't—" She nuzzled the spot under his ear, and delivered a protracted, mind-numbing lick that had his cock twitching with anticipation.

Wait a minute. Sam stiffened as a trickle of unease in his gut competed for his attention. What if this molt thing drove her to scratch the itch with other men, strangers eager for a mindless, faceless fuck? "So what do you do? Who . . . ?" He stumbled to a halt, the breath clogging in his throat.

The temperature of her skin increased, burning right through his shirt. "I take a few days off and I, uh, masturbate," a panting breath, "but it's never enough, *never*. It drives me crazy." She sounded as though she was going to cry.

Sam grinned. He wanted to sing, to shout. His blood fizzed and sparkled, his cock pulsing happily in his jeans. Rolling Gina onto her back, he brushed his palm over her sexy little belly. Her eyes went wide and dark, tiny red lights flashing in their depths. Delighted with the reaction, he furrowed his fingers through her springy curls, into the dripping cleft of her sex. She was incredibly wet, delectable juices slicking her thighs, her labia searing hot and so smooth.

His, all his.

"Ssam?"

Gently, he kissed her forehead, even as he worked two fingers inside her. "This time you'll get enough. I promise, sweetheart. I'll be here for all of it, the pain as well as the pleasure."

Ruthlessly, he stroked, sweeping his thumb over her clit again and again, sealing his lips over one furled nipple, then the other, relishing the sweet, agonized sounds she made, the way she arched clean off the bed and into his hands. With his name on her lips, a lovely deep growl, she shattered, first going rigid, then collapsing back onto the pillows, shuddering.

Hugely pleased with himself, Sam waited until she calmed, studying her expression. His balls actually hurt and his cock was strangling in his jeans, but it didn't matter. He'd wait if it killed him, Gina couldn't. "Better?"

A slow smile broke over her face, her cheeks still suffused with color. He loved it. "Oh, yess," she murmured. But as she reached up to stroke his cheek, she winced.

Chapter 8

Gina gasped. God, she'd forgotten how much it could hurt, especially at the beginning. But as she blinked up into Sam's worried face, the pain eased. Somehow, his presence made all the difference. Not just because he was sympathetic, but because he was *Sam*—Sam with his sexy drawl, his clear-eyed, ocean gaze, and his calm good sense.

She wanted to leap off the bed and dance around the room, she wanted to rain kisses all over his face, hug him to death, shout to the world that she loved him, *loved him*—

Oh.

More than a little dazed, she peeped up at him from beneath her lashes, but he was already disengaging, pulling away. Before she had time to panic, he smiled. "I'm going to run a warm bath. Will that help?"

Dumbly, she nodded, her brain spinning with discovery.

A few minutes later, he returned, scooped her up in his arms, and carried her into the bathroom. The warm water felt wonderful on her aching body, and she relaxed with a long sigh. Sam rolled up his sleeves and leaned over her, a fluffy sponge in one hand, Gina's favorite baby soap in the other. "Not too hot?"

"No. Ssam?" She sat up, pressing a desperate kiss to his lips. Stretchy tremors of sensation traveled over her skin.

"Yeah, darl?" Squeezing the sponge, he trickled water over her breasts.

"Off." Gina tugged at his shirt, but she misjudged, and buttons shot in all directions. "You'll get all wet, anyway. Heck, I want you naked."

Sam's eyes glowed, astonishingly bright in his tanned face. Without a word, he stood and ripped off his jeans and boxers, kicking off his boots. His cock bobbed at eye level, magnificently erect, the broad, velvety head flushed a deep rose pink, already shiny with excitement. Gina reached out with eager fingers, unable to help herself.

Dropping the shirt, Sam danced aside. "Nu-uh. Touch me and it's over. Lean forward, love." He climbed in behind her and water sloshed on the floor.

Gina laughed, even as painful sensations traveled over her body. She'd never realized what a difference it would make, sharing. *Loving.* Sam drew her back between his knees; his erection welded to the small of her back, an iron bar hotter than the water. She clasped her arms over his long, brawny thighs and hung on as the molt began.

It took two hours. Sam emptied and refilled the bath several times. He found Maeve's stash of bath oils and poured them in with a lavish hand, joking about the "pong," a reckless mix of lavender, jasmine, and patchouli. He stroked, he massaged, peeling the dead skin away with blunt, gentle fingers. In between, he told stories about growing up in the Australian outback. Most of them were at his expense, and Gina found herself giggling through her physical discomfort.

He showed no trace of embarrassment or revulsion.

Gina looped one hand behind his neck and pulled his face down beside hers. His stubble rasped her cheek. She rubbed her lips over it, savoring the tingle. "It's finisshed," she whispered. "Now fuck me till I die."

In complete silence, Sam set his hands at her waist and turned her around. His eyes glittered, his jaw was set hard. Gladly, she reached down to guide him to the greedy mouth of her body, but he shook his head, holding her off him. "Not yet," he rumbled, his chest heaving.

Carefully, Gina straddled him, catching her breath at the exquisite feel of their heated flesh sliding together in the water, aided by her natural lubrication. God, it felt as if he'd oiled her there, too! She rode him in a slow drag of wet satin, back and forth, the collar beneath his cock head bumping sweetly over her clit. "When?" she purred.

Sam nipped at her lips. "Remember what I said about next time?"

"Mmm?"

"I want to do it slow, watch my cock sliding into your pretty cunt." A shuddering breath. "Fuck you from behind."

Speechless, Gina let her head fall back, opening her mouth for the assault of his tongue, wrapping hers around it, tapping and caressing. Sam groaned as if the heart was being ripped from his chest, pulled away, and grabbed a towel. "Jesus, I'm dying. Quick!"

He bundled her up in the towel, taking her back to the bedroom. There, he set her down before the mirror and dried every fold and crease of her body with meticulous care, despite the trembling of his hands. Gina writhed and whimpered, her new skin so soft, so sensitive, that each gentle swipe of the nubbly fabric sent hot chills racing up her spine and stiffened her nipples beyond bearing. Finally, he tossed the towel aside and pulled her back into his chest, towering over her, his hands on her shoulders. "Look at you," he murmured over her head, his deep voice choked with something very like awe. "Dragon lady, you're fucking gorgeous."

Her eyes prickling with tears, Gina watched him sink to his knees. Beginning at her hip, he licked his way up the pattern, one scale at a time, while his palms skated up and down her torso, caressing her, claiming his territory. For the first time in her life, Georgina McBride looked at herself without prejudice, as though she was brand new. All those years ago on prom night, she'd been more right than she'd realized. Dragons had an enduring place in the human consciousness because they *were* beautiful, with a magical, perilous power. The more Sam worshipped the dragon in her with his hands and his mouth, the more she glowed, the pattern flexing, illuminating her skin with drifting trails of phosphorescence.

Sam kissed his way around to her front and nerves fluttered in her pelvis, delicate silvery wings of sensation. Shivering, she buried her hands in his thick hair, watching the tension in the powerful muscles of his buttocks, his scrotal sack drawn up tight and plump between his thighs. "The darker they are, the hotter they taste." He dipped his tongue into her navel. "Did you know that?"

But he'd reached up to feather her nipples, and she could only gurgle. The orgasm gathered in her belly, a dark, fiery tide, a demanding pressure. Sam shifted, wrapping firm, warm lips around a nipple, tugging.

Gina roared. And came.

Her knees went, and Sam caught her in his arms. He didn't waste words. The moment she'd stopped shaking, he pressed her down to her hands and knees on the rug. Her pulse thundering so loudly in her ears she could hardly think, Gina caught the crackle of foil. She turned her head, finding Sam's eye in the mirror. "Don't," she said. "I take the Pill. Jusst you. Pleasse, Ssam."

"God, yes." Sam tossed the condom over his shoulder and surged forward. He grasped her hip with one hand and aimed his cock with the other. "Watch, Gina." He fed her the first inch, the broad head a tight fit. "Watch it . . ." He rocked forward, the thickness of his shaft disappearing inside her body, the pink lips of her sheath stretching to accommodate his girth, "go in." Flush against her, his balls swung hot and heavy.

She saw his jaw muscles bunch as he gritted his teeth. Then he pulled back and his cock reappeared, fat, slick, and shiny with their juices. He rammed back in. She'd never seen anything so gorgeously lewd in her life, never felt crammed so deliciously full. She laughed, breathless with lust and love, and wiggled her hips. "You're wicked, Sam Jones."

"Aren't I though?" He shot her a tight grin in the mirror. Then he reached around to caress her clit, slicking his fingers with her moisture. "You have no idea, dragon lady."

When he rubbed his slippery fingers over her asshole, she reared back with shock.

"Do you like that?"

"No. Yes. Don't know."

Sam chuckled and pressed with his thumb. He set up a firm, jolting rhythm with his hips, one that rammed the head of his cock over a sweet spot she hadn't known she had, at the same time circling his thumb just inside her ass. Involuntarily, Gina's internal muscles clamped down on his shaft, and he swore. "Fuck, darl, don't—"

She giggled. "Don't what? Do this?" Rejoicing in her own strength, she rippled her pelvic muscles around his stone-hard bulk.

"Aaargh!" Sam exploded into action, hammering into her body, all ruthless masculine power. "Shit, I can't—"

Gina gave herself up to the storm, to the blood-heating sensations in her ass, the hard flesh spreading the succulent walls of her sheath, his iron grip on her hip. "Me neither," she gasped. "Oh God, Ssam. Harder, harder!" Her clit burned. Lord, it felt as if it was the size of her fist.

Sam shouted something unintelligible. He jammed himself so high and hard inside her, the rug slid forward on the floor, taking them with it.

She wasn't sure who yelled the loudest, but the little cabin reverberated as Sam rode her down to the floor. Gina lay with her cheek pressed to the rug, feeling the hot wash of his seed in her dark, secret places, a series of luscious spasms rocking her with delightful aftershocks.

Sam nuzzled her hair and rolled aside, allowing her to breathe. "So much for slow," he panted. "You're a menace, Gina McBride."

Gina collapsed across his chest. "Never mind," she said. "There's always next time."

Sam went very still beneath her, but all he said was, "Do you realize what time it is?" He nodded at the clock radio on the dresser—it read 12:10.

"Oh." Gina fought to clear her head. "We missed it. Happy New Year, Sam." She gave him a misty smile and a peck on the cheek, her heart full. She was a whole new being, as new as the year. Life stretched ahead, beckoning with possibilities.

He pulled her to her feet. "No, we didn't." His arm snug

around her waist, he led her over to the bed. Though he flashed her a cheeky grin, his level blue gaze was surprisingly serious. "Bloody fine way to see in the new year, if you ask me."

She settled into the pillows with a sigh. "Sure was."

"Gina?" He wound a long curl around a finger.

"Mmm?"

"Did you mean it? About next time?"

"Sure." She smiled, certain her foolish heart was in her eyes. "The wedding's not till four." Turning her head, she pressed a kiss to his wrist. "Plenty of time to practice going slow."

"I meant next New Year's." Startled, she stared up into a bottomless blue gaze, drowning. Sam leaned right over her on his elbows, bracketing her head between his forearms. He looked a little pale, but determined. "And all the ones after that."

The air had evaporated from her lungs, but her heart sang hallelujahs. Gina threw her arms around his neck. "Oh, Ssam! Yess, pleasse!"

Denise Rossetti

When **DENISE ROSSETTI** was very small, she had an aunt who would tell her the most wonderful fairy stories—all original. Denise grew up, as little girls do, but the love of stories has never left her. All hail the guys in the white hats, she says—unless the ones wearing black are more . . . um . . . *interesting*?

Denise is small, noisy, and dreadfully uncoordinated. She tends to wave her hands around a lot, which can be unfortunate if the tale she's telling happens to have explosions in it!

She loves to hear from readers. *http://www.deniserossetti.com*